volume two
when murder becomes mayhem
some people need to die

lar e hale

Happy reading. ☺

for E

Copyright 2019

ISBN-13: 9781985826052

This is a work of fiction. Characters and incidences are the product of the author's imagination and are used fictitiously.

Published August 2019 by lar e hale

acknowledgements

I'd like to thank Karmon, a kindred spirit who has many bodies of her own buried in Money Bayou.

I'd also like to thank Julia and Vince for allowing me to use their real names instead of Victoria and Ramone.

I'd especially like to thank my editor who encouraged me to dig for the rich yellow metal in my writing and not settle for the pyrite I sometimes try to pass off as such. She might say *Ooh, shiny* every so often to mollify me, but she's not buying this fool's gold – not for a second.

And I appreciate her for that.

Books by Lar E Hale

The Murder Series

making a case for murder
doing what has to be done

when murder becomes mayhem
some people need to die

murder in the light of day
right and wrong are relative

good evening

She thought about her first time.

It was bloody and messy and scary, but the fear soon transformed into a pleasure she couldn't have imagined, a thrill she determined to experience again.

And again, and again.

If she had known then what she knew now, Cassidy would have given it to her drunken mother's boyfriend. Not her body – he took that against her will time after time.

No, it was the knife.

The first time she used it had been unintentional. The man grabbed her hand after she'd lifted his wallet and wouldn't let go. She pulled and pleaded, but he held on and tried to call the police. Cassidy couldn't be arrested again, couldn't spend any more time in jail, so she knocked the phone from his hand and it shattered on the sidewalk.

"You bitch," he said, and bashed her to the ground. When he yanked her up by the hair, she instinctively reached into her jacket and stuck it in his chest. They watched as the blood spilled, and then stared at each other. She saw something in his eyes, something exhilarating.

He was afraid of her.

A lifetime of feeling helpless evaporated as she vented her failures and frustrations at the man lying on the ground. Afterward, she knew two things she didn't before – money wasn't the root of all evil, men were.

And she liked destroying them.

Cassidy killed indiscriminately, choosing the time and place with thought and planning. But the men were chosen at random.

Like the one walking toward her.

She glanced around in feigned alarm, appearing nervous of the man to put him at ease, to make him feel safe.

It helped that she was a wisp of a woman and pretty to boot. Men had a natural inclination to help an attractive 'lady in distress,' and she exploited that inherent weakness.

Cassidy smiled when he nodded hello and immediately swung her knife at the back of his neck after she walked by – but the blade whistled through empty space.

Her eyes widened as he plunged his own deep, cutting her from pelvis to sternum.

"That's not a knife. *This* is a knife."

She was stunned by the sudden twist of fate and didn't have the presence of mind to remember where she'd heard that before as she tried to keep herself from spilling out.

"How . . . Why?"

Cassidy watched the man walk calmly down the sidewalk and tried to reconcile the answer he'd given as her life ebbed away.

"You needed to die."

chapter one

To some, it might seem strange to hang Christmas ornaments on a palm tree and an artificial one, at that. You might think he would be offended by Florida's version of the traditional evergreen, but Kris Kringle is fine with it. He has been vacationing in the Sunshine state for centuries and currently has water-front homes in Miami and Sarasota.

Having lived in the Panhandle her entire life, Mary didn't find it odd at all. She enjoyed placing the fish, beachball, and pineapple decorations on the bent branches along with her favorite tree topping ornament – a Hawaiian shirted Santa sporting sunglasses and riding a surfboard.

Ho-ho-ho and cowabunga, dudes and dudettes.

She looked over as they laughed at Watson who kept removing the reindeer antlers Dax kept putting on him. The Golden Retriever rolled his eyes when he glanced her way, but she knew he loved the attention.

And the scratching that always followed.

Dax patted him on the rump before walking down the hallway to his room, and Tasha asked if she minded her birthday being on Christmas.

"No, not really," Mary said. "I think Jesus is a *more the merrier* kind of guy, so he's probably alright with divvying up the day. And it's sure better than sharing it with Hitler. Or having it on the same day as the Nine-Eleven attack."

Mary knew kids whose birthdays were forever ruined because of the terrorists' assault on the World Trade Center. On the upside, they got more presents and attention than they might normally receive by parents who still grieved the loss of those killed by cowards who had the temerity to call themselves *soldiers* of Allah.

"And, being an only child, the quality of the gift was always high. Like the Martin." Mary referred to the D-28, an acoustic guitar she treasured.

It was the last present her father gave her before he went missing, the last good thing she had to remember him by. Because after that he'd raped her over and over while she was gagged and tied to her bed. The first time she'd screamed, he put his hand over her nose and mouth until she passed out. When she came to, he said he'd kill her if she yelled again or tried to escape.

Tasha saw a cloud pass over her face. While Mary seemed to have overcome the horror of her experience, it was only natural to become agitated at this time of year, worrying he might come back someday and try to take her.

But she would never let that happen. He'd be charged with molestation, aggravated rape, assault, and attempted murder the moment he showed his face.

Mary had been devastated by what her father did, and Tasha knew she'd be dead if Dax hadn't found her. He stopped her from killing herself, nurtured her self-esteem, and gave her a home and his heart. In return, she loved him with a fierce devotion.

"Are you alright, Mary?"

"Yup. Why?"

"You looked elsewhere."

"You're right. I was contrasting this Christmas with last year's. What's interesting is how different things are and how much better my life is – not for the obvious reasons but because of how important you and Dax are to me. Again, not for the obvious reasons."

Tasha's confusion made her smile.

"I loved and felt loved by my . . . by that evil son-of-a-bitch. If he hadn't done what he did, I would have been a happy girl thinking the love he gave me was the pinnacle of parental affection. But compared to what I receive now, it makes that pinnacle seem more like a muddy ditch. So, is that the result of my abuse or because of who you and Dax are? And if it's the latter, should I accept how the bad brought me the good in the context of a divine being altering the course of my life?"

Tasha grinned but felt the seriousness of her query. All three of them had given considerable thought to God or, more specifically, if there was one.

As a detective, she'd seen first-hand the evil that men, and women, do. It was hard to believe in a loving Being who'd tolerate it, let alone allow it to flourish.

"Well, that's a good question, hon. And a heavy one. I'll tell you this, you're right about life being interesting. I think you were always going to be special. You're bright and compassionate, and your inner strength is evident by the decision you made to escape," Tasha said and paused.

"But all of those qualities have both deepened and fortified the bedrock of your character. It's made you more, more than you might have been if he hadn't . . ."

Mary nodded and looked at Tasha with affection.

"You can say it. If he hadn't raped me. And you're right; I do feel more. Stronger, more aware, more caring of others, and more willing to intervene on their behalf."

Tasha remembered the time Mary stepped in and put a man on the floor because he wouldn't leave a woman alone.

"It's hard to find a silver lining in that kind of abuse Tash, but sometimes I wonder if I had to go through it in order to get here. I like who I am, how I feel about things, how much I care about you and Dax, and how much y'all care about me. But such a metamorphosis from abuse to abundance, like the caterpillar and the butterfly, begs the question I alluded to earlier. Is there a God?"

"I don't know, Mary. It makes me say *Hmmm* for sure, but, if God exists, I'd be pretty pissed at Him, or Her, for letting that son-of-a-bitch touch you in the first place. I swear, I wish I could get my hands on him. I'd . . ."

Mary saw the anger build and slipped an arm through Tasha's. "Thanks."

"For what?" I asked, placing the bowed, wrapped boxes I'd kept hidden in my closet under the brightly lit palm tree.

"Tasha was about to tell me what she'd do to the *son-of-a-bitch* if she got ahold of him."

"Oh, yeah?" I said and cocked my head at Tasha. "First off, you'll have to get in line. And secondly, you are a detective in good standing with the St. Vincent police department. Other than curtly read him his rights and maybe cuff him too tightly, whatchu gonna do, girlfriend?"

My fingers snapped back and forth, and she cracked up like she always did whenever I *worked* it.

"Thanks, Dax, for always being such a rich source of amusement for me."

"You are welcome, Tash, and ... wait. Are you laughing with me? Or at me?"

Mary and Tasha looked at each other and snickered. Not a giggle, chuckle, laugh, chortle, or guffaw, but a snicker. Of all the related connotations, snickering was by far the least detectable and most effectible when making fun of someone. Not that I cared because I loved to see them enjoy each other – even at my expense.

"Why don't you ask *me* that question?" Mary asked with a wide-eyed expression of mirth.

I chuckled and choked on my soda. "Smartass."

"Well, y'all, I have to go," Tasha said and stood to leave. "I have an early meeting in Panama City, and I need to be somewhat bright-eyed. The morning's coffee will take care of the bushy tailed. Thanks for dinner. And the company." She gave Mary a hug and kissed her cheek.

"Thanks for coming. Hey, how about a sleepover, sometime? We could do a pajama party. What do you think?" Mary said, eyes beaming with excitement.

"Sure. How about I come and get you Friday after work? Then we can go out on the boat and catch some fish early the next morning."

"How about you come over *here* for the sleepover, and then we go fishing?" Mary asked and raised a brow my way.

"Sounds good to me, but how come I never get invited to go out on the boat with you two? Are you even fishing?"

They grinned at each other.

"It's a girl thing, Dax. You know how it is," Tasha said.

"No, I don't know how it is. And why does Watson get to go? He's a guy. A furry one to be sure, but still a guy. You probably just don't want to get shown up by a fishing stud such as myself, and, now that I think about it, it makes sense. Still, if we're going to have fish for dinner, I better go out in the kayak and catch us some."

Mary piped up right away.

"That smells like a challenge. You want to go biggest or most? Loser has to clean the fish and the dishes by himself."

"Himself? What about herself? Or herselves?"

They laughed at my use of a made-up word but more so because I inferred the loser would be a *her*. We agreed to terms and conditions, and I made a mental note to stop by the fish store in the event I got skunked.

"And no going to the St. Joe Shrimp Company to supplement your feeble fishing attempt," Mary said.

I have long suspected her of reading my mind, and it has fascinated me and made me feel stupid at the same time for considering it. She probably just knows me well and gets lucky, but come on, it was a little eerie. And a little cool. What if she really could?

"Why, whatever are you implying?" I asked with a contrived expression of wounded indignation.

"I'm not *implying* anything," she said with a grin.

Tasha laughed, said she had to leave, and asked me to come outside to retrieve some things to put under the tree.

After handing me the presents, she gave me a kind of hug and reached up to kiss my cheek. I leaned down to make it easier, and she put a hand to my face and kissed me on the lips – a soft kiss that sparked and caught fire. It was everything I'd imagined, and when I responded, she gave an involuntary groan that fanned the flame of my desire.

Tasha stepped back and looked at me with an expression I thought I understood but probably didn't. Her eyes were smoky and her smile knowing.

"So you liked that then?" she said.

"Why would you think otherwise?"

"Because you haven't made a single move on me in all this time, even though I'm fairly sure you like me some. Am I wrong?"

I liked her a lot, loved her in fact and had for months. But those feelings had been suppressed to keep from losing her because if she knew the truth about me, I would.

"You're not wrong, and I'd rather not talk about it now, but if you don't mind . . ."

I set the packages on down and took her in my arms. When our lips met again, she moaned and pulled me closer.

~~

"What do you think, Watson?"

"Why suck her mouth? It seems an odd thing to do. Why not lick her face, instead? Or rub noses?"

Mary grinned and agreed it was very un-canine like.

chapter two

The Onesie felt tight across her chest as Mary reached inside the freezer for the frosty mugs.

She *over-developed* months before her father raped her and used to wonder if his attack was triggered because of it. But she stopped caring about his reason a long time ago and only felt contempt for him now.

And the horse he rode in on.

"Sorry, but you should have thrown his sorry ass," she mumbled to the imaginary mare as she poured the drinks.

Tasha's silk pajamas, a Chinese design with vivid colors, full sleeves, and long-legged pants looked *smooth*, according to Dax, and he asked to feel her.

"Sure, but where are *your* PJs?"

"I don't wear any."

Her face grew warm, and her pulse quickened when his fingers brushed the underside of her wrist as he felt the fabric, leaving Tasha torn between wanting Mary to stay in the kitchen and wanting her to come back.

"Here we go. A&W root beers all around."

Mary set a tray on the coffee table, and, after everyone took a glass, they raised them, clinked them, and emptied them, laughing when Dax held a pinky finger up and out.

"It denotes class and cultivation," I said and carried the mugs into the kitchen for a refill.

They continued to make fun of my redneck etiquette, chuckling as they tuned the guitars. I thought about their impact on my life and began to consider my good fortune, but they'd call dibs on the solos if I didn't get back out there and stake a claim.

We played for hours, loving the music and the way it made us feel – free and alive, in touch with the universe, ourselves, and each other.

~~

Mary offered the bed again before lighting the wick and turning off the light, but Tasha shook her head and fell back on the air-mattress. It was queen-size, nineteen inches tall, and felt like a cloud.

"This will be just fine. Thanks, though."

The smell of the scented candle permeated the room, and the flame cast flickering shadows on the walls.

"This feels like camping out in the woods," Tasha said, patting the mattress and calling Watson. He jumped up and snuggled against her as she scratched behind his ears.

"You know, I've never been. What's it like?"

Tasha told her about the sights and sounds and smells and smores – and bugs and bites and bears.

"Then you gather around the campfire, and someone tells a story about a ghost or a crazed killer lurking in the forest. It's fun and a little scary. I always slept with one eye open, not wanting to be caught unaware when the killer reached into the tent to claim his victim."

Mary chuckled when Tasha tried to grab her arm.

They'd bonded over similar experiences of abuse, and, over time, and in many ways, their affections for each other sometimes felt sisterly.

"Hey, Mare? I'd like to talk to you about something, if it's alright."

"Sure. What's up?"

Tasha hesitated, anxious about how Mary might react. "It's about Dax. About how I feel."

"With your fingers, right?"

"Well, I've also been known to use my hands, feet, nose, toes, even my elbows."

"And your lips?"

"I, Uh . . ." Tasha blushed, feeling self-conscious.

Mary thought to have some fun with her awkwardness. "You, uh, what?"

"I think I'm in love with Dax."

"You're what?" Mary said, a slight edge to her voice.

As much as she enjoyed putting Tasha on the spot, she almost stopped when apprehension appeared in her eyes – but instead decided to test the sincerity of her declaration.

"Just what are your intentions concerning my father?"

Mary tried to be funny by flipping that age-old question but was surprised by the unexpected way it made her feel. Dax really *was* one to her.

"I love him, Mary. And I hope you're alright with it."

She saw the truth in Tasha's eyes and plopped down on the mattress, causing Watson to pop into the air before landing on his back. They laughed and hugged each other.

"That's great, Tash. And you know what? It turns out I love my *Dad*, too," Mary said with a shine in her eyes.

~~

The girls had been quiet for a long time, and I missed the sound of their voices. I couldn't make out what they'd said, but the laughter warmed my heart.

I'd thought about Tasha a lot since the other night. My reasons for keeping her at arm's length were legitimate, but her affections were like an avalanche waiting to *whumpf* and create a slide I'd never be able to outrun.

It didn't help that I wasn't sure I wanted to.

When she came into the room and closed the door behind her, I could have said something but kept my mouth shut and my eyes barely open.

Tasha stood next to the bed a moment before moving her fingers from button to button until the silk shirt hung open. Rather than take it off as one might, she slid a hand under the material, coaxed it to slip from one shoulder, and then the other. When her top fell to the floor, I hoped my intake of breath would be regarded as an apnea.

Because, you know, I was sleeping.

She slipped out of her bottoms, lifted the blanket, and lay next to me. When I *woke up* acting surprised, she shook her head.

"Too late for that. I knew you were awake."

"What? No, I . . . How? I thought I did a rather good job of peeking through my eyelashes."

"Oh, you did," she said and twirled her fingers through the hair on my chest.

"Well, then, how did you know?"

"I'm a detective, with keen observational skills. I noticed a small protuberance under the sheet as I undid one button after the other."

She was that rarest of creatures – a classy, intelligent lady with smoldering sensuality. I could almost hear the snow and ice roaring down the mountain toward me.

"Well, I have a thing for buttons. And yes, as fetishes go, it's not . . . What do you mean a *small* protuberance?"

She slipped her hand behind my head and kissed me long and deep. I'd be in serious trouble if she moaned so I pushed her away – just as one escaped her lips. A throaty, *I want you* rumble.

"Tash, wait. Mary's in the other room."

"We're not going to have sex, Dax. I just want to lie next to you, maybe kiss a little and let you give me a back rub. Unless you'd like me to leave?" she said with a grin.

"No. It's too late for that."

I pulled her close and ran a finger down her spine.

~~

Tasha was introspective when she left his house before sunrise, thinking herself ready for love but frightened by the want of it. Inevitably, her father came to mind. His was the longest relationship she'd had with a man, and, if not for his twisted nature, she might have found love much sooner.

He'd touched her as long as she could remember, and not once did she think it wrong because he hadn't raised her that way. When the truth finally dawned, she left for Florida to live with an aunt and didn't tell anyone.

But she'd been haunted by what he'd done, reliving his abuse through recurring nightmares that finally ended after finding Dax and Mary. Theirs was a special relationship.

And when they invited her into their lives and hearts, she'd been renewed.

Tasha never gave herself to anyone, not really. Many men wanted her, but she'd never been interested.

Until now.

There was something compelling about the way Dax treated the women in his life – as gifts to be cherished and nurtured rather than played with and discarded.

And, of course, there was also how he made her feel. Her face flushed just thinking about him.

These feelings were new to her, and she thought about calling Jeri to get perspective and advice. Tasha loved her friend and trusted her opinion.

~~

"You know one of the things I like about you most, Dax? You'll eat cold leftovers for any meal of the day or night," Mary said, grinning. "It makes it easy to get up and out on a morning like this without having to make breakfast."

She fussed with her fishing gear in anticipation and couldn't wait to get a line wet and win the bet with him.

"Have I ever made you feed me, girl?"

"No. I didn't mean to imply you did. I like to cook, and you are the lucky beneficiary. I'm just saying I appreciate how easy you are to please. You're what they call *low-maintenance*, and I like that. And I like you."

The twinkle in her eye revealed more than her affection for me. She was celebrating a victory she had yet to win.

"Well, thanks hon. I like you, too. But I'm still gonna kick your butt. And watch you clean fish. I might help you with the dishes because you worked in an *I like you*, but I'm going to smirk while I dry."

She laughed and shook her head. "Yeah, good luck with that. You might be able to out-fish me, but not Tasha. She's a fish-catching machine."

"I know, right? Is she using a special bait or scent?"

"I'm not saying yes, and I'm not saying no, but as she told me, 'My boat, my rules. Don't tell anybody, anything. Especially Dax.'"

"Did she really say that? I thought she liked me."

"Oh, she does. But just because she kisses you doesn't mean she's going to share her fishing secrets."

'Uh, what?"

Mary didn't appreciated how amusing it would be to tease him until she saw the expression on his face.

"Why are you *Uh, what-ing* me? Did my eyes deceive me? Weren't you two kissing the other night by her truck?"

"Well, yeah. I was trying to figure it out before I told you, but now that you know, what do you think about it? And keep in mind, while I can see the fun you're having, I'm serious about knowing your thoughts."

I *was* serious and tried to look it.

"Okay," she said with a somber voice. "If you really want my opinion, I'll tell you. I'm sorry, Dax, but I'm . . . happy about it. Happy for you, happy for her, happy for me."

She burst out laughing when I called her a smartass and said it took one to know one.

"So, how do *you* feel about it?"

"I've cared about her for a while now, but I think you knew that already," I said, and received a nod. "But I'm afraid of hurting her."

Mary raised her brow.

"Your father."

"Is that all?" she asked.

"That's enough. If Tasha knew, she'd never look at me the same. I don't want her to find out I'm someone she wouldn't like much. Or respect."

Mary nodded. "I understand. Don't know if it helps, but, for what it's worth, I know what you've done, and I like and respect you just fine."

"Thanks, sweetie. It does."

We looked into each other like we did sometimes, communing without saying a word.

Knock, knock, knockin' on Heaven's door.

The audible alarm for the front gate announced Tasha coming to take Mary and Watson fishing.

"Hey, Mare. I forgot to ask where y'all are going? Indian Pass, I'm assuming?"

"Yup. We're going to try Dry Bar first, maybe head over to L.A. later. I don't think Tasha would mind me giving you that info seeing as you don't have a boat to get out to her honey-holes. How about you?"

"The Maze. St. Joe Bay doesn't hold the fish this time of year. Well, good luck then. Hope you catch fish. Just not as big as mine." I smiled and she did the same.

The other alarms sounded as Tasha got closer to the clearing, and Mary grabbed her fishing rods and backpack.

"Oh, by the way. I know you had a girl in your room last night and I'm okay with it because I trust your judgement. I hope you'll be as understanding when I have a boy in mine."

She gave me a grin and walked away.

"That will be a completely different situation," I called after her, "and I will not be at all understanding. Stop laughing, you little shit. It's not funny."

But it was.

When she got into the truck, Mary looked at me with a full-on twinkle and I cracked up.

~

Tasha heard his laughter as she pulled away and said, "What's that about?"

"I was giving Dax grief about your being in his room."

"Uh, I . . ."

"What? *Et tu, Tasha?* Dax gave me the same response when I mentioned the two of you kissing the other night."

She grinned as Tasha's face turned red.

"We, uh . . ."

Mary thought the two of them were acting like they were the kids and she was the parent. "You guys are adults, you know. You can do whatever you want."

"You're right, Mary. We are. But it doesn't mean we can do anything we want because it's not just about us." Tasha looked over and said, "It's about *all* of us."

"Well, yeah. I know, but . . ."

"And what you know but maybe don't fully understand is that Dax doesn't just love you, he loooooooves you. You're the apple of his eye, and your needs outweigh all others. He'd do anything to protect you, and, although I shouldn't tell you this, I think he'd do almost anything to please you."

Mary nodded and grew quiet.

"We aren't hemming and hawing because we've forgotten who the adults are, we're doing it because we care

13

about you. If our being together is a problem for you, it's a problem for us, and, more specifically, for Dax. He'd drop me in a heartbeat if he thought you didn't want me around. And just so you know, I'd leave of my own accord if you felt that way, because . . ."

Tasha looked over and saw the tears in her eyes.

"Oh, Mary. I'm sorry. I wasn't trying to come down on you or make you feel bad. I was just explaining why . . ."

"I know, Tash, I know. You just reminded me how lucky I am. Thank you," she said, scooching closer to give a hug.

"Don't forget about me," Watson chimed in and stuck his head between them from the back seat.

~~

Where St. Joe Bay was sand and grass, Indian Pass Lagoon was mud and oyster bar. The Maze referred to an area behind the campground at the end of Indian Pass Road.

I caught a red on my first cast and put it in the cooler behind me, letting the fish firm up on the ice before being filleted. It was a quarter-inch shy of the maximum slot size with some weight to it, and I grinned knowing I wouldn't be doing dishes tonight.

The peacefulness of kayaking, especially fishing from one, is hard to articulate. The connection to nature is gratifying and intimate. You can reach out and touch it. And sometimes, it can reach out and touch you, too.

Last year, I'd meandered through the back waters of Money Bayou, appreciating the wilderness beauty of a road less traveled. It's secluded, and if you got into trouble no one would know about it.

Those were my thoughts exactly when I heard the noise behind me, one made by a twelve-foot alligator sunning himself on the bank – a bank three-feet away.

An interesting thing about gators is, they don't move quickly. Until they do.

Did I panic?

No.

Did I piss my pants?

Come on.

Did I reach for the knife?

Oh, hell yeah.

Fortunately, he backed down. And by backed down, I mean he let me paddle away from the bank and meander my ass out of there. He did, however, follow me and slip under the kayak a few feet from shore.

Do I now own a pair of alligator boots?

Uh, no.

I jumped out and ran like a little girl.

chapter three

"Are you in my quadrant, Lieutenant Yar?" Jeri asked when she answered the phone.

"No, Seven, but I could be. Unless you have plans to come to this sector anytime soon."

They were both huge Star Trek fans and liked to use the show's lexicon whenever possible. Tasha's middle name really was Yar, and back in their academy days she'd named Jeri, *Seven of Nine,* because of her Borg-like ability to function rationally in stressful situations.

They'd been best friends ever since.

"No, sorry. I'm trying to catch-up with the workload left by my former boss who was recently killed in the field. Rightfully so, I might add."

Robert James Thompson was the former Assistant Deputy-Director in the Atlanta field office. He headed the Sex Trafficking division and had been doing an exceptional job – for those kidnapping and selling human beings for sex. He not only protected the criminals involved and facilitated their efforts; he'd raped hundreds of stolen young girls.

He also turned out to be Mary's uncle, and, after her father went missing, Robert tried to take her, as well. But she ended up surprising him – to death.

"How is everyone doing?" Jeri asked.

She'd known Tasha a long time, and the sound of her voice as she talked about Dax was like music to her ears. "Am I still funnier than he is?"

"You are singularly unique, Seven, especially to me, and have always given me the utmost joy and laughter. But Dax also tickles my funny bone, and . . ."

"And? What else is he tickling, Tash?" Jeri said as a joke. But when her friend didn't respond, she became serious. "Really?"

"Jeri, I'm in unfamiliar waters, and I'd like to talk to you about it if you don't mind."

"Of course, girlfriend. Fire phasers when ready."

"I'd rather do it in person. I could come this weekend."

Jeri wore a big grin on her face which, of course, Tasha couldn't see. "Oh, it's like that, is it? A see me, hear me situation? Interesting. Text me your itinerary, and I'll pick you up in the shuttlecraft. Maybe we'll beam on over to Darwin's Burgers and Blues, if time permits."

"Ooohh, yeah. I haven't had a decent burger in ages. Thanks, Seven. See ya when I see ya. Love you."

"Back at you. Live long and prosper."

~~

"I'm very sorry for what I done, and I wish I'd had the time to make it up to her, to make things right." The sweat traced down her drawn face as she wobbled on the chair. She sounded sincere to me.

Maybe she was?

"Still, you have to admit some things just can't be forgiven, Dot. Things that cause irreparable harm or death. Like what happened to your little girl."

The wobble got worse as she'd been standing a while.

"I mean, it's difficult to overlook the actions of a mother who'd molest her own daughter, rent her out to strangers, and then sell movies of what they did. Wouldn't you agree?"

I sipped some ice-water from the glass in my latex-covered hand and asked if she'd like a drink. When she nodded, I stood and held it to her lips.

"Try to keep still, now. You're going to fall if you're not careful." I sat back in the chair and asked how she could atone for the damage done to her daughter.

"God has forgiven me. He has. And it's not for you to judge me. Only He can."

"Hmmm. I often wonder about the existence of God. While I can appreciate a Being of superior knowledge and intellect, I have trouble understanding why that entity would allow so much evil to go unpunished. Or better still, why they refuse to intervene on behalf of the innocent in the first place? It troubles me, it really does. I guess it's why I'm here with you. Is it fair for you to live after Sara killed herself because of the humiliations you heaped upon her?"

She started to cry and, in doing so, almost lost her balance. I reached out to steady the chair.

"I'm not the same person I was then," she said as a sob heaved from her chest. "I've changed. I'm sorry I hurt Sara. Really! I wish I could go back and change things, but I can't."

"You bring up an interesting point. Second chances. Should a person like you have one? My initial reaction is no. The person you *were* abused your daughter and caused her to suffer, culminating in her death. But you seem believable in your regret, and therein lies the rub. Can a person move beyond who they were and go on to help make the world a better place for others?"

"Yes, yes they can. I have. I want to atone, to make things better. I want to save others from people like me."

I nodded and walked to the sink, washed and rinsed the glass, and then set it in the rack to dry.

"This is great news, Dot. Great news. It makes it easier to give you a second chance, and I thank you for that."

I pulled out my phone and pushed play.

Dottie stood white-faced and still. The video showed her and an eight-year old girl drinking from teacups, pretending it was a 'fancy affair.' When Dottie filled their cups the second time, she poured from an unlabeled bottle. After a few minutes, she moved closer and touched the girl more affectionately as they laughed and told stories.

"We're in a *good news - bad news* place here, Dot," I said and put the phone back in my pocket. "The good news is you haven't molested her yet. If you had, I'd have taken the knife to you the moment you walked through the door. The bad news, well, you know what the bad news is and why you're standing on a chair with a rope around your neck."

I looked her in the eye with the knife in my hand.

"You haven't changed, and I can't let you hurt anyone else. You understand, right? But I'll give you a second

19

chance. Kick the chair out from under you. You said you wanted to save others from people like yourself. Prove it. Validate God's forgiveness and save girls like Rachel - from *you*. Otherwise . . ."

~~

"Thanks again for waiting. I had a little trouble finding the place. Guess I should embrace the twenty-first century and start using GPS technology, but I like to go from here to there the old fashion way – with maps and intuition. And, of course, being a man, we don't admit we're lost or ask for directions till we absolutely have to." I looked at her with a smile and she returned a nod.

"My husband and father are the same way. Frustrating sometimes, but it's a *gotta love 'em* deal," she said. "So, this is a Christmas gift, huh? For your daughter?"

"Yes. Well, a Christmas-Birthday present."

"She must be something. I like her already."

I nodded, took the receipt, and shook her hand. "She's a special girl. And thanks again. You take care, now."

She waved and gave me a thumbs-up as I drove away.

The sun had already set, and the opportunity to see the green light some people said blinked the moment it slipped below the horizon was gone. I'd been seeking that flash for decades and only seen sunset after beautiful sunset.

Dammit.

On the way home, I thought about Dottie, her daughter, her daughter's death, and her own.

She surprised me by taking the second chance I offered. After a minute or two, she said a prayer and wobbled the chair until it fell over. I'd never seen anyone hang before, and she stared at me the whole time.

Dottie seemed sorry for what she'd done to Sara, and I think she acknowledged what she was by killing herself, knowing she'd molest the little girl next door, eventually.

I felt some sadness for her, but she had come to that realization far too late, and I didn't give her any more sympathy than was fair – to her and to Sara.

As it always did, the question popped into my head, the one I'd asked myself the first time I considered eliminating as much evil from the world as I could.

Can I live with it?

The answer is always the same. *Yes.*

If the police, the courts, the politicians, the people, or the oft prayed to but probably non-existent God would step up and tell the wicked 'NO MORE,' then I wouldn't have to take matters into my own hands.

If you kill the innocent, you die. Molest a child, you die. Rape, you die. It's that simple.

And that hard. Suspecting and knowing are not the same, and I won't take a life unless I KNOW. Unfortunately, I've known too many since Mary's father.

~~

Watson looked up, and there she was. His effort to reach her came from concentration and belief that he could. Mary tried to teach what came naturally to her – the ability to fly. She flew into the air with her arms extended, and Watson began to have similar success by using his tail.

"Not bad. Not bad at all. You're really getting the hang of it. Or the tail of it," she said and giggled at her joke.

"If I don't question the impossibility of it, I seem to do fine," he said and jumped around on the cloud they were perched on.

Mary let her feet dangle from its edge.

"There's Yvette's house. Want to see what she's up to? Maybe it's movie night," she said with a wink and a grin.

Watson rolled his eyes and shook his head.

When he and Mary used to live across the street from each other, Yvette was his adopted guardian. And she'd talk to him as if he understood her, which he did. She did not, however, understand him.

English was her primary language, and she knew some rudimentary Spanish. But Retriever? Unlike Mary, who was fluent in all three, Yvette didn't get it. Or him.

Movie night was a case in point. Yvette would ask what he liked to watch, but regardless of his pick, she always played an 'oldie but a goodie.' It became a sore spot for him, and when he'd left her house to find Mary at Dax's, he vowed never to watch another *oldie* again.

Mary laughed and leaned back. They were close, best friends, and telepathically connected since childhood.

Or puppyhood, depending on your point of view.

"Well, it wasn't a fun time," he said.

"Oh, I know. Why do you think I didn't come over then?"

"You said you had to iron on Thursdays?"

They laughed some more until Mary glanced down at her old house. Her lips pinched and her eyes narrowed.

"Mary? I'm not sure that's a good idea."

"I know. Still, I think I'll go have a look. By myself, though, okay? I don't want you to see me that way."

"I get it," he said and rubbed her face with his snout. She kissed him and scratched behind his ears for a bit.

"Even in our dreams, it feels sooooo good," he said and jumped from the cloud, flying through the air using his ears like the wings of a plane.

Mary flew inside and saw herself in a series of visual snippets: before, during, and after her father's betrayal. The sickening way she convinced him to remove the restraints gave her the chance to escape, but she'd been undone when the time came because he'd recorded them and threatened to show everyone if she told anyone. She couldn't live with people knowing, so she went to the woods to die.

And then Dax found her.

Mary flew away thinking about the man who raised and raped her. She didn't know precisely where he was, but she knew exactly what happened to him.

~~

I pulled into the clearing after midnight and wondered if the 'Big Guy' had already come and gone. Although my gift traveled by trailer rather than a sleigh, I felt a little bit like Santa Claus – albeit a less tolerant incarnation. Where he'd leave coal in your stocking for being naughty, I might take something from you instead.

Mary will be surprised.

In addition to celebrating Christmas and her birthday, next week would also be an anniversary for us. A year had passed since I'd accidently knocked her out trying to keep her from killing herself.

After bringing her home that night, I looked through her phone for answers as she lay unconscious on my couch. The hopelessness in her eyes on the videos her father made broke my heart, and I'd resolved to do what had to be done to end her suffering and hold him accountable. In less than twenty-four hours, she was free, and he was dead.

I suspect Mary knows what I've been doing since then, but she hasn't said anything. Maybe she feels the same way about the people who inflict cruelties upon the innocent. They have to go.

And I have to do it.

chapter four

Watson's head lay on the mattress as he sat by the bed. His stomach growled and he needed to go outside, but he wasn't going to let her get the best of him. He could wait for as long as she could pretend to sleep.

The smells coming down the hallway begged to differ, and, before long, his tongue touched the tip of her nose.

"What's making you crazier? The peeing, the presents, or the pancakes?" Mary asked without opening her eyes.

"Why do you test me so?" he said and nudged her.

"Cause it's fun, and you'd feel the same way if I'd been the one who'd cracked first."

She patted and scratched him up before getting out of bed to open the door. Watson stepped around her and made a beeline for the back door and yard.

"Guess it's the peeing." she said and moseyed down the hall, yawning and scratching her head. A bluesy two-part harmony with acoustic guitar backup heralded her arrival.

"Happy Birthday to you. Merry Christmas to you. Happy Birthday, dear darlin.' Mary Christmas to yaaaaa."

They kept playing and humming and grinning until Dax played a solo with too much, Dax.

Tasha stopped and looked at him while Mary cracked up. They'd been here before.

"Why, Dax? Why do you always take a simple song and turn it into a solo soliloquy? Didn't you get enough guitar time when you were a child?"

"He's still a child, Tasha," Mary said, chuckling. "Don't let his 'who me?' expression fool you. He'll snatch a song right out from under you if you let him."

"I don't think you two realize the pressure I'm under to improve. Being the worst guitar player in the room is a difficult cross to bear."

I placed the back of my hand against my forehead in an *Oh, woe is me* pose expecting them to fall out laughing at my pitiful pantomime. But they took a different approach.

"You know, Mary, he's right. It can't be easy for him to play in our shadows knowing that even if we lost an arm or most of our fingers, he'd still only be second fiddle to us."

"It's sad, that's for sure. But I'd rather not imagine the caterwauling sound his fiddling would make."

I could tell they thought I was special. Maybe the short, yellow bus kind, but I could work with that.

"Do we want presents or pancakes first?" I asked. Watson walked by licking his lips so that answered that. After breakfast, we sat around the Christmas coffee table and opened our gifts.

I expected Mary, who was tidy and organized, to open hers carefully to protect and save the wrapping for another day's use, but she ripped the paper with abandon and acted every bit the little girl I fell in love with. Her smile was infectious and her cuteness undeniable.

Tasha's eyes glistened through unshed tears as she sat back and watched. I couldn't help loving her more, even as I considered how to end things between us.

"Thanks," Mary said, giving them both a hug and a kiss. "For everything."

Tasha got up to leave. She was going to work early so her partner could spend the morning with his wife and kids. He'd come in around noon and stay late so someone else could have Christmas dinner with theirs.

We followed her outside, and Mary saw the big red bow around a bright yellow machine on a coal black trailer. She grinned and raised her eyes.

"For me?"

"What? Oh, no. Sorry, hon. It *is* a sweet-sixteen present for a sweet sixteen-year old, but, as Tasha can attest, you have the maturity of a much older young lady. Why, what would you do with a three-hundred sixty degree, zero turning radius, riding lawn mower?"

"Work!" She punched my arm, hugged me, punched me again, and then ran to the trailer.

Tasha chuckled and shook her head. "You know, most girls get that excited over a new car or a trip to Europe. But she's not most girls, is she?"

"No, she isn't," I said and put my arm around her. The vanilla scent in her hair reminded me of a root beer float when she stretched to kiss my cheek.

"I like you, Dax."

I nodded but didn't reply till she raised her brow at me. "I like you, too, Tash."

We looked at each other for a few moments before she walked to her truck.

"Bye, Mary. Have fun."

"Are you coming over for dinner?"

"Depends on if I end up covering for someone. Save a piece of cheesecake just in case, okay? Might stop by later. See ya."

Mary waved and continued to inspect the mower – *her* mower. She hadn't expected it, but it was the perfect gift. It satisfied a lot of wants and needs: a desire to work and save money, to be free and independent while doing so, to be outside in the sun with the birds and the bees and the snakes and the trees.

She liked the idea of being her own boss, as well as the physical benefits outdoor labor offered.

Since Dax began training her, she appreciated the need for stamina and strength more. If the body is strong, the mind is clearer – both necessary components to accurately assess and solve situational problems.

It helped her disable and defeat the FBI man who shot Dax in the back and tried to kidnap her. After shoving an ink pen in his eye, she picked up his gun and put three bullets in his head to ensure he'd never hurt anyone else.

The training was part of the reason she'd finish the rest of the school year at home. The incident in the locker room made that necessary . . .

She'd been staying after school to attend an advanced math seminar offered by the university. On her way to class, she heard sounds of distress from the boy's locker room and found a girl laid out on a bench with her arms stretched and pinned by a boy who sat on them so he could fondle her as another boy knelt between her legs.

"Stop, please. Don't," the girl begged.

"Hand me that towel so I can shut her up."

"I've got something better," his friend said and reached under her skirt to pull them off.

The boy on the bench was big, but the one on his knees was huge. If he got up, Mary knew she'd be in trouble.

She moved in and punched him in the throat. When he gasped, she drove her elbow into the side of his head and sent him crashing to the floor. As the other boy stood, Mary caught him by surprise with her shoulder, knocking him down and putting him in a choke hold.

The girl was slow to react but quick to leave, running out and away without a word. Mary noted it but didn't judge or hold it against her.

The boy in her arms went slack, and she checked him and his friend for a pulse. They'd live but given what they would have done to that girl, she wasn't sure they should.

Mary long suspected what Dax was doing and believed he meted out a much needed form of justice – permanent punishment. The lives of those abused were positively impacted when their abuser was finally, forever eliminated. Like hers had been when he put her father in the ground.

They'd later discussed the locker room attack in detail – situational awareness, risk assessment, use of force – to better develop and hone her conflict resolution skills.

It was always about learning with Dax. And she came to realize that, while teaching her to defend herself, he was also teaching her to think, to be measured in her response, to be aware of her surroundings and the evil in the world. He was open to the goodness in folks but prepared for the badness, and he wanted her to do the same.

'People are difficult to know,' he'd told her, 'and, unfortunately, not to be easily trusted.'

She said no when he asked about involving the police. "If the girl comes forward, I will for sure. But she might not want anyone to know, and I have to respect that. For now."

But it left her in a tough position.

Was she enabling those boys to continue to hurt others by protecting that girl's privacy?

When Dax asked for their names, she balked and said she'd like to keep them to herself for the time being.

"Your call, girl," he said. "But watch your back."

She asked about being home-schooled again for the next semester, and Dax thought it a good idea.

So had the principal.

It wasn't her first incident since going back.

"Well, what do you think?" I asked, watching her sit on the mower, fiddle with buttons, and pretend to cut grass. "You wanted a way to work by yourself."

"It's a great gift. Perfect, really. I could have worked on the Cape or in town without any trouble, but . . ." she said, grinning when he said *uh-huh*. "I could have, Dax."

"Well, you know how I feel about what happened with those boys in the locker room."

"That all's well that ends well?"

"Uh, that's not an accurate recitation of what I said, now is it?" I looked at her and waited to hear the truth.

"Not exactly. You said you were 'Proud as shit,' and 'Those assholes got what they deserved.'"

We laughed and then talked turkey. "How much longer does that bird have to be in the oven?"

We took a chance the residents and snowbirds would stay home with family and friends on Christmas morning and drove to the Piggly Wiggly parking lot to practice maneuvering the trailer.

Mary reminded me she only carried a learner's permit after pulling out of the driveway.

"So, you're going with me when I cut grass?"

"Yeah, funny thing about that. I got a good price on the trailer and mower and made the deal thinking Florida had a work waiver that allowed a youngster with a permit to drive by themselves in certain conditions. Turns out they don't. So I'm working on a couple ideas. Meanwhile, yes. I'll come with you, maybe cut the grass while you weed whack. We'll get done in no time."

"Huh."

"What?"

"Well, you've mistakenly put yourself in the driver's seat, as it were. I see you as the weed whacking variable in this equation. And secondly . . ."

~

No sooner had we sat down to dinner than my phone rang. Usually, I'd let it go to voicemail but saw the call was from Julia. I showed Mary who enthusiastically nodded her head. Two minutes later we were clearing the table after shoveling some food in our mouths.

Julia owned and operated the Scallop RePUBlic with her husband, Vince. It was a nice place to go for drinks and live music on the Cape, and Mary's favorite place to play. The acoustics were good and the ambience cozy. She'd been asked to play there quite a bit, and every time was a thrill. Nothing brought her more joy than playing and singing, and the applause she received was the cherry on top.

By the way, St. Joseph Bay is THE place to find the most succulent scallops in the state, maybe the entire country, so a lot of businesses have scallop names: Scallop Rentals, Scallop Dock and Dive, Scallop Auto repair, Scallop Nail Salon, Jet Ski and Scallop . . .

I know, I know. But whatchu gonna do?

We arrived to find a nice reception of people who'd had a good day and were looking to enjoy a good Christmas night. Mary was a minor celebrity in the area, and the locals clapped and cheered when we walked through the door. She was a talented musician who played from the heart and invited others to feel the music and love it as she did.

I didn't know if she was a prodigy or not, but her guitar skills far exceeded my own. Not that I was awful. I'd been playing gigs in the city and around the state for a long while.

Watson walked to the stage and watched us set up. Julia didn't normally let animals into the bar, except maybe the stray cat who oversaw the construction of the place and now guarded the vehicles in the parking lot – by catnapping in the seat when a window was left open. But in order to get Mary, she had to take him as well.

Watson smiled and nodded when Julia glanced his way and tried not to laugh as she turned toward me.

"Did you see that?"

"See what?" I asked.

"That dog. He smiled and nodded, and then winked at me, too. That can't be right. Right?"

"Well, Julia, I'll tell you what he told me one day when I asked the same thing. 'There are more things in Heaven and Earth, Dax, than are dreamt of in your philosophy.'"

I grinned when confusion creased her brow.

"What?"

"Apparently, he's well read and fancies himself a canine King. In this case, Hamlet."

"What?"

"Dax is just having fun with you, Miss Julia," Mary said, giving me a twinkle only I could see. "I want to thank you for having me. I always love it here. It's like a big living room where friends gather to have fun."

"We love having you come play for us, Mary. People ask for you all the time. You're incredibly talented. Do you know how good you are?"

Mary opened her mouth and then blushed. Her love for music was a passion and her ability a gift she recognized but didn't fully understand. It came as easily to her as drawing a breath. How could one be esteemed for doing something as simple as breathing?

"Don't go giving her ideas, Julia. I've spent months telling her she's just *okay*, and you'll undo all my efforts to keep her humble and at home if you tell her the truth."

We all laughed, and Mary mouthed a *Thank you* to me after Julia left to help a patron.

"She's not wrong, you know. You're good."

"I know," Mary said and turned red again.

An hour of play and audience appreciation later, Tasha walked through the door. I'd texted and asked her to join us if she could. After Mary and I finished the song, I called her on stage with a nod.

There was a time when she'd have begged off, but not anymore. We'd played so often, at home and around town, it was now second nature to her. She picked up a guitar, and I asked her to play *Summertime*.

Tasha and Mary grinned knowing how much I loved to hear them sing it. Knowing also how I might try to highjack the song when it came time to play my solo.

But I didn't mess it up this time – Watson did, when he turned two-part harmony into three.

~~

She ran to her bedroom and threw herself on the bed. Isabel had been criticized and belittled by her mother for years, ever since her father left them. But tonight's tirade was particularly hurtful, and Isabel could feel despair tug at the remnants of her self-esteem.

Maybe she was as worthless as she'd been told?

Isabel heard her mother's boyfriend say, "Stop talking to her that way," as she cried into her pillow. He knocked and came into her room. After closing the door, he sat on the edge of the bed and began to stroke her hair.

"Honey, I'm sorry. Your mom had no right to say that to you. I don't know what she was thinking, but I have a good idea why she said it."

Isabel turned her head and looked at him with wet, wounded eyes. She choked back a sob and wiped the snot from her nose with the back of her hand.

"Why? Why would she say something like that?"

He brushed the hair from her face and smiled.

"She's jealous of your youth and spirit. You're free to become whoever you want to be, and she isn't. It makes her angry and vicious. I won't let her get away with calling you names. Especially when they're lies." He wiped at her tears and gave her a tissue to blow her nose.

"I *am* fat. Well, not really, but I'm not thin like she is." Isabel took another tissue to wipe her eyes.

"Izzy, she wishes she looked as good. That's why she gets so mad. She knows men like girls who have a body like yours. Maybe I should dump your mom and be with you?"

He smiled and she did, too.

Frank kissed her forehead and then her nose. When his lips brushed hers, Isabel was stunned and unable to form a coherent thought. She kissed him back, not understanding what was happening or what she was doing.

"We should keep this to ourselves, don't you think? After all, it's private and belongs only to us."

Isabel nodded, confused but uplifted. Frank didn't think she was a fat worthless slob. He cared about her.

And when he started coming into her room late at night, he made her feel loved, special, and wanted.

chapter five

Tasha decided to drive to Atlanta to visit her friend. She thought the time alone on the road would be relaxing, and it was – for the first four hours. Then she wondered why she hadn't just flown. Was it because of the time spent travelling, or the crowds of people trying to reach their New Year's Eve destination?

It would have taken an hour and forty-five minutes to drive to the airport, an hour of waiting before takeoff, about an hour of flight time, and another half hour before her tired bottom relaxed in Jeri's car.

So, yes, she'd already be there by now instead of having another hour to go. But no. It was the people. She saw enough of them, at the office, out on the street, and needed a break. Except she already missed Dax and Mary.

What was it about those two? The conversation, the fun, the music? The sense of belonging – and wanting to belong?

Goose bumps played hopscotch up and down her spine thinking how Dax rubbed her back with a soft sensual touch that said he enjoyed it as much as she did. Maybe more. His yearning for her was evident, and she was both appreciative and disappointed in his hesitance to go further.

Maybe it was like he'd said – Mary was across the hall. She understood but suspected there might be other reasons. Would he have done anything if she hadn't kissed him first? Or snuck into his room?

Her face flushed. She'd never done anything like that, and it embarrassed and excited her.

What is it about Dax?

"What?"

Jeri smiled, shook her head, and took a sip of wine.

"Where are you, girl? I *said*, what is it about Dax you find so appealing? He's not funnier than me, is he?"

It was Tasha's turn to shake, smile, and sip.

"Seven, I've told you many, many times you are a hoot. Maybe the hoot of my life. To paraphrase a late seventies E. F. Hutton commercial, 'When Jeri Ryan jokes, people laugh.'"

Jeri asked where she'd seen a seventies commercial.

"Dax showed it to me on YouTube. He's a little weird that way and uses a lot of movie and television quotes. Kind of like we do with Star Trek. He's even got Mary doing it."

"I don't know about *his* TV lingo, but our Trek lexicon is legit," Jeri said and lifted her glass.

"Too legit to quit," Tasha said, lifting and clinking. "Dax can be as funny as you, but the quality isn't as consistent. What really makes me laugh though, is when he thinks he's clever as shit but really isn't. The look in his eyes when he sees the one in mine and Mary's is, I don't know, endearing. And cute."

Jeri grinned at her friend.

"Damn, Tash. You sound like you're smitten." She reached for the bottle of chardonnay and filled their glasses. They clinked again and took another gulp of the grape of life.

"I'm afraid it's worse than that, Seven. I'm in love."

"Damn, really? I mean, damn. Have you told him?"

In the decade-plus they'd known each other, Jeri never heard anything even close. Tasha barely dated, and the longest relationship she'd been in lasted three months.

"I've had feelings for him for a while but only came to terms with it recently. And yes. I've mentioned it."

"What did you say?"

"I told him I liked him."

Jeri cracked up, spilled some wine, and licked it from her arm. It was the good stuff and not to be wasted.

"Sounds like you bared your soul."

Tasha said she'd waited weeks before kissing him, and Jeri called her a hussy for making the first move. When she mentioned crawling into his bed, Jeri spilled more wine she didn't reclaim.

"What? You slut."

"I know. Can you imagine? I was bold as all get out . . . Until the morning when I woke up with him looking at me. He kissed me, I mean kisssssed me, and I left lickety-split." Tasha quit talking when her face warmed at the memory.

"You tease. What the hell?"

"I got scared. I didn't know why then, but I do now. I've never felt this way and I don't trust it. Even more so because I want it so badly."

A quiet moment passed before Jeri spoke up.

"If you want my opinion, Tash, you have no choice but to follow your heart. You've already become a tramp and a wanton woman – and I couldn't be happier for you. I love you, girlfriend, and hope he doesn't take long to say it, too. Remind him I work for the FBI if he doesn't treat you right."

They hugged and drank and drank some more.

"Speaking of your work, do you think you're going to get promoted? Do you want to be?"

Jeri was the Section Chief in the Sex Trafficking division of the Bureau's Atlanta office. She'd worked directly under the man who tried to kidnap Mary.

"Well, if they offer me the job, I'll take it. But honestly, I love what I'm doing now as Chief. I have good women and men under me, and we've accomplished a lot. Of course, we could have done more if Thompson hadn't protected those slave-trading bastards. I'm so glad Mary beat the shit out of him before punching his ticket."

Tasha nodded. They were on the same page when it came to people who sold human beings.

"How is she, by the way? Any trauma or behavior problems since then? I really like that girl and her pluck."

"She's doing good. Better than good. You'd think there'd be some emotional repercussions, but she's solid. Some of that has to do with her relationship with Dax, but Mary has a lot of innate strength. Remember what she did to get away from her father?"

It struck Jeri the three of them were not just friends – they were a family. A strong, tightknit, loving family. Maybe Tasha was ready for more than just a romantic relationship? When her phone rang, Tasha left for the bathroom.

"Ryan."

She listened as a parole officer gave her information on a parolee she'd asked to be kept informed about, and then asked a couple of questions before hanging up. When Tasha came into the room, she poured some wine and told her.

"Dorothy Walton was found dead. Apparent suicide.

"Sara's mother? My Sara? How?"

"She hung herself. The note said, 'I'm sorry.'

~~

Mary declined to play the Raw Bar with Dax, choosing instead to update and organize the spreadsheet for her fledgling lawn care business. She'd taken advantage of the time between Christmas and New Year's to acquire enough clients to hit the ground running come springtime. More than enough, actually.

The people who rented out their million-dollar homes, condos, and cabins typically left their upkeep to realtor management groups. They were responsible for hundreds of houses and took a percentage of the rental rate as service fees. In addition to cleaning the interior from top to bottom every week and making minor repairs, the lawn needed to be maintained as well.

Mary first thought she'd subcontract with one or more of the many real estate concerns in St. Vincent – there were seven on Cape San Blas alone – but Dax told her a lot of the owners spent the holiday season in their beautiful homes and suggested she might gain more autonomy for herself by appealing to them in person.

He was right.

Many were impressed with her *moxie* and seemed genuinely interested in helping a young entrepreneur get started. Mary sensed some of that interest might have to do with her being a *pretty young thang,* as Dax would sometime call her, and she didn't know how to feel about it.

'Well, are you going to do the work?' he'd asked.

'Of course,' she told him. 'Just because they think I'm cute, it doesn't mean I'm not going to do my best.'

'Well, there ya go.'

Mary figured she could work a hard three days a week and make enough money to feed a college fund. She'd work more days if Dax let her, but he insisted she at least pretend to be a teenager, maturity notwithstanding, and that meant time for play. When she asked if it also meant time for dating, he held onto his smile. But just barely.

She thought of the day last summer when Dax was bothered by her talking to an older boy. He trained her and knew she could defend herself but was still perturbed and didn't understand why – until he did.

He'd become paternal in his feelings toward her, and Mary began to tease him as any daughter would – by making him think about her and boys. Which was funny, because she already decided not to have sex for a long time.

There were too many things she wanted to do with her life, and they didn't include getting pregnant or emotionally ensnared until she'd learned all there was to learn and seen all there was to see.

Dax knew of her ambitions but not of her abstinence, and she was having too much fun to tell him, right now. Besides, he'd teased her about using coffee table coasters far longer than she teased him about boys, so it was his fault. *He'd* started it.

So much for my maturity, she thought and chuckled.

~~

One of the things I liked about playing a gig outside was the relative inattention of those who listened. They mostly talked, laughed, and had their good time with each other – not me. Which was fine because I made mistakes. Not so bad as to make one cringe, but I wasn't like Mary. She was so good; she was *too* good. That little shit.

Oh well, back to me.

As I stood on the newly built stage at the back of the parking lot, I remembered the old one. It had only been ten feet from the pavement and the large crowds used to sprawl into the road, particularly during the Singer-Songwriter Festival. In fact, the bar used to put up signs that read, 'Caution: Drunks Ahead.'

The Indian Pass Trading Post, or as we locals called it, the Raw Bar, served alcoholic beverages with their oysters. I'm told they're pretty good, but I have yet to eat one.

To me, it seemed like swallowing a huge booger – but without the flavor. I have two friends who tell me they taste great, especially when baked with cheese, and they've made it their mission to get me to try one.

Good luck with that.

Even if it had the supposed aphrodisiacal effect, I still wouldn't give it the time of day. And I didn't need the boost. Just thinking about Tasha was sufficient.

Although I'd 'fallen and I can't get up' in love with her, I believed I could still keep her at an emotional arm's length. After all, I'd been pretty successful in doing so for months. Until she kissed me. Now, I thought about her too often and in too much detail. Like the way she moaned.

I thought I'd thought out loud when the crowd gave me a look, but the sour note I struck screeched like fingernails on a chalkboard. Guess I *could* make one cringe.

"Just seeing if y'all were listening."

A few people laughed and went back to their lives. I decided to finish my set by playing songs that required my undivided, un-Tasha thinking attention.

Good luck with *that.*

~~

Isabel felt a soft caress as she woke to see him kneeling on the floor by her bed.

"Happy New Year, Izzy."

Usually there was a hurried, almost frantic few minutes of activity when he'd come in her room, but now his fingers tracked a lazy line from her face to her breasts before he kissed one, and then the other with a slow deliberation that deepened her desire.

Frank pulled the nightgown over her head, and then did something he'd never done before – remove his shorts. Isabel's eyes were wide open, and the feel of him made her … wet.

And worried. Then she remembered her mother said she would be an hour late getting home.

He touched her the way she liked, and when he rubbed and prodded, she thought about giving him what he wanted – before the realness of it scared her.

"No, wait. Don't, Frank. I can't. I'm a . . . I can't."

She expected him to be angry but saw a gleam in his eye as a grin raised his lips.

"Not ready for the big time yet? That's alright, honey. Let me show you something else."

Isabel didn't appreciate the trouble she was in when he kissed her *there*.

~~

Dax sent texts at midnight wishing Happy New Years.

When Tasha received hers, she shared it with Jeri who did a decent impression of Sandra Bullock in the movie, *Miss Congeniality*.

"He really likes you; he thinks you're gorgeous. He wants to kiss you; he wants to hug you. He wants to *feel* you, he wants to fu . . ."

Tasha laughed and threw a pillow. She thought about calling him but chose to text instead.

"Why don't you sext him?" Jeri wasn't tipsy or even slightly inebriated – she was drunk.

"What? Are you crazy?" Tasha said, cracking up at Jeri's expression. "Besides, he's already seen me naked."

"What? You didn't tell me that. Weren't you wearing pajamas at your pajama party?"

"I was. And then I wasn't."

"You slut."

"I know. I'm also a hussy and a tease, remember?"

The memory of unbuttoning her pajama top knowing Dax was awake and watching made her blush.

She sent a picture of her and Jeri with a text of New Year hopes and wishes.

~~

Mary smiled and sent a text wishing Dax the same. She'd already given Watson his New Year's hug and kiss. He lounged on the bed at her feet and didn't mind doubling as a foot warmer while he fell asleep to the rhythm of her toes squishing his fur between them.

She thought about the new year ahead and the old one behind, particularly the school year.

When Dax brought her home from the woods, she'd been a freshman. Instead of going to the police and telling them about her father, they handled it themselves and kept her hidden until a suitable plan could be implemented. This gave her months to accrue the knowledge necessary to meet her high-school educational requirements so she could take on-line college courses under an assumed name.

Mary was determined to learn, come hell or high, and studied hard to achieve her goal.

After Tasha found her with Dax and her ordeal became *nightly news*, he asked if she wanted to go back to school. She said no, at first, and then reconsidered.

While it might be more comfortable to remain in the relative safety of her new home, she couldn't accomplish the things she wanted to do from a position of avoidance.

In order to overcome life's upcoming adversities, she'd have to learn to cope with the reactions of people who knew her story. And as high school was a microcosm of attitudes and prejudices she would encounter in the real world, Mary thought it a good place to start.

She had been optimistic based on her experiences with those who came to hear her play. They embraced her for who she was, a girl with a love for music. She never heard a derogatory word and hoped her fears of being ridiculed or judged were unfounded.

Because of her accelerated home schooling, she'd been promoted to the senior class with enough credits to graduate in June. Most of her classmates had been kind but standoffish – not spending any real time with her. Others were resentful of a nerdy freshman hobnobbing with students above her social station. Some girls were catty. Mary encountered their kind of spitefulness during her *over-development* period, so she just ignored them.

But a few of her new peers were just plain mean . . .

"She knew exactly what she was doing. Probably threw it at him every chance she got and then cried rape when he gave her what she asked for."

Mary stopped in her tracks and walked back to the four girls. Two of them had scorn in their eyes, and she asked if they were talking about her. The other two moved from one foot to the other and glanced at the redhead.

Mary looked at her, too.

"Well? You said it loud enough for me to hear when I walked by, but you're quiet now. How come?" she asked, but already knew the answer.

Since her return, she'd broken two noses, three fingers, one arm, and pulled an ear so hard there was tearing. All of them were boys who tried to touch her or said something that caused her to give them the attention they wanted, though not the kind they had in mind.

She thought their knowing she killed somebody might give them perspective, but high school boys were stupid. And soft.

"You don't scare me, Mary Stewart. I'll say whatever I want, especially the truth. You probably pranced around in your underwear and got just what you deserved."

In her mind, Mary had already smacked her across the face, thrown her to the floor, and dragged her by the hair down the hallway.

"Is that what y'all think?" she asked the other girls.

The one with the same narrowed eyes as the redhead nodded, but not the other two. One stood quiet, and the other seemed embarrassed but shook her head.

"I hope you never have to know what it's like to be so violated. It's not just the pain, which ends soon enough, but the feelings of helplessness and humiliation, which doesn't. Those stay with you for a long time," Mary told them and walked away, hurt and pissed.

She didn't feel any satisfaction when those boys had that redhaired girl on her back in the locker room a week later – although the karmic irony was not lost on her.

After that, she decided to end her social experiment and finish her schooling at home. People were going to do and say what they would, and she resolved to take each one individually and treat them accordingly.

Mary looked forward to the New Year.

chapter six

A little after one in the morning, I finished the final few bars of Jimi Hendricks' *Voodoo Chile – A Slight Return*, using the Wah-Wah pedal for the last time.

The sound always brought out the rocker in me, and I reached into my blues-face toolkit for a tuned-in, far-out, scrunched-up expression that matched my mood.

I appreciated the smattering of applause and thanked the thinning crowd for coming out, adding the obligatory, "Y'all drive safe, now."

After breaking down the equipment and loading it into the van, I saw the New Year's wishes the girls sent. Tasha's had a picture of her and her friend giving a rock-n-roll salute – middle fingers down leaving thumb, index, and pinky fingers up and waving. I wanted to reply but knew she'd be asleep by now.

Me too, in just a little while.

I leaned against the van after closing the side door and looked at the stars looking at me. The beauty and majesty of the seeable universe was an elixir in its ability to invigorate my spirit. Anything seemed possible, and everything seemed attainable. It gave me hope the world could be better, that people could be.

Of course, that feeling lasted all of six seconds before it was shattered by the sound of drunken human interaction. I glanced around the nearly empty parking lot for anyone who heard what I had. A couple in a truck were going at it hot and heavy and didn't seem to notice the disturbance.

The woman was talking louder, and I considered going over when he grabbed her arm. I didn't have a problem sticking my nose into someone else's business but preferred to keep a low profile if possible.

Except for Mary's father, all the others had been dealt with at least fifty miles away from St. Vincent, and I didn't want my involvement in those killings to cross anyone's mind by being seen acting aggressively.

Suspicion was dangerous. It led to observation, scrutiny, complication, and possible incarceration.

The woman wrenched her arm free, and then stabbed a finger at the man's chest. When the situation escalated I reached for the phone. It would take at least fifteen minutes for a patrol car to arrive, unless one was in the area. I dialed 9-1-1 when he raised his hand, pressed send when he slapped her, and then walked over to the SUV.

She'd been shoved back onto the seat while the man stood between her legs and tried to muffle her cry for help. Two others watched and egged on their buddy who still had his pecker in his pants but was fumbling to release it. His friends stepped forward when they saw me approach.

"Y'all best leave her alone."

They looked at me with disdain. "This ain't none of your business, guitar man," one of them said with a sneer.

"Yes, it is." I moved toward the man on the left trying to draw the one on the right closer.

When *Lefty* put his hand on my chest, I put mine over his wrist and brought my fist up to his elbow, bending but not breaking it. I quickly sliced my hand and struck *Righty* in the throat after he reached for me, and then hit *Lefty* under the chin with the heal of my hand before driving my knee into his crotch – hard.

Righty's hands were around his neck, and I stomped the outside of his knee with the heal of my foot, hearing the crack of bone before the cry of pain. *Pecker* reached behind his back, and I did the same. He beat me by a half-second, and it was all over after that as I recalled that old cliché about bringing a knife to a gunfight.

Lefty was unconscious, *Righty* writhed on the ground, and the man with the knife might die if he weren't careful. I began to explain it to him when my head exploded.

Time is a funny paradox in that it could be both fast and slow at once – relatively speaking. I don't think it took more than three seconds before I crumbled to the ground, but it was the longest three seconds of my life. And the clarity of mind was incredible.

The gun I'd aimed at his head dropped when my knees buckled, and I contemplated shooting him in the chest on the way down but worried the bullet might pass through and hit the woman lying on the seat. So I shot his knee thinking he would reach for it reflexively and drop the knife.

I guesstimated the position of my assailant based on the angle of attack as my knees hit the gravel and moved the gun under my left armpit, twisted my body to the right, and got off two shots before I fell forward.

My last thought was of the spaghetti Mary said she'd leave in the refrigerator for me. She knew I liked it cold and knew I loved her sauce.

I was pretty sure she knew I loved her, too.

~

A sharp pain sounded at the back of my head when I put feet to floor and sat on the edge of the bed.

Jesus!

I don't know why I said His name because He hadn't ever answered me. Guess it was just another way of saying *gee whiz*, which was a much too genteel way of saying *ouch*. It felt like my skull was cracked wide open, and I reached behind to see if it was.

Ouch, dammit. Shit!!

Standing up took five whole minutes, and I almost fainted getting to the medicine cabinet in the bathroom. The child-proof cap on the aspirin bottle had apparently reached adulthood since I'd last twisted it because it held on with gusto, unwilling to share its contents. Just as I was ready to throw it in the toilet, a chuckle resonated and a voice said, 'Go on. I'm just funnin' ya.'

The cap twisted easily, and I poured seven small tablets into my hand and swallowed them with cool water. The throbbing stopped instantly and I glanced at the label – *Pain Away*, manufactured by a company called Mar E, a division of the Farm A Sutical Corporation.

I'd never heard of them but thought about leaving a testimonial on their website.

On my way to the kitchen, I heard a noise in Mary's room. She was sobbing, and Watson had an arm around her trying to hold back tears of his own.

"What's wrong, sweetie?"

They looked for a second before jumping up and on me. Mary hugged tighter than she ever had before, and Watson stood and licked my face, something he'd never done either.

"What's going on, guys? The affection is nice but a little much. What'd I do to deserve it?"

Mary looked at me in a way that broke my heart, and I wiped her face of the tears she'd shed.

"I love you, Dad. Please don't leave me."

She called me *Dad*. Suddenly the room began to spin.

"Dax! Wake up. Wake up!!!"

~~

Tasha washed her face and started to cry again. She didn't look in the mirror knowing what she'd see – a woman desperate to keep the man she loved alive.

They were going to operate in a few hours after waiting days for the swelling to recede and the coma to end.

Her ringtone reverberated off the ceramic walls of the small hospital bathroom and should have made her jump, except she almost didn't hear it because of worry. She turned off the phone and cried some more.

Mary and Watson were still asleep in the chairs when she returned to the room, and Dax smiled at her from the bed. She didn't believe her eyes until he moved a hand back and forth, snapping his fingers as he did.

"Whatchu up to, girlfriend?"

Tasha grinned all the way as a tributary of tears ran down her cheek. He crooked his finger and pointed to his lips. If she thought she was in love before . . .

"What the heck?" Mary said. "I fall asleep a few minutes and then find you kissing a girl? In bed, no less? I hope you remember this when the time comes. I thought you were hurt. I mean, geez, I could have stayed home and played my guitar. You scared Watson to death, you know," she said with a stiff upper lip and circles under her eyes.

"Only Watson?" I asked, trying to make her smile. "And he better be the only one I find *you* in bed kissing."

"I might have been a little concerned, but he was the frightened one. I knew your head was too hard to break."

Her eyelashes were wet when she kissed my cheek, and I patted her hand. "I'm okay, honey."

She raised her head and nodded. "I have to go to the restroom. I've been needing to for a while."

Watson followed, watching her lean back against the wall and slide until her bottom touched the cold tile floor. When she pulled her knees to her chest, a sob let loose.

Mary couldn't hold it in anymore.

~

Fireworks of pain exploded in my head as I brushed my teeth with the hand still able to do so. But it was a small price to pay if I wanted her to kiss me like they did in France.

"Hey, Tash?"

"Yeah?"

"How long are we going to pretend I'm not handcuffed to the bed? Is this official or personal?"

She nodded and took a key from her pocket then smiled and looked at me with mischief.

"What if it were personal? Would you mind?"

Before I could answer, a doctor came in and asked how I felt. She unlocked me and left while he did an examination.

Seems I'd been lucky.

The doctor expressed disappointment in not getting to perform brain surgery and laughed when I offered him a raincheck, but he grew serious when discussing my injury and the need to take it easy.

"We'll know better after more tests, but for now, rest is best," he said and left when the nurse came in with drugs.

Tasha returned and picked up right where she'd left off. "Well? Would you mind?"

"Have you always been this brazen? Because honestly Tash, I like it."

Rose pink crept from her neck to her face.

"Uh, no, Dax. Not really. Not about romantic stuff. I'm usually very *not* this way. It's you. I don't understand it, but I'm drawn to you in an almost feral way."

I felt the same but decided to keep it to myself. At least until I'd made up my mind about letting her go.

"Tash, there's no reason to feel embarrassed. I have a hunger for you as well, and a worry I can't explain."

For crying out loud! Why not tell her how I *really* feel?

"What worry?"

"Hmmm. Could we postpone that conversation for another time, please?"

She nodded and I asked about Mary.

"I sent her to get some food. She's hardly slept or eaten since you've been here and wouldn't even have gone to the cafeteria if I hadn't played the *Dax* card. You know, 'Let's not give him anything to worry about, like you not eating.' Of course, she saw right through it but went anyway. She's been worried about you. Me, too."

I opened my hand and she gave me hers.

"Sorry for the scare. It might have been prevented, but I couldn't let it be. So, tell me. Why was I cuffed to the bed?"

"You want the good or the bad news first?"

"Always the bad," I said and yanked on the white sheet tangled around me.

"Hang on. I almost forgot I have a job to do."

She pulled a recorder from her bag and glanced around before giving me the European kiss I'd hoped for.

"Don't tell anyone I did that. The last time I kissed a suspect it caused quite a fuss."

Her eyes were a playful romp – then she turned on the recorder, noting date and time before taking my statement.

"Mr. Palmer. Would you like an attorney present?"

"Am I under arrest?"

"No sir, you are not."

"Can you tell me why I was handcuffed to the bed?"

Tasha looked at me with some irritation and turned off the recorder. "What are you doing? I thought we'd discuss that after your statement."

"Well, you didn't say so, and, if you had, I wouldn't have agreed to it."

She glared at me, Detectively. It was disconcerting and not at all how she looked at me a few minutes earlier.

"Tash, I have nothing to hide, and I'm going to tell you the truth. But I'm also going to exercise good judgement and common sense as a citizen being questioned by the police. I hope you can accept that."

She looked at me a long moment before nodding. I put my hand on hers when she reached for the recorder.

"By the way, if it were anyone else, I'd say no. But if *you* wanted it to be personal, I wouldn't mind. It could be fun."

Tasha's confusion gave way to understanding, and her face hued as she flipped on the devise.

"We put you in protective custody. And the handcuffs also helped alleviate your family's worry about your getting up and leaving with a serious head injury."

My family. Mary, Watson . . . And Tasha?

"Thank you, Detective Williams."

"You're welcome, Mr. Palmer. Now, would you tell me what happened at the Raw bar in the early morning hours of January 1st?"

I told her everything, from the time I gazed at the stars to thoughts of Mary's spaghetti waiting for me at home.

"Did you have to beat those men so badly?"

A retort about beating them *goodly* came to mind, but I thought it best not to share. It was funny, though.

"The circumstances determined the level of force. Those men were actively involved in urging their friend to molest that woman. I didn't know if they were armed or could fight, so when they stepped up to prevent me from helping her, I put them down as quickly and as harshly as I could. I needed to get to the man before he violated her, and I couldn't let them interfere."

After she finished with a few more questions, I asked for another one of those suspect kisses.

"Or are they only given to get us to spill the beans?"

Tasha leaned in but stopped when Mary and Watson entered the room.

51

"Hey Tash? Have you ever read a book called *If you Give a Mouse a Cookie*?" Mary asked and set a sandwich and juice on the table for her.

"No, I don't think I have."

"Are you sharing or warning, Mare?" I asked.

Her face was a wide-eyed expression of innocence.

"I'm just trying to give my girl a heads up, is all. Or is she *your* girl now?"

I felt flushed and hoped Mary would take pity on me. Given my injury and her affection, I was fairly confident she wouldn't purposely embarrass me in front of Tasha.

"Dax and Tasha sitting in a tree. K-I-S-S-I-N-G. First comes love, then comes marriage, then comes. Hey, have you two given any thought to having a . . ."

The pillow hit her square on the nose. Mary emitted a squeak, and her mouth formed a perfect circle. Mine too, because I didn't throw it.

I looked at Tasha with gratitude for protecting me but had to bite my lip to keep from laughing because she was beet red and as cute as could be.

"Oh, Mary. I'm sorry. Did I hurt you?" Tasha said, and then glanced at me with raised eyebrows. "Wait, what? I just saved you from your evil step-child."

I held it together until a pillow struck her back. Thank goodness the drugs kicked in then, because I laughed hard enough to hurt as they turned the room into a battlefield littered with pillows, cushions, and a sandwich.

Everything came to a halt when I started to cough.

"I'm alright. Just catching up on catching my breath." They both watched me with nervous apprehension. "Really. I'd let you know if I wasn't."

"Yeah, right."

Mary held on to my hand like she meant it and looked at me with a love as deep as the ocean. I'd scared her, and it hurt to see her so exposed. When I pointed to my cheek, she grinned and shook her head.

"If you give a mouse a cookie . . ."

She patted my arm instead and began to pick up the pillows. Tasha moved to help, but I kept her next to me.

"So, why was I handcuffed?"

It was time for the truth, and it must have been serious because Mary stopped picking up and peered over. Even Watson looked at me with a pillow in his mouth.

"There *was* a protective custody element involved, and Mary and I *were* afraid you'd wake up and get out of bed. But there was also a possible suspect element. So, until we got your side of things, we had to 'incarcerate' you because the other side claimed you attacked them for no reason."

"So, you really *do* kiss your suspects? Interesting."

Tasha grinned and explained why I'd been under arrest – or more accurately, arrest adjacent.

The woman who'd been assaulted was married to the man assaulting her. She told the police her husband was just being a *drunken ass* and thought some romance in the parking lot might be fun. She didn't really want to, even though they'd done it before, but said she didn't scream until a crazy man shot her husband.

"Does she usually let her husband's friends watch them have sex? Because they had a front-row seat," I said.

"She said she didn't see them until after he got shot and she jumped out of the SUV."

I nodded and Tasha continued.

"The men said *you* were the voyeur and attacked them without provocation when they confronted you."

I nodded again and asked for some water. Mary was there in a second with a glass and turned to go find ice.

"That's alright, sweetie. The water's fine."

"No, you like ice. I'll be right back."

Tasha shook her head and sighed after she left.

"She's been so afraid, Dax. More than the last time."

"I can feel it. It'll be okay once I get out of here."

"I hope so. Are you tired? Do you want to stop?"

"No. Tell me all of it."

Mary returned with the ice and filled my glass.

"Thanks, hon. I appreciate it."

"You're welcome," she said and continued to pick up the room while Tasha told me the rest.

"A woman was killed. The sister of the husband, the man you shot in the knee."

My heart dropped. I must have missed my target. The woman making out in the truck, perhaps?

What had I done?

"She's the one who clobbered you in the back of the head with a crowbar."

The downward spiral of my depression stopped in its tracks and held its position. She tried to kill me, huh? Well then, she got what she deserved.

Or did she?

Maybe she was just saving someone from an attack – like I'd been doing. Maybe she acted correctly by trying to help her brother and his friends? Maybe they were her friends, too?

Had I been wrong to intervene? Should I have turned away when that frightened woman cried out for help?

How could I have left it alone?

Married or not, the man didn't have the right to rape her, or the other men to protect him. If they'd stepped aside, they wouldn't have been hurt – maybe no one would have.

That woman's death was going to haunt me.

What a mess.

It would be my word against theirs, and, on the surface, mine should suffice given the facts. But someone was dead, which meant things could get complicated. The police would look into all of our lives, and there were things in mine I didn't want seen.

I watched Mary finish her work and asked the question that was surely on her mind, the one keeping her heart full of fear even though I was out of danger. At least, physically.

"Were there any witnesses?"

Tasha shook her head.

"Not as of an hour ago. Someone heard a woman scream but couldn't say for sure if it was before or after the gunshots. But as of forty-five minutes ago, yes. In fact, there's a video. Everything you said in your statement matches what Dominic told me when I called him back. I think everything is going to be alright."

She expected them to *woohoo* or *yea* or something but got nothing instead. Not even a *huh*.

I was incredulous, and Mary appeared to be stupefied. Tasha was more blasé.

"What?"

"You didn't think to tell us that after you found out?"

"Yeah, I thought about it. But you said you wanted the bad news first, remember? Always the bad? Besides, it was more dramatic this way, don't you think?" she said with a sparkle in her eye.

A shoe was flung from across the room.

chapter seven

For the third time in as many minutes, I opened and closed my left hand in an attempt to make it work properly. There was a lag in response from the brain to the fingers as they fretted the strings. It was frustrating, and Mary voiced what I already knew.

"Now, Dax. The doctor told you this would take a while. Maybe six months, and you've only been out of the hospital two days. He didn't want you to leave early in the first place. Remember?"

I'd left after being scanned, poked, prodded, and tested the day after coming out of the coma.

"Hey, that reminds me of something interesting," I said. "First, do you want anything to drink?"

"Sure. I'll take a Dew," Mary said.

She continued to play while I went to the fridge and got a Mountain Dew. I was in a beer drinking mood myself, so I grabbed a couple of cold mugs and poured our beverages.

I set hers by the stool and took mine to the big chair – a rocking, rolling, swiveling, reclining, Barcalounger beast with an impression of my behind imprinted in the cushion.

"I had a dream," I said, and took a long swig of A&W. Theirs was THE root beer. Others were good, but not as.

"What are you, Martin Luther King now? One clunk on the head and you're a cultural icon?"

She's a funny girl, and it's why I keep her around. That, and her spaghetti sauce. Oh, and the *I love her* thing.

"In the aforementioned dream, I had a killer headache and went for aspirin, which worked instantly by the way. It was called Pain Away – I should see if it's a real product. Anyway, when I came down the hall you were crying in your room. Then you hugged me, said wake up, and I came out of the coma. Isn't that interesting?"

Mary stopped playing and nodded.

"Yup, it is. Because I had a similar dream. You know, Watson and I share dreams all the time. Maybe you and I did, too? In mine, I said, '*Don't leave me.*'"

"Mine, too. Huh. Did you call me anything in yours?"

"You mean like a song-stealing, solo-playing, big shit who needed to get off the pot and wake up?"

I smiled. "Something like that."

Mary had told me many times about her and Watson hanging out in the nether world, and I thought it fanciful. But this time I wanted to believe.

"That's not what I called you, though. Was it?"

I shook my head, tipped the mug, and wiped the frothy moustache from my lip.

"No. It was something else," I said and went for a refill.

"Wanna share?" she called out.

I considered it. What she'd said was precious to me, and I wanted to hold on to it, treasure it. It wasn't everyday a girl called a father *Dad* for the first time.

"I think not," I said and sat back in the chair. "It was sweet and meaningful, and you'll just roll your eyes, like you're doing now, because you hate being thought of as soft and cuddly. Don't you, Pooh Bear?"

I cracked up when her face scrunched like she'd bitten into a lemon, and she laughed when root beer came out of my nose. That was how Tasha found us when she opened the front door.

"What did I miss?"

We filled her in, and, after I brought her a frosty mug of her own, she did the same for us.

"It looks like there aren't going to be any charges filed. Thank goodness for that witness. And his video."

A man parked along the road recorded what happened, although he forgot about doing so because he'd been drunk as a skunk. He'd also been high as a kite with a bag of weed stashed somewhere in the car he couldn't lay his hands on to toss out the window. So he drove off when he heard the police siren.

When the police questioned him later, he told them he heard the woman cry for help, but not the words spoken between the men before the fight broke out. He couldn't say how it started but saw Dax knock them down and pull a gun before the woman clocked him from behind.

"He started shooting as he fell to the ground, and that's when I got the hell outta Dodge."

"Why'd you wait so long to come forward, Jack?"

"I'd been drinking and didn't trust what I'd seen. Then I remembered I recorded it on my phone."

"You have a video? Why the hell didn't you say so in the first place?"

For the most part, Jack did a good job of capturing the whole of it. The woman's cry could be plainly heard, as well as Dax's comments to the men and their responses. It was clear they put their hands on him first and that the husband reached for the knife before Dax pulled his gun.

"The state's attorney said she'd never in all her years seen a statement about an incident match so precisely with video of the actual event," Tasha told them. "She was impressed. Me, too. We both believe you."

She grinned and lifted her mug before emptying it, and Mary took the glass to the kitchen for a refill without asking if she wanted one. Tasha and Dax loved A&W root beer and one was never enough. Or two or three.

"The video probably saved my ass. At least from doubt and speculation. Without it, the pendulum of prosecution might have swung against me."

"You might be right. Thanks, Mary," she said, taking the mug. "It's an interesting case of perspective, isn't it?"

I nodded. "On one hand, you have a person who says he came to the defense of a woman under attack, and on the other, four people who swear they were attacked while they were just fooling around minding their own business. Not so easy to get to the truth, is it? Especially if someone lies about the facts."

"You mean four *someones*, don't you?" Mary said.

"You're right about that," Tasha replied. "A four against one story usually carries more weight, but their account of the event was already suspect. Even before the video."

"How so?" Mary said, rubbing up Watson.

"Everything being equal, who is more credible? A sober person who's never been arrested and calls the police for help, or those with alcohol levels well above the legal limit and arrests for aggravated assault?"

"How do you know I was sober, Tash?"

"The hospital checked when y'all were brought in."

"Y'all?"

"When the police arrived, six people were laying on the ground – one dead, two unconscious, and three screaming bloody murder. Dom said the two who told him what happened reeked of beer, so he called and got an order from a judge for blood tests. Everyone went down the road to Sacred Heart hospital. You ended up staying there, and the others were taken to Bay Medical in Panama City – except for the sister. Who, by the way, *was* the one making out."

I rocked in the big chair while Tasha answered some questions from Mary. It was difficult to reconcile the death of the woman who tried to take my head off. I was conflicted about what I'd done, and how I'd live knowing she might have done the right thing from her point of view. For all she knew, I was going to shoot her brother. She didn't know why and didn't have time to find out.

"Dax? What's wrong?"

"He's bothered about killing that woman," Mary said.

I hadn't said anything to her, but she knew.

"She tried to kill you," Tasha said. "The doctor said you were lucky to be alive, let alone walk and talk. That woman and her brother had been in and out of trouble for years. She'd been convicted of beating the hell out of a girl for flirting with her boyfriend. Put *her* in the hospital, too."

My head nodded but my spirit wasn't comforted.

"Yeah, but it's that perspective you mentioned earlier. What if she was just protecting her brother instead of looking for another head to bash? She saw me beating up his friends and tried to help. Would we do differently? Even with her history, she could still be right in this instance. I mean, she'd have to *know* her brother was going to rape his wife, maybe his friends too, and not care before I could even begin to . . . The truth is, she was trying to save someone from harm. Just like *I* was doing."

The room became quiet except for the clock on the wall, and we found ourselves alone with our thoughts.

"Perspective is a bitch."

Mary hardly ever spoke that way, and my expression reflected that fact. Tasha also looked at her with surprise. Mary then doubled down.

"A *fucking* bitch in this case."

Watson stopped licking himself and peered at her with hound-dog eyes. They just had a conversation the other day about the difference between *his* saying the B- word and humans, who use it inappropriately and derogatorily.

"Mary . . . . Well, hell. I want to say your full name the way parents do when their kids act up, but I can't recall your middle name. How come I don't know it?"

"Because I never told you.

"Oh, yeah. Care to expound on your expletive?"

"Hang on. What's *your* middle name? I'll tell you mine if you tell me yours?"

"That's what you said a year ago, so I'll just come up with my own. How about Mary *Little Shit* Stewart? Kind of rolls off the tongue, yes?"

She smiled and nodded.

"So does Dax *Big Shit* Palmer. Hey, let's keep those, okay? It'll look good on college admission forms."

Tasha knew them both and suspected they did as well. They just liked to play, especially when tensions needed to be eased.

"The wife and husband are going to keep lying," Mary said, "keep saying they were only having role-playing fun. Those men will follow suit because from their *perspective*, they were trying to keep Dax from sticking his nose into something private, even though they were doing it in public. And their failure to just say *Hey, man. It's all good* can be explained away because they were stinking drunk – making them more belligerent and less cordial."

Watson stuck his head under her hand for attention.

"It's a tropical shit storm that could turn into a category five hurricane of headaches," she added and gave him some.

"That's both an excellent and poetic statement of fact, Mare," Tasha said. "They could stir up a hornet's nest of trouble, maybe even bring a civil case if a criminal one isn't forthcoming. And even though the D.A. isn't filing charges against Dax now, she could be pressured to later."

"Could charges be brought against *them*?" I asked and took up scratching duties when Mary went to the kitchen.

"Well, like Mary said, the wife claims it was a game. So the husband didn't legally rape her if she gave consent. As for the men, they could be charged with assault, but because of the condition you left them in, it might be difficult to win in court – even with the video. The jurors will consider the same perspectives we've talked about in reaching their decision, and they tend to expect the victim to look worse than the assailant."

"I know the standard for conviction in a criminal case is beyond a reasonable doubt," Mary said as she sat on the sofa with a soda, "but are the facts enough to protect Dax in a civil case with its preponderance of evidence threshold?"

She patted her leg and Watson left my fingers for hers.

"Yes, I believe so," Tasha responded. "He acted to save someone from injury or possible death, and the use of force was justified. But a jury could be instructed on the law and its meaning and still come to their own conclusion based on feelings instead of facts."

"That's some bullshit there." Mary said, and I gave her an *am I going to have to start a swear jar* look.

"I agree," Tasha replied. "And Dax, I understand your feelings about that man's sister, but you would have been vulnerable and at deadly risk if you hadn't shot her. I truly believe she would have kept hitting you with that crowbar. I've seen way too much to doubt it."

She took a long drink of her beer and finished it without meaning to. Mary raised a brow and Tasha grinned, nodded, and handed her the mug.

"Hmmm, I hadn't considered that she might have tried to kill me after I was out cold."

"It might add some objectivity to your assessment of *her* perspective if you do," Mary said when she returned. After handing the root beer to Tasha, she kissed my cheek. "Give it some thought."

We left our worry alone to spend some time laughing and luxuriating in each other's company. When Tasha had to leave for work, we all walked to the door. She hugged Mary first, and then held onto me a bit longer, digging in her nails for good measure before letting go. When I pointed to my lips, she leaned in and started to blush.

Tasha didn't know why, but she felt like a kid caught kissing on the porch as the light flickered on and off.

"If you give a mouse a cookie," Mary said, a subtle twinkle in her eye as she walked whistling to her room with Watson following.

"Do you think she minds?"

"Minds what?" I asked, playing dumb.

She cocked her head. "You want that kiss or not?"

"I want."

A tear fell down her cheek when she touched my face. "Dax, I was so worried. I've just found you."

I kissed her lips and sparked a flame. As our passion ignited, we were serenaded with a song.

"Dax and Tasha, sitting in a tree . . ."

chapter eight

Barbara Bedford sat in the cushioned hospital chair and listened to the ambient noise as her husband slept. She remembered how he'd made her feel when they first dated: beautiful, cherished, respected.

That all changed.

She'd never been a confident woman to begin with and building self-esteem had always been a challenge. Still, she ought to have stood up for herself more.

But Hale was strong-willed, self-assured, aggressive. And he'd done things in the bedroom that roused a want in her she should've tried harder to overcome but couldn't.

Not even on her wedding night . . .

They returned to the honeymoon suite after a night of dining, dancing, and drinking. Hale had teased her at the reception in subtle ways - a knee between her legs as they danced, an arm brushing her breast as he reached across to shake a hand, a finger caressing her thigh under the table as Brett gave the best man's speech – and when she walked out of the bathroom wearing a wisp of white satin, the look in his eyes made her shiver.

"Come sit on my lap."

Barb did as she was told and began a slow grind that worked her into a lather as the pace quickened. He pinched her nipples when the orgasm crashed over her like a tidal wave, and she leaned back to savor the sensation.

His was held in reserve, again, and she was the grateful recipient of his ability to do so. Hale liked to have his fun with her and liked to take his time having it. He smacked her behind as she continued to quiver and told her to go and get ready for the main event.

"Don't forget the accessories," he added.

She found them on the nightstand next to the bed. After a shower, she slipped the mask over her eyes, put the gag in her mouth, dropped to her knees, and cuffed her wrists behind her back. Hale liked her to wait in this position, and, in spite of the humiliation, she tingled with anticipation.

Barb was addicted to the arousal of her desire, the primal passion he'd discovered and exploited. She'd done things that filled her with shame, but the resulting pleasure overwhelmed her disgust and as long as they kept it to themselves, she could live with it.

She uttered a guttural groan when he opened the door. After leading her to the bed and placing pillows under her head and hips, Hale made himself a drink and sat nearby to peruse his personal playground.

"I have something for you. Let's call it a wedding gift." When he snapped his fingers, her legs drew up and open. "Tell me."

"Ow wan eehd."

"Come on, now. Make me believe it."

"Ow waaan eeeeehd."

Her face burned with indignity, but she *did* want it. She was like dry kindling waiting to be lit, needing to be. He liked to torment her by bringing her close but no cigar, letting the ebb and flow of her need build until she pleaded for release. But this time he did something different, and she was more than amenable.

His touch was light, soft, and his tongue experienced. She'd never felt anything like it and came again and again.

Before she could catch a breath, Hale took her hard and fast. She panted as he drove deeper with every thrust and soon found herself caught in an unrelenting climax that drove her to the very edge of reason.

Afterward, he sat her up on the edge of the bed and removed the gag. She thanked him the way he liked, the way they both did, and he lifted the mask when she finished.

Except it wasn't Hale. He'd been watching his sister and best man play with his new bride.

Barb was confused, hurt, angry, and shouted at him until he walked over and slapped her across the face.

"Knock it off, dammit. Don't raise your voice to me."

She looked at Haley, who licked her lips, and at Brett, who winked.

"How could you do this? You said this was ours. You promised it would stay between us," she screamed. Hale balled his fist and she stopped, knowing he'd hit her.

"It *is* going to stay between us. You're part of the family now. And in this family, we share. Understand?"

Barb hated how submissive she'd become to his will but wanted the pleasures associated with it.

And she hated herself for wanting them.

"I said, do you understand?"

"Yes."

After that night, Haley and Brett took her frequently. And, to her detriment, she was more willing than not. Barb became a junkie who would do anything to satisfy her addiction, and that fact took a toll on her psyche. Thoughts of suicide began to surface a few weeks before Hale took the 'family' to Florida for a New Year's vacation.

He rented a house on the Cape north of the rocks, and the combination of sun, beach, and Bahama water eased her depression. When someone suggested they go to the Indian Pass Raw Bar, she was up for it.

Haley kept her eyes open for a boy-toy to play with and everyone drank, laughed, and listened to a guy who played a pretty good guitar. They danced and drank, celebrated the New Year and drank, and stayed long after most everyone else left and drank some more.

After Haley picked up her toy and took him to his truck, Hale and Brett reminisced with an old friend while Barb excused herself and left to use the bathroom.

When she returned, the men were watching something on Brett's phone. She heard herself say, 'Please ... Fuck me,' and broke into a cold sweat after the friend looked up from the video and gave her a drunken smile.

"Would you like to hear her say that to you, Scott?"

Alcohol always brought out a cruelty in Hale that made Barb fearful of what he'd do – or make *her* do. He might not have offered her to another man if he hadn't been so drunk, but she was probably fooling herself in thinking he'd honor his promise to keep it in the *family*.

"Hale, no. I won't do that," she said and stormed off.

He went after her, followed shortly by Brett and Scott, and grabbed her by the arm.

"You'll do what I tell you," he said, and whispered in her ear. "Because we both know you like it. You like it a lot."

It was true. But if she gave in to this, she would be lost. Maybe forever.

"You told me this belonged to us, the two of us. Then you gave me to Haley and Brett and said it would only be the four of us, just the family."

She felt her anger build and her voice began to rise. "I'm not going to do it, and I'm not going to let you make me."

Barb emphasized her point by poking a finger on his chest with force, something she'd never done before. He responded by slapping her and then marching her to the SUV where he opened the passenger door, pushed her back on the seat, and positioned himself between her legs. She felt the twisted mix of revulsion and excitement ignite and might have let it burn if not for what he said next.

"Get your tickets ready, boys. We're going to ride this train all – night – long."

She screamed and tried to fight him off. When Hale pulled the knife, she thought he was going to use it on her. The sound of gunshots fed her fear, and she scrambled over the console and dove out the driver's window to escape.

Now, her husband laid in a hospital bed while she reflected on how they got there and who was to blame.

Hale's knee was shattered and needed to be replaced. The ligaments around Brett's elbow were distended, his jaw and several teeth broken, and a testicle crushed. Scott's knee could be repaired, but he would be laid up for weeks. She had a broken wrist, and Haley ... Haley was dead.

The death of Hale's twin sister hit her harder than she expected. Even though Haley took every advantage of her, she was more giving of her affection in a way Hale was not.

Of course, she still made her do things, but Haley didn't debase her to the extent her brother had.

Was that what she now considered affection?

Barb's story to the police was what Hale told her to say, but they weren't going to charge that guitar player, and she was thankful for that.

Hale would have raped her, although she'd long since given him permission. But he would've let the others do the same after she'd said no, and Palmer saved her from them. And herself.

Who *was* to blame for the carnage that night?

~~

"What?"

"In the hospital, remember? You said you had a hunger for me and a worry you can't explain," Tasha said. "What was the worry?"

"Could you not move for a minute?" I asked her.

Like the night of the pajama party, she stood next to my bed after unfastening a many-buttoned blouse. Her eyes glistened in the moonlight, her smile both naughty and nice.

"Damn. You're beautiful."

Tasha suddenly felt shy and naked. Her face flushed, but Dax didn't know until he pulled her onto the bed.

"Sorry, Tash. I didn't mean to embarrass you; I've just never seen anyone so stunning."

"I ... Thanks."

"It could be the way the light catches you just right. Of course, you can't depend on that light, can you?" he added and with that she was herself again.

He smiled his smile, and her heart skipped a beat when his lips touched hers. What started as a slow burn grew in intensity as his hand slid under her shirt, until he quit when she sighed from want.

"Tash, I'm sorry. We can't. I can't, not yet. Sorry."

"I thought it was us girls who played hard to get. What, do you think you're all that and a bag of chips?"

"I'm a bag of chips for sure, but I might not be all that."

"Is it Mary? Because that I can understand."

"Yes. That's most of it. The rest is, well, I like you. And I want you to like me, too."

"Given where your hand is, do you doubt I do?"

When I tried to remove it, she said, "Uh-uh."

My fingers casually caressed her breasts, providing a needed distraction to keep from telling her what I couldn't.

"There are things about me you don't know anything about, Tasha. Things you wouldn't understand."

The sensual delight of feeling her, even in a slow and measured way, was only surpassed by her reaction to it.

"Mmmm," she purred and closed her eyes. "Try me."

"Things you couldn't understand."

"Why not?"

"Things you *shouldn't* understand."

"I don't understand," she said with a knowing grin and moved my hand down the length of her.

"You don't wanna get involved with a guy like me, Tash. I'm a loner. A rebel."

When we reached the destination of her longing, she moaned in my ear as I touched her for the first time.

~~

Tasha snuck back into Mary's room well before dawn, and we all enjoyed a good breakfast before she left for work. While I did dishes, Mary went to the garage and returned with a small fan.

"Is the one on the ceiling in your room not working?"

"No. It's good," she said and grabbed the last piece of bacon from the plate.

"Not getting enough air from the conditioner? I've been meaning to swap out the filter."

"No, it's plenty cool." Mary chewed the last of it and washed it down with some *Dew*.

"Watson needing more airflow?"

She looked over, and Watson shook his head.

"He says no."

I rinsed the skillet and set it in the rack, dried my hands and hung the towel.

"Well, then. What's the deal, Lucille?"

Mary was patient, enjoying his confusion and waiting for it to clear. She saw the first flicker of understanding in his eyes before his face began to turn the crimson color Tasha's did when *she* got embarrassed.

It took a lot to get to Dax, and Mary had looked forward to playing with him all morning, until she saw his distress. He was uncomfortable in a way she'd never seen.

"Dax, I'm sorry. I thought I'd have some fun with you, but I see this is different. I barely heard anything. Really."

I was completely caught off-guard. What did she think about what she'd heard? How did it make her feel? How would I feel knowing how it made *her* feel? Was she uncomfortable now? With me? With Tasha?

With me and Tasha?

"Mare, for the record, you did good. The tease was righteous and the delivery perfect."

Mary smiled but her twinkle was subdued, and my anxiety began to build. I was afraid of having a conversation I wasn't ready for with the girl whose opinion of me meant the most.

"I don't know what to do, kid."

"Didn't sound that way last night. But if you'd like, I could give you the *birds and the bees* talk."

My guffaw made Watson jump and Mary crack up.

"I'm half-tempted to call you on that talk just to see who'd cry *Uncle* first."

"Ah, let's not and say we did," she said. "Okay?"

We shook on it, but I still needed to know.

"Are you alright?"

"You mean, am I traumatized? No. Is it a little weird? I don't know yet. At the most, it might be *icky* after I process it all, but that's to be expected. I mean, no girl wants to think of her dad having sex."

"No, I guess not," I said and kissed the top of her head. Twice now she'd referred to me as *Dad*. Course, I'd been dreaming the first time. Maybe this was one, too?

I pinched myself to find out.

~

Soon after Mary came to stay with me, I'd installed a rudimentary alarm system to warn us if anyone approached the house. Electronic eyes similar to those used to prevent an automatic garage door from squishing your cat stood guard along the driveway.

The *green* eye was positioned a hundred feet from the road, the *yellow* halfway down the almost hundred-yard length of the drive, and the *red* a hundred feet from the end. They each had a corresponding light and song that lit and played inside the house: *Green Onion, Yellow Submarine,* and Jimi Hendricks' *Red House.*

When Mary's story caught the attention of the media, I put up an electronic gate with its own song. I'd also added another warning for fun and function.

In addition to the alarms, the wooded acreage was replete with NO TRESSPASSING signs, leaving no doubt that anyone wanting to talk to Mary about her ordeal was not welcome. Anticipating the lack of respect for my obvious declarations, I placed small explosives called squibs in the trees near the house.

The *black* alarm was a triple-threat.

A voice shouted a warning, immediately followed by the sound of a shotgun blast made real by the exploding squibs. Everyone hit the ground to keep from being 'shot,' and most of them got up and ran back to their vehicles.

While relatively effective, the real fun came when the inquisitive and stubborn, mostly news crew journalists, pushed on toward the house where they were treated to a high-pressure spray of water and paint mixed with gasoline. It left them a sticky, smelly mess that kept Mary and me in stitches when we watched the recorded episode with a bowl of popcorn between us.

It had been awhile since anyone received a *black eye,* but news vans and looky-loos again began to loiter at the front gate because of what happened at the Raw Bar.

The video went viral, and it would only be a matter of time before someone tried to breach the property. I was out walking the perimeter and considering other measures to dissuade them when the front gate opened.

An SUV followed Tasha's truck down the driveway, and I went up to the house to meet them. Mary was taking drink orders and asked if she could get anything for me.

"Coke, please. Thanks, Mare."

She turned toward the kitchen and then turned back when Tasha introduced the woman with her.

"Dax, this is Barbara Bedford."

Mary harrumphed and left to get the drinks.

"It's nice to meet you." I extended my hand and she gave it a shake – then hugged me.

"Thank you, Mr. Palmer. Thank you so much for helping me. I needed it. More than you know."

"You're more than welcome, Mrs. Bedford."

She was still holding on when a miffed Mary set a tray on the coffee table and sat in her spot on the couch.

"Please. Call me Barb." She pulled away and dried her eyes, set an envelope on the table and took a seat.

Tasha explained how Barb came into the station to give an affidavit about what happened, and to apologize for not being more forthcoming at the outset.

"I'm so sorry, Mr. Palmer, for the difficulty I've caused. I should have told all of the truth in the beginning."

I looked at Tasha who nodded her head and saw the tension drain from Mary's face. She left the couch to follow Watson outside and patted my shoulder as she passed by.

"Call me Dax, Barb."

She tried to tell me about that night, and I could see how difficult it was for her. After a few minutes, she seemed too embarrassed to continue and Tasha stepped in.

"Mrs. Bedford wanted us to make a copy of the written affidavit as well as the video of her statement. She wanted you to have them in case her husband tried to make trouble. The state's attorney has read the statement and reiterated her decision not to file charges. She's closing the case."

I nodded. "Thank you, Barb. I hope . . . May I ask you a personal question?"

She set her drink on the coaster. "Of course."

"Is your husband going to hurt you because of this? Are you safe?"

"I don't think he'd beat me or anything like that, but when he's capable of caring for himself, I'm going to leave. I can't keep living the way I have. It's too destructive."

Barbara thanked us again and stood to leave.

"Be careful, Mr. Palmer. He's full of hate. Haley was more than a sister to him. He loved her more than anything or anyone, and he's already said things that make me afraid for you. I'm sure he's struggling with his grief and needs a place to direct his anger, but . . ."

I asked about Haley, trying to get a feel for who she was – or could have been. Barb didn't say much except she had a temper and was devoted to her brother.

Unfortunately, that did nothing to lessen the burden of my guilt. I'd killed a sister trying to save her brother and had to live with it. It wouldn't be easy.

Nor should it be.

We said our goodbyes, and Tasha put an arm around me as Barb drove away.

"Dax, the sister might have killed you."

"Yeah. Maybe."

Tasha knew it would be with him for a long time. It said something about his character that he was full of self-recrimination. She didn't doubt he'd done the right thing.

The sister could have yelled *Stop* or *What the hell are you doing?* or anything to get Dax's attention to keep him from shooting her brother. But she used a crowbar instead, and that said something too.

His being alive was a miracle and it was still too early to know if he'd stay that way. If that woman had killed him, Tasha thought she might have killed her back.

"We still on for dinner and muzak, tonight?"

"Muzak?" I said. "Are you saying my playing is only appropriate for elevator venues?"

"Not at all. Those musicians are pretty darn good. But maybe someday, if you keep practicing."

74

chapter nine

Because of a warm winter and high overnight temps and dew points, Mary began cutting grass in late February. She still had a learner's permit, so Dax had to drive the truck and trailer. If she were to move it a foot by herself, a ticket could be issued, prolonging the time needed to get licensed.

To avoid driving to every yard, Dax cobbled together two lightweight aluminum fishing carts she could attach to the backside of the mower seat and pull behind her.

One side of the wagon carried gas, oil, water cooler, weedwhacker, blower, etcetera, while the other carried Watson. The cart's rod holders were used for an umbrella to give him shade as Mary worked, as well as a cool space to slumber, should he wish. And according to Mary, he wished. A lot.

Dax would park the trailer on Cape San Blas or Indian Pass roads, and then come move her to the other peninsula when she was ready. Riding the mower from one lawn to the next along Indian Pass road didn't present a problem. The speed limit was low, the traffic light, and the shoulder wide enough to accommodate the mower and wagon.

But traversing the Cape was different.

Fortunately, a bike path called the Loggerhead Run ran the length of it. Although motorized vehicles were not supposed to use it, the police turned a blind eye and let her be. All of them knew her story, and most had a good deal of respect for her.

Besides, she was from *around here*.

~~

News of the shooting at the Raw Bar reached a national audience after the video was posted on YouTube. As a result, local business boomed in what was normally a slow economic season when so many people came to St. Vincent out of nosy curiosity. Most ended up parked or standing on the side of the road in front of Dax's house at one time or another, and the police had their hands full. They'd also seen a boon as tickets were issued left and right.

They hunkered down the first week until Tasha arrived with packages from Amazon. Dax had them sent to her place to save the UPS driver from being hassled.

"Well this should be interesting," Tasha said after the boxes were emptied.

"And fun, too."

Mary read the manual while Dax went to the garage. Tasha picked up the guns and followed him. Thirty minutes later, they were ready.

"Going to join us?" he asked.

"I might observe from a distance. Don't want to get in the line of fire. You both sure about this?"

She saw nodding, smiling faces who were eager to restore some normality to their lives by going to the Piggly Wiggly for the best fried chicken in the area.

~~

A small group of people formed round us in the parking lot when we came out of the Pig. Some were news crews, some protesters, and some simply curious.

I set my weapon in the buggy and pushed it toward the truck. As the people impeded our progress, I reached for the gun. Mary brought hers up, ready to shoot if necessary. A part of her hoped it would be.

"I understand some of you are just doing your jobs," I told them, "but I don't want to talk. And while I appreciate it's frustrating, that's just too bad."

After being bombarded by questions and comments coming from voices getting louder, I pointed the firearm.

"If y'all don't move and let us by, we're going to have to use these. So please, step aside."

A man rushed forward, and Mary let him have it. The solution of water, paint, and dish soap from the Super Squirt Gun caught him flush in the face, and he yelled and stumbled to the pavement with burning eyes.

I opened fire in front of me and pushed the cart through a hole created by the skedaddling news team.

Mary brought up the rear and shot two more who got too close. The rest stepped back and out of the way, some of them open-mouthed. She thought about shooting them anyway but held her fire, keeping her gun up to cover Dax as he put the groceries in the back seat

"Boy, don't even think about eating that chicken."

After ruffling Watson's ears, I grabbed another gun and joined Mary at the back of the truck to survey the damage. The news crew recovered and was pointing their camera at us from what they estimated was a safe distance of about fifteen feet. The squirt guns shot twenty.

"Y'all go on now and have a good day."

And with that, we stepped inside and drove away.

~

Tasha observed the whole thing and saw the episode as another example of their kindred spirits. They liked to have fun, especially in stressful situations, and she brought that up later as the three of them laughed between bites of pizza while watching the body-cam videos.

~~

A giant squirt gun hung on the rack where Mary could get to it easily just above the weedwhacker.

Most of the looky-loos left town, moving on to other shootings of other people in other places, and the national news got caught up in reporting the tweets of a twit – so the Raw Bar incident fell off the media radar. But some still tried to get a shot of Mary or Dax.

Her story was retold in the local news, and she had to shoot a reporter and a few photographers who pestered her while she worked.

As she came to the end of a driveway on her way to another lawn, Mary saw the man standing by his car taking her picture. She must have shot him before, because he was just outside the thirty-foot range of the Super-Duper Squirt.

Watson growled.

"It's okay. We'll get him if he gets closer."

The yard she just cut lay a significant distance from the next one on her list, and Mary had been meaning to see if a house or two in between might like to hire the services of *Quite Contrary LawnCare*. She decided now would be a good time to try the next-door neighbor.

When Mary knocked, a girl she recognized opened the door. She'd stood behind the redhead at school who baited her, the one who shook her head when Mary asked if they thought she got what she deserved.

"Hi, Isabel. How are you?"

Isabel had thought a lot about Mary since the day in the hallway, wishing she'd spoken up at the time and said how sorry she was about what happened to her. Especially after seeing her story again on the news.

"Hi, Mary. I'm doing alright. How about you?" She saw Watson in the cart and walked over before Mary answered. "Can I pet him? Would he mind?"

"You'd have to ask him," Mary said and grinned at the light in Isabel's eyes.

"What's his name?"

"Leroy."

Watson cocked his head and rolled his eyes at Mary.

"What do you think, Leroy? Mind if I give you a pat? Maybe scratch you up a little?"

Watson started to object until he heard her say *scratch*. He stuck his tongue out at Mary as Isabel did an adequate job of finding the spot that made him go, *Aahhh*.

"Mary, Leroy is a beautiful dog."

"That old mutt? I don't know. Maybe."

Mary laughed when they both looked at her in disbelief. She reached over and joined Isabel in giving Watson an unexpected afternoon delight.

"Yeah, Watson's a cutie, all right. I just don't want his head to get so big it doesn't fit in the wagon anymore."

Mary explained she was just having fun by calling him Leroy when Isabel said, "Huh?"

"You should hear some of the things he's called me," she said and laughed again when Isabel repeated herself.

Mary filled his bowl with water and asked if Isabel wanted a Gatorade as she reached into the cooler to fetch one for herself.

"No, thanks. But why don't you and Watson come around back to finish your drinks? There's shade and a pool to wet your feet. And paws."

"I have to get back to work. I appreciate it, though."

"You can take a few minutes. I mean, you came here for a reason, right?"

She picked up his bowl and walked along the side of the house. Mary shrugged, took a business card from the pouch, and followed Watson who followed Isabel to the backyard. The water looked inviting as she sat in the chair under an umbrella that didn't hinder the breeze from finding her.

Isabel urged Watson to cool off by jumping in the pool, and he could already feel the water washing over him as he looked at Mary with puppy-dog eyes.

"Oh, that's good, Watson. I haven't seen those since, well, since you *were* a puppy. Isabel, that's kind of you, but I'm sure your parents don't want dog hair in their pool. Besides, he usually jumps in the Gulf when I weed whack the boardwalk from the house to the beach."

Watson shifted his eyes to Isabel and got an *Aww*.

"It's okay, really. My mom is at work, and my dad doesn't live with us anymore. And, as I'm the one who actually cleans the pool, it's not a problem for me. How can you resist those eyes? His expression is precious."

Watson looked back at Mary with a beam in his pitiful, puppy eyes and jumped in as soon as she nodded.

Isabel laughed and Mary swallowed some Gatorade, letting her head lean back against the chaise. It felt good, and she relaxed a bit before having to get up and back at it.

"Mary, I want to apologize for not speaking up when Camille said those things about you. I've felt bad about it ever since and thought I'd see you in class after Christmas vacation so I could tell you. But you didn't return."

"I appreciate that. Really. I don't know why she said it, but it did trouble me. Maybe she feels differently now."

She watched Watson attempt a breaststroke and saw Isabel looking at her in her periphery.

"Camille is a pain in the ass, and I don't hang around her anymore, but she stopped running you down after what happened in the locker room."

Mary nodded and started to call him out of the water when Isabel stopped her with a question.

"Why would a father touch his daughter? I mean, even if you let him, he would still be wrong, right?"

The thought of Isabel thinking she'd *let* her father do those things made her angry, and she searched for the calm Dax taught her to find. After a deep breath, she saw distress in Isabel's eyes. But it wasn't fear of retribution.

With serenity covering like a shroud, the point of her question became clear. Isabel was asking if responsibility rested with the adult, regardless of the actions of the child, and Mary saw her differently in the realization.

Had something happened to her, too?

Maybe that's why her dad was gone.

"There isn't any justification for a father to treat his daughter as a lover. None. Not even if she begs. It's wrong, and it's evil - and it's *always* the father's fault."

She watched Isabel consider her words and felt kinship for a fellow processer.

"I didn't mean to suggest you wanted him to do that."

"I know. Well, I do now."

They talked about shared interests, school, music, even boys, and it was a little past one o'clock when they left the sanctuary of the pool and walked to the front.

A truck pulled up alongside the mower as she prepared to leave, and a man Isabel called Frank introduced himself. When Mary asked about taking care of his lawn care needs, he looked her over and smiled.

"Can you start today?"

After mowing the yard, she pulled the cord and the weed-eater fired up. Mary loved to whack. It was gratifying to see the result after the nylon string touched the grass.

By the time she worked her way to the backyard, Isabel had donned a swimsuit and was in the water with Watson.

Frank watched them as he ate what looked like a lunch. Mary stood by and waited, but he waved her up so she could whack. They jumped out of the pool and Frank gave Isabel an empty glass with a smack on her bottom, sending her into the house laughing.

After Mary finished blowing the porch and patio, Isabel joined them out front to say goodbye.

"Maybe y'all could come by, sometime?" she said and ruffled Watson's fur. "We could take another dip."

"Maybe. See ya, Isabel."

Mary rode up the driveway thinking about her. Other than Tasha, she didn't have any female friends. Or any other friend, except for Watson.

And Dax, of course. But he was so many things to her: friend, confidant, accomplice, mentor. Dad.

Mary saw the man before he saw her see him and moved her hand behind the seat, brought it to her side, and told Watson to sit tight. When she drew near the road, he popped out from behind the tree and started clicking

He'd correctly calculated she couldn't reach the Super-Duper on the rack without getting off the mower. What he didn't count on was the Side-Arm Squirt she used to soak him and his camera with as she rode by.

One of the pictures captured was of a beautiful young girl with a Mona Lisa smile and a glint in her eye. That shot earned him two-thousand dollars and landed on the cover of the National Enquirer.

~~

Tasha thought about the all-consuming, hair-pulling, back-scratching quality of what just happened and rubbed herself soapy with a wide grin on her face.

We're like kids who can't keep our hands off each other.

Dax was generous with his pleasures and attentive to her wants. The passion that burned whenever he kissed her never failed to spark, and she already wanted to feel that flame again.

They didn't have sex when Mary was in the house, and Tasha stopped leaving her room for his during sleepovers. While it hadn't been wrong, it didn't feel right anymore.

Although Mary seemed fine with their relationship and loved to tease them into embarrassment if she could, Dax wanted to give her time to 'acclimate to her new reality.'

Tasha suspected it was more for his sake than hers, but they'd decided to wait until Mary cut her lawns to be alone and together. They could then explore the breadth and depth of their sensuality with patience and thoughtfulness.

Or go at it like rabbits as they did this afternoon. Except Dax wasn't fast, she thought.

And he's certainly not soft and fluffy.

~

The ice-cold peach-flavored soda tasted good, and the burning sensation satisfied as the liquid slid down. My eyes closed as I rocked and listened to her shower.

I pictured the individual beads of water falling from her chin to form a creek that meandered through the valley of her breasts, joined by other droplets cascading from her nipples, creating a river that flowed down her navel and led inexorably to the reservoir of her passion before rushing rapids roared over the cliff into a writhing waterfall that crashed into a misty climax.

Alright, I might be in trouble. Here I was thinking about a woman I'd just been with fifteen minutes ago as if I hadn't just been with her fifteen minutes ago.

I craved her, and the mystery of it went uninvestigated because I didn't want to muck it up by thinking too much about it. My Michigan friend said I did that sometimes and told me to knock it off, mostly because she'd been tired of listening to me analyze things to death.

Tasha walked down the hallway wrapped in terrycloth and joined me in the living room. She lifted the A&W I left on the coffee table and finished it in one tip of the mug.

"Thanks. Guess I worked up a thirst."

Her eyes smiled in a *cat who ate the canary* kind of way, and I patted my lap and bid her to come. The chair squeaked as she straddled me like she'd been doing it for years, and I kissed her as if it were the very first time.

"Dax."

The way she said it made me squirm beneath her.

"Mary was right," Tasha said as she opened the towel. "If you give a mouse a cookie . . ."

"He's going to want a glass of milk."

She nodded and put her hand behind my head.

chapter ten

Tasha poured the russet colored liquid in the Keystone Cops coffee mug Dax gave her for Christmas. She felt *Hazel-Nutty* this morning and stirred the milky creamer as she watched her partner and Johnson talk with the large young man about the Alabama game.

When they'd finished, Johnson walked the youngster to the door and Dominic filled a cup before sitting at her desk.

"Again with that kid?" Tasha asked.

"Yeah. Sam asked him to come in."

Another parent demanded the police arrest the boy they said raped their daughter. Sam Johnson spoke to both girls in the course of his investigation and their stories were similar – they *did* consent to physical contact but insisted they did *not* want to have intercourse, swearing they'd told him to stop.

It didn't help that the girls had been drinking prior to the alleged attacks, with one smoking 'a doobie' as well. While those facts shouldn't have mattered as it applied to a question of assault, it did cast doubt on their credibility considering five other girls he interviewed said they'd also been with the boy and the intercourse was consensual.

Despite the parents' anger and insistence, there was nothing that could substantiate their daughter's claims and it devolved into another *He said - She said* sexual assault allegation without any charges being filed.

"Do you think he hurt those girls, Dom?" Tasha asked.

"I don't know. The kid is likable and seems genuine, but I just met him. Sam says his Spidey sense isn't tingling, so he's not sure either. Hard to tell with the promiscuity of today's youth. You know, I heard ten percent of sixth graders in Texas have had sex. Can you believe that?"

Tasha could but didn't want to.

"I heard that, too. Something's going on out there, but I don't know what or why. Or how to stop it."

She saw the short, slight girl standing off to one side and got up to meet her.

"Well, hello, Miss Rivera. I'm so glad to see you. And so happy to hear about your success."

Maria Rivera, aka, Chica Sanguine, was a student at Gulf Coast Community College and came to the attention of the St. Vincent police when her artwork was displayed on the outside walls of many business establishments from Mexico Beach to Eastpoint along the coast - all illegally.

Tasha admired both the artistry of her painting and the content, or at least what it was trying to convey – the police need to serve the citizens instead of themselves.

When Maria was caught tagging an old airplane hangar down Rutherford road, Tasha gave her a choice of jail or job. With her help in finding more suitable canvases, Maria began to paint legitimately and her work was later heralded as 'important and timely' by People magazine. The mayor, who'd become a staunch supporter, asked her to create a mural for the city.

"You know better than to call me Miss Rivera, Detective." She reached for the hug Tasha offered.

"As do you, Maria."

"You started it, Miss Williams. And don't ask me to call you Tasha. My mother would smack the back of my head for such a lack of respect toward my elders," she said with a wry smile. "And in this case, my betters as well."

Maria thanked Tasha again for the opportunity she gave her to pursue a dream she didn't know she had instead of arresting her. "Although, I could have done a pretty good job on those jail cell walls."

"There's no doubt about that, Chica."

Maria told her about being asked to go to New York by an uptown art gallery, and the respect she'd received from her mother.

"I've been wanting it from her for a long time, and I don't know if it would have ever happened if not for you. Thank you, Tasha. Thank you so much."

"You're welcome, Maria. But remember, your talent has too much shine to go unnoticed. You were always going to be found out. Don't quit telling it like it is, Chica. And how it could be. Alright?"

Dominic returned to Tasha's desk when Maria left and said he heard her being sweet. "I blame Palmer. Ever since you found that kid with him your demeanor has been . . . Nice. Where's the disappointment in your fellow man? The pessimism for the people, and the look you'd give when they gave you shit? Yeah, that one."

He remembered when she came to work tired and gray. She'd been civil but bemoaned the state of the human condition, expressing serious concern for its future. Now, she smiled more, laughed more, and gave humanity at least a fifty-fifty chance to survive themselves.

"Good morning, Detective Williams."

Tasha smiled at Dominic before turning to respond. "Hello and good morning, Miss Harris. How are you today?"

Donna Harris worked for Child Protective Services and drove from Panama City to handle cases in the area.

"I'm well, Detective. And you?"

"Except for my smart-aleck partner, I'm having a good day so far. Do you know Detective Greer?"

Miss Harris nodded and shook hands with Dominic. She sat in the chair he pulled out for her and set a purse on the floor by her feet.

"Tash, I've got some phone calls to make so I'll leave y'all to it. Nice to see you again, Miss Harris."

"You too, Detective," she said and turned her attention to Tasha. "I'm hoping you can give me an update about Mary Stewart's father. Has he been apprehended?"

Tasha told her what she knew. There'd been no credit card activity, cash transfers or withdrawals from his bank accounts, no calls to or from his phone, and no one had seen or heard from him. He seemed to have vanished.

"You remember his brother was an FBI director, so maybe he helped obtain a new identity or got him out of the country somehow. But I think he's probably dead. It's been a year and a half and given what he did to Mary and what he and his brother did to those other girls, it's logical to assume he was involved with some unsavory people. And bad people do bad things to each other."

Donna nodded, knowing full well what people were capable of. Bad parents in particular.

"I've been out to visit them three times since that awful mess at the Raw Bar, and I always come away thinking how well they seem to handle the hardships they face. Especially when you consider they've both had to kill to survive. You'd think the stress alone would cause problems, but they're amazing together. And their humor is downright infectious. They make you laugh."

"That they do," Tasha said. "And you're right. They are amazing."

Donna rose from the chair and extended her hand.

"Thank you, Tasha. I would like to see the two of them become a permanent family. Sooner, rather than later."

Tasha took her hand and nodded.

"In their hearts, they already are."

~~

"I'm sorry, Hale. I know it's not what you want to hear but bringing a civil case could end up doing you more harm than good, even if you could get it before a judge. Though not insurmountable, the video is harmful to your claim, and coupled with Barbara's affidavit . . ."

Hale nodded his head and looked out the window. His lawyer wasn't telling him anything he didn't already know, but hearing it released him to move forward. As he watched a hummingbird flit up and against the pane, he knew a judgement wouldn't be enough anyway.

He wanted Palmer to pay, but not with money or a court ordered finding of fault. He wanted to break him, to beat him down, to make him suffer.

To make him dead.

Rational thought implored him to turn away from his intended course of action, but he'd turned a deaf ear and banished it to the dark recesses of his mind.

Palmer *would* pay for taking his sister's life, with his own. And so would Barb, although hers would be a more degrading journey to the grave.

"Thanks for your time, Charles," he said, and shook his hand. "I appreciate your input. How about coming over Friday night? I'm sure Barbara would love to see you again."

Hale grinned as his friend blushed. Barb hadn't *seen* Charles because of the mask, but she knew he wasn't her husband and opened herself to him all the same.

Her fate had been sealed soon after his knee operation. She sat cuffed above him, arching her back when he'd pull the chain between her breasts, seeking the pain it caused and its subsequent pleasure.

As he tugged harder and harder, she moved toward her climax with enthusiasm. When it came, she lost her balance and experienced an intensity like no other after he caught her by the throat – and squeezed.

He encouraged her interest in erotic asphyxiation, as a means to her ultimate demise, and began to systematically debase his wife by giving her to Charles and many others while she was bound and blindfolded. They used to be quiet to give Barb the illusion of fidelity, but he knew she'd known all along when she *thanked* all who stood before her.

Even after the mask was removed.

~

Hale stopped by the store on the way home and saw the pretty girl on the cover of a tabloid magazine. But it was Palmer's name that caught his eye, and he put it with the other items to be rung up.

~~

"Watson, what the heck are you doing?"

He was trying to accomplish a feat that had never been done in the annals of canine calisthenics – position oneself on a floating raft in a backyard pool.

"But you're going backwards. That's not gonna work," Mary said. "Want me to hold the raft for you?"

The look in his eyes forbade her to speak further. Not only was she breaking his concentration, but she was also undermining his confidence by questioning his form.

Isabel watched him inch closer and clapped her hands and giggled in delight when he made it onto the raft.

"You did it! You did it, Watson. What a smart dog."

He stuck his tongue out at Mary and then tipped and dipped and fell into the water. They were laughing as his head broke the surface but stopped when he looked at them.

Well, they tried to.

Watson wasn't one to get mad or hold a grudge, but he waited until he stood next to them before shaking the water from his fur. Isabel squealed and Mary grinned.

"Okay, we had that coming, but it was funny."

Frank took a swig of his beer and stepped through the sliding screen door. He'd watched the attempt and laughed when the dog hit the water.

"He almost had it there for a minute. Hi, Izzy. Mary."

He kissed the top of Isabel's head and looked over at her friend. She wore a bathing suit that fit her to perfection. The swell of her breasts accentuated a slim waist, and he thought about her in ways he shouldn't have.

"Hi, Mr. Frank. Isabel, mind if I use the bathroom?"

"Of course not, silly. You know where it is."

Watson jumped into the pool, and Mary went into the house before remembering she forgot her backpack. More specifically, the monthly item inside. She turned back, and then stood still in the middle of the kitchen.

The way Frank was rubbing lotion on Isabel shoulders made her uneasy. His hands were too familiar. When she let him slide them over her breasts, Mary spun around and marched to the bathroom.

What the hell? What is going on? What is he doing? What is she doing? What should I do? What can I do?

Questions bombarded her brain, and she tried to corral her thoughts but couldn't. She needed time, and distance, to process. Mary saw a girl in the mirror fighting to remain calm in the midst of an emotional storm.

"Hey, Isabel?" she said when she went back outside. "I completely forgot the two new lawns I'm doing today."

Mary reached for her clothes hanging over the railing and started to put them on over the swimsuit. Isabel looked at her with disappointment.

"Well, shoot. I was hoping we'd play some music. Maybe you could come back after you're done?"

Watson thought it sounded like an idea with promise as he got out of the pool and shook himself dry.

"I don't know. This is the first time cutting them, and I'm not sure what needs doing or how long it'll take. How about if I call you later?"

Watson picked up his bowl and started to take it to the wagon when Isabel got up and knelt in front of him.

"Thanks for sharing your trick with me. Maybe you'll get it next time." She rubbed and scratched till his foot moved then patted his head and kissed his nose.

Frank went into the house after saying, *see y'all*, and Isabel carried Mary's backpack and walked with them to the front, giving Watson another scratch for the road.

"Thanks for staying, Mary. I had fun. And thanks for the math tutoring. I need it. Maybe I could pay you for it?"

Mary shook her head. "Thanks for letting us enjoy your pool. Maybe we should pay *you*?"

They chuckled and Isabel gave her a hug.

"I'm so glad for your friendship,"

Mary didn't know what to say and patted her back.

"Are we friends, Mary?"

The easiest thing would have been to say yes. Isabel was fun to be with and had a tender heart toward Watson. But Mary didn't give herself away easily and needed time to consider what she'd seen.

"I think we're on our way to becoming friends, Isabel. Maybe good ones."

Mary reached out and touched her arm, trying to soften her words. She saw the hope in Isabel's eyes and wished she'd just gone ahead and told her they were.

Maybe Isabel really needed a friend right now?

"Would you like to come over some time? Meet Dax and Tasha? We could play music and sing, have dinner. Maybe you could stay the night? A pajama party, perhaps?"

Isabel's face lit up. "That sounds like fun. When?"

"How about next weekend? Friday night? Maybe Tasha will take us fishing on her boat Saturday morning? Do you fish?"

"Fish? Yes. Catch? Not so much. But I'd love to try it from a boat."

They cemented their plan with a firm handshake, and then Isabel grabbed her for another hug. She hugged back this time and it felt okay.

Mary called Dax when she reached the road and told him she was done for the day and ready to be picked up. Watson asked about the new lawns, and she told him she'd been mistaken about the day and didn't realize it till now.

She didn't know if he saw what she did, but she wasn't ready to talk about it

chapter eleven

My hand throbbed, and no amount of squeezing eased the pain. I'd only played for an hour or so, and everything was fine until the last part of the last song.

The Thirsty Goat was bustling tonight, and people were shaking my hand, slapping my back, and giving me words of well-wishing and support. It was the first time I'd played in public since the Raw Bar, and the comments were good.

For the most part. I heard one or two negative remarks, albeit, from a distance, but it was fine by me.

The freedom of speech we enjoy in this country is an awesome thing, and I'll fight to defend anyone's right to voice their opinion. I'll also fight for my right to confront those anyone *assholes* who disparage me unfairly.

Preferably when they grew a pair and said it to my face.

On the drive home, I thought about the young man in the audience whose face I'd seen on the news.

He'd been acquitted of a crime he committed – robbing, raping, and killing a woman in her home. After spending the better part of a year in jail awaiting trial, he was released due to a technicality. The police conducted a search of his house before the warrant arrived and the man was set free because of it, despite finding her jewelry in his closet.

As outrageous as that seemed, it was necessary to protect us from those in law enforcement who would plant incriminating evidence and then lie about it – even after video to the contrary turned up on the evening news.

That didn't mean he was going to get away with it . . .

I pulled into the garage well after midnight and poured some Dr. Pepper into a glass of ice before heading into the living room. Mary swiveled around in the big chair and asked for a sip that became a couple of swallows.

"Want one of your own?"

"No thanks," she said and began to rock as I sat on the couch. When the Pepper touched the coffee table, the chair stopped. The glower she cast looked ominous in the dimly lit room and I stifled a grin and put a coaster under the glass. The rocking resumed and the glower transformed to a glow. She shook her head and cracked a smile.

"I like you, Dax."

"I like you too, kiddo. Why are you up, Buttercup?"

"Processing. How was your gig? Did you play well?"

I told her about my night but not about the pain.

"Want to share your thoughts?"

"I think so," she said. "But under certain conditions. I'd like to invoke a modified *don't ask–don't tell*. I'm seeking guidance, so, I'll tell you a little bit and let you ask a question or two when appropriate. However, I retain the right to reign you in at any time. Agreed?"

A *don't ask–don't tell* had only been invoked once, by me. It was meant to be used sparingly and only for things of a serious nature, providing a way to ask something of the other without giving the reason why – like I'd done when I asked her to drop me on a street corner and pick me up a mile away from a house I'd been surveilling.

One of my reservations was that she might request one someday because of a boy – and I was not ready for that.

"And Dax, before you answer, I'm going to present this as a hypothetical. We could treat it like a possible scenario or a contingency plan, instead. Will that work for you?"

"Sure."

"It's about a boy."

My face fell, but before I could ask a question I wasn't supposed to, she smiled and shook her head.

"But it's not about me."

I called her a name when she twinkled at me.

"Bet you wish you'd put a coaster under that glass now, don't you?"

We shared a moment and some soda before she began.

"Let's say there's a boy whose mom left some time ago. The dad brought a girlfriend into the house, and she's been living there for a while. The girlfriend touched the boy inappropriately, but he didn't seem to mind at all."

"How old is the boy?"

"Older than me. Old enough to stop her, but he doesn't. I don't know what to do, or if it's mine to do anything about."

"How old is the girlfriend?"

"She's old. Almost ancient. About your age."

I loved that kid and her little shit ways.

"Mind telling me what you've processed so far?"

"Well for me, the reason to get involved would be if he's being harmed, regardless of how it appears. The girlfriend has only been there about a year, so she hasn't molested him since childhood. But she could still be hurting him, couldn't she? He's withdrawn and insecure but sweet, and I can't help thinking he's being taken advantage of."

I heard the apprehension in her voice.

"He thinks she loves him like a mother, but Dax, that's the part hanging me up the most. To me, that so-called mom is abusing her son, even though he seems okay with it."

"I assume you've already thought about talking to him but decided against it?"

She nodded, got up from the chair, and took the empty glass into the kitchen with her.

Besides the humiliation and scandal that would follow if Isabel's mother found out what was happening under her roof, there were too many unknown consequences that could come from asking why she let Frank touch her. Mary couldn't know how Isabel would feel or what she might do and didn't want to hurt her.

A sleepy Watson walked into the room and laid next to me on the couch. I asked Mary to bring a treat back with her and began to scratch and ponder.

The situation was disturbing. Even a willing teenager wasn't psychologically or emotionally prepared for the consequences of an adult's attentions. I shared her concern about his vulnerability and thought it a good place to start.

Mary set the glasses on the coaster covered coffee table and I rubbed Watson's belly before giving him his treat. We clinked our drinks and leaned back.

"May I speak freely?"

She nodded and sipped.

"Getting involved in another's business is serious and sometimes necessary. If a person needed saving, I'd be inclined to help them – even against their will. They might not have anything to do with me ever again, but I could live with that rather than letting them suffer without my trying. The issue is knowing if your friend is being abused or not. I assume having that information will help you help him?"

"Well, I didn't say he was a friend. And yes, I think so. If she ... *he* wasn't being pressured or made to do anything he didn't want to; I'd still think it was wrong. But I might be willing to let it go. Or at least consider something other than breaking the girlfriend's neck."

Mary grinned before asking how she could verify it.

"Would you recommend using remote observation to assist in the knowing? And would doing so be unethical?"

I might have questioned her using a *don't ask – don't tell* when she could have easily asked for my help, but I had to trust her judgement and her reasons for the invoking.

See how that works?

"An argument could be made about the unethicalness of letting an allegation of abuse go uninvestigated."

"That was certainly a mouthful," she said and smiled.

"I use trail-cams up at the cabin. They can be set for motion detection or you can watch in real time. You can also record. Might that work for your hypothetical knowing?"

Mary nodded then shook her head. "Those might be too big. Do we have anything smaller?"

When I showed her what *we* had, Mary didn't ask why, and I didn't tell. She just took what she needed and gave me a hug before going to bed.

~~

Eddie glanced around before hiding behind the bush. From here he could peek into her bedroom and watch. She was younger than the one he robbed a year ago, the one he'd raped. And killed.

He hadn't meant to, but she wouldn't stop screaming.

You'd think she'd like the idea of a young man wanting a woman her age and would've been more appreciative of his attentions. But she fought him harder than the others. If she would've just gone with the flow, he would have been in and out of her and her life in less than an hour.

It was her own damn fault she was dead, but as much as he hadn't intended to kill her, it seemed the smart thing to do from now on. So the police wouldn't have a witness to hold over his head one day.

Eddie had an obsession for older women. Much older women. The fact they were weaker and less likely to report a sexual assault wasn't the reason he preyed on them, although it had proven to be an unexpected bonus.

It was stupid to take that woman's jewelry, even more so to keep it in his house. He'd been lucky the cops screwed up or he'd be shit-canned and in prison. From now on, he'd stick to stealing their cash like always.

She came out of the bathroom and reached for the skin moisturizer on the nightstand by the bed. He watched the woman's practiced ritual and imagined his hands all over her still alluring body.

Eddie could hardly wait to make her acquaintance.

~~

The phone rattled as it vibrated. With the volume off, Tasha wouldn't know if it was a call unless it rattled again.

It didn't. She picked it up and noted the time. It was late, but she couldn't sleep and sent a return text.

It rang before she set it back on the stand.

"That's great news," Tasha said when she answered. "Congratulations, Seven. Do I address you as Deputy-Director now? Does Starfleet have an equivalent rank?"

"It's Assistant Deputy-Director, Lieutenant Yar. And yes, there are Deputy Directors in Starfleet's Internal Affairs department. Hey, girlfriend, how come you're not sleeping? Is Dax keeping you up on a school night? Are you doing your part to keep *him* up?"

"Jeri, you're incorrigible. No, he's not here, and yes . . . I do my part. And I do it well," she added with a hint of blush Jeri couldn't possibly see but would know was there.

Men thought women didn't talk about sex as much as *they* did, and they were right. Women talked about it more.

"Did you ask him about that three-way?"

Tasha shook her head and laughed.

"No, not yet. I'd be careful what you ask for, Seven. He might say yes, and then what would you do?"

"Ain't that the truth. Listen, they're making me take a two-week vacation before I step into the position. Said I hadn't taken one in ages and probably wouldn't get another chance any time soon. They want me rested and recharged before throwing me to the wolves. So, I'm thinking a week in St. Vincent to hang with you and your family and another with you and me in Mexico. We could go back to that place where we had so much fun. How about it?"

Tasha loved the idea and told her she'd try to get the time off work. She hadn't taken a vacation in a while, either, not a real one, and the thought of spending a week with her friend made her heart sing – until she realized it would be a week without Dax.

"I can't wait, Seven. It's been a long time since we were footloose and fancy-free. Remember those great cigars we smoked at the seaside bar?"

They reminisced into the late hours of the early morn.

~~

Frank stood quietly in the hall listening to his girlfriend sleep. Monica was home almost every night, which made it risky but incredibly exciting when he left her bed for her daughter's. His time with Isabel was measured in minutes, but they were intensified by the anticipation and nature of their relationship.

He'd shown her things she didn't know she wanted but had sense enough not to take her virginity. That was a can of worms best left unopened right now. He fostered her yearning and was content to wait until she gave it freely, thinking it her idea.

If and when the shit hit the fan, he'd quit Monica and take Izzy to Texas. She was old enough to leave, and he was sure she'd come. He'd cultivated her love along with her desire, and, while he sometimes felt a twinge of guilt for his intrigue, the reward of having a mother and daughter under the same roof outweighed the occasional prick of morality.

He was living the dream, as the fantasy was now reality.

Monica's snoring was steady when he opened Isabel's door and slipped into her room.

chapter twelve

Monica was unsure about letting Isabel spend Friday night with Mary and Dax. Her apprehension stemmed from a fuzzy understanding of the incident he'd been involved in. But her worry eased when Isabel said Detective Williams would also be there. Frank looked up from his dinner when Izzy mentioned her.

"Mary says she's a friend of theirs and visits a lot. She plays music and fishes. In fact, she's going to take us out on her boat the next day to catch some. It'll be fun."

"Don't forget to take along some sunscreen. You know how you burn. Oh, I'm going to swap my afternoon shift and work Saturday night, so you and Frank are on your own for dinner when you get back. I'll be sleeping."

Monica took her plate to the sink and began to clean up.

Isabel's cheeks burned when Frank winked at her, and she left the table to help with the dishes.

The thought of spending a whole night alone with him stirred conflicted emotions about what she'd been doing – or allowing to happen. She didn't initiate anything between them, didn't seek his attention or ask him to come into her room, and so had minimized the extent of her responsibility. He was the adult and, despite her willingness, the bulk of it rested on his shoulders.

But did it really? When she asked Mary about a father touching his daughter, she was thinking of Frank. He'd always been kind throughout her mother's cruelty and gave what she thought was a parent's love and attention.

But the kiss he gave on New Year's was not a father's, nor was hers to him a daughter's.

Had he taken advantage of her?

Had she let him?

It troubled her to think she might have, but the reason for it was murky and she couldn't, or wouldn't, see it clearly. Regardless, she felt complicit now.

Isabel wondered if any of this would have happened if her mother loved her, maybe treated her differently. Or hadn't called her a fat worthless slob that night.

What kind of mom does that?

~~

Pajamas consisted of shorts and shirts and were judged based on disparate design and clashing color with bonus points given for absurdity. These were items of clothing you'd rarely wear in private, let alone in front of anyone. So when they whistled at my outfit, I thought the trophy was in the bag, confident that my neon and knee-high socks had put me over the top. Until Tasha called a foul.

"Uh, uh. This is a shirt and shorts competition, and, while we can all agree about the absurdity of those socks, I'm not sure we can award any points for them. What do you girls think?"

Isabel sat quiet, so Mary weighed in.

"I concur. Although, I'm inclined to give him a point for originality. It would be a shame to discourage this kind of outrageousness in future competitions. What do you think, Isabel?" Mary asked and took a picture of Dax, who posed as if it were a *Cover Girl* photo shoot.

Isabel got up from the couch and walked outside.

I looked at Mary who shrugged and then smiled when she came back inside wearing sunglasses and earbuds.

"Ah, yes, that's much better. Those socks were too loud to think and too bright to see your ensemble."

We all started laughing and Watson went over and gave her a fist-bump with his nose.

"That was nicely done, Isabel."

"Thanks, Mr. Dax. Your wacky is catchy."

"It's amazing how quickly Isabel has succumbed to the sickness of our silliness," Mary said, looking at me. "It's only been, what? Forty minutes?"

I gave her a wide-eye of incredulity.

"Are you saying it's me, girl? That I'm an infectious disease, a carrier of craziness, an imp of insanity?"

"Don't forget Ambassador of absurdity, Duke of daftness, and a Sultan's ass," Tasha said, and then added, "Sorry, that was supposed to be Sultan of sass."

Isabel cracked up and Mary shook her head.

"See what havoc your socks have wrought, Dax? You've taken an otherwise normal girl and turned her into a Mad Hatter of merriment."

"A Frankenstein of folly," Tasha said chuckling.

"A Jack-O-Lantern of jocularity," Isabel uttered, and everyone fell out.

When Watson called her a *Shih-Tzu of shenanigans*, Mary nodded and stuck out her hand. "Give me four."

After the laughter quieted, I said what seemed obvious. "Guess this means I win."

Three pairs of eyes turned, two heads shook, and one voice said, "Uh, no."

Isabel's pink My Little Pony shirt and green Teenage Mutant Ninja Turtles shorts won the day, while me and my socks came in dead last. I'm not saying it was a girl versus boy thing, but, clearly, I was robbed.

Those socks rocked.

After a dinner consisting of fish, risotto, and the last of last year's scallops, we played and sang songs till the cows came home. Or in this case, Watson tugged on Mary to go for their nightly walk up and down the driveway before bed.

Isabel tagged along, and I waited until they were out of sight before turning to Tasha. We reached for each other and started making out like bandits.

"How much time do you think we have?" she asked in a raspy whisper. I activated the driveway alarms – not the audio but the lights. The yellow one flashed on their way to the road and the mailbox, so I took Tasha's hand and led her down the hall.

When the red light blinked, the one thirty-yards from the porch, we flew out of my room in separate directions – me to the bathroom and a shower and Tasha to the rec-room to inflate and sheet her mattress.

The girls were laughing when the door opened, and Watson ran back to jump on the mattress after hearing the air pump. Tasha gave a smile and a pat and told him to be patient. Mary followed and watched for a moment before asking if she'd like some ice cream before bedtime.

"I'm buying."

"Sounds good, Mare. Thanks."

Tasha thought Mary could see right through her and started to feel like a caught kid. But it had been worth it.

They sat around the coffee table enjoying easy banter with their ice cream, and Isabel felt appreciated and valued in a way she never had before. After good-nights, sleep-tights, and bedbug-bite admonitions, she followed Mary and Watson into their room and was given the guest option of using the bathroom first. Isabel cleaned her face and teeth before brushing her hair while sitting on the air-mattress next to Mary's bed.

A multi-colored Dreamcatcher hung on the post of the headboard, and Isabel reached over and felt the intricate design of stitched material, feather and wood. She was transfixed by the decoration.

"You like it?" Mary asked from the bathroom door.

"It's beautiful," Isabel said. "Does it work?"

"It seems to, as long as it's on the bedpost. In fact, I can't remember the last time I had a bad one. Now, Watson and I fly around in our dreams all the time."

Isabel looked at her with big eyes and a smile.

"You fly? Me too! But what do you mean *our*?"

Mary took a brush to her hair and looked at Watson, who grinned and nodded.

Isabel thought her leg was being pulled when Mary told her they could enter one another's dreams but said it in a way that made it seem possible, and she wanted to believe it could be.

"Thanks for sharing your family with me, Mary. Y'all are great. And so much fun. You must laugh all the time."

Mary nodded and said she did.

"Dax and Tash are pretty cool. I'm lucky to have them."

Watson cocked his head and then raised his bushy brows. Mary raised her own and asked if his neck was stiff. He said no and squinted his eyes.

"Eyes a little scratchy then?"

He rolled them and asked Isabel if he looked like chopped liver to her.

Isabel looked at Mary who chuckled.

"There's no sense asking her. She doesn't understand Retriever. Do you, Isabel? Besides, you know how special you are to me and how lucky I am to have you, too."

Watson nodded, and Isabel grinned in confusion. "You two talk to each other, do you? Am I crazy or are y'all?"

They spent the night getting to know each other before the sandman sprinkled dust in their eyes. As they finally closed for the night, Isabel's thoughts were of Dax.

Did he come to Mary's room like Frank came into hers?

~~

Breakfast was an all hands on deck affair as everyone contributed to its making, eating, and cleaning up.

"The tide waits for no woman," Tasha said, "and the best fishing starts in an hour and a half."

The major Solunar time was a two-hour period with the moon either directly above or below the earth and was excepted by hunters and fishermen to be the optimal time to catch their prey. Some believed, and some did not, but 'Those who don't usually go hungry,' Tasha said when Dax questioned its veracity one day.

Watson would rather go with the girls, but the chances of getting snagged by a treble-hook lure was too high. So he would tag along with Dax, though not before obtaining some affection first. Isabel's turn came after Mary went to her room. When she returned with two backpacks, they said *Cya's* and *Later Gators* and left.

"Guess it's just you and me, boy," I said and grabbed drinks, treats, and Watson's bowls for the road.

My trip was a multi-tasked mission requiring visits to Lowes, Wal-Mart, and the Blue Moon Bar and Grill. After we cleared the bridge in Mexico Beach, I found a sweet tea in the cooler and asked Watson if he wanted a Snausage.

105

Which, of course, he did.

The wind swirled around the open windows as we rode in silence along the wooded stretch of road through Tyndall Air Force Base. Two F-22 Raptors landed as we drove past the runway, the noise from the jets loud and patriot proud.

After stops in Panama City and Callaway, I pulled into Lynn Haven's Blue Moon parking lot around noon. A pretty decent lunch crowd was laying siege to the place, so Watson and I went for a walk to stretch our legs.

We turned into a subdivision after a few minutes and ambled down the sidewalk until Watson found a suitable place. He gave me a *Do you mind?* look, and I turned around so he could do his doo-doo business.

The houses weren't as far from each other as I'd hoped, but the foliage offered some privacy from nosy neighbors. While the luster had long since left the neighborhood, most of the yards were clean and cut, and the vehicles white, washed, and in the driveway.

Watson walked over and stood next to me with a grin that reflected the humor in his eyes.

"I know. Humans think they're in charge, but who's picking up after whom?" I retrieved the smelly deposit with the plastic bag worn inside-out on my hand.

After tying the knot, I asked if he'd mind a walk around the block before heading back. He started to crack wise about my taking his poop out for a stroll until I threatened to affix it to the underside of his collar.

"We may not be the superior species, but we do have opposable thumbs."

After being overwhelmed with patrons earlier, the Blue Moon was now empty save for the couple in the booth at the back. I ordered a couple burgers, some fries, a cold Coke, and asked for some ice to take outside and put in Watson's water bowl.

"He can come inside as long as he's quiet. Just move over to the table closest to the stage," the waitress said.

"Thanks. You're very kind."

Watson's wagged his tail when the approaching aroma reached his nose, and he licked his lips with a question.

"I ordered two."

Her nametag was pinned low on her shirt, making it difficult to ascertain her name without looking at her chest. Fortunately, she only had eyes for Watson, and I was saved the embarrassment of explanation.

"Ooohh. He's so cute," she said and set the tray down. "What's his name? Can I pet him?"

After introductions were made and affections given, she left to get my drink as Watson made short work of his burger. I broke off a piece of my own and gave it to him with some fries, asking if he'd like some ketchup with that. The question was rendered moot in a matter of munches.

"Thanks, Jocelyn," I said when the soda arrived.

She asked if we wanted another burger and smiled when Watson nodded. He rolled his eyes when I asked if he was buying and tried to maneuver her fingers to a scratching position that offered the most satisfaction. Just as nirvana seemed within his grasp, Jocelyn was called away to attend to another customer.

"Sorry, boy. So close, and yet . . ."

I reached down and gave him some commiseration and comfort. When he tried to move my fingers to Mary's spot, I acquiesced and called him a *loose goose.*

"Don't look at me like it's not true. You'll let anyone scratch you – anytime, anywhere."

I smiled and began to think about how it could be done when the front door opened and three guys walked my way. One nodded as he stepped on the stage and began to setup.

Must be a practice session.

Watson barely noticed until I stopped scratching.

I thanked Jocelyn for bringing another burger and gave Watson half while the guys tuned up.

The volume was low compared to how they'd sound at showtime, and I sang along when they played a Stevie Ray Vaughan tune – until the drummer looked over.

I shoved some burger into my mouth and tapped my fingers to the beat. They weren't bad, but the guitar player wasn't killing it. His rhythm was spot on, though. Halfway through the song, the bass player quit to answer his phone and, based on what I overheard, an unexpected opportunity presented itself. Or would in another minute or two.

"Dammit. Where in the hell are we going to find another guitar guy who can sing?"

"What about Larry?"

"Larry? Are you crazy? He's a metalhead, and a coke snortin' one at that. What about Carl? He's not bad and knows most of our songs. Maybe we could get him down here to practice before we go on?"

"Carl's in Texas visiting family. What about Bob?" His friends looked at him like he'd said something stupid and after he thought about it, he agreed.

"Well, shit. Johnny can't make it, and that's that. And if we don't play, they'll never ask us back. We're screwed."

"Maybe not," I said.

Three pairs of eyes looked at me. Four, if you counted Watson who had a French fry dangling from his mouth.

After some discussion, I jumped on the stage, played parts of a few songs, and, for some reason, got embarrassed when the couple in the back hollered for more. We reached an agreement, and one of the guys went to get Johnny's gear so I could use it for tonight's show.

I sent the girls a text and apologized to Watson. We wouldn't be getting home until well after midnight, and he'd be one tired puppy before then.

"The good news is there will be food, music, and drink. You might even receive some stranger scratching."

We practiced for a long while and sounded pretty tight. The Blue Moon filled with people as day became night, and I took Watson for another walk before we started the set.

The moon hung low in the sky, and the dark only gave way when pushed or shoved. Watson wanted to run free, so I bent down and removed his leash.

"Have at it. But we need to be back in fifteen minutes. Meet me where the neighborhood ends in ten, okay?"

He nodded and turned to go.

"Don't go back without me, now. Without a leash, you might get ticketed, dognapped, or hit by a car. If that happens, Mary will kick my ass. Or kill me. Or both."

Watson grinned and took off, stopping by a tree to lift his leg before sprinting from yard to yard.

I walked quickly with purpose and determination.

~~

Eddie put the pot to boil and finished setting the table for a quiet dinner with the memory of his grandmother. They always dined together before he left to *love* someone the way she had him.

He'd watched the woman from the bushes long enough and couldn't wait to make her acquaintance. Whether she screamed or succumbed, lived or died, would be up to her. If she were smart, she'd lay back and let it happen. Hell, she might like it. Some had.

He always did. *Nana* made sure of that.

The knock startled him, and he jammed the weapon in his pants before opening the front door.

"Good evening, Mr. Taylor. May I come in?"

The man walked in and closed the door without waiting for a response, and Eddie was about to go off on him until a flash of recognition crossed his eyes.

"I know you. You're the guy who killed that woman in St. Vincent on New Year's Eve."

The man nodded.

"And you're the guy who raped and killed a seventy-six-year-old grandmother of five, great-grandmother of twelve, yes?"

The tone was friendly, but the smile was cold and the eyes even colder. A phrase Eddie must have heard or read somewhere popped into his head and chilled his heart.

Harbinger of death.

But he didn't think the man a foreshadowing of things to come – he was the instrument of his destruction. Eddie turned to run but something wrapped around his neck and held him in place. By the time he remembered the gun in his waistband it was too late.

~

I removed the leash and heard a sound coming from the kitchen. A pot of water boiled next to a pile of shrimp on the counter, and I turned off the stove in shock.

The table was set for two.

I'd only seen men's jackets and shoes at the door and took the calculated risk he was alone before walking in. If there was someone in the house, I wasn't looking for them because I wasn't killing anyone just to save my own ass. They didn't rape and murder that grandmother. Eddie did.

I left by the back door and jumped over the fence. I hadn't intended to deal with him until Tasha left for Mexico in a couple weeks, but the chance to act now was the very definition of serendipity.

Who'd think a man having lunch with his dog would murder a stranger a few minutes before performing with a band he'd just met and offered to help out?

Of course, there'd only been a fifty-fifty possibility he'd be home and another fifty he would be alone. I'd been lucky. Unless someone was there. Then not so much.

Watson sat waiting by the road, and I gave him a rub and a scratch before attaching the leash. He looked at me quizzically and cocked his head.

"Ask me no questions, and I'll tell you no lies."

~~

The Dreamcatcher hung on the wooden post of her bed, its colors vibrant in the glow of the full moon. Mary put it in her backpack with a note, and Isabel got misty eyed when she discovered it after a day of fun, fishing, and catching!

She'd hooked a monster Tripletail, and Mary and Tasha whooped when she landed the giant fish. Tasha filleted it at the cleaning station and sent the steaks home with her.

After eating their fill, Frank made a lunch of what was left for her mother to take to work. As Isabel laid in bed, she thought about Mary, how much she was loved, and couldn't help wanting the same. Frank gave her love – maybe not the way he should, or the way she needed, but it was more than she ever received from her mother.

So why not give herself, all of herself, to the one person who cared for her?

Would it be so wrong?

~~

A twisted grin appeared that couldn't be seen by the object of his lust as Frank took her offered innocence. But Mary saw it through the camera in the Dreamcatcher and her anger burned. That grin confirmed her worst fear – Isabel was being used.

Mary jumped from the bed to run to the house, reached for the phone to call her instead, and then plopped down on the floor to think.

Isabel thought she wanted what Frank was giving her, but Mary knew how destructive her choice was. How could she help her? What could she do?

What *should* she do?

chapter thirteen

Hale twirled the ice in his glass and watched his wife writhe and groan as Charles, Carol, and Carol's friend used her for their gratification. Barb's appetite for pain, pleasure, decadence, and domination was insatiable as she'd become a captive of her carnal existence and a servant to its desire – a fact he exploited to her detriment.

When they began to play in earnest, he rose from the chair and Brett followed him into the living room.

"All set for Florida?" Hale asked.

Brett still felt pain from the broken jaw he got the night at the Raw Bar, and the loss of a testicle was a constant reminder of his humiliation. Like Hale, he wanted the guitar player to suffer for what he did, and hatred fueled his need for revenge.

"I'm not opposed to hurting Palmer. Or killing him, if it comes to that. But I'm not killing the kid."

"I'm not suggesting we do. I only want him to feel the agony that comes when a terrible thing happens to someone you love, someone you should have protected. And no matter how hard he tries; he'll never be able to live with it. She could be a means to that end."

"How?"

Hale indicated the bedroom with a tilt of his head, and they listened to Barbara submit to her shame.

"We *take* his little girl."

~~

'What do you think?"

"It sounds like a great idea," Mary said with eagerness, suppressing a smile that might give her away. "Watson and I would love it!"

Tasha looked at Mary, and then at Dax who looked at Mary and then back to Tasha, who looked at Mary and said, "Uh . . ."

"What? Were you only asking Dax to go? What about me and my little dog?" Mary and Watson gazed at her with puppy-dog eyes that were unrepentant and unrelenting.

"Uh . . ."

"You said that already." Mary dodged the pillow Dax threw before letting Tasha off the hook.

"I'm just teasing. Although, I can't imagine what you're going to do all night on an island by yourselves."

She raised her brow with a look of innocent inquisition, wanting to see Tasha's blush deepen.

"I thought I might jump his bones as the moonlight glistens on our wet, naked bodies."

Mary's smile froze even as her face began to warm. The room got quiet, and the sparkle in Tasha's eyes burned bright as Mary was caught in the proverbial headlights.

"Touché, Tash. You got her good."

I kissed the top of Mary's head and she slapped my arm.

"I didn't get got. I just, uh. I just . . . Oh, hell."

She threw a pillow that started a melee we'd later call *The Great Pillow Fight*, which eventually was renamed Pillow Fight One as we failed to learn from the past and repeated our mistakes many times over.

"When y'all thinking of going?"

"Well, he hasn't accepted my invitation yet, so maybe you and Watson will get to go after all. Dax?"

They both looked at me and waited for a reply.

"Sounds like fun, Tash. I'd love to *join* you," I said. "Tell me again about that glistening moonlight."

"Aaahhhh," Mary said and left for the kitchen.

Watson followed and was rewarded with a treat and a scratch. He smiled when she stuck out her tongue even though they couldn't see her and wagged when she grinned.

"Yeah, she got me."

Mary brought a chilled mug of Tash's favorite beer into the living room and set it on the coffee table in front of her. She lifted and tipped the glass to Mary, who nodded.

"Do you have any plans for Graduation Night?"

"Isabel asked me out for dinner and maybe a party. Might be some cute boys there," she said, looking at me.

Mary loved to get under my skin by acting like a normal girl with a natural curiosity about boys, but I knew better. First off, she was *not* normal – no way, no how. Secondly, I knew she was trying to get a rise out of me. And she knew I knew she was. Did all daughters torture their dads this way?

I wondered and tried to call her bluff.

"Why limit yourself? Don't overlook the not-so cute. They need attention too."

"You're absolutely right. There are tons of good but not as cute guys who are nice and respect a girl and her feelings. But there's something about a cute boy, a bad boy with eyes full of mystery and lips you just have to taste."

I wasn't going to win this hand, so I folded and raised my palms in concession. She collected her winnings by giving me an impish grin.

Tasha asked her to elaborate on bad-boy cuteness, and I shot a glance that struck her square between the eyes. They hooted and hollered at me till I asked if Mary planned to speak at her graduation.

"Thankfully, no. Christine Merriweather is giving the valedictorian speech for the both of us, which is only right. She spent four years earning the honor, and I only went a couple of semesters. Besides, what could I say that would have any meaning to kids almost two years older than me?"

Before I said a word about the challenges she'd met and overcome, Mary shook her head and said no.

"I'm not talking about that. Not to them."

"Anybody getting hungry?" I said, changing the subject and leaving for the kitchen.

"Are you going to stay the night, Tash?" Mary asked.

"If it's okay. Thanks."

"You're always welcome to. Right, Dax?"

"Right."

"You want the air-mattress in my room or the spare? Or maybe Dax's?"

115

I stopped snapping green beans and backed up a step to look in the living room. This was unexpected, and I didn't know how to feel because I didn't know if she was serious.

"Would you mind if I said Dax's?" Tasha asked.

"Not at all. Watson and I would be happy to don our jammies and join y'all in another sleepover slumber party," Mary said, trying to regain the upper-hand.

"Uh-uh. Not this time, girl."

Tasha had a pillow locked and loaded and ready to fire. Mary raised her hands and began to walk backwards.

"Yes, ma'am."

It was hard not to crack up, and I saw Tasha struggling as well as Watson raised his ears and retreated with Mary. When they reached her bedroom, I let loose a laugh.

Tasha's eyes glowed in triumph, and a victorious smile lit her face – until Mary came out armed with a hamper full of pillows, towels,, nerf balls, and other throwables.

I tried to remain neutral, but they eventually ganged up on me until I sued for peace by crying *Uncle*.

It was a hell of a good night.

~~

"All units, all units. Shots fired at 453 Pecan Way."

"Shit, that's two streets down."

Dom responded to the dispatcher as Tasha turned and stopped the car in front of the house. They drew their guns and hurried to the door. After listening for a couple seconds, they knocked, announced themselves, and listened again. Nothing.

"Did you hear that? Sounds like someone's hurt," Tasha said, though she hadn't heard a thing.

"Yeah," Dom replied, satisfying the legal requirement of probable cause. He turned the knob and they walked inside. A woman lay on the floor, a bloody baseball bat next to her.

Dom knelt to check for a pulse as Tasha kept her gun up and ready. When he shook his head, they went from room to room looking for the killer but found another body, instead. A young girl with multiple gunshot wounds.

They cleared the rest of the house before Dom left to call it in, and Tasha took a few moments to calm herself.

That girl can't be more than eleven.

She could have cried, but the anger wouldn't let her. Still, a tear formed when she saw a drawn picture of a hand-turkey hanging on the refrigerator. The back door opened and a young man, maybe twenty, walked in and stopped. He was covered in blood and started to point a gun at her.

"Don't. If you raise it one more inch, I'll shoot." Tasha watched him consider her words and saw the resemblance. He was family. "Why did you kill them?"

He sneered and said, "Robbie told Mom what I did to her, and she went off on me and wouldn't knock it off. So, I shut her up. Robbie, too."

Tasha couldn't see any remorse or reflection of thought about what he'd done, and she knew he never would. He was heartless and would stay that way for the rest of his life. How many others would suffer because of it?

"What did you do to Robbie?"

The gleam in his eye told her everything, and he smiled when she asked how long it had been going on.

Tasha shot him once in the head.

~~

As Mary rode the mower along Indian Pass Road, she thought about how subdued Tasha had been last night. She didn't talk about the shooting and all attempts to make her laugh were unsuccessful. She also declined to eat dinner, play music, or even stay over. Mary tried to tease her by asking if Dax had already lost his appeal, but the sad smile was pitiful, and she hurt for her.

Goodbye hugs were longer, and Mary saw the depth of Dax's love for Tasha in the way his fingers stroked her hair. It both warmed her heart and made her hurt for him, too.

When she reached Isabel's house, her thoughts turned to what *she* had to do today. After Watson jumped from the wagon and ran to the back where Isabel was waiting, Mary checked her watch and started to cut the grass, considering the correctness of her intended course of action yet again.

Two weeks ago, she couldn't say she was Isabel's friend when asked, and, now that she could, she feared she might jeopardize that friendship.

117

Maybe lose it altogether.

Twenty minutes later, she finished weed-whacking just as Frank pulled up the driveway, right on time. Mary smiled and waved as she traded the whacker for the blower and shouted *yes* when he asked if she was swimming today. She blew the pool area so Watson and Isabel could resume their lounging, and the boardwalk from house to beach and back.

Mary stowed the blower in the wagon and grabbed her backpack. Watson and Isabel swam in the pool, and Frank sat in a chair watching them play.

"Okay to go inside and change?" Mary asked, knowing Isabel would chide her for asking.

"How many times are we going to do this? Mi casa es su casa."

Mary went to Isabel's bedroom and undressed.

Normally, she changed in the bathroom but not today. The Dreamcatcher on Isabel's bedpost winked at her as the ceiling fan made it dance. She'd already swapped out the dime-sized camera in the center with the original piece soon after seeing the two of them together, confirming what she suspected but now wished she didn't know.

Isabel seemed to give herself to Frank willingly, and maybe it was all none of her business, but . . .

Mary slipped on her bottoms and spent a few seconds reaching around inside the pack for the top. It was too small by half, and it made her blush. She'd meant to wear it for reasons thought long and hard about but faltered in a moment of modesty – until she heard him watching by the door left open a smidge for that purpose.

Instead of covering herself, she pulled the top from the pack, turned around, and raised her eyebrows. Frank took her in, all of her, and his jaw literally dropped. He didn't look at her eyes until she ambled over.

"No fair peeking, Mr. Frank."

She closed the door, frowned and finished dressing.

While planning for the possibility of his coming inside to catch a *glimpse*, the probability factor wasn't nearly as high as his eyeballing her at the pool. But what she failed to do was bring a back-up top to wear in the event he saw her half-naked first. It wasn't a serious oversight, but she might need to take Dax's Contingency Planning class again.

She'd given thought to his reaction to her plan if she had run it by him and had a good idea of what he'd have said – 'Oh, hell no. Absolutely not. Go to your room, young lady, and don't even think about coming out. Ever!'

Mary went outside and sat by the pool with her legs in the water. She nodded when Isabel's eyes widened.

"Sorry. I usually wear a one-piece but thought I'd get some sun on my stomach for a change and just threw this in the backpack. Guess I grew out of it."

"No need to apologize. If you got it . . ."

Frank mapped every crease and crevice of Mary's body in the matrix of his memory, from the firm bottom he'd admired before she caught him looking, to her large breasts, taut stomach, and legs he longed to open.

He wondered what she would be like.

~

Mary loaded the mower onto the trailer and took a long drink from the cooler. It quenched her thirst, and she used some to wash the dirt from her hands, face, and the back of her neck. But it would take more than water to cleanse the stain on her spirit.

While Isabel didn't say anything, Mary knew she'd been bothered by Frank's attentions towards her, especially after he offered to rub suntan lotion on a place she pretended she couldn't reach.

Everything she'd said and done was contrived to tweak his interest and Isabel's irritation, with the intention of driving a wedge between them by exacerbating one of the most primal and volatile of emotions. Jealousy.

Of course, that bitterness could turn on her.

But more than the possibility of Isabel's anger was Mary's worry of hurting her by destroying the illusions she had about who and what Frank really was. For the second time today and about the hundredth since conceiving her plan, part of her wished she could have stayed out of it.

But she couldn't. Not if there was a chance to save Isabel from that immoral man.

Mary called Dax to come get her and then tried Tasha. It rang four times before going to voicemail.

"Hi, Tash. Just wanted to say *Hey* and hope you're doing okay. You might think it's better to be alone with this, but it's not. You have family who loves you, and you should be with us. I know of what I speak."

Tasha called back right away, and when Dax arrived to hook up the trailer, Mary was laughing and crying.

And crying from laughing.

chapter fourteen

"Kids. They grow up so fast. One semester they're bright-eyed freshmen and the next, high-school graduates with the world at their feet. Where did the time go?"

Tasha nodded and said, "I know. It seems like only yesterday she was a freckled-faced teenager. Okay, she's still a teenager, but now that she doesn't need us anymore, I'm afraid our girl's going to spread her wings and fly away. What ever will we do?"

Mary giggled in the back seat. "Guys, I'm not..."

"You know, maybe it's just as well she's leaving. After all, she's not that adorable little thing we found a year and a half ago. She's getting old. Sure, she's still got some cute on her, but how long's that gonna last? What do you say we fill that empty nest with someone bright and shiny new?"

"Dax..."

"It might be nice to start fresh, maybe not make the same mistakes we made with this one," Tasha said and tilted her head toward the back.

"Tash, stop. I'm going to pee."

I looked in the rearview at a beaming little girl.

"We did the best we could with what we had to work with, Tash. So let's not beat ourselves up about it. Besides, I've got my eye on this low mileage, pretty little pre-teen I'd like to take for a spin, and... Wait. That didn't sound right."

The truck exploded in laughter, and it was miles before we returned to a semblance of ourselves.

"I'm not going away to school. At least not yet," Mary said. "I'll take online courses until I can't anymore, and let you feed and house me until you won't anymore."

"What about clothe you?" I asked.

"I'll let you keep buying them for now, just to make you happy, then wean you slowly so it won't be a shock to your system. But Tasha and I will do the shopping. How does that sound?"

"Expensive."

Mary smiled because he always said how little she cost to have around, and that she'd been *cheap* and *a real bargain.* She said he'd been lucky he did his shopping in the woods instead of Sears & Roebuck, because catalog girls cost a pretty penny. To which he responded, 'Ain't no penny ever been prettier than you, girl.'

He was corny like that, but she wouldn't change him for anything. Besides, she liked corn.

"That's great news about those scholarships," Tasha said and turned in the seat to look at her. "Any idea which one you'll use?"

Mary shook her head, and then nodded.

"Probably one closer to home. I can't trust Dax not to turn my room into a man-cave. But having choices I didn't have a week ago is pretty cool. Thank you, Mrs. Hunter."

Tasha raised her brow, and Mary explained.

Mrs. Hunter was her freshman math teacher and her biggest academic champion. She encouraged Mary to apply herself to higher mathematics, was responsible for getting her into the online classes offered by the university and worked tirelessly to promote her favorite student. Her efforts garnered scholarships from colleges and universities – two offering full rides.

"Sounds like she cares about you, Mare. I'm sure you'll make her proud. As you do me."

Mary touched her shoulder and Tasha patted her hand.

"How about some affection for me?" I asked.

"I don't know. Are you proud too?"

"Hmmm."

"Well?"

"I'm thinking, I'm thinking."

Tasha slapped my arm, and Mary punched it.

"There's your affection. You big shit."

I smiled and thought about Tasha as they kept talking. She seemed better this morning but still wasn't herself. I couldn't blame her for being so bothered by what happened. Killing, even in the line of duty, shouldn't be easy on the soul. It still bothered *me* from time to time. Especially the woman at the Raw Bar.

"Earth to Dax?"

I'd been thinking about her instead of listening to her. "Huh?"

"Do you still want to go to the island tonight? It might not be everything we planned, but I'd like to sit and watch the sunset. I might even let you hold my hand."

A hopeful melancholy echoed in her voice.

"A quiet night on the beach sounds great. We can listen to the water lap the shore, feel the balmy breeze on our faces, and watch the moonlight glisten on our wet and naked . . . hands."

Tasha grinned when Mary punched me again.

~~

She put the supplies in the boat, climbed into the truck, and drove out of town to pick up Dax.

Tasha had mixed feelings about tonight because he might ask questions she didn't want to answer. Or couldn't. She knew he'd been concerned about her reticence since the shooting but was glad he hadn't pressed her to talk about it.

How could she tell him? Or anyone?

She murdered that boy, and the fact he raised his gun didn't matter because she was already squeezing the trigger when he did. The injustice of allowing him to live and breathe and recall the pleasure of destroying his family had become unbearable, and her *rightness* in the moment felt absolute. But not anymore.

Tasha was riddled with doubt, guilt, and confusion. Her moral compass was askew, and she felt lost and adrift. She was an enforcer of the law and a believer in due process – not judge, jury, and executioner.

How did this happen? Had she temporarily lost her mind? Why did she do it?

That gleam in his eyes . . .

It embodied the delight of evil people doing evil things. Her father wore one just like it when he'd tell her how lucky she was to have him love her the way he did.

What am I going to do?

Tasha didn't feel any remorse that he was dead, only that she killed him. How could that be? How could she reconcile what she was with what she'd done?

Who had she become?

~~

Mary watched as Dax and Tasha drove away, and then glanced at a pouting Watson before heading in to get ready. "Come on, I'll only be gone a few hours."

"Do you know how long that is in dog years?"

"Yup. A few hours," she said and grinned.

"Well, yeah, okay, but . . ."

He nudged her leg as they walked to her bedroom then jumped on the bed. Mary picked out a sundress from the closet, held it up to herself and asked his opinion.

"It's pretty. Maybe a little short."

"Really?"

She tried it on and looked in the mirror hanging on the back of the door. "It doesn't look too bad. A little tight in the chest, maybe. Then again, everything is anymore."

Mary started to change but stopped when she heard the alarms sound as Isabel drove down the driveway.

She put on socks and tennis shoes, ran a brush through her hair, swished some mouthwash, spit it out, said *Eckk*, and hurried to the front door as the horn beeped.

Watson ran through when she opened it and gave Isabel the opportunity to scratch him up before they left. She obliged while he leaned into the open window.

"Thanks, Watson. I like you, too," she said when he licked her face.

Mary rolled her eyes at his attempt to garner an invite and voiced a hardy *Harrumph* soon after. He looked back at her and grinned.

"Doesn't hurt to ask," he said when he walked into the house. Mary gave him a hug and kiss.

"No, it doesn't. Be home after-while, Crocodile."

Watson watched them leave from the window and then went to the kitchen, took a drink from his bowl, grabbed a few snacks, jumped up on the couch and made himself comfortable. He pawed the remote buttons to the E network to watch a rerun of *Keeping Up with the Kardashians*.

He wasn't interested in the sisters, although they could be a hoot – and a headache. But two of them had dogs, and Watson had a crush on one of Kylie's.

~~

Peppers is a Mexican restaurant with big plates and big servings for big appetites. The food is good and the atmosphere pleasant but loud, especially tonight. Most of the recent graduates would visit one of the local eateries before attending any number of festivities scheduled for the evening. Two of Isabel's friends sat with them as their food arrived, and one told her about a party.

"Everyone's going. Should be lots of boys there. *College* boys," Diane said, drawing out the word. She smiled at Mary before getting up to leave with her friend. "You're welcome to come. If it's not past your curfew."

Mary noted the sarcasm and smiled with a warmth she didn't feel, making the girl fluster before saying goodbye.

"Sorry, Mary. I don't know why she would say that."

"It's okay, Isabel. Dianne's just reminding me of my age. No harm, no foul," she said and took another bite of the beef burrito covered with refried beans and rice.

"What's funny is you're older at sixteen than Diane and most of her crowd are at . . . whatever it is they are."

Mary swallowed and took a drink of her soda. "Thanks.

Isabel stuffed the rest of the quesadilla in her mouth. She was hungry and finished her plate well before Mary, who asked if she wanted to go.

"Where? To the college party?"

Mary nodded but didn't speak. She had a mouthful and didn't want to drop a tasty morsel. After finishing, she said, "Mmm, that was good. Yup, the big boy party."

"I don't know, should we? And will Dax let you?"

"Sure," she said and meant it.

He might have balked or tried to talk her out of it, but she didn't think he would say no. That's not to say he'd like it, though. And truthfully, she didn't need to go, curiosity notwithstanding. But if Isabel wanted to, she didn't want her to miss out.

"Maybe we could stop by and see what the hype's all about? If we don't like it, we'll go to the beach."

Mary agreed, and they headed to their first college party to live *la vida loca*, the crazy life, for an hour or so.

~~

Dax finished putting up the tent and blowing up the mattress while Tasha started a fire with the kindling and logs she loaded in the boat. They were quiet in their work, enjoying the feel of the sand, the last rays of the sun, and the occasional touch from one another.

The island was devoid of anyone or anything save the birds that gave it its name. Bird Island was essentially just a long sand bar behind St. Vincent Island, a 12,000-acre wildlife refuge that was home to alligators, snakes, Sambar and white-tailed deer, ospreys, falcons, turtles, and bald eagles – in addition to flies, mosquitoes, and other biting insects they hoped to avoid by camping on the sandbar.

They sat in folding chairs with a cooler between them and watched the sun begin its downward trek. Dax poured a glass of her favorite wine, a Kendall-Jackson Chardonnay, and Tasha sipped, closed her eyes, and listened to the birds, the crackle of the fire, and the wind as she pushed her toes into the sand.

"This is wonderful."

I reached for her hand and she turned it over to give me access to her palm and fingers.

"Mmmm. That feels good."

We watched the sun set and the sky darken. The fire licked at the logs, and the only words spoken were *thank you* after Tasha wiggled her empty glass and I filled it.

There was a blissful quality to the time spent in silence that beckoned the spirit to rest and renew and extolled the virtues of the possible. Tranquility washed over me, and I felt closer to Tasha as each moment passed. But eventually that intimacy unnerved me, and I patted her arm and went for a walk and a pee.

~

Tasha watched him amble off and began to cry.

Could she tell him what she'd done? Would everything change between them if she did?

Would it change if she didn't?

~ ~

Mary was reminded of the Stevie Ray Vaughan song, *The house is a rockin'*, as they walked into a madhouse of people who were talking, laughing, dancing, and drinking.

She recognized some, but most she didn't. A boy, a *college* boy, presented each of them with a whistle and a plastic cup of Kool-Aid.

"Welcome, ladies. Glad to see you. There are drinks in the kitchen, bathrooms on every floor, and the whistles are in case someone gets stupid. We don't want you to be hassled, so if someone bugs you, blow it. Got it?" he asked but didn't wait for a reply before walking away.

Isabel lifted the cup, but Mary put a hand on her arm.

"We probably don't want to drink anything we didn't pour ourselves; don't you think?"

She nodded and they moved through the boisterous crowd until Isabel ran into some friends along the way. Mary took her cup and went into a kitchen full of activity.

A makeshift bartender drew beer from a keg while another mixed drinks. Mary poured the beverages they'd been given down the sink and tossed the cups in the trash. She found bottles of sweet tea in the fridge and took two.

Isabel had another cup in her hand when she returned and was laughing with some friends. Rather than intrude, Mary watched the partygoers and their interactions.

It was interesting.

The boys were like hunters, or better yet, fisherman, because when they didn't get a bite, they just moved on and fished the next hole. The girls, on the other hand, huddled together. Better to stay with the pack than get picked off from the herd.

I've seen way too many National Geographic specials.

Mary caught herself tapping her feet to the music, and someone from school asked her to dance. It occurred to her she hadn't danced with a boy before and instead of being nervous, she was unexpectedly excited.

"Sure. My name's Mary." She stuck out her hand and he took and shook it.

"I know who you are. I'm Zack." He put his hand above her elbow and walked them to the middle of the room.

Mary frowned when she saw Isabel take another cup from an older boy she didn't know. Maybe Isabel knew him?

After three songs, she followed Zack to a couch. He offered to get her something to drink, and she asked for an unopened can of Coke. When he left, Mary considered how he held her during the slow dance. He'd been a gentleman, considerate and appropriate. They talked about high school and teachers, college and opportunities. He was going to pledge the fraternity throwing the party.

Zack was a nice boy, which shouldn't have been such a surprise to her. Mary looked around for Isabel and in doing so noticed an anomaly.

An oddity of Solo cups.

Most were red, but eight boys had blue ones and four girls had yellow, five counting the one Isabel was given. She wasn't sure what it meant but it vexed her.

Mary walked over to Isabel's friends, but they hadn't seen her for a while. She thanked them and searched the ground floor before climbing the stairs.

A couple on the landing pointed when she asked where the bathrooms were, and Mary looked in each one but found them empty. She decided to open every door. The first was a linen closet and the second was locked. She considered knocking but opened another, instead.

Inside were two girls she recognized and three boys she didn't. The girls were making out on a bed as the boys watched and took pictures. One of them looked her up and down and asked if she wanted to join in the fun.

Mary glared at him with contempt and saw yellow cups and whistles on the dresser. A warning began to sound in her head, and she rushed back to the locked door.

"Isabel," she said and knocked. She thought she heard a girl groan but couldn't be sure. Mary kept pounding until the door flew open.

"Who the . . ." he yelled and then hollered *Hey* when she walked past and yanked his friend off of her by his hair.

"What the fuck," the buddy howled.

Isabel was partially undressed and looked bewildered. Mary saw the yellow Solo and told him to get out. When he put a hand on her, she bent it backward until he screamed.

"I can break it, if you'd like," Mary said and walked him out of the room. The boy who'd answered the door kept recording with his phone but stepped back when she threw his friend into the hallway and closed the door.

"Isabel? Are you alright?" Mary's concern rose as her friend tried to focus. "Izzy?"

"Only Frank calls me Izzy."

Isabel pulled up her shorts and sat up. She clutched at her bra and blouse but had trouble clasping and buttoning. Mary helped and asked if she knew what that boy was doing.

"I . . . Yes."

"Really? You wanted this to happen? They were filming it, Isabel. Did you know that?" Mary sat on the bed and tried to hold her hand, but she pulled it away.

"I think they put something in your drink."

Isabel shook her head. "We were just kissing, and it went too far. I don't know why I let him touch me so much. I've never let anyone do that before. Well, except for Frank. But he loves me."

Mary didn't think it the right time or place, however now that it was said . . .

"Are you letting Frank touch you, Isabel?"

She nodded. "But not since he . . ."

The hurt in Isabel's eyes made Mary's heart bend, but it broke when they filled with humiliation as she realized her secret was out.

Isabel stood quickly and then vomited. She fell to her knees and continued to wretch as Mary held her hair and rubbed her back till it was over. When she left and returned with a wet washcloth, Isabel was gone.

Mary looked everywhere but couldn't find her. As she walked through the front door, her name was shouted over the raucous crowd. It was Zack, and she thought of asking for his help. Until she saw the yellow cup in his hand.

The car was gone. And so was her ride home.

She reached into her back pocket, wanting to call the police about her suspicions and to see if Isabel was okay, but remembered she'd forgotten her phone at home.

Well, crap.

It was at least six miles to her house, all of it in the dark. Mary thought about Isabel as she walked down the long driveway. At the end of it, she crossed to the other side of the road and began to jog against whatever traffic she might encounter. If a car were going to hit her, she'd rather see it coming than be struck from behind.

~~

When I came back from my stroll along the sandbar, Tasha was still sitting in the chair staring at the fire as the flames caressed the starless night. Her eyes shimmered, and she wiped her face before I sat down.

After filling her empty glass she let me hold her hand, and my thumb moved lazily across the back of it. My need to fix a problem was DNA engrained, and, as I did my best not to pry or express concern, a bolt of lightning flashed in the sky followed by a thunderous clap.

"Jeee-sus!"

Tasha looked at me with tear-stained cheeks. The edges of her mouth lifted, and a grin formed on an otherwise uncooperative face. A sparkle in her eye peeked around the corner of her sadness.

"Scaredy-cat."

"Am not."

"Are too. Wait till I tell Mary. Or does she know?"

"I am not; you better not, and she doesn't. Because there's nothing to know."

Tasha's grin turned into a smile that seemed to induce otherwise disinclined muscles to comply.

"Dax, you said Jesus like you needed saving. I might go so far as to say you were on the verge of . . ."

"What? I wasn't on any *verge*. I just . . ."

"The verge of squealing like a . . ."

"Don't you even."

Tasha's eyes were tinged with glee. She mouthed the words and snickered when I responded.

"I did not almost squeal like a little girl. I was . . ."

We both saw the flash, but only one of us moved.

"Fraidy-cat, fraidy-cat, I see you. Jumps like a frog, when I say *boo*."

"Tasha, now, I didn't jump. I flinched. Barely."

"Barely? I swear there was an inch of daylight between your behind and the chair."

The level of her levity made me smile. "An inch of daylight? At midnight?"

She took a long drink from her glass and said, "Fraidy-cat, scaredy-cat, peek-a-boo . . ."

Tasha was having fun, and I was happy to be the butt of her joke. "I am neither scaredy or fraidy, nor did I squeal or verge. My reaction was a reflection of a highly developed sense of awareness to the possible dangers . . ."

"Buck-buck, buck-oww."

I cracked up and tried to make a stand.

"I am *not* a chicken, *or* a scaredy-cat. I'm a man. A manly man. With manly . . . Manliness."

Tasha looked at me at length and nodded.

"You do have some nice manliness going for you. Still, how can I love someone who is so easily frightened?"

Her eyes twinkled in the firelight, and I knew then I'd never be able to let her go.

"Eeeeehh," she squealed and jumped out of her chair onto my lap. A ghost crab looked at us, and I swore it shook its head before scurrying off. Tasha pretended otherwise, but we knew she'd freaked out when it walked over her foot.

They say revenge is a dish best served cold, but I think it's just as satisfying with a warm woman sitting in your lap. I decided to take the high road, however – mostly because I couldn't think of a rhyming little ditty as good as the one she teased me with.

"You were saying?"

"Umm, how can I *not* love someone who is so easily frightened?"

"Nice recovery."

I kissed her cheek, and she took my face in her hands.

"I do, you know. Love you."

Knowing felt altogether different than wondering, and a myriad of emotions raced and whirled inside of me.

"I love you, too, Tash."

Well, we'd said it. Out loud. And though heavy in its implications, I was surprisingly light-hearted. The weight of the world seemed to lift from me and thoughts of a life with her flitted about like fireflies. Tasha, on the other hand, started to cry.

"What . . . You didn't want me to love you back?"

She laid her head in the crook of my neck and sobbed. I was going to say something flip and funny to try and *fix* it, but the sage words of my Michigan friend came to mind – 'Just shut up and let us cry.'

I rubbed and patted and took my friend's advice. In time, her sobs turned to quiet weeping, and then, just quiet. I held her for a long time before she spoke.

"I killed him."

Her voice was muted and devoid of emotion.

"I'm sorry, Tash. But he didn't give you any other choice. You see that don't you?"

"Why did you say it like that?" she said, lifting her head. Do you know?"

"Know what? You had to kill him. Otherwise, he might have killed you."

"Your right. I had to. But it wasn't self-defense."

She left his lap and walked to the water's edge. The wind blew through her hair and dried tears shed for the loss of what they could've been. Dax wouldn't want to be with her once he knew the truth.

When he came up and slipped his arms around her, she leaned back and told him everything. Whatever she thought his reaction might be, she wasn't prepared for her own.

"What the hell are you talking about? I killed him. How is that okay?"

Tasha was furious in a way she couldn't have imagined earlier. His words of support should have made her feel better, but instead, they pissed her off. It didn't help that he was calm and unaffected by her outburst.

"Tash, I didn't say it was okay, I said it was justified. And I'm at a loss as to why you're angry at me. You were on my lap loving me three minutes ago. What's up with that?"

My smile was meant to diffuse the situation, but it only made her madder.

"Damn it, Dax. This is serious. I'm a killer. A murderer. I'm going to have to turn myself in and . . ."

I pushed her in the water.

She surprised me by taking my offered hand, and *insisted* I join her by pulling me in. We splashed and dunked and tried to keep the other from reaching the bank. But when something brushed against our legs, we called *shark* and skedaddled to the safety of the sandy shore.

I put another log on the fire as Tasha dried off, and she poured some chardonnay in our glasses while I toweled. We sat easy for a spell and listened to the night.

"If you weren't a detective, what would you do if you saw your neighbor beating his wife or molesting his child?"

"Call the police."

"What would they do if they couldn't confirm the abuse? Even after talking to them?" I asked.

"Not much, I'm afraid. And not right away, either. Without corroboration from the victim, our hands are tied. As is the prosecutor's – unless it could be documented."

"And if it couldn't?"

Tasha shifted in her chair and looked at me.

"What are you getting at?"

"Some people believe what happens in another's home is none of their business and has no effect on *their* family. I disagree. At the very least, that molested child will grow up with emotional problems that could affect other children and other lives, not to mention their own. From that perspective, it should be everyone's *business* to stop that man. Even if we have to do it ourselves."

Tasha was quiet – listening, thinking.

"But the suffering of that wife or child is the real issue, Tash. It's what has to be stopped. Not later but now. Some people need to die to save the ones they're killing. Or will. Or already have."

The conflict of conscience in her eyes was evident. "There's no question in my mind you did the right thing. That boy molested his sister and murdered her and mother. He needed to reap what he'd sown."

"Dax, I . . . It's not that simple."

"What if Mary's father got his hands on her again? Would you just . . ."

"I'd kill him."

It wasn't what she said that had the most impact; it was the strength of her conviction. At that moment, Tasha knew she would step outside the law to protect Mary. Where she was concerned, it *was* that simple. And yet . . .

We sat and sipped our wine, alone with our thoughts. I was unsettled by the uncertainty of what she'd do, whether she would turn herself in or turn herself inside out looking for a way to live with what she'd done.

I wanted to tell her it could be alright, that she didn't need to hold herself in contempt, and that the principles she lived by were still valid. I wanted to say a lot of things to make her feel better but told myself to shut up – before she told me herself.

The sun found us holding hands, awaiting its arrival.

"Want to try and get a couple hours sleep?" she asked.

"First, tell me what you told me earlier."

"You were an asshole for shoving me in the water?"

I shook my head and said, "Before that."

"Fraidy-cat, scaredy-cat," she sang.

"After that. And I am not afraid of lightning."

"Buck-buck."

"Smartass."

Her eyes reflected her feelings.

"I love you, Dax."

I kissed the palm of her hand and led her to the tent.

chapter fifteen

She heard the doorbell and then the knocking. Isabel peeked through the blinds and saw Watson, who seemed to see her. She stepped away from the window and jumped when her phone rang.

It was Mary.

Isabel let the call go to voicemail and walked down the hallway. She stopped when he barked for her and almost opened the door.

But she couldn't.

When the mower started, she went to her room and the empty suitcases lying on her bed, wishing she could talk to Mary but knowing she'd never be able to.

The embarrassment from telling about Frank led to her decision to get an early jump on her college career by taking summer semester classes – not to get ahead but to get away. From her mother, from Mary, and from Frank.

She wiped her eyes and began to pack.

The great irony, she thought as she folded her clothes, was the reason for her leaving was no longer an issue.

The last time Frank came into her room he went on and on about how Mary looked in her tiny bikini. She'd been crushed and cried herself to sleep. Not because he thought her attractive, because she was. But it was clear he wanted to touch Mary the way he did her, and Isabel's feelings for him were a tortured, twisted mess.

She hadn't let him have her since then and probably never would again.

Probably . . .

Watson barked once, twice, and she went to see. Mary was mowing near the road, and Watson sat in the cart, shaded by the umbrella. He cocked his head and looked right at her.

Isabel put her hand on the window and a tear fell.

"I think I'll miss you most of all, Scarecrow."

~~

Mary read the email again and closed the laptop.

"Well, hell!"

Watson jumped.

"Sorry," she said, setting the computer on the floor and lying on her side next to him. She planted an elbow on the mattress and propped her head with her hand.

"She's gone. On her way to Tallahassee."

"I know." He lifted an ear to accommodate her fingers.

"How do you know? I just got the email."

"She told me."

"When?" Mary said and stopped scratching. "I've been trying to talk to her for a week."

He nudged her fingers, but they didn't move.

"Two days ago when we cut her lawn. She stared at me from her bedroom window."

"And how did she tell you she was leaving? And why didn't you tell *me*?" Mary pulled her hand from his ears and laid it on her hip.

"I deduced it from the sadness in her eyes. Looked like she was saying goodbye."

"Deduced, you say. And you didn't tell me, why?"

"I . . . Well, shoot. I forgot until you reminded me." Watson looked at her fingers and wondered if they'd ever scratch him again, especially when she gave him *the look*.

"Hey, I'm not an elephant. I forget things, sometimes."

"Just not dinner or lunch or breakfast or brunch, right?" she said with a grin and picked up scratching where she'd left off, contemplating Isabel's message.

Mary knew her revelation about Frank was the reason. If she could just talk to her, convince her she was her friend.

At least she'll be away from that son of a bitch.

"I'm really going to miss her, Watson."

"Me, too."

~~

They'd chatted non-stop since leaving the airport, and the time flew by with the miles. After talking about what they'd do in St. Vincent before going on their trip to Mexico, Tasha asked her tentative question.

"We haven't talked about that since the academy," Jeri said. "Oh, will you pull into that Burger King drive-thru? I haven't had a Whopper in forever."

Tasha took a hard pull on the curly-Q straw when they left the burger joint and was rewarded with sweet chocolate bliss. Jeri offered a bite of flame-broiled perfection and her stomach growled *yes*, wishing for a Whopper of its own.

"Well, tell me. Do you still think vigilantism has merit?"

"There's nothing inherently wrong with it as long as the guilty have it coming," Jeri told her. "Except people as a rule don't have the judgement to dispense that kind of justice. Present company excluded, of course."

"But what about the law?" Tasha asked.

"Yes, there is that. But when it fails to protect and punish, what then? Just tell the victim nothing can be done? Can I have some of that shake?"

Tash handed it over, and after a long sip, Jeri continued.

"Now, I'm not advocating vigilantism, but I understand the desire for an out of the box solution to injustice, maybe even the need for it. If one does evil, one should . . ."

Jeri stopped and gave her back the king-sized cup.

Tasha took another pull and considered her best friend. Something wasn't right.

"What's happened, Seven?"

Jeri didn't want to spoil their time together, but it was Tasha she turned to when troubled.

"We found two young girls who'd been kidnapped and missing for months. They'd been raped, beaten, and sold. We know who's responsible but can't prove it in court without the girls' testimony. And they won't give it because they're traumatized and afraid. I'm heartbroken for those kids and angry with the discrepancy between doing what's right and what's legal. Traffickers don't respect the law, man's or God's, and I find myself wondering more and more if they shouldn't just be eradicated from those of us who do. A vigilante, now that you mention it, might hit the spot right about now."

Tasha reached over and patted her hand. She also hurt for those abused children and thought about their damaged lives, and those who'd caused it.

Maybe Dax is right? Maybe some people need to die.

"Is it okay if we don't talk about it, right now?" Jeri asked. "I'm a little weary and jaded."

"No problem, mi amiga."

The warm breeze kissed her cheek as she lowered the window and thoughts of spilling her guts flew away.

Tasha didn't think she could tell her, anyway. Despite Jeri's frustration with the law's limitations, she was adamant in its adherence. She might understand, but then again, maybe not? It could ruin their friendship, and Tasha wasn't willing to take the chance.

Which made her telling Dax all the more intriguing. Why him and not Jeri?

"We've been invited to play a beach concert tomorrow afternoon with Dax and Mary. We played a few last year and had a blast. You wanna?"

"It sounds like a good time, but, damn, Tash. I haven't done anything like that since we were off the grid."

"No worries, mate," Tasha said, channeling her inner Australian. "We'll just stop by the bottle shop, get your favorite plonk, and throw you in some togs. You'll be a real ripper, spunk as you are."

Jeri grinned and shook her head in perplexity.

"Say again?"

"Don't worry, you won't have to drink with the flies." Tasha laughed when Jeri scrunched her face.

"Huh?"

~~

The visit flew by in a flurry of fun and frolic. They played in public twice and Jeri became an official member of the band when she threw herself off the beach-stage into the arms of the crowd who hoisted her above their heads and passed her around like a Rockstar.

Tasha was surprised at how quickly Jeri warmed up to Dax, expecting her to be overly protective and reserved in her judgement. But the two of them became fast friends and kept everyone in stitches with funny repartee.

"It'll only be a week," Jeri said.

"What?" she asked, lost in thought and only hearing.

"I said, I know it's hard to leave your family, but . . ."

"It'll only be a week." Tasha finished her sentence and nodded. "They *are* my family, aren't they?"

"Uh, duh."

"Duh? Is that the kind of articulation you'll be using as Assistant-Deputy Director?"

Jeri grinned and took a swallow from her wineglass as Tasha slipped into the kitchen.

"She loves you, you know."

"Who, Mary?" Tasha asked, returning with the last of the Kendall-Jackson.

"Yes, Mary. Your *daughter*."

"Seven, she's not . . ." Tasha got a faraway look in her eyes, gazing inward rather than out. "Jeez Louise."

"What?"

"She does feel like a daughter. Or how I imagine one might. Gee whiz! When did that happen? I thought we were like sisters just a few months ago."

"Why can you say *gee whiz* but my *duh* is disparaged?" Jeri said and sipped her wine as Tasha came to grips with her new perspective.

"Do you think Mary feels that way?"

"Yes," Jeri told her

"Really?"

"Why do you think she calls me Aunt Jeri? Because I'm her mama's *sista*."

"Geez, me a mom?"

"Maybe a wife, too?"

Jeri's eyes were full of mirth and mischief. She enjoyed seeing her normally unflappable friend flap a little.

"I . . . We haven't . . ." Tasha saw Jeri having fun and tried to have some back at her.

"Would you be my best girl at the wedding? Or object when the minister asked?"

"I don't know, Tash," Jeri said and raised the stakes. "I might stand up and claim you for myself. You know how attractive I think you are."

"What would you do if you had me, Seven? What with you all the way in Atlanta and me down here? And what about my dearly betrothed?"

Tasha had played this game with Jeri over the years but never won, not really. No matter how hard she tried, Jeri always pushed it one step further than she was willing to go. She kissed her on the lips once for the win, but Jeri opened her mouth, and that was that.

"I don't mind sharing you with Dax, as long as you *come* when I call," Jeri said and smiled. "See what I did there – with the double entendre?"

Tasha rolled her eyes. "And how do you intend to bring about the entendre of your dreams, dear girl? I don't think a call in the hand is worth Dax in my bush."

Jeri raised an eyebrow and chuckled.

"Nice wordplay, Tash. Sassy. But I can see by the hue of your crimson cheeks that I would getchu before too long." She took a long drink before a grin lit a spark in her eye. "Oooh! Let's call Dax. Have him come over."

"I don't know, Seven."

"Oh, come on. It's my last night here. Let me play with your boyfriend, girlfriend."

Tasha reached for her phone and handed it over. "Tell him we're out of wine and ask if he'd mind bringing some. Say, pretty please."

~

"Wow."

It wasn't what he said but the way he'd said it. That and how he looked at her. Tasha wished Jeri back to Atlanta so she could take him into the bedroom. She groaned when he kissed her and thought this might be a big mistake

"Thanks for coming over."

She led him to the living room and watched his eyes widen. Jeri had insisted their attire match the occasion.

"Dax!" Jeri said, and threw her arms up and around him. "Thanks for rescuing us from ourselves. We would have perished of thirst. Maybe you could join our little party? Does Tash have a pair of your PJs in a dresser drawer?"

"Dax doesn't wear pajamas, Seven." Jeri's reaction gave her some unexpected satisfaction.

"Uh . . ."

Tasha took the bag and asked if he'd like a nightcap.

"A small one, maybe. Thanks."

She left them on the couch and went to the kitchen. The corkscrew on the countertop sat in triumph, as previously slain bottles stood in silent defeat.

Holy moly. Maybe this is not a good idea.

She lifted the corkscrew to do battle once again. The laughter from the other room hastened her pour, and some precious Kendall-Jackson spilled on the counter. If Dax hadn't brought an extra bottle, she might have . . .

She used a paper towel instead.

Jeri sat next to him with her feet tucked, leaving enough room for Tasha, who chose to sit opposite them. He tipped his glass with a glint in his eye, and Tasha followed suit.

She watched her friend enjoy Dax. Jeri flirted in a friendly way, teasing and touching, sometimes skirting the line but never crossing it. He didn't mind and neither did she, even when Jeri's words began to slur and the proximity to him narrowed. By the time Tasha left to fill their glasses again, she was practically leaning against him.

What the hell? Jeri thought.

Tasha would've easily caved an hour ago. But despite her best efforts, Dax seemed oblivious to her attempt to rattle him. She might not be as pretty as Tasha, but she still looked damned good.

Maybe he thinks I'm drunk and harmless?

Which, of course, she was. Jeri was only fooling around, trying to make him nervous and get a rise out of him.

Did she mean that last as a double-entendre?

She hoped not. Jeri was tipsy for sure but would never do anything to hurt her best friend. Her flippant jokes to

Tasha about the three of them together had been just a jest between gal-pals.

Maybe Dax just didn't find her attractive?

'Well that can't be,' she told herself and set about one last time to make him fidget.

She nudged even closer as he told a tall tale about a ton of Tarpons, and he finally stopped talking when she rested her head on his shoulder – except the reaction she hoped for wasn't the one she received.

Dax smoothed a wisp of hair behind her ear with his fingers and began to caress the contour of her face.

Jeri froze when he looked into her eyes.

"So . . . A three-way, huh?"

"Uh . . . I . . . uh . . ." she stammered, unaware that Tasha was sitting beside her until she whispered in her ear.

"Gotchu, girlfriend."

"What? I wasn't . . ."

Tasha's warm breath made her quiver, and she flushed in confusion as Dax brushed his thumb across her lips. Only for a moment did she think of calling their bluff, if indeed it was one. Either way, she was got and could only get *gotter* if she didn't stop. Right now.

"Well played, guys."

Dax leaned in when Tasha groaned in her ear.

"Alright, you two. Cut it out. I give."

When they finally stopped, their eyes sparkled with playful delight. A hint of curiosity crossed Jeri's mind – until they looked at her in a way that made her squirm.

"Uh, guys?"

chapter sixteen

"You mean like that?" Mary asked, her eyes laden with laughter. She'd held onto my wrist after throwing me down and gave it a slight twist when I considered a countermove. "Ah-ah."

My arm burned and began to protest. I thought about biting her ankle but changed my mind when the pressure on my arm increased.

"Dax?"

"Okay. I yield."

The ache in my shoulder only amplified when released, taking a minute or so to subside. I didn't grouse or attempt to massage the pain away. Don't know if it was a man thing or a dad thing, but damned if it didn't hurt.

I'd been teaching her to *dance,* to flow seamlessly from defensive to offensive positions, minimizing her exposure to maximize her efficiency by introducing unpredictability into confrontational events.

Mary thought the *Arthur Murry School of Ass-Whooping* was less wordy than my description and more fun to say.

Anyway, after I'd grabbed her she twirled and drove an elbow into my ribs, snatched my arm and yanked me over her shoulder. Her execution was swift, unexpected, and beautiful to behold.

"That was great, Mare. I don't know if you're getting quicker or I'm getting slower, but your commitment to the attack was impressive. It's kind of like your guitar playing – no hesitations, no mistakes."

She grinned and curtseyed. "Well thank you, kind sir. But Dax, I make mistakes. Believe me."

"You sure? I don't hear any." I stood up and tried not to wince or groan.

"That's because you love me," she said and started to rub and knead rubbing my aching shoulder.

"Where did you ever get that idea? I mean, you're likable enough, sure, but . . ."

I expected her fingers to remind me of the pain I'd tried to hide, but she smiled instead.

"I like you, too." A few minutes later, she said, "Better?"

"Yes. Thanks, hon."

"Welcome."

Mary left the room to get us some water, and I rolled the mat against the wall. After our thirst was quenched, I asked if she would like to take a bike ride to cool-down.

"That sounds good."

~

Watson kept up for the first few miles before jumping into the padded fishing cart behind her bike. He lay in quiet comfort, the wind soothing as they rode down Indian Pass Road to the boat launch. When he saw Isabel's driveway, he let loose a mournful howl.

"I know. I miss her, too," Mary said.

"Heard anything?" Dax asked.

"No. She won't take my calls or return a text."

Mary already told him about Frank and Isabel, what she saw when she spied on her, and how Isabel appeared to give herself freely. He was concerned, as she knew he would be. Dax believed as she did that an adult had no business having sex with a teenager, regardless of their willingness, and his frustration was evident as they'd discussed what, if anything, could or should be done.

She *hadn't* told him about her attempt to provoke a lustful reaction in Frank to prick Isabel's jealousy. Although he might have agreed the strategy had merit, he'd not like his little girl showing herself half-naked to a man like that. Or anyone else, for that matter.

But she'd needed to do something to save Isabel, even if from herself, and Dax might have stopped her.

She also hadn't mentioned the college party and the yellow cups. He'd be pleased she didn't drink anything she didn't pour herself and proud of her observational skills.

144

But a seed of worry might settle in a furrow of his mind – one that could grow into a thicket of over-protectiveness.

Dax had never put his foot down in a way that caused her to chafe. She knew his directives came from an honest place and never felt the need to challenge his choices for her. But she had known too much freedom with him to have it curtailed now, so she kept those things to herself to avoid his ... Concern.

Still, not telling him felt a little like a betrayal.

"Maybe time alone with her thoughts is what's best right now," he said, looking over at her. "Might give her a better perspective, one that reveals that S.O.B's true colors."

She nodded and noted the hard edge around *S.O.B's.*

"You're right, but I hate her having to wrestle with it alone. I could help if she'd let me, I think. Of course, helping her hasn't *helped* so far."

When he asked for clarification, she shook her head, remembering the way Frank looked her all over.

"Sorry. Just lamenting."

"Lamenting?" he asked as they came to the boat launch. "That word's pretty antiquated. Where'd you get it?"

Mary grinned at Watson who rolled his eyes before jumping out of the cart and into the water. When Dax raised an eyebrow, she explained.

"Watson and I have been exposed to your, how can I say this, eloquence? Allow me to give an example. You have a propensity to use an inordinate number of highfaluting words, the preponderance of which could be said more succinctly. Now, I'm not saying your pretentious ..."

"But you're not saying I'm not, right?" he chuckled. "Highfaluting?"

"Haughty, hoity-toity."

"Snobbish, snooty?"

"Pompous, ostentatious."

"Oooh, that's a good one, Mare. Kind of rolls off the tongue. Os-ten-ta-tious. Hey, I'm just doing my best to give you as much conversational expertise as I can before sending you out into the cold, hard world on your own. Which could be sooner rather than later, you little shit."

Mary laughed and punched his arm before continuing. "I haven't even mentioned the made-up words – gooder, betterer, carefuller . . ."

~~

Isabel stopped and gazed at the cloudy sky. Her ears were burning, yet the sun was nowhere to be seen.

Someone must be talking about me.

When the hairs at the back of her neck tickled, she looked around to see if someone was watching her too. A boy nodded hello and gave a welcoming smile. She returned his nod and continued on her way to class.

Isabel had seen him around the campus and thought he was beautiful – tall, muscular, powerful. She felt her face grow warm and thought herself a floozy. But since she had only been with Frank, the word probably didn't apply.

Frank.

He'd come to visit after she refused to return his calls, driving over a hundred miles while her mother was at work. She'd been torn between wishing him away and wishing . . .

It embarrassed her to admit how much she missed their time together in the dark quiet of the night.

In the weeks since leaving home, she came to believe what they did was wrong – he shouldn't have touched her; she shouldn't have let him, and they shouldn't have betrayed her mother regardless of her derision.

However, she began to question that belief after Frank expressed how much he needed her. Wanted her.

Loved her.

If not for the timely return of her roommate to their dorm room, she might have given more thought to giving in. But when he tried to persuade her to come to a motel as she walked him to his car, it brought clarity to her confusion. What had been sensual in the middle of the night now felt unseemly in the light of day.

She needed to let him go, and so she did. Though not without regret. Wrong as it might have been, she loved him and the things he'd shown her.

Isabel couldn't reconcile the contradiction but knew she didn't want to be with anyone else until she could. In the meantime she'd let her awakened sexuality slumber and concentrate on her studies and college life.

"I'll become a born-again virgin," she said with a grin.

~

He watched her cross the courtyard after returning his hello. She wasn't up to his usual standards, but there was something about her that appealed to him – she was Mary Stewart's friend.

Troy had a seething hatred for Stewart ever since she'd knocked him down and out when he was playing with the girl in the locker room. And more than anything, he wanted to give Mary not only a taste of what that red-haired slut had asked for, but the whole, damned meal.

"Maybe you should just leave it alone. She might kill your ass like she did that guy from the FBI," Gregg told him months ago with a stupid grin on his face.

"Fuck that," he said. "When I get my hands on her, I'm going to tear her a new one. Literally."

But the opportunity had never materialized despite his efforts to settle the score whenever he visited St. Vincent. She didn't go out much by herself except to cut lawns or ride her bike, and never at night. He couldn't snatch her up and throw her down in broad daylight without being caught, especially since the police already questioned him about those high schoolers who'd said he raped them.

'I'll get that bitch,' he told himself. Someday, somehow. Until then, he would take it out on her friend.

~~

After landing in Atlanta, Jeri accompanied Tasha to the departure gate and hugged her, afraid to let go. Only when she gasped did Jeri release her.

"Sorry. Didn't know I was holding on so tightly."

"It's alright, Seven. It only hurts when I breathe," Tasha said light-heartedly. "We should take another trip. I had a great time. Well, except..."

"Except for almost getting yourself killed? Yeah, let's not do that anymore. I want to be pissed at you, but I'm too happy you're alive. I'll be mad at you later, though."

"Come on, now. The doctor said he missed by a good two inches. I was never in any real danger of dying."

Tasha's smile made Jeri grin until the reality of what could have happened showed in her eyes.

"Don't know if I ever said it before, but I love you, Tash. Always have."

"I know that. I love you, too. Always will." Tasha wiped a tear from Jeri's cheek. "I'll be alright. And it's okay to get mad. I'd do the same if you got yourself almost killed. Which, by the way, don't. I know how competitive you are, trying to one-up me and all."

"I'll bet I could get almost killed by an inch and a half. Maybe even an inch! That way I'd come twice as close to biting the dust as you did. *Almost* did."

They laughed, hugged, and said their goodbyes when Tasha's flight was called to board. Jeri's phone beeped, letting her know the car and driver had arrived.

"Must be nice to be chauffeured home. One of the perks of being a Deputy-Director?" Tasha asked.

"Assistant Deputy-Director, Detective Williams. And the car is taking me to the office. I want to know who those men worked for. I doubt if they were freelancing."

"Let me know what you find?"

"Of course. Give my love to your family, girlfriend. Especially Dax," Jeri said with a wink full of wicked glee.

Tasha grinned and cocked her head.

"You're going to get into trouble if you keep playing that game with him, Seven. He'll eat you alive."

"Hmmm."

~

Tasha closed her eyes and reclined in the seat, thinking about Acapulco as the pain settled into a dull ache.

Her time in Mexico had been festive. They'd cut loose like college girls on spring break and danced and drank and played and partied. All was well and wonderful until she'd strolled down the beach one beautifully moonlit night.

Jeri had retired to their cozy suite, tired from the day's cavorting, but Tasha had a little energy left to spend and took a walk along the shoreline. The crash of the waves and smell of the salty air reminded her of the two people she could no longer live without.

She began to give serious thought to building a life with Dax and Mary. Up till then she took each day one at a time, enjoying their love and friendship, a part of them but not part of them. But now she wanted more. In fact, she wanted it all. And it scared her. What if...

The sound floating on the wind drew her attention to a new home under construction. Tasha moved toward it and stopped when its cause became evident. A young man and a much younger girl were fooling around, still dressed but not for long it seemed to her. She recognized them both and frowned, unsure of what to do.

The young man worked at the hotel, was in his mid-twenties and gorgeous. He had a disarming smile, and she'd seen many women respond to his charm. While that was good for him, the reason for her displeasure was the young lady. She was Mary's age but without the savvy and maturity, and Tasha couldn't help thinking about the girl's parents who were probably asleep and oblivious to the poor decision their daughter was making.

As she debated whether to intervene or not, an older man emerged from the shadow of the house and grabbed the teenager by the hair. He said something in Spanish and smacked her when she screamed.

"Shut up, puta, or I'll kill you now."

The young man ran off, and Tasha instinctively reached for a gun she didn't have. She looked around for something else and picked up the only thing in sight.

The man slapped the girl again, hoisted her over his shoulder and took off after the boy. Tasha hit him from behind and the driftwood shattered, leaving a piece in her hand. When the man fell to the sand, she pulled his head back until the girl underneath was free.

"Run to the hotel. Now!"

He tried to grasp her as she scampered away, but Tasha yanked harder, falling backward as the hair ripped from his scalp. The man hollered and reached into his pocket, but she shoved the splintered driftwood into his neck before he could use what he'd been after.

Tasha fell on top of him thinking the pain she felt in her back might be a muscle strain, but when she rolled over, the agony was excruciating and the reason for it stood over her.

The gorgeous young man with the disarming smile was holding a knife, only he hadn't come to help her.

He'd tried to kill her.

Blood glistened in the moonlight and his smile turned into a sneer. But it faded when she lifted the gun his partner pulled from his pants and squeezed the trigger.

The police later suspected the men of sex trafficking after searching a cargo van parked alongside of the house. Recovered evidence implicated the two in other abductions, all young girls who'd never been seen again.

But the investigators didn't have a suspect to question because both were dead.

And if that knife were two inches longer, I'd be too.

When the captain announced their final approach into Panama City, Tasha thought about Dax and Mary. They had no idea what happened, and she wasn't exactly sure how to tell them. It was hard to imagine a casual way to bring it up that might ease the fear that would follow.

Oh, hey guys. A funny thing happened as I strolled along the beach one night . . .

When she arrived at the baggage carrousel, they were there with smiles on their faces and a large McDonald's cup she knew would be filled with ice-cold chardonnay.

Mary threw her arms around her and then began to cry.

Dammit, Jeri, Tasha thought before saying, *Thank you.* She actually relieved her of the burden of telling and helped alleviate most of the initial shock.

"I'm alright, honey. It's just a scratch, really."

A muffled *bullshit* made her grin, and Dax chuckled.

"She's got you there, Calamity Jane. Welcome home."

He leaned in and touched his forehead to hers.

"You good?"

"I am now."

~~

Marcus sat quietly after telling his boss, knowing his reaction might be calm contemplation or murderous rage.

"You're saying it was coincidental circumstance?"

"Yes, sir. It appears that way."

"How is it a Florida detective and the newly appointed Assistant Deputy-Director happen to be at the same hotel?"

"Apparently they're close friends and have been since their police academy days," Marcus said. "According to reports, they're highly regarded in law enforcement and said to have impeccable integrity."

"They said the same of Ryan's predecessor," Dimitri scoffed, "and Robert Thompson was the best friend we ever had. I still can't believe he got himself killed by a little girl. How old was she? Seventeen, eighteen?"

"Fifteen. And," Marcus handed over a photograph, "not only does the detective live in the same town as the girl, she seems to be involved with her guardian."

"Interesting . . . This gives us some leverage should the new Director become a problem. Speaking of problems, where are we with those girls that got away?"

"We've let the parents know what will happen if they talk to the FBI. Or we could kill them now if you'd prefer."

"No," Dimitri said. "Leave them be for the moment. Can't fault them for escaping. That blame belongs to their handler. He needs to appreciate the position he's put us in."

"Would you like me to speak with him?"

"Have Anthony do it."

Marcus nodded, knowing what that meant.

chapter seventeen

Tasha looked out the window as they drove through town, hearing but not listening to her partner. For the first time in a month, she was back on the streets instead of being stuck behind a desk. Her body may have benefitted from the light-duty imposed by the captain, but the mundane activities of the office had been mentally exhausting.

She took a deep breath and sighed.

"Good to be out and about?" Dom said.

"You know it. I'll tell you, though, I have a lot more respect for our office colleagues. It takes a special kind of fortitude to do what they do. I swear, if I had to listen to one more ridiculous complaint from an obnoxious citizen, I might have killed somebody."

Dom chuckled.

"Looks like you've already started. Three people in three weeks? Isn't that what the kids call *trending*?"

Tasha looked at him but didn't respond. The men in Mexico hadn't left her any choice, but the boy in the kitchen? He still haunted her thoughts.

"Sorry, Tash. I didn't mean anything by that. For what it's worth, I don't have a problem with your killing anyone who needs it. I *do* have a problem with getting yourself killed in the process, so knock that off. Alright?"

Tasha saw the distress in his eyes and before his tone became more serious, she smiled and said, "Why Dominic, are you saying you'd miss me?"

"What I'm saying is, I don't want to have to break in a new partner. It's a pain in the ass."

"I thought I broke you in. You're right, though. I was a pain. But you were the ass."

They expressed both their anxieties and affections with professionalism and could now move forward, something not so easily accomplished with Dax and Mary.

Not that she didn't understand their reasons.

They'd asked her to stay for a weekend that turned into two weeks of familial bliss before she left. Mary tried to keep her close and safe and melted into her arms whenever Tasha hugged her. The bond between them deepened, but it broke her heart to see the fear in Mary's eyes.

Dax on the other hand was, Dax – calm, playful, funny. He was more willing to except her claim of being okay, but she felt him worry as his fingers caressed her to sleep.

Their intimate moments were tender and tranquil, as if they had all the time in the world together – or fervent and frenetic in their need to have all of each other before it was too late. It was sad and wonderful at the same time, and she began to lose herself for love of him as their hearts began to beat as one.

Jeez Louise, that's sappy as shit. Get a grip, girl.

Tasha laughed out loud, and Dominic raised his brow.

"I was just thinking . . . Never mind," she said as her cheeks warmed.

"Is this a Dax related thought?" he asked. "How's that going, by the way? You still liking that guy?"

"Yeah," she said and turned to look out the window. "I'm still liking him."

~~

I sat in the big chair with my morning Mountain Dew while Mary showered before work. She'd have her license soon and wouldn't need me to drive the trailer anymore. What if a day came when she didn't need me at all?

Damned unsettling, unsolicited random thoughts.

The television gave the news, but I muted the sound, not wanting to hear anything that might make me have to do something to someone. It was pure selfishness, but I couldn't care about anyone right now, except my girls.

I'd been fooling myself thinking I could continue to do that *voodoo* I do with Tasha in my life, supposing a modicum of physical and emotional distance would be sufficient. But having and eating that cake was no longer an option.

Tasha could have been killed, and, just like that, my priorities shifted. I wanted time to explore the possibility of who we could be together, who all of us could. And that wouldn't happen if I kept up my evil-killing ways. While Mary might accept it if she knew, Tasha never would. She'd leave me, shoot me, or arrest me – maybe all three.

The choice was clear

"Well then? What's it going to be?" Mary asked as she walked into the living room.

"Oh, come on now. You can't possibly know what I was thinking."

"No?" she said and went to the kitchen to get a Dew of her own. After a long swallow from the cold can, she sat down and twinkled. "What are you talking about?"

"What are *you* talking about?" I asked, giving Watson a sought-after scratch.

"Are you going to work with me today or no?"

I looked at her with an expression of total disbelief. "That's what you meant?"

"Think I'm reading your mind again?" Mary patted the couch and Watson abandoned my hand for hers.

"Are you?"

"I can tell you what you're thinking now, if you want." She took her fingers from behind Watson's ear and stroked the furrows of her forehead.

"I'm picking up some fragments. *Can she really? No. That's silly. She's just a little shit. Little shit. Little. . .*"

I lunged and her leg came up in an instant to defend. I grabbed her ankle and pulled off her sock. She started to giggle before my fingers touched the soft bottom of her foot.

"No, wait. Sorry, I'm sorry. I'm . . ."

Mary squealed with laughter as I gave her a much-needed tickling, her first, and Watson joined in by nudging her ribs with his nose. She cried *Uncle*, and I stopped moving my fingers but didn't let go.

"What am I thinking now, you little shit?"

She grinned and answered with absolute certainty. "How much you like my smartassitude."

"Lucky guess. Nice made-up word, by the way."

I picked up her sock and handed it over. Watson looked disappointed that we were done playing.

"I know, but now that we know she's ticklish, we can do this again if she gets out of line."

"I think not," Mary said.

Watson followed me to the kitchen for breakfast. After filling his bowls with wet and dry foods supplemented with pieces of torn bacon, Mary and I sat down to eat before starting our day.

"Mare, I want to talk to you about something."

"Shoot," she said, stirring a piece of pancake in a lake of syrup before shoving it in her mouth.

"It's about Tasha."

"Okay." A piece of bacon waited its turn in her hand.

"I . . . What if . . ." I was suddenly nervous and took a bite of eggs to compose myself.

Mary washed down the bacon to make room for an egg and pancake combination. "Go ahead, 'I . . . What if . . .'"

The only way for me to proceed was directly – ish.

"On a scale of one to ten, how much did you like having Tasha stay with us?"

She knew where I was headed but would still make me jump through many hoops to get there. Strangely enough, it was one of her most endearing qualities. Mary liked to watch me fidget, an inexplicable aspect of her affection.

She took a Dew drink and answered my question.

"A hard eight, maybe a soft nine. Why do you ask?"

See what I mean about making me work for it?

"Well, how would you feel if she stayed more often? Maybe permanently?"

Mary set down her fork and looked at me directly. I couldn't discern her feelings, which didn't bode well, and it occurred to me I'd neither given enough thought to this conversation nor adequately calculated the consequences.

What if she didn't want what I wanted? What if she liked things the way they were? What if . . .

156

"Are you asking for my permission?"

"I wouldn't put it quite that way, but there's an element of truth in your question. And now I see the pitfall of asking because you might be influenced to accept something you don't want out of love for me. I can't have that. It is imperative you know it's about us, first and forever. If you don't want things to change, they won't. Understand?"

The seriousness of what I was asking her hit me hard. I'd screwed up and put pressure on her in a way that could have unforeseen drawbacks. She loved Tasha, sure, but as a mother? Could she ignore my feelings for Tasha if she needed to protect her own? Would it cost her if she did?

"That's a lot of power you're giving me, Dax."

I nodded and shrugged my shoulders.

"Alright then, here's what I'm going to do with it – give it back. And don't offer it to me again. I trust you to consider me and my needs, to make decisions for my benefit and well-being. If you want Tasha to live with us, whether I like it or not, it's your decision to make and mine to accept."

Was she a remarkable young lady, or what?

"That's a lot of power your giving *me*, sweetie."

"You've earned it. You saved my life, remember? And I'm grateful every day. Besides," she said, picking up the fork and dipping her egg into Syrup Lake. "It just so happens I love the idea of Tasha becoming a permanent part of us. She already is, you know."

I tore a piece of bacon and gave Watson half.

"You could have told me you were alright with it right off instead of making me anxious."

"Yup. But where's the fun in that?" Her eyes sparkled as she chewed. "So, when are you going to do it?"

I took my plate to the counter and started to fill the sink with dishwater.

"Maybe tomorrow when we're playing the Fourth of July blowout at the Tip. That way, you'll be there for moral support if she says, *Thanks, but no thanks.*"

"Well, hopefully, she loves you in spite of your foibles – like I do," she said with a smirk. "But how can you ask her to marry you without a ring?"

Mary drank the last puddle of syrup before licking the plate clean. How can you not love a kid like that?

"I already bought one."

"Really? What would you have done if I'd said no way, Jose?" She slid her fork and plate in the sink before grabbing the towel to dry.

"Well, they have a two week, no questions asked return policy, so . . ." I said and raised my hands

"Always the contingency planner," she chuckled.

~~

Dax whacked the weeds leading to the backyard, while Mary mowed the front. Isabel peeked out of the window, careful not to be seen, especially by Watson. He would tell Mary, and she couldn't talk to her. Not now.

Thank goodness her car was in the garage.

She'd been home over a week, struggling to understand what happened and why. A month ago, a boy she couldn't imagine being interested in her, was . . .

After bumping into each other four times in two days, he asked if she was stalking him.

"Of course not."

When he asked *Why not,* she said he wasn't quite cute enough. Where she'd found the courage to say such a thing was a mystery, but he looked astonished before grinning.

"Well, thanks for setting me straight."

"You're welcome," Isabel said, heartened by his humor. "Just so you know, you're not hideous. I wouldn't . . ."

"Throw me out of bed for eating crackers?"

A gleam in his eye made her blush.

"I was going to say; I wouldn't cross the street just to avoid having to look at you." She didn't know why she felt so at ease with him but decided not to question it.

"My name's Isabel."

"Troy." He held on to her hand for a few moments after shaking it. "Listen, if you don't think it would sully your reputation to be seen in public with such an unattractive person, how about joining me later for a drink? Maybe after sunset? I'm much cuter when the light is low."

They laughed and talked for hours and seemed to form a connection that grew as the days passed.

She was surprised at his gentle manner, especially given his physical size and stature in the college community. Feelings for him began to develop. He was supportive of her decision to abstain from intercourse and respectful of the boundaries she set – boundaries that kept shifting despite her earlier resolution to let her sleeping sexuality lie.

He had earned her trust by not taking advantage. Once when they were making out, his fingers traced from her breast to her navel, and she worried he wouldn't stop. But he didn't *touch* her, or even try, until she asked him to.

Troy saw her naked for the first time on the night she left the school, though that hadn't been her intention. He'd come to pick her up for a date an hour earlier than expected, time set aside to shower and get ready.

He apologized, offering to leave and return later, but as her roommate was gone for the weekend, she didn't see the harm in his staying. After stepping out of the shower, she noticed her outfit wasn't on the hook and called out, asking him to wait in the hall while she got dressed.

"No problemo."

When Isabel opened the bathroom door, the room was bathed in elegant shadows as candles flickered. Cheese and crackers sat beside a bottle of wine, and a single rose stood tall in one of two stemmed glasses.

Troy stepped forward and kissed her forehead.

"Happy three-week anniversary, Isabel."

She was deeply moved and stood on the tips of her toes to kiss his cheek.

"Thank you."

Isabel felt a tear tumble that he quickly kissed away. His lips tracked the slope of her neck, and she didn't realize the towel had fallen off until he picked her up and set her on the bed. "Troy, I don't think . . ."

He slipped off a Polo shirt, and then removed his jeans. Isabel had never seen so much of him and was stunned by his beauty – broad shouldered, chiseled chest, slim waisted, long-legged, and muscled in every way.

He was huge.

"Troy, wait. We can't," she said as he laid next to her.

If he'd done anything else, she might have jumped from the bed, but his fingers traced her face with the gentleness she adored and trusted.

"It's okay, Izz. I know the rules. Just kissing, touching, and rubbing, right?"

She writhed as he kissed her. Their nakedness fanned an already inflamed desire, and she quickly found herself on the precipice of a too profound pleasure.

When he touched her, she gasped.

"Ooh, Troy. We ... we need to stop."

"Just a little more," he said, rubbing himself against her.

"But ... Oooohhh."

Isabel lifted her hips in spite of herself, not wanting to stop but knowing she had to. For reasons not understood, having sex with someone so soon after Frank would make her feel worthless, like she was a whore.

"Okay, okay. No more. We have to ..."

She tried to heave him off of her when he sought entry. "Troy, no. Don't."

He began to push himself inside, and Isabel started to panic as the pain began to build.

"No, please, Troy. Stop. You're hurting me. Don't do this. Please, no. Don't. Please ..."

She didn't know she was begging until the tears rolled down the side of her cheeks. He withdrew without saying a word, turned her over, and shoved her face into the pillow as he took her from behind.

The pain she'd felt earlier was nothing compared to the agony of his being fully aroused and firmly seated. Her muffled screams went unheeded and continued unabated until she passed out.

She felt the stickiness between her legs when she came to but didn't know it was blood until she saw the sheets. The pain pierced as she tried to walk to the bathroom before crumbling to the floor. She crawled in the tub and curled into a fugue state long after the hot water gave way to cold.

She stripped the bed, threw the sheets in a trash bag, and tossed it in the dumpster before leaving campus. After hours of driving aimlessly, she found herself parked in the driveway of her house, sitting in the dark of early morning and asking the same questions over and over.

Why would he do that? What should I do?

When the blaze of sunrise burned through the fog of her desolation, a debilitating question reared its ugly head.

Was it somehow my fault?

~

Her confidence had plummeted since returning home, going from holding him fully responsible to blaming herself and making her question if she'd really been raped.

Why would he take what he must have known she'd give eventually? Maybe he didn't believe she was serious about abstaining because of how she'd let him touch her?

But she had said no and tried to push him off.

Didn't he hear the pleading in her voice, or see the tears on her face? Did he turn her over so he wouldn't have to? Or was he unaware of her fear and overcome by excitement, like she almost was. Had her muted screams sounded like groans of pleasure?

He hadn't called or texted. At first, she thought he got what he was after and was done with her. Now she wondered if he was just too embarrassed, knowing he'd lost control but not what to do about it.

Isabel heard Watson barking and thought he'd sniffed her out. A peek through the window showed a cat teasing him from the safety of a tree branch, and a smile crossed her face until the question that worried her most asked again.

Was she a whore?

Frank had turned her on.

And, though she shut herself off, Troy had no trouble finding the switch – because she'd shown him where it was. But she cared for them both and thought they cared for her.

Maybe that was the difference?

A whore would let anyone have her. And Isabel would never do that. She'd kill herself first.

But you wanted Troy to touch you, and it was what? Two whole days before you let him feel you up.

"I'm not a whore!"

She'd been fighting with herself all week, and her self-worth had taken a beating.

Frank and her mother hadn't helped, but in fairness, she didn't let them know she needed any, instead saying she'd come home early for Independence Day celebrations. Her mother seemed irritated by the sudden intrusion.

And Frank thought she missed him.

She'd been crying when he came into her room. He sat on the edge of her bed and asked what was wrong, but she didn't say anything. He wiped the tears and tried to comfort her by stroking her hair and face. His touch was soft and soothing, and Isabel felt better: soothed, loved, cared for.

She drifted to sleep only to be awakened by a searing pain. His fingers were inside of her and she burst into tears. He left her alone and hadn't tried to touch her since.

In fact, he avoided her entirely by spending more time at work. Perhaps he feared she would make trouble for him, but she never would. Frank was the last man she'd ever love for the first time.

She wasn't in love with Troy, but thought she could be. He shared qualities with Frank she cherished – patience in expressing desire, thoughtful consideration as her passion was explored. But now she wondered if they only cared for her because of what she let them do.

Was she just a toy for men to play with?

Is that all she'd ever be?

Standing at an emotional crossroad, desperate to know the truth, she sent a text to Troy hoping to find the answer. 'We need to talk.'

She went to the window and watched Mary drive the mower onto the trailer while Dax put the blower in its place. Watson jumped in the truck when the door was opened, and they pulled away a few seconds later.

Her phone sounded and she read the incoming text.

'I miss you, Isabel. Watson, too. We're playing out at the Tip tomorrow around two. Come and join us. Please.'

Mary somehow knew she was inside but respected her privacy rather than invade it.

Why don't I just talk to her?

Maybe it would help with how badly she'd been feeling about herself? But humiliation kept her from thinking on it any further, reminding her what she revealed about Frank. How could she ever face Mary again?

A text from Troy interrupted.

'Yes, we should talk. I'd like to explain. Can you meet me at Sutter's? I'll be there around eight.'

Sutter House was an off-campus residence along the St. Joseph Bay owned by a wealthy alum, available to both past and present fraternity members.

An explanation was exactly what Isabel wanted, what she needed. Then she'd know.

One way or the other.

chapter eighteen

Sipping his coffee, Hale sat on the early morning beach in contemplation. They'd been staying on Cape San Blas for the last couple days and would leave first thing tomorrow, giving them only twenty-four hours to get it done.

Or more precisely, to get it started.

He intended to steal something precious from Palmer tonight and come back in a few weeks to take his life. Brett didn't know about the latter, but he was more than willing to participate in the former as retribution for what Palmer had taken from them. Haley.

There wasn't a minute Hale didn't miss her, the way she laughed, the way she looked, the way she felt . . .

Palmer hadn't just murdered his twin sister; he'd killed everything that meant anything to him.

Why didn't he just mind his own damned business?

In the six months since her death, his only respite from misery came from thoughts of making Dax Palmer suffer.

And subjugating Barbara. He'd stripped her of most of her dignity, and tonight he would take the rest.

Then he'd take *her* life as well.

~~

Mary glanced at the phone once more before shoving it into her pocket and climbing aboard. When I lifted a brow, she shook her head.

"Too bad. She would have had fun."

"Yup," she said, and sat down as Tasha backed the boat away from the city dock.

"Why do you girls stick the phone in your back pockets? And why don't the screens crack when you sit on them?"

"Special tissues in the contour of our behinds allows for and conforms to . . ."

I grinned as the rest of her concocted explanation was lost in the wind after Tasha pushed the throttle forward and headed to the northern end of the Cape.

Every Fourth of July, the public-at-large converged at the tip of the St. Joseph Peninsula State park for a party that had grown in size over the years. Well over a hundred boats of different shapes and sizes made the annual pilgrimage to beach-up and anchor-down.

This year, an unofficial sponsor asked a few bands to perform – providing generators, sound equipment, and a makeshift stage. We were playing the two-to-five slot which worked for me. I'd already committed to playing the Raw Bar before the Tip offer came up, and a power nap between the two gigs should get me through the long day into night.

A power nap is different than the regular kind needed by those who were old or getting there. Just so you know.

Tasha swapped out her workday for a night shift, so she would be a tired puppy as well before her day was done. I wondered if she'd need a . . . *take* a power nap, herself?

~~

Isabel sat up and put her feet on the floor. She yawned and stretched for what seemed an eternity, and then rubbed her eyelids to induce them to lift.

Why am I so tired?

Every attempt to get out of bed this morning had been thwarted by a lethargy that pulled her back to sleep and into dreams she didn't remember but felt as real as the rug fibers scrunched between her toes.

She listened to the birds, some calling, some answering, others just singing. The warmth of the sun felt good on her face, and she opened her eyes to a bright, sunny afternoon.

"What?"

The clock said it was three-thirty, but she didn't believe it till her phone told her the same. She'd never slept so late, not even when she was a flu and fevered child.

How did she get home? When?

Isabel opened her door and listened. The house was quiet as she meandered into the kitchen and saw the note – *Looks like you had a late night. Hope you used protection.*

Leave it to her mother to think the worst of her. Why didn't she just have an abortion? It would have been better than raising a child she obviously didn't want.

Would have been better for me, too, she thought before thinking she liked herself, even if her mother didn't.

So did Mary and Watson. Dax and Tasha too, even.

Frank for sure.

And Troy?

She made some coffee and went out to sit by the pool.

The caffeine helped her weariness but didn't clear her head. A figment filled her imagination, one where familiar faces did unfamiliar things. Things she'd seen in her dreams. But the hallucination vanished as quickly as it appeared, leaving an uneasy feeling in its wake.

Isabel couldn't remember leaving the Sutter House or driving home. And except for a fleeting image, didn't recall sex with Troy, which would explain why she was so sore.

She sipped at her cup and recollected what she could in an attempt to evoke what she couldn't.

Troy met her on the porch, and they'd left his friends milling around downstairs for the privacy of his room. She'd been glad he left his door open, a sign he understood her reluctance to be alone with him.

He'd taken responsibility for his conduct and asked for her forgiveness, said his inability to contain his enthusiasm was the *reason*, but stressed that it was in no way an *excuse* for his behavior. She'd been overwhelmed by his sincerity and willingness to take the blame – all of it. When she told him she wasn't a whore, he nodded.

"I know that, Izz. I'm sorry if I made you feel that way."

One of his friends stuck a head in, offering to get them something to drink. She recalled feeling relaxed afterward and lying down when Troy went to take a leak.

The last thing she thought she knew for sure was being aroused by hands touching her everywhere and all at once. Someone kept moaning; she didn't know who, but a vague memory hovered over her like an apparition.

"Ooohh, Troy."

"It's Gregg, baby doll."

The coffee cup crashed on the patio cement when she remembered her response.

"Mmmm . . . Don't stop, Gregg."

~~

"Not now, Mare. Maybe later," I told her.

"Okay," she said. "How about now?"

"Funny girl. She's preoccupied with work and the press briefing. It's not the right time."

"Chicken-shit."

"Who's a chicken-shit?" Tasha said from behind me.

"Dax. He's afraid to . . ."

"Mary Elizabeth," I said and gave her my best glare.

"Nope. Try again."

"Mary Louise?"

She shook her head and grinned.

"Sure you want to keep going? You know what happens when you say *Beetlejuice* too many times."

"What's he afraid of, Mare?"

"Sweetie?" I said, and Mary laughed. She'd had her fun and stepped up on the stage.

"I'm going to play a couple more songs while you guys start packing up." The crowd came alive when they saw her and cheered when she started to play.

"Do I get that kind of response?" I asked.

"Sure. Don't they cheer when you're done?"

"Yeah, but . . . Wait. You mean because I'm finished?"

The glimmer in Tasha's eye was the first I'd seen all day and her sassiness was as sharp and appreciated as Mary's. She was a bigger shit than Mare but a smaller one than me.

A big, little shit.

"What?" she asked after putting her bass in its case.

"What?" Had I said that out loud?

"Did you call me something?"

"*Let me call you sweetheart, I'm in love with you,*" I sang and put my guitar in its case as well.

"I thought Mary was your sweetheart?"

"Mary's my sweetie. However, the job of sweetheart is available. Would you be interested in the position?"

"I'd have to clear it with my husband first."

She guffawed when my smile evaporated, causing Mary to glance over from the microphone.

"When did you get so easy to get?" Tasha asked.

"I'm not easy. I just . . . Have you been married?"

"No. Never wanted to be."

"Oh."

The people erupted in applause after Mary finished her second to last song, and I tried to hide my discontent.

"Dax?

"Yes?"

"I don't know, you know? I mean, I've thought about it. But I'm afraid. Afraid of having it and afraid of losing it. Does that make any sense?"

"It might," I said with a grin. "If I knew what the heck you were talking about." Whatever her fears, it seemed to me she wanted it more than she didn't.

Tasha leaned in close and whispered. "I love you, too. You big shit." Then she bit my ear. "Can I think about it?"

"Sure, but I may rescind the offer in a couple weeks."

"What? Why?"

~

Mary saw them laughing from the corner of her eye and assumed it a done deal when they slipped their arms around each other. She hadn't expected to care so much, and a wave of emotion swept over her.

She was happy, until she saw Troy Allison staring a few yards from the stage. The way he looked at her gave her pause. Smug, satisfied, and angry.

Maybe he still held a grudge?

She might, if a little girl got the best of *her*. She'd been lucky to put him down in the locker room, him and his friend, and knew a full-on confrontation with such a big guy could be problematic. He didn't scare her, but she wasn't stupid. He could hurt her if she weren't careful.

When she finished her song, Troy sauntered away as the applause began. The feelings usually experienced by an audience's praise were tempered. His being there probably didn't mean anything, but she would have to be on guard. Maybe even talk to Dax.

She left the stage when the people let her and gave a hearty congratulations to Dax and Tasha.

"For what?"

"Yeah," he said with a wide-eye. "For what?"

Mary looked back and forth between them and said, "For . . . What?"

~~

Tasha turned off the television and got ready for work. The press conference had failed miserably in its attempt to calm tensions and allay suspicions, ending up becoming another indictment of police misconduct and incompetence. One reporter even accused the Chief of Police of blatantly lying to the public to protect his officers from being prosecuted for murder.

The chief hadn't helped himself by being combative.

The shooting occurred when she was in Mexico. Two patrolmen went to the home of James Cantrell in the early evening to talk to him about a friend of his who'd been arrested. Within minutes, the fourteen-year-old was dead.

The officers said he had a gun and they were forced to shoot. James' cousin, who ran away after James was shot, said the cops got pissed and pulled their guns for no reason.

The discrepancy between the two accounts should have been easily resolved by reviewing the video from the bodycams, but . . .

~~

". . . both officers failed to turn them on, as required by departmental policy, resulting in rampant speculation and accusations of a police cover-up," the newscaster said.

It was all bullshit, I thought as I rolled out of bed feeling worse than I had before lying down.

Those cameras should be left on all the time. At least then wed know what happened and justice could prevail. Then again, Rodney King might beg to differ.

Me, too.

The channel flipped to Jeopardy! when I stepped into the hallway. Mary must have picked up on my reluctance to watch the news of late.

"Grand Teton National Park," I said and followed my nose to the kitchen. "Damn, Mare. This smells great."

"Thanks. But your answer's incorrect because it wasn't given in the form of a question. And it's Final Jeopardy, so I hope you didn't wager it all."

I uttered a *ha-ha* with a mouthful of gumbo from the pot, and then reached for a paper towel to wipe the counter of spillage before retrieving my favorite bowl.

"Have you eaten?"

"Yup. But I wouldn't mind another three or four bites."

She left the couch and grabbed a spoon.

I savored the supper by shoveling it into my mouth. That's how we give praise to the chef in this house, which is a lot more amenable than passing gas like some cultures do.

"Sure you don't want to come and play a few songs? I can drive you back during a break."

Mary dipped into the crock, collected a shrimp, and blew on it while shaking her head.

"Is that an example of killing two birds?"

She nodded and put the crustacean in her mouth.

"Where's Watson, by the way?"

She glanced at the backdoor and then scooped herself some rice and a slice of sausage.

"Mmm, that's tasty," she said.

"It sure is. This is as good as your spaghetti sauce. You keep this up and you'll make someone a fine wife someday – in about twenty years."

"Twenty?"

"That's when I'm thinking of letting you start dating."

Mary grinned and took another couple of bites before reaching into the fridge. "Want one?"

"Please." She handed me a soda and asked if I wanted a glass with ice. "No, thanks."

"So?"

"So, what?"

"Did you ask her? And don't say ask who."

I popped the top of the can and took a quick drink. "Yes and no. I never actually said the words, but she picked up on what I didn't ask. She's almost as quick to discern what I'm thinking as you are. Of course, you cheat."

Mary didn't bother to ask what I meant but smiled. "And?"

"She was tentative. I took her response as a maybe." When Mary raised an eyebrow, I told her Tasha might be right to protect herself from getting more involved.

"Why?"

If she could really read my mind, she already knew. If she couldn't, she didn't need to know how much I worried about Tasha being devastated if she ever found out that her maybe-could be-husband was a murderer. Albeit one with a penchant for justice and a killer sense of humor.

"It could get, complicated," I said, expecting her to ask how. But she nodded, instead.

"Maybe. But Dax, she's going to hurt just as much without you as she will with you. And so will you. You guys might as well hurt together."

Her words resonated with meaning.

"That is cryptic and, or, profound, depending on your understanding of what I meant by complicated. But you're not going to clarify that for me, are you?" I asked with a grin.

"As George H. once said, as parodied by Dana Carvey, *'Not gonna do it. Wouldn't be prudent at this juncture.'*"

The imitation was damned good, and it cracked me up. "Where'd you hear that? That goes back a ways."

"YouTube. It's a lot like you – old, but still funny."

I got up to wash my bowl, but Mary took it from me. "You'll be late if you don't get a move on. Sleepy head."

"It was a power nap, Mare. Emphasis on *power*."

"Uh-huh."

~~

Hale raised a glass, and Brett clinked it before downing the double shot of hundred-year old cognac in a single gulp.

"Interesting way to treat such an expensive brandy, but understandable. Given the circumstances."

Brett grinned and ask him to, "Hit me again."

Hale poured another shot and said good luck.

"For what?" Barbara asked, walking into the room.

"I'll catch up with you two later," Brett said, cupping her breast before he left.

"Where's he going?"

"How come you're not dressed?" Hale asked her.

"Why can't we go somewhere else? Or just stay here?"

"And miss seeing your knight in shining armor play the blues?"

"Hale, he's not . . . I don't . . ."

A feeling of anxiety came over her. He filled a glass to the brim and held it out. She didn't want it but knew better than to refuse. When she sipped at it, he gave a look that made her tip the tumbler until it was empty. He poured a little more and watched her empty it again.

"Now, go and put on that low-cut sundress. And Barb?" he said when she turned to go. "Wear the thong. And make sure it's pulled high and tight."

She nodded as the toxic mix of dread and desire, fueled by the liquor, began to burn. The loathing of what she had become yielded to her need to be controlled.

He owned her.

And that was that.

~~

The beauty of the setting sun didn't soothe her troubled soul as she had hoped.

Isabel spent the day processing, reclaiming memories and examining facts in order to understand what happened. And what she needed to do.

Troy *had* raped her.

He'd willfully violated her trust and took her brutally without permission a week ago, and then given her to his friends last night. They'd taken her repeatedly, individually and collectively, as he watched and filmed the spectacle.

The depth of his betrayal was nothing short of evil and would have been enough on its own to crush her spirit. But she'd also done things she couldn't have imagined with boys she neither knew or cared about.

Why?

Maybe something was in her soda? She'd never been drunk before, but it would have taken more than a mixed drink to make her that way, right? And besides, she hadn't smelled or tasted anything other than Coke.

Isabel heard stories of taste-free, date-rape drugs that made you weak and confused before they knocked you out. But, although she'd forgotten most of it until this afternoon, she had been aware of what they were doing at the time.

The thing she couldn't understand was how her arousal flared with such intensity.

Can a drug do that?

Could it make someone do things they didn't want to? Or did it free them to do what they *did*?

Drugged or not, she hadn't done anything to stop it. Quite the opposite in fact, a truth confirmed by a video sent a few hours ago.

In it, she saw a whore who'd do anything with anybody. Like Frank. Troy. Gregg, the boy with black hair, the one with the moustache, the two brothers . . .

She went over it all in detail, from the first time Frank touched her to the email she received with an implied threat of exposure if she didn't come see them again.

Mary's text said she'd be at her front door first thing in the morning, but Isabel would be long gone before then.

chapter nineteen

A protest march for the black teenager killed by white police officers had been peaceful so far, but Tasha worried it wouldn't stay that way. Too many people were too upset, impatient for a justice too long in coming.

Who could blame them? she thought.

Things were changing in America but not fast enough. Not long ago white men, women, and children would meet in town squares across the country to watch and cheer the hanging, burning, and mutilation of their black neighbors.

How is that not our version of a Holocaust?

Tasha believed one of the men who'd shot that kid was a racist. She'd heard him make a derogatory comment a few months earlier and thought it only a regurgitation of the vile diet of ignorance many southerners were fed as children.

She thought differently now.

That man was a *good ol' boy,* raised by parents who had themselves been taught to believe a distorted view of their southern heritage based on a revisionist history passed down for generations. Pete Miller was a product of bigotry, and she suspected another black boy died because of it.

"Damn," Tasha said when the call came over the radio.

~~

In addition to food, drink, and a guitar played to near perfection by a humble yours-truly, the Raw Bar patrons saw fireworks, an ambulance, and heat lightning in the sky. They may have seen an X-rated peep show, too.

No, I didn't flinch at the flashes. Not much, anyway. And yes, I saw her on her knees a few times.

Because I was meant to.

I'd noticed them an hour or so earlier but didn't let on. Regardless of the sincerity of my sorrow in killing his sister,

I couldn't see any good in tearing open that wound by trying to express my feelings. So I acted as if he wasn't there.

Imagine my surprise when the waitress handed me a beer during a break from *that man and his wife.* "He said they've enjoyed your playing and wanted to show their appreciation."

"Thank you, JuliAnne."

I don't usually drink when performing, and, if I did, it wasn't beer. But I nodded a thanks to Hale Bedford and took a long pull, hoping his gesture meant something.

It had. He'd been trying to get my attention.

There wasn't any compassion in his eyes, only spite. And he'd never listen to a plea for forgiveness, let alone give it. He was comforted by his animus and always would be.

And maybe he was entitled.

He leaned over and spoke to his wife when I started the next set. She looked at me forlornly and left the table. I watched her flirt with a stranger before whispering in his ear and coaxing him to the relative privacy behind my van, out of sight to most. Unless you happened to be on stage.

You'd think I'd be flummoxed or at the least, distracted. But no. I could play, sing, engage, emote, and peripherally peek without missing a beat, figuratively and literally. It was an impressive display of multi-tasking, if I say so myself.

After she went down, I gave the devil his due by glaring at him. Hale tipped his glass; confident I'd understood the point he was making. She was his to do with as he wished.

"Thank you, folks," I said, grateful for their applause. "Now, how about a slow one for all you lovers out there?"

~

Barb groaned when the music started, not because of what Palmer said, but because Hale kept pushing her button – the one that activated the micro-vibrator in the thong pulled high and tight. The stranger grasped her hair and held on, intensifying the moment of release. It came when he did, and she was engulfed in a tsunami of pleasure.

She stood and adjusted her dress after the man patted her head and left. The guitar man faced the audience as he sang his song, but Barb felt him looking right at her.

A whiff of shame flitted about like a butterfly before returning to the confines of its dark cocoon.

~~

Norman Greenbaum's *Spirit in the Sky* drew Mary and Watson from her bedroom. The song meant someone had deactivated the alarms and was coming up the driveway.

"It can't be Dax. He still has hours to play.

"It's Tasha," Watson said and pushed the curtain aside with his nose.

"Oh really? And how do you know that?"

"I can smell her."

"And just what, exactly, are you smelling, Pal-o-Mine?"

Before he could answer, a car stopped in front of the house. A smile he shared with Mary crossed his face.

"Oh, ye of little faith," he told her and moved quickly to keep from being hit by the opened door.

"Hey Tash. What's up?"

"It's Isabel. She's ... Mare, she's ..."

"What? Tell me."

"She's at Sacred Heart. She tried to kill herself."

"Oh my God. No!"

Mary grabbed her tennis shoes and sat to put them on.

"Mare, honey ..."

"I need to see her. I have to go."

"Wait," Tasha said. "She's in intensive care. They won't let anyone see her until ..."

Mary stood and faced her. "I'm going."

The tone of her voice convinced Tasha that Mary would not be impeded. She'd leave by foot, bike, mower, or Dax's truck if need be, but she was going.

"Alright, hon. Okay. I'll drive you. But we can't stay long. I have to get back to work."

Mary didn't nod or move.

"Just hold on a second until I use the bathroom?"

Tasha hugged her and felt trembling. She wished she'd spoken to Dax before coming by but hadn't wanted Mary to hear it on the news without someone around who loved her.

"I'll be right back."

Tasha hurried down the hall, hurried to finish, and hurried to return only to find Watson locked in the bedroom with Mary nowhere to be seen.

"How come you didn't let me know she was leaving? You could have barked or something," she said on the run.

"She told me not to," Watson called out but knew she wouldn't understand. Tasha didn't speak Retriever. Or any other canine dialect he was aware of.

~~

Brett had to hustle to get back to his car.

Just as he was ready to go in and get her, a truck pulled up to the house. He thought he'd been discovered, but after a few minutes, the girl ran up the driveway and down the road. After trailing her for a mile or so, he pulled over when flashing blue lights appeared in his rearview mirror.

But they weren't for him.

He saw the girl get into the truck and followed her to a hospital where he parked to collect his thoughts and nerve.

~~

Tasha spoke with the head nurse on duty while Mary walked down the corridor to the room, riddled by guilt. By texting she would be at her house first thing in the morning, Isabel must have felt trapped with no other option.

It was her fault. Hers and Frank's.

He sat next to Isabel's mother by the bed. They barely acknowledged her when she entered the room and walked directly to a chair back against the wall. She found it difficult to contain her anger toward Frank and wanted to hurt him, maybe even kill him.

But she was bewildered by his behavior.

He cried openly, holding onto Isabel's hand, and Mary was struck by how distraught he appeared. Her mother, on the other hand, was a different story. Except for a single tear in the corner of her eye, Mary couldn't detect any concern for her daughter. She could be hyper-stoic, but . . .

Was Frank the loving parent to Isabel? The thought perplexed and was hard to accept. Was he a pedophile or a caring influence in her life? Or both?

Did it matter?

Tasha came to the door and asked to speak to Frank and Isabel's mother. When they stepped into the hall, Mary got up and stood next to the bed.

"I'm so sorry, Isabel. I wasn't going to make you talk about it. I just wanted you to know I was your friend."

Tears began to form, and she sat down in Frank's chair. "Don't die, Isabel. Please. Don't give up. Let me help you."

Her phone dinged and she pulled it from her pocket. It was a text from Isabel.

'I'm sorry, Mary. Something happened, and I can't be here anymore. I should have talked to you, but I couldn't.'

She looked at Isabel in astonishment.

Wild imaginations of other-worldly abilities filled her head until a more logical reason shooed them away. Texts could take hours to arrive, sometimes even disappearing – like socks from a dryer.

An email had also been sent, but before she opened it Isabel's backpack began to sing *She's in Love with the Boy*. Mary reached in to turn it off and saw a text from a *Troy*.

'Hey, Superstar. You were great last night. Come on over. The guys miss you. Bet you miss them, too.'

An uneasy feeling crept over. It couldn't be the same Troy she'd seen today, the one who'd molested that girl in the locker room. Could it?

Mary looked through Isabel's phone for a picture she might have taken of *her* Troy but found the video first. For reasons she couldn't explain but didn't doubt for a second, she knew what she would see if she pushed play. The anger began to churn even as her heart began to break.

"Is that why you're here, Isabel?"

She sent a copy to herself and turned off Isabel's phone before putting it back into her pack, not wanting Frank or her mother to see anything indelicate if they answered it. When the conversation in the hall ended, Mary went back to her seat against the wall.

"Thank you again," Tasha said as they walked inside. "I'm sorry to have bothered you." She looked at Mary and tilted her head to the hallway.

"I want to stay, Tash," she said when they were alone. "At least for a little while. I can't leave her just yet."

The crack in Mary's voice made Tasha pull her closer.

"She's going to be alright. The doctor says she can go home in a day or two."

"I still want to stay. I need to. Please?"

Tasha noted the stubborn resolve displayed earlier had given way to imploring. That Mary asked was significant, and she hugged her tighter before letting go.

"They've given me permission to go into the house and investigate, so I'll be gone about an hour or so, depending on what I find. Will that work?"

Mary nodded.

"I'll stop by the Raw Bar and tell Dax what happened – unless you want to?"

"No. I don't want to talk right now. I'll catch-up when he gets home," she said and gave her a hug. "Thanks, Tash. I love you."

"I love you too, Mare."

Tasha's heart swelled as Mary's words filled a void she didn't know she had, and a paraphrased utterance from a beloved actress accurately expressed her feelings.

She likes me. She really likes me!

~~

There's nothing quite like the feeling you get when you connect with an audience. Everyone is engaged: tapping their feet, singing along, dancing the blues fandango. They love you, and you love them right back. It's exhilarating.

I was playing *Say What!*, a great Stevie Ray tune, and as the entire crowd sang the only three words in the song over and over, my goosebumps got some of their own.

After passing the musical baton to a kid playing the hell out of the keyboard-organ, I looked up and saw her swaying to the music at the very back of the parking lot. Even from a distance, the sensuality of her movement stirred me.

I missed my cue when her tongue slowly wet her lips, but no one noticed my lapse except the woman who grinned to confirm it. I smiled at Tasha and wrestled the solo back, playing us to an end that had taken twenty minutes to reach.

The people were reluctant to sever the bond we'd formed, and the applause was loud and long. Like me, they knew this had been a magical moment, one we might never experience again.

"Thank you so much," I said and turned to the kid. "Todd? You were fantastic. Todd Emerson, everyone."

The crowd roared their approval, and Todd took it all in with the aplomb of youth – too cool for school.

"Ya'll are a great audience, and your appreciation is, well, appreciated. Thank you," I told them. "And now we're going to take a pause for the cause. Cause I have to go pee."

Laughter and cheers greeted Todd as he stepped off the stage, and I looked around for Tasha before following. She was talking to a couple guys sitting at a table full of them, so I left for the bathroom, receiving words of praise on the way.

Praise is good. Transitory, but good. Unfortunately, it didn't always translate into confidence, and I was never able to rest on my musical laurels. It's similar to the Roman conqueror who rides in a triumphal chariot while a slave stands behind him and whispers over and over in his ear, *'All glory is fleeting.'*

Except in my case it was more like, *'Don't get cocky. You're not as good as they think you are.'*

Tasha was sipping what I assumed was sweet tea when I returned. She'd never drink while on duty. Tease me from behind a noisy crowd, yes, but imbibe? We sat on the steps of the stage and watched the people move about.

"I liked how you said *hello*."

Tasha started to say something, didn't, and then did.

"I was going to say my lip-licking wasn't for you but for Todd. But up-close, he's just a kid. What is he, twenty?"

"Seventeen. I wonder if he saw you?"

"No. He was totally absorbed in his playing. Man, you two were on fire. I couldn't keep from dancing a little."

"Yeah, I saw that. What is it about the way you move?"

Tasha blushed in spite of trying not to. "Don't look at me like that, Dax. You know I'm working."

"Speaking of which, were those the two cops you were talking to? The ones who killed that kid?"

181

Tasha nodded. "They really shouldn't be partying, not with what's happening in town. It's insensitive."

She mentioned the protest and its violent potential.

"Something's not right about that shooting. It feels off."

"I agree, Tash. But what can be done?" Something in her eyes said there was more. "What?"

"Isabel tried to kill herself."

"Jesus. Is she okay? I have to tell Mary."

Tasha put a hand on my arm when I tried to stand.

"Isabel's going to be alright, and Mary already knows. I'm sorry, Dax, but I . . . Shit!"

I grinned despite my worry for the girls.

"Well, me too. But I don't feel the need to apologize."

"What are *they* doing here?"

I followed her gaze but already knew who she meant. "He's letting me know what's what and who's in charge."

"And how is he doing that?'

Tasha rolled her eyes after I explained.

"Yeah, right."

"Really," I said.

"Uh-huh. And just how many guys has she serviced?"

"Three."

"Come on."

"And one girl."

She glanced over, trying to reconcile what Dax had seen with the woman who'd insisted she was going to leave her husband before it was too late. 'I guess she didn't make it,' Tasha said to herself.

"Sorry, Dax. Thought you were bullshitting me."

"Wish I was."

"So, you've seen quite the exhibition tonight. Makes my little demonstration seem pretty tame."

I wanted to kiss her, or at least hold her hand, but we liked to keep our public displays of affection to ourselves, particularly when she was on the job. I did, however, look at her longingly.

"Tash, I got more of a thrill watching your body move to the music than seeing anything that woman did."

The smile in her eyes warmed the cockles of my heart. "The girl she was with, though, did this one thing."

Tasha cracked up and pinched me before standing up. "Just couldn't help yourself, could you?"

"No really, this thing was..." I grinned and stood when she cocked her head. "On second thought, maybe I should shut up and stop trying to be funny."

"You can try shutting up, but Dax, don't ever stop trying to be funny. It's your best feature."

"Really? You find nothing else to your liking?"

"Well..." Tasha leaned forward, whispered in my ear, and stepped back when she finished.

"Wait. You can't just say those kinds of things and then leave me like this. Stand here for a minute, okay?"

Her grin tantalized and made it worse.

"Stop it now. I have to get up on stage in a few minutes."

"Tell me again about that girl who did that thing?"

"What girl? What thing?" I said, and we basked in our humor and allure for each other.

"I'm sorry I didn't talk to you first before telling Mary. I just didn't want her to hear about her friend accidently."

"No, I'm glad you did. Thanks."

Tasha told me how Mary reacted to hearing the news about Isabel, and that she was waiting at the hospital.

"I'll take her home, then it's back to the law and order thing. Later, Dax. I like you."

"I like you, too. See ya tomorrow?"

"If you're lucky," she said and walked away.

Ain't that the truth.

~~

"Don't. I'm not... No."

Mary looked up from the phone and watched her toss and turn in the hospital bed as she slept. The seething anger she felt when reading Isabel's email transmuted into an ice-cold hatred after seeing the video.

Just as Isabel had done earlier that day, she processed – examining facts in order to know what needed to be done. When Tasha opened the door and asked if she was ready, Mary nodded. She was more than ready.

chapter twenty

"Dude. There's three bathrooms in the house. Why are you always going outside to take a piss?"

"It's a call of the wild, thing. Only in this case, I'm the *wild thing* being called. I gotta go where I gotta go, and man, I gotta *go*," Troy said on his way to the door.

"Well hell, man. We ain't waitin'. That girl's raring to go, too. She's been giving it away since we made her a '*star*.'"

A friend of theirs was a chemist, a gifted one, and he'd created a drug to lower the inhibition and raise the libido. They'd used it sparingly on a few girls, and its success had exceeded expectation. Sex was now a limitless commodity.

"Yeah. A ruined reputation will do that, sometimes. When nobody believes you didn't do anything, you say *fuck it* and end up doing everything. And everybody," Troy said and stepped outside into the backyard.

"Besides, you don't want me to go first. She's not gonna want any of y'all once I give it to her."

"Fuck you," Gregg called out, laughing his head off. "Let me know if it's *deep*, you freak of nature."

Troy chuckled and gave a backwards wave of his hand. He followed a trail over the dune and through the sawgrass that ended near a copse of trees by the water.

The bluff was his favorite place to relieve himself, and the reason for Gregg's retort. His comment referred to an old joke about two guys peeing off a bridge late at night into the river below, arguing about who was bigger.

"Man. The water's cold."

"Yeah," his friend says. *"It's deep, too."*

To say Troy was well-endowed would be a significant understatement. At six-foot four, two-hundred thirty-five pounds, he was an impressive physical specimen. But it was his attribute that defined him. Friends on the baseball team said he was a double-threat at the plate – he could hit the ball out of the park with the bat in his hands or lay down a bunt with the one between his legs.

He was an elite athlete and played many sports at the university, but the game at which he excelled was *women*. Troy could have anyone and gave to those who wanted him. And from those who didn't, he took.

Not like Gregg or some of the others. They'd *take* a girl by chemical means, get her on video acting like a pornstar, and threaten to tell friends and family if she didn't play ball. Troy didn't have a problem with how they got their rocks off, but he liked to take his women the old-fashioned way. By force.

A girl who didn't want him revved his motor, and he set about putting her in a compromising position by whatever means necessary – charm, respect, and, most importantly, empathy. Validating a female's feelings nurtured her trust. Then the fun began.

He never spiked a drink or gave a girl any sort of drug. It wasn't sporting. A little alcohol maybe, but not enough to inhibit her ability to make an informed decision.

Troy was all in favor of a woman's right to say no. He believed in it, supported it, and in fact preferred if she did – because taking a girl against her will was the high he craved. And she'd know he owned her for the rest of her life.

Of course, she might call it rape. And it was. But that would be difficult to prove because she'd be bloodied and bruised even if she gave herself freely. He was big, and most women were not.

He'd violated more than thirty girls and had never been arrested, though the police had spoken to him several times. He was charismatic, believable. And as a 'star' athlete at a major university, the administration tended to protect their financial interests by maligning the victims.

Life was good, damned good for Troy who at nineteen had the world by the balls, and the girls by the . . .

He pulled himself loose from his shorts and took a wide stance, placing fists on his hips and looking out at the dark.

When the waterfall of his stream cascaded into the bay, he closed his eyes and imagined himself feeling the bottom.

It's deep, too.

A branch fell through the limbs of a tall tree to his right, and an explosion of hurt made him double-over. He reached between his legs in agony and toppled into the water.

Someone jumped in after him, and he thought it might be one of his house brothers come to help. But when Troy peered through the pain, he saw who it was.

"You?" he said, falling backward as he stepped forward and slipped. He swallowed some water and started to cough then felt an arm across his neck and started to choke.

"Yup," he heard behind him.

He tried to stand but was shoved under as he struggled to break free and breathe. After a few minutes of thrashing, he finally managed to lift his head to keep from drowning, but the stranglehold had now become a death grip.

Troy slipped into a coma, unaware he'd been released to help repair some of the cellular damage to the exterior of his neck by allowing the heart to pump and circulate. He didn't feel the sharp slash of the pen shell or mind that his blood spilled behind the kayak as it towed him away.

And soon, after his lungs swapped out air for saltwater, he would never mind about anything else ever again.

~~

Pretty late to be fishing, Brett thought.

He watched her put the rods in the holders and load the kayak in the truck before strapping it down. She didn't put anything in the cooler so the bite must have been slow. Unless she was a catch and release kind of girl. Kind of what he intended to do with her.

He'd been lucky.

After following her home from the hospital, she pulled out of her driveway within minutes of being dropped off and drove to the secluded spot down a semi-hidden trail.

The original idea had been to kill the dog and leave the girl abused in her bed for Palmer to find. But while she was fishing, he found a place nearby where he could *do her* that was hundreds of yards from the nearest house.

Brett meant what he'd told Hale before they came – he wouldn't kill the girl. But he didn't have any qualms about touching the hell out of her. It wouldn't bring Haley back, but Palmer would suffer. Like he had.

When she yawned and stretched, he realized she would be heavier to carry than expected. She was tightly packed inside a lightweight wetsuit, lean but muscled. He worried the gun might not penetrate the neoprene until she reached behind and pulled down the zipper strap.

After peeling the suit off and tossing it in the truck bed with the water-shoes, she took off the hair-tie and removed her one-piece before toweling off.

Damn! No wonder her father put his hands on her.

The order in which she dressed made him grin – socks, shoes, underwear, t-shirt – but she never got to the shorts because he pounced when the shirt covered her eyes.

Brett was taken by surprise when she kicked him in the plexus, driving the breath out of him. He grabbed her leg and tried to use the gun, but she jumped up and threw a kick that caught him on the chin.

He saw her head push through the neck opening as his temple struck the bumper on its way to the ground.

~

Mary scanned her surroundings before looking at the body crumpled at her feet. A mask covered his face and he held a stun-gun in his hand. As she considered what to do, Dax's words echoed in her mind.

If someone tries to take you, subdue you, or kill you, and they're down and vulnerable? Don't hesitate to do what has to be done. You kill them. Immediately and permanently. Otherwise, they'll try to take you or someone else another day.

She didn't know the man but could guess his intention. Unfortunately for him, he'd picked the wrong girl on the wrong night. Mary placed her hands how she'd been taught and broke his neck with a quick twist. The sound unsettled her, but she had to hurry before Dax got home.

Her curiosity gave way to pragmatism. Rather than leave unintended clues by lifting his mask or dragging him clear, she moved his arm and leg just enough to drive away. Whoever he was, she'd find out soon enough from the news.

She didn't feel bad about leaving him dead. He got what he deserved, just as Troy had.

And maybe later, the boys who'd used Isabel would too.

~~

When I told them this was the last song, the audience responded by booing. "I appreciate that. It's a lot better than hearing 'about time.'"

That got a laugh.

"I'd like to thank y'all for making this night special. It's been awhile since I've been back, and you've made me feel right at home."

The cheering surprised me in its seeming sincerity. Or it could just be their inebriation talking. Either way, it felt good. I plucked an arpeggio introduction and then stopped.

"I just want to say, for what it's worth, there's not a day I don't think about her and wish it hadn't happened."

His expression didn't change, but the intensity of his animosity shimmered like waves off of hot asphalt. Bedford was never going to except my regret nor adjust his attitude. He would hate me for the rest of his life.

I began to play *Bridge of Sighs* and glanced at the cops. They were still drinking, still loud, still insensitive. The whirling thoughts since Tasha left had coalesced into a plan. It was damned risky, but an old Latin proverb asserted that fortune favored the bold.

I'd also seen it favor the lucky.

And sometimes, the stupid.

~~

They walked, or rather staggered from the Raw Bar to the dark parking lot of the soon-to-be new store across the street. The sound of exploding fireworks made Dennis jump even though he'd seen them climb in the sky.

"Don't be such a pussy."

"Fuck you, Pete," is what he tried to say, but it came out mumbled and muted.

"And you keep your mouth shut. You're in too deep, so just let it play out. It'll all be over in a week or two. Ain't no white cop gonna go to jail for killing a nigger down here."

"Shut up, Pete. Damn! What the hell's wrong with you? He was a kid."

"Yeah? Well, now he's a dead kid. He shouldn't have been smarting off. Shouldn't have pulled a gun on us."

Dennis stopped and stared at his partner. "You know damn well he didn't."

"Then why'd you shoot him?" Pete said with a smirk.

"Because you yelled *gun* and shot at him. But he didn't have one in his hand."

"He did when back-up arrived, though, didn't he?" Pete looked at him hard. "Didn't he."

Dennis had panicked and fired his weapon, striking the boy in the head. When he saw a gun in the teen's waistband, his panic escalated. He'd killed an unarmed kid and his life was forever ruined – until Pete put it in the boy's hand. His objection to the illegal and immoral tampering of evidence was weak, and he failed to tell his superiors the truth.

"Why, Pete? Why didn't you just leave him alone?"

"Why? Because it was bad enough that little fucker told us to go screw ourselves, but when he turned his back on me? No. That boy needed to learn some respect."

Dennis knew the respect he referred to went beyond that for the police. Well beyond.

He watched Pete drive off before stumbling to his car, knowing he'd get a pass from a brother officer if pulled over. It was another aspect of the Thin Blue Line that tied him to men like Pete. Whether he liked it or not.

If they didn't look out for each other who else would?

A bang followed a burst in the sky, and he looked up to watch the firework fizzle. Something bit him from behind and he fell twitching to his knees.

~

The odor of wet dirt prevailed as Dennis came to. Lying face down, head covered, mouth taped, hands and feet tied, his first reaction was to cry out.

"Don't."

He tried to move but felt a shoe on the back of his neck.

"Officer Hartley, let's understand one another. I'm not going to waste my time hoping you'll be cooperative. I'll just drag you on over and let the alligators have at you. Speaking of which, hang on a sec."

He heard a rustling, and then three whispered spits.

"Sorry about that. Guess they're hungry tonight. So, you must be wondering why you're here."

His heart sank as he listened to the conversation he had with Pete. While other slithering critters moved about, he tried to speak. But the man told him to shut up.

"Any chance of seeing your family again depends on your compliance and your willingness to do what needs to be done. You and your partner are not going to escape punishment like so many of your brethren have for so long. Do you understand?"

Dennis grasped a sliver of hope and said yes as best he could. The man then lifted him with ease and sat him down on what felt like a tree stump.

"You are in a promising position here. By chatting it up with your buddy, you've avoided getting killed right off the bat by trying to lie to me. Now you have an opportunity to do the right thing, before the town tears itself apart. Not to mention you might get to live a little longer. Is that a thing you'd be interested in, Dennis?"

"Eth," he said.

"Good. This is what you're going to do . . . Shit, wait. Don't go anywhere."

Dennis heard four more spits before the man returned.

"Don't worry about my running out of bullets. I have extra clips. As I was saying, you're going to tell me exactly what happened after pulling into James Cantrell's driveway. Everything you and Pete did and why. In detail, without lies or omissions. You won't get another chance to tell the truth. Do you understand?"

"Eth. Leeze. Eth."

The man removed the tape from his mouth with a knife but left his head covered. When the tip of the blade poked the side of his neck, he told it all. Whatever thoughts Dennis had about being deceptive were abandoned as the pressure from the sharp blade reminded him of what he had to lose. After he finished, the knife was withdrawn.

A long minute later, the man spoke.

"My preference is to believe you. It's not easy to admit to panic. But that's exactly what you are going to do if you want to keep breathing. In the morning, I want to see you on television repeating what you told me. And don't worry you might forget something because I recorded it to your phone and sent a copy to the Panama City news department. They'll be at your house in an hour or so, I imagine."

"You bastard!"

"Now, is that fair? You need to be held accountable for your actions. And you will be, one way or another. You'll either tell the truth and pay the price, or . . ."

"I'll go to jail, lose my family, everything."

"What if something were to happen to them, Dennis? Something terrible?"

"You son of a bitch. Stay away from them!"

He felt the knifepoint beneath his chin.

"Keep quiet and calm down. I am not threatening your family. I'm only posing a question. If a man came to your house and killed your child, would you be satisfied with his going to trial? He might be set free because of a technicality, or because the jury had a bias. Or because he was a cop. See where I'm going here? My inclination is to kill you now instead of waiting for you to be exonerated. At the very least you're guilty of panicking and shooting an unarmed kid. But Dennis, you let your partner get away with murdering an innocent young man, and then participated in a cover-up to save your own ass. Where's the justice in that? What about your oath? Tell me why I shouldn't just feed you to the gators and call it a night?"

Dennis opened his mouth to scream but felt the knife pierce his skin. What could he do? *What . . .*

". . . can I do?" he whispered.

"Go home and talk to your wife. Tell her what you did and what you're going to do to make it right. Tell the truth, take your medicine, and do your time. Do it to restore the public's faith in our system of justice, maybe even find some redemption for yourself. Or hell, just do it to stay alive. Because Officer Hartley, if you tell anyone else about our conversation, or make a deal that lets you off the hook, you will die. And don't try to run away. That'll piss me off."

The man slipped the knife into his hands.

"Watch out for your partner. I don't trust him not to kill you. And don't take all night cutting yourself loose. There's a gator about thirty yards away and getting closer."

Dennis was frantic to free himself, slicing his wrists and drawing blood as he heard something crashing through the brush. He pulled the hood from his head just in time to see an armadillo walk into the clearing.

His relief was short-lived though, falling off the stump after being frightened by a family of raccoons perched on a wooden picnic table beside him.

He cut the binds from his ankles and looked around. There weren't any alligators, living or dead, but his car was parked nearby. Dennis ran toward it, needing to get home before all hell broke loose

~~

"Where the hell is he?" Hale muttered. He should have been back hours ago. In fact, Brett was supposed to join him at the Raw Bar after he finished with the girl. Maybe he ended up killing her and was on his way to Georgia?

Wouldn't that be something!

Hale grinned at the possibility of Palmer's pain, not for a moment disturbed at how his anguish might have come about. A deep satisfaction coursed through him hoping he'd no longer have to suffer alone.

His spirit lifted, making him feel what the Brits called *randy*. He finished his drink and walked upstairs to have some asphyxiation fun with his wife.

chapter twenty-one

"The coastal community was stunned when the officer said he fired in confusion after his partner shot the unarmed teenager. He claimed Pete Miller took the gun tucked in the young man's pants and placed it in his hand shortly before other units arrived on the scene. Hartley apologized for his part in the needless death of James Cantrell and the cover-up that followed. In other news, the body of Troy Allison was discovered in St. Joseph Bay this morning after going for a swim late last night. Although the cause of death hasn't been determined, one eyewitness said there was evidence of an aquatic encounter. For more on this story, we now go to Phillip Cummings standing by in St. Vincent. Phillip?"

"Sounds like they're trying not to say shark attack," I said strolling into the room.

"Yup," Mary replied and turned off the television. She was dressed and ready to go.

"Do I have time to eat?"

"Six minutes," she said.

I opened the fridge and grabbed a couple cans of Dew and a few hardboiled eggs from a shelf inside the door.

"Voila. A redneck, continental breakfast."

My attempt to elicit a smile was unsuccessful and she tapped her watch, wanting to be there before visiting hours began. I cracked and peeled the eggs, tossed them in a bowl and sprinkled some salt and pepper.

"Let's go."

She was quiet on the way, and I uncharacteristically followed suit, spending the time in rumination.

Officer Hartley had stepped up. It took the threat of death to persuade him, but still . . .

I have a great respect for those in law enforcement and the job they do, but those officers' conduct required a swift and just punishment, even more so because they were cops. Fortunately, the vast majority of those who protect and serve didn't share a similar disregard for human life.

Hartley might survive his ordeal. Miller, on the other hand, was the proverbial dead man walking. Incarceration was his only hope – unless he fled the country.

"Dax? Would it be okay if Isabel stayed with us for a while? I mean, if she'd want to."

We'd been up late last night talking about Isabel, Frank, and the love he seemed to have for her. Mary worried about Isabel's vulnerable state of mind, and I suspected she wanted to keep her close and protected.

"Sure. Her mother may object, though."

Mary shook her head and looked out the window.

"It's not going to be up to her."

I recognized that tone and smiled in understanding. Isabel would be staying with us for a while.

When we pulled into the parking lot, she kissed my cheek before opening the door.

"Thanks. I'll text you."

~

She ran through the rain and stepped inside. The nurse at the main desk told her she would have to wait another ten minutes, and Mary sat in the appropriately named room.

They must not have found him yet.

There had been nothing on the news about a man in a mask with a broken neck. While curious about the who, she was sure about the *why.*

Like her father, and her uncle, that man wanted to have his way with her. It was troubling to imagine him waiting in the dark for his chance.

What is it about some men who think women are theirs to do with as they will?

Are they defective? Was their evil innate, or chosen?

She stayed up late, long after Dax went to bed, waiting for the remorse she thought would come but never did.

Perhaps she was still too angry.

She'd like to talk about it but that was an impossibility. While Dax would commend the way she'd protected herself and even appreciate her reasons for wanting Troy dead, he wouldn't approve of her decision to kill him. The fact he'd been making the same kinds of decisions could be argued as a double-standard, but she knew better.

Dax was a grown man who made his choice after a lifetime of experiences, and he'd say her life was all ahead, unknown and full of possibility. If he thought her clean slate was marred because of him, she knew he'd never forgive himself. And she couldn't bear that.

Besides, it's not like she planned to go into the family business. Troy needed to pay for what he did to Isabel, and now he had. It was a one-and-done deal.

But what about those other boys? And Frank?

~~

Hale turned off the news and stared outside. After sprinkling all morning, the rain intensified and pounded the metal roof with what sounded like baseballs.

Many arrests were made overnight due to civil unrest, protesters were sent to the hospital, a young man drowned, and a fire was set and fought at the Dollar General Market. But no mention was made of a girl being attacked or killed.

Brett hadn't returned his calls or texts. He could have chickened-out and left, but that didn't sound like him. Brett missed Haley about as much as he did and had been eager to get back at Palmer by spending time with his little girl.

Whatever happened, he'd find out in a few hours. They were leaving for home as soon as Barbara finished packing.

Hale almost killed her last night.

She had been riding him hard and started to suffocate after leaning into the scarf wrapped tightly around her neck. He became inflamed and chased his sister's memory long after Barb passed out. She was hardly breathing when he finally removed the scarf and the handcuffs.

He hadn't planned to kill her yet, but if she'd died, oh well. She wasn't long for this world anyway.

Neither was Palmer.

~~

Tasha stepped out of the shower and into her room, preferring the cool caress of the ceiling fan to a bath towel. She drew the curtains to keep out the sunlight, set the alarm, returned Jeri's text, and got into bed bone-tired and curious.

Why did Hartley come forward? she wondered.

Guilt? Concern for the community? She commended his decision to tell the truth – it gave the protesters a ray of hope, a flicker that halted the violence in its tracks. But his revelation was a mystery.

Usually an officer wouldn't give a confession unless the evidence against them was irrefutable or a favorable plea-deal was offered.

Perhaps his conscience got the better of him?

Tasha had been tasked to investigate his assertions, something she didn't look forward to. But bad apples like Hartley and Miller needed to be removed from the basket before their rot spoiled the bushel.

Waxing a little poetic there, aren't you girl?

She fell asleep with thoughts of Dax rubbing her back.

~~

After days of rain and strong winds, Scotty could finally take the new kayak out and get his *fish on.* He pulled down a path few people knew about, or so he thought, and saw something lying on the ground

~~

Isabel listened to the water sprinkle as she rubbed and scratched a sprawled Watson lying next to her. Mary had insisted she take the bed again last night, preferring to sleep on the air mattress – *It feels like camping out.*

She didn't buy it but hadn't objected too emphatically, appreciating Mary's attempt to ease her anxiety since being 'raised from the dead.' The humiliation of not dying was as unbearable as that which had compelled her to want to die.

She didn't give the hospital psychologist any specific reason for the attempt. She only told her an act of betrayal overwhelmed her desire to live, and the therapist's efforts to delve deeper came to naught as Isabel stubbornly held on to the little self-respect Troy hadn't stolen.

"Why'd he do that, Watson? I thought he liked me. Am I just stupid or what?"

He told her she wasn't stupid – unless she already knew he was an asshole. Then it was on her. But Isabel didn't understand. Mary did, though.

"Couldn't have said it better myself, Watson."

She ambled from the bathroom with a towel draped over her shoulder and sat beside him. After a quick scratch, she began to dry her hair.

"What did he say?"

"Loosely translated, he said it's not your fault Troy was a piece of shit."

Isabel grinned and watched her attack the thick mane. It was the first time she'd said anything about him.

Mary came to the hospital every day and stayed as long as the staff permitted. Sometimes she'd crack a joke or talk about Dax and Watson, but mostly she would sit quietly.

Her support was just what Isabel needed, and she loved her because of it.

"Mare? Why are you staring at me?"

"Are you going to try to kill yourself again?"

Isabel was startled and began to fidget.

"I ... I don't know."

"You are not a whore, Isabel."

Her face flushed with embarrassment and she tried to move, but Mary put a hand on her arm.

"You're not."

"But I let them ..."

"Is having sex with multiple strangers anything you'd thought about before? A fantasy, maybe?"

"No! Never. I'm not like that." Isabel was hurt Mary would even think it. "It was dark, and I thought it was Troy. But then I ... Why didn't I stop them?"

"Remember the party we went to on graduation night? The bedroom? You had the same glazed look in the video, kind of there but not. I think they gave you something."

"I wondered. But could a drug make you feel ..." Isabel stopped and turned her face aside. Only a whore could have experienced pleasure in such a demeaning way.

Mary felt her shame, remembering her own struggle to understand what happened with her father.

"Yes, it could. And once your inhibitions are stripped, who you're with and what you're doing seems far removed from who you are."

Isabel glanced at Mary, thinking she might have been talking to herself. "I'm sorry."

"Why?"

"You always seem so strong and confident. I forget sometimes what it must have been like for you."

"I forget sometimes, too. More often than not, now. And you will too, someday."

"How? How can I? How did you?"

"I was lucky to have Dax." A tail slapped at her leg until she added, "And Watson, of course."

"I don't have a Dax," Isabel said.

"You have me."

Mary patted her arm and the tail slapped at her again. "And Watson."

"But people will see the video? And ... Wait. How did you know my eyes were glazed? I didn't send it to you."

When Mary explained, Isabel jumped from the bed. After a long minute passed in silence, a quiet voice spoke up.

"I didn't want you to see me like that."

Isabel's melancholy tweaked the desperation Mary felt after her father threatened to show the videos of them. The humiliation of being seen *like that* had driven her to suicide – just as it had Isabel.

"I said the same thing once," Mary mumbled to herself, and then got up to stand in front of a puzzled Isabel.

"Belle, I know exactly how you feel. You'd rather die than have anyone see you that way. But the girl in the video isn't you, and the sooner you accept that the better."

"But it *was* me," she said and teared up.

"No. You wouldn't have done it if you weren't drugged. And you wouldn't have tried to kill yourself if you were fine with what happened. A whore would've been okay with it."

Isabel fell into Mary's arms and started to cry. Watson hopped from the bed and rubbed against her leg. When the tears dwindled, she looked at him through wet eyelashes.

"Thanks, Watson. You're a good friend."

She kissed Mary's cheek and gave her a heartfelt hug.

"I wish I had talked to you earlier."

"Me too. I could have told you about Troy."

"What about him?" Isabel said, taking the offered towel to dry her eyes.

"He was one of the boys attacking Camille that day in the locker room."

"What? That was him?" Isabel was shocked.

"Yes. And a couple girls at school said he raped them. You didn't know?"

"No. But . . ."

"But?"

"My roommate at college. She said something about him once but dropped it when I got upset. Wow."

"There's more," Mary said.

"What?"

"Gregg Thurman was with him."

Isabel looked at her for a long time before speaking.

"This can't be the first time they've done this sort of thing. How many others, I wonder?"

"We might have to find out. Maybe do something to prevent it from happening to anyone else."

"What could we do?"

"Talk to Tasha. Maybe Dax, too."

Isabel turned around, holding herself in her arms. The thought of them knowing filled her with dread, and she moved from side to side, back and forth.

"It's your choice, Isabel, and I'm not going to push you, but people are going to talk about you regardless. It's a chance to reclaim your life. Believe me, you don't want to live with this any longer than you have to."

The rocking slowed and then stopped.

"Belle," she said softly.

"What?" Mary asked and put a hand on her shoulder.

"I like your calling me Belle. Makes me feel special."

Mary hugged her from behind.

"Well, you are. To me, at least. Don't know about Watson." A nip on the ankle made her jump. "Ow! Damn. That hurt."

Isabel laughed at their silliness, and soon they all were. "Let me think about it," she said, after they stopped. "Okay?"

Mary nodded and said *come in* to a knock at the door.

Watson moved quickly when it opened, jogging down the hall to get to the backyard.

"What? No *good-morning* this morning?" I called after him before addressing the girls.

"And how are you good ladies this fine morning? Or should I say you fine ladies this good morning? Or how about..."

I could have ducked when Mary threw the pillow, but I'd have missed out. Isabel cracked up as it laid precariously on my head, covering one eye and half a smile. She looked at the bed then back at me.

"Go ahead," I said with my best Clint Eastwood accent. "Make my day."

No sooner had the words left my lips than she grabbed another pillow and heaved ho. In the next thirty-seconds I was pummeled with whatever they could lay their hands on, including puffy animals and a wet towel.

"Don't move," Mary said and reached for her phone. Her smile widened as she took a few pictures of the carnage. "Man, I wish I'd filmed that."

The girls got quiet, and the air in the room seemed to gain weight. They looked at each other, and then at me.

"What? Do I have teddy bear innards in my hair?" I asked, trying to lighten their mood with humor – you know, because I'm such a hoot.

"I'm sorry, Mr. Dax."

"For what, hon?"

Maybe it was the way she looked at me, but I didn't fully comprehend what was coming until it hit me in the face. The stuffed kitten exploded at the seams and feathers flew and floated on and around me. The girls fell out laughing.

"Too bad you didn't get *that* on video," Isabel said.

After Dax retreated to make breakfast, they made the bed, folded the air mattress, and tried to put Humpty Kitty back together again. As they collected the foam and feathers, Isabel asked what he knew.

"I haven't said what happened or the video – I wanted to talk to you first," Mary said. "But I did say a boy raped you at school."

Isabel scrunched her face.

"I had to, Belle. He thought Frank was why you tried to kill yourself and was going to beat the crap out of him.'"

"Why would he think that?"

"I told him I'd seen Frank fondle you by the pool, and what you said about his touching you."

A blush overwhelmed Isabel's cheeks ability to quash. "God, I'm so embarrassed. Why the hell did you do that?"

"Because my father raped me, damn it! And I wasn't going to stand by and let another man molest another girl. Especially someone I cared about."

The intensity of her anger surprised Isabel, and she wished she hadn't stirred up old feelings.

"I'm sorry, Mary."

"Me too. I didn't mean to get so riled. But I have no tolerance for the evil that people do. Neither does Dax. And Frank is . . ."

"He's not, Mary. Really. Except for kissing me that first time, he never did anything I didn't let him."

"You didn't feel taken advantage of?"

Mary hadn't meant to talk about him but couldn't help trying to reconcile the pedophilic nature of what he'd done with the anguish he displayed in the hospital.

"No, not really. I believed he loved me. I still do. And I loved him. I still do, too."

Mary saw the truth in her eyes and looked away. She was confused and disheartened and didn't realize she was shaking her head until Isabel put a hand on her face.

"I know you're afraid for me. And it means a lot. But you don't have to worry about Frank anymore. I've already decided that what happened between us shouldn't have. But more than that, it's not right. For me."

A burden Mary hadn't been aware of lifted, and she slid her arms around Isabel and hugged.

"You don't know how glad I am to hear that. Really, Belle. Frank's a lucky man."

"How do you mean?" she asked, holding on to Mary and her affection for a little longer.

"I was going to have to kill him."

"That's funny," Isabel said before letting go. "You know what else is? Not *ha-ha* funny but strange?"

"What?"

"Troy was a strong swimmer. He was strong, period. It's hard to believe he could have drowned."

"He must have run into trouble," Mary said.

"A shark, you think? Like they're saying?

"Something like that."

chapter twenty-two

"Well, what do you think?"

"I think he's dead, Detective," the coroner told her.

"Ha-ha," Tasha said and took a sip of her coffee.

"Before I begin do you have any donuts your profession is known to consume in the line of duty? I have a hankering for a Sourdough glaze."

"That's a very stereo-typical question, Doctor. And no. I finished the last one before coming in. Sorry. How about I bring a dozen next time?"

Dr. Bishop nodded and began his examination. Tasha donned a pair of latex gloves and inspected the items on the counter – clothes, shoes, zip-ties, gloves, mask, stun-gun, phone, pocketknife, wallet.

Dumbass. Who brings identification to a crime scene? She tried to access the cell phone, but it was dead.

"Do you have an iPhone charger, by any chance?"

"Try the second drawer on the right."

Tasha found one and plugged it into an outlet.

"Hmm."

"What?" she asked.

"Neck is broken. Appears intentional. Temple injury looks ancillary. Were there stones or rocks near the body?"

"A few yards away. But the rain obliterated any usable evidence." She looked at the dead man's driver's license.

"Hmm."

"Detective?"

"I thought he looked familiar. His name is Brett Vander. He was part of that mess at the Raw Bar on New Year's Eve."

"The woman killed by your friend?"

"Yes," she replied, powering up the phone. "It looks like he got clocked on the chin pretty good. Was it a fight?"

"If so, it was one-sided. There aren't any scratches, cuts, or other offensive wounds I can see."

She nodded and saw that Brett received messages from *Hale*. Nothing in them gave a clue to what he'd been up to, but a text from Brett raised her antenna.

'Won't be long now.'

He sent it around the time she'd seen Bedford and his wife sitting at the Raw Bar. Was he saying, *see you soon?* There was no reply, and Hale's texts asking his whereabouts weren't sent till hours later.

As her mind moseyed down the path of possibilities, she remembered something Barbara Bedford said when she met with Dax at his house – *He's full of hate, Mr. Palmer and he's already said things that make me afraid for you.*

Tasha floated the idea of Hale and Brett wanting to hurt Dax. Maybe even Mary by extension. But he'd been playing at the bar, and she'd been at home with Watson.

Won't be long now.

What wouldn't be long?

On the face of it, Brett's motive seemed sexual in nature with the intention of violating the *stunned* where he stalked them. If not, and if it were an abduction instead, he'd have to carry them almost a quarter mile. Unless he intended to drive the victim's vehicle, but then why park his own down the road if he'd meant to take theirs?

Why would anyone be out there at that hour?

Perhaps a couple looking for some intimate time alone? Brett could have followed with the intention of taking the object of his desire but ran into an unexpected problem.

Why hadn't anyone come forward?

A few reasons sprang to mind, including the obvious – they killed him. Hiding an affair or avoiding outstanding warrants, a shakedown gone sour . . .

Blackmail could explain an out-of-the-way rendezvous, and why Brett wore a mask to conceal his identity. But not the stun-gun. Extortion being a dangerous occupation, why not bring the nine-millimeter in the console of his car?

What about a drug deal? Again, why the stun-gun? And the mask? It didn't make sense.

"Not easy to reconcile, is it?" Dr. Bishop said.

Tasha thought she'd been thinking out loud. "What?"

"Those officers killing that kid with implied impunity. Makes you wonder if we'll ever survive as a species."

She nodded in agreement. "It's hard to believe rampant racism still exists in this country. And yet, look at the cesspool of bigotry the recent election uncovered? I worry that insidious swamp will never be drained."

After Officer Hartley's admission and accusation, Miller told everyone it was his partner who shot the boy first and then planted the gun, and that he'd just got caught up trying to save his friend from prosecution for a mistake caused by a panicked response. His story gained traction, particularly within the department, until Hartley sent another recording to the press that refuted Pete's account with his own words. An arrest warrant had been issued, but Pete was gone when Dom and Tasha went to serve it.

"We can, I guess, only continue to strive toward 'the better angels of our nature,'" he said as the scalpel sliced. "Lest we dissolve into desolate desperation."

"That's some fancy alliteration, Doctor."

Bishop grinned and pulled the flaps of skin apart to give him access. "Would you care to give it a try, Detective?"

"Uh, no. So, cause of death is a broken neck?"

"Seems to be, but I won't know definitively until I'm finished. Same with time of death."

Tasha put the items in an evidence bag and dated it. "Sourdough glaze, then? No Bear Claw or fritter?"

"An apple fritter sounds good, too," he said, reaching for the saw. "Maybe throw a couple in? Thanks, Tasha."

"You're welcome. You'll call me when you know more?" she asked, getting ready to leave.

He nodded and started the saw before turning it off. "There's something about that football player. An anomaly."

"What? Didn't he drown before the sharks got to him? Geez, I hope so."

"Cause of death is still drowning, but barely. Those sharks must have gotten there pretty quick. They might have even been the reason he swallowed so much water, by getting pulled under or fighting for his life. It's somehow comforting to think the high levels of alcohol and cannabis in his system may have eased his suffering. But I digress. There was bruising on his neck – what was left of it."

"Do you think it had anything to do with his death?"

Bishop looked at her a moment before answering.

"There's not quite enough to speculate about its cause. Maybe he'd been wrestling around or got a high tackle from a football game. Could you ask about it when you talk to the people who saw him last? It'll niggle at me until I know."

Tasha smiled. "Of course. I am no stranger to niggling. Mine manifests as an itch at the back of my neck. You?"

"Twitchy eyebrows."

He raised them up and down, making her chuckle. "Now, it's back to work for me, Detective."

"Me, too."

On the way back to the station, Tasha thought about the cameras worn by Officers Hartley and Miller. The national news was replete with stories of unacceptable behavior by some in law enforcement, and the use of bodycams had become necessary to protect both the public and police.

Of course, they needed to be used properly, otherwise *transparent accountability* were just empty words.

Some thought the cameras should be turned on all the time, taking the discretion of when to use them out of the hands of the individual officers. But there were issues of privacy to be considered. They should be able to use the bathroom, pick their nose, or have personal conversations without being 'wired.' Tasha thought a possible solution might be for central dispatch to have operational control.

Dominic was out tracking down a lead to Pete Miller's whereabouts when she arrived. After pouring some coffee and cream, she took the cup to her desk and removed the phone and wallet from the evidence bag.

The taste of hazelnut teased her tongue as she debated whether to call Bedford from the station phone or Vander's.

If Brett's, Hale may inadvertently say something upon answering that might . . . What? Did he know what Brett was doing? If so, would he reveal it? Did Hale already know Brett was dead?

Did *he* kill him?

She'd prefer to question him in person so his reactions could be observed. Asking for help in identifying his friend's body might be the way to induce him to come. Tasha took a sip from her cup then picked up the wallet. It was old and frayed, wanting to fall apart as she opened it.

A couple pictures landed on the desk.

One showed Hale and Brett on either side of Hale's sister, the woman Dax killed, the one who'd tried to kill him with a crowbar. The first picture was odd in that each man had a hand firmly planted on Haley's behind, while hers were shoved down Brett's and her brother's pants.

The wickedness of her smile was also evident in the other one as she looked up lasciviously, naked and on her knees. The inscription on the back made Tasha blush. More so because the girl in the photo looked younger than Mary.

It appeared as if they'd all known each other intimately for decades, a supposition that was confirmed when she looked through Brett's phone.

In addition to many provocative pictures of Haley, he also had an extensive video library which left no doubt about their appetites and aberrations. A movie named *Wedding Night* showed Haley and Brett with Hale's wife, who submitted to anything and everything she was told.

As Tasha watched Barbara Bedford being used for their pleasure, she thought about her father and became angry.

"Williams."

She looked up at her captain standing by the desk.

"Sir?"

"From our body this morning?" he asked, referring to the evidence bag.

"Yes. I'm doing some preliminary investigation before notifying next-of-kin. Looks like he's the bad guy."

"How so?"

"He was found wearing a mask and carrying a stun-gun. Someone broke his neck for him. It might be an attempted rape or abduction."

"How are you going to play it?"

She laid out her thoughts on how to proceed.

"Good. Let's hold the mask and stun-gun from the press for the moment. See if anything shakes out first."

"Yes, sir. I agree."

Tasha saw what looked to be a fidget in him she'd never seen before. "Is now a good time for you, Captain?"

He nodded slowly, some apprehension in his eyes. "As good a time as any, I suppose. Should we wait for Dominic?"

"We can if you'd like, but I'm not sure when he'll be back. He's following up a lead."

"Miller?"

"Yes. He's still in the wind, but we'll find him. We want to, right?" she asked to get a reaction.

"Yes, Detective. I want his ass nailed to the wall. There's no place in this department for policemen like him."

Tasha nodded, hoping his words accurately reflected his feelings. He'd asked them to look into *OfficerGate*, as it was being called, and she felt resentment from those who thought investigating a fellow cop was a betrayal, pure and simple. Even the recorded words from Pete himself telling what he'd done and why did little to change the hearts and minds of some. She could only surmise that they shared his racism, and their anger stemmed not from his actions but because he'd been so openly exposed.

Fortunately, she'd never seen the captain exhibit the slightest hint of prejudice, except for criminals in general, and her esteem for him was high – until he closed the door to his office behind her.

"I erased the memory cards from the bodycams."

Stunned by his admission, Tasha sat down and took a deep breath while he took his seat behind the desk.

"Except," he said, "I did no such thing."

"Hold on," she said, and cocked her head to the left. "As statements go, that's by far the most intriguing I've heard. Sounds like the first two lines of a good mystery novel."

She grinned a bit, and he returned it ever so slightly.

"Is this a tactic designed to disarm your suspects?"

"Could be, but in this case, no. It just struck a chord. Now, Sir. You were saying?"

"The night of the shooting, I collected the SD cards and brought them to my office to see what happened. But before looking at them, I had to ..."

"You had to what?" she asked when he hesitated.

"Use the bathroom. I couldn't wait. So, I left the office for about twenty minutes."

"You had to pee for twenty minutes?"

"No, Detective. Diarrhea. The kids brought home a flu-funk. After a few days, I thought I'd escaped unscathed, but it got me in the end."

Tasha bit her lip to keep from laughing.

"In the end, you say. That's where it got you?"

Captain Doyle cracked a smile. "You surprise me, Tasha. I didn't take you as a bathroom-humor enthusiast."

"Oh, I'm not. Why grown men think farting is funny I'll never understand. However, I do appreciate a good pun. Particularly when spoken so eloquently. So what happened after you left the bathroom?"

"Before returning to the office, I stopped by and did a cursory interview with Hartley and Miller. When I asked if the cam-vid would support their story, they got quiet. Now I know why."

"What reason did they give for not using them?"

"Miller didn't say squat, and I'd decided to put a reprimand in his jacket. That was the third time he failed to follow proper procedure and it was three times too many. Hartley said they hadn't even thought about it because their visit wasn't an official interaction issue."

Policy dictated the use of body-cameras for any and all interaction with the public.

"Their *being* there made it official," she pointed out.

"Yes," he said, "but because they were just going to ask a couple questions with no intention of arresting anyone, their mindset was one of no harm, no foul. At least that was their thinking, so they said."

Tasha shook her head, and the captain nodded.

"Yes, I know," he said. "And no, we don't."

When she raised a brow, he added, "Have a remedial thinking seminar."

She smiled and asked him to continue.

"The Chief ran into me on my way back to the office and asked about the body-cam footage. When I told him they hadn't been turned on, he proceeded to ream me good."

"Why you?"

"Everything that happens under my command is my responsibility, one way or the other."

"I guess," Tasha said. "But that's not quite fair, is it?"

"It is what it is, and part of the job. Anyway, when I got back, I put the memory cards in the computer, wanting to cross that T as it were. And there was nothing on them."

"Well, there wouldn't be if the cameras were off."

"No," he said, leaning back and looking deflated. "There was *nothing*. Nada. La rien. They'd been formatted, and, as a result, were wiped clean."

"La rien. Is that French?" she asked with a grin.

"Oui," he said with a straight-face and an eye glint.

In addition to sharing a last name with the fictional character, Popeye Doyle, and a first name of the detective the movie was based on, her captain also had a major drug bust under his belt. But he'd been affectionately nicknamed 'Pappy' instead of Popeye because his gray hair gave him a grandfatherly quality. And, unlike the character, he could speak the language – although rumor said he only learned it in order to complete the French connection.

"Why did you say *you* erased them?"

"My computer and password were used, ergo . . ."

"Assuming you didn't do it," Tasha said, receiving a shake of the head, "or they weren't already wiped before you retrieved them from the vests. . ."

"I doubt it."

"So someone just happened to break into your office and erase a crucial piece of evidence, all while you were unexpectedly indisposed in the bathroom? Sounds . . ."

"I know what it sounds like." Doyle ran a hand over his face. "To make matters worse, I broke evidentiary protocol by not securing those cards before I left to use the facilities. I didn't even lock my office door."

"Yeah, that's a no-no. Why are you telling me this?"

"I'd like you to believe me."

Tasha did believe him – or wanted to. She could at least give him the benefit of the doubt for the time being.

"You checked the camera across from your office?"

"It's broken."

"Still?" she asked incredulously. "I thought that work order was sent in months ago?"

"Yes, but the money from this year's budget has already been spent on other essentials. Like body-cams that aren't being used."

She considered the facts and asked her question.

"Why would someone erase an incident that wasn't even recorded, according to Hartley and Miller?"

"You tell me," he said, wanting to hear her thoughts.

"Well, the easy answers are someone didn't know they weren't turned on, Hartley and Miller are lying, or you are."

"Yes. Which one seems more likely?"

"If they're lying, so are you," Tasha said definitively.

"How so?"

"You *did* take the cards from their vests when they arrived – I've already verified that with Goodwin. At no time did you speak with them alone when they were here, even your cursory interview was witnessed, and according to their phone records, they didn't call you from their cells. They could have used a different phone, but it would show up on *your* records if they had, right?"

Doyle nodded. "Go on."

"Of course, they could've reached out another way, and you could have made up the diarrhea story as an ad hoc alibi to cover your tracks. In fact, this entire conversation could be an elaborate ruse to make you appear innocent by way of openly confessing your guilt."

"But you don't believe that." Something in her voice said she didn't.

"I don't want to, but an investigation is warranted."

lar e hale

"Yes, it is. Now, assume, as you did earlier, that I didn't do what you've just outlined and someone did in fact see me go to the bathroom and seize the opportunity. Can you tell me why that individual would erase those memory sticks if they didn't know there was nothing on them?"

"To protect Hartley and, or, Miller. Or someone else. Or something else."

"The department, maybe?" he asked, watching Tasha follow where he led.

"Who knew your password? Was it easy to crack?"

"No, and the only person who might have access to it is someone I have no reason to suspect. Nevertheless, since *I* didn't do it . . ."

His inference took Tasha by surprise.

"Are you serious?"

"I can't think of any other explanation."

"Assuming it wasn't you, of course," she said.

"Of course," he replied. "What do you think?"

"All things are possible, I suppose. But that's a hell of a risk. And for what? To protect someone like Miller? Or the department? He'd be hung out to dry if it were true."

"Not really."

"And why not?" Tasha asked, before it dawned on her. "Ahh. Your fingerprints are all over this mess and any attempt to shift blame to that *dog* without proof won't hunt. Especially after Pete tried the same thing on his partner."

"Your metaphor is convoluted but accurate. I look much better for this than he does."

"I agree," Tasha said and waited to see if he would ask. To her relief, he didn't.

"Sir, I think it's clear you're in it up to your eyeballs. And if it is a mess of your own making, you'll still be stuck in the stink of it when the time comes. For now, and because you didn't ask me to, I'm going to take a look at the Chief. But just so you know, I'll be looking at you, too."

She considered that he could be playing her by being so forthcoming but knew there'd be plenty of will on her part to bring him down if that was where the chips fell.

214

"Thank you, Detective. I appreciate your willingness to search for the truth. Wherever it takes you."

Tasha stood and moved to the door before asking.

"Did you know Miller was a racist?"

"How is that relevant?"

"With respect, Captain, please answer my question. Were you aware of his feelings toward people of color?"

"No," he said and looked her square in the eye. "If I had, he would've been pulled from the street, and bounced the second his union options were exhausted."

"Thank you, Sir," she said and went back to her desk. After texts to Dom and Dax, Tasha left for home and lunch.

~~

As soon as the deadbolt slid into place, he moved in and grabbed her from behind, holding her still.

"Don't move."

Something hard pressed against her backside and he ordered her to step back before making her lean forward and place her palms on the door.

"Wait," she said but fell silent when the something hard prodded. He lifted her skirt and told her to widen her stance, then slapped her sharply on the bottom when she didn't.

Her compliance was swift and unexpected, much to her surprise. She didn't hesitate when he said *wider,* and her burning behind was quickly soothed by gentle caresses . . . Until he discovered she was soaking wet, the sound of which reverberated in the confines of the small foyer as his fingers touched and teased.

Without being told Tasha pushed back hard against the something pressed against her.

~

"That was far more exciting than it should have been. Why do you think that is?"

"A few thoughts come to mind," I said, following her to the bathroom. "A strong woman longing to be tamed by a strong man?"

Her *Ha* made me grin.

Tasha turned on the shower and asked, "Where did that whole role-playing thing come from, anyway?"

215

I watched her breasts sway under the blouse as she reached in to test the water temperature, likening her body to a work of art as exquisite as any found in the Louvre.

"It was a happenstance, as I just happen to walk by the door when you opened it. I jumped out with the intention of saying *Boo,* but you reached for the gun. So I held on tight until you knew it was me. And then . . ."

"Yes?" she asked and began to take off the rest of her clothes in that innocuous way I knew was meant to entice.

"And then, it became the chicken or the egg question. Were you responding to what I was doing, or was I doing according to your response? Either way, it was exciting."

She stood in naked splendor with a half-grin on her face watching me struggle to maintain eye-contact, when what I wanted to do was look her up and down and all around.

"Dax, I'm going to tell you something I don't expect to say to anyone else. Ever. I love the way you lust for me. It provokes a passion that's beyond my ability to explain. Thankfully, it's not beyond my ability to express."

She winked and stepped into the bathtub, closing the curtain behind her. "That smack on the ass, though."

"Yeah, sorry about that. Seemed like a good idea at the time. It won't happen again." She pulled back the plastic and looked at me with steamy eyes.

"You misunderstand. I liked it. But I'm damned if I know why. Must have been the context."

"Which was?"

"You had me right where I wanted you."

Oddly enough, I knew exactly what she meant.

"You definitely put me in my place, that's for sure."

Her throaty chuckle invited me to join her, but when I reached for the curtain, she said no.

"Sorry, Dax, but if I let you in, I'll never want to get out. Your quickies always become longies." She looked at him wistfully before adding, "And I thank you, kind sir, for your thoughtfulness in that regard."

That last was murmured with the syrupy sweetness of a Southern Belle, and she saw the delight dance in his eyes.

He was enamored by her, and it gave her goosebumps and chills in all the right places.

As Tasha stepped from the tub, I offered to show her a little known but highly effective drying process.

"Which is?" she asked before reaching for the towel.

I began to lick the beads of moisture from her neck.

"Mmmm. Is this a full body service?"

"Yes, Ma'am, with special attention given to nooks, crannies, and places in between."

She let the tingle tantalize before pushing him away. "Down, big boy. I have to get back to work. And your technique will *not* make me dry."

"Why Tash, whatever do you mean?"

"I'm wise to the rise in your Levi's, Dax."

The twinkle in her eyes sparked one in my own.

"You little minx. Did you actually see that movie?"

"Movie?" she asked coyly and began to dry off.

I was intrigued by the thought of her watching a cheesy R-rated film from the early seventies, but before I could ask about it, she told me they'd found a body.

"Any one I know?"

"Brett Vander."

"Name sounds familiar. Oh, yeah. What happened?"

A look of concern creased his brow when she told him. "I know. The thought crossed my mind too, but he was killed miles away from you and Mary. Did you see him at the Raw Bar that night?"

I stepped into the bedroom and watched her dress, the sight never failing to satisfy.

"No. Where was he found?"

She buttoned a blue blouse, wondering what she would say if Dom or the captain asked about the change of clothes. *An unexpected nooner came up?*

"A trail off 30A."

There were quite a few such trails in St. Vincent, mostly used by those who preferred the access to shallow water fishing most boats couldn't reach. I'd launched my kayak from the end of many of them over the years.

"Broken neck is interesting," I said.

"How so?" she asked and slipped on her shoes.

"It indicates training and discipline. As well as a willingness to . . ." I stopped short of saying *do what has to be done.* Something began to wiggle around in the folds of my brain, a thought not yet realized but forming. When it came into being, I dismissed it almost immediately.

"Willingness to what?" Tasha asked.

"To permanently eliminate a threat."

We looked at each other for a second before she spoke.

"Some people need to die?"

I didn't know her thoughts but assumed some of them were in the kitchen with the boy she killed. We hadn't talked about it since the night on the sandbar, but I knew it weighed on her – the way Bedford's sister did on me. Doing what had to be done didn't necessarily make one immune to emotional repercussions.

"Better him than who he was after. Or the one after that. Don't you think?"

Tasha let him take her in his arms. He stroked her hair without saying anything more, his silence more meaningful than any words he could have spoken. He knew what she'd done, understood her struggle to live with it, and gave her unconditional support. She doubted if she'd be as generous if the roles were reversed.

"You're a good man, Dax. And lucky to have me."

She kissed my cheek and turned to leave.

"Thanks. But didn't you mean *I'm* lucky to have *you*?"

"Isn't that what I said? You're lucky to have me?"

"Yeah, but you meant *you're* lucky to have *me*. Right?"

"Did I?"

The way she looked at me underscored what I already knew – I *was* lucky to have her. Damned lucky.

"There's a part of me that wants to put you over my knee for your insolence, young lady," I said with a grin.

"Well, I'd be careful there. I might break your arm for you. Then again . . ."

I raised my brow and she smiled that smile.

chapter twenty-three

No matter how many times she lifted the folder, Jeri couldn't get used to how thin it was. Dimitri Anatovich's file should have been at least an inch or two thick, but thanks to her predecessor, only five pages were inside.

Robert Thompson had not only protected him from scrutiny, but he partook of the fruit that Dimitri harvested – young girls plucked and purchased for sex. Thompson's activities were a terrible embarrassment to the Bureau, and Anatovich's incarceration was a high priority for the new Assistant Deputy-Director.

Jeri began to build a case after returning from Mexico. While there wasn't enough evidence to get a wiretap, she authorized surveillance to monitor his movements to help uncover the extent of his trafficking operations. More resources could be brought to bear as the case solidified, but for now, her options were limited.

Even though she *knew* he was guilty, guilty, guilty.

But knowing isn't proving, she thought. And proving took time and money, persistence, patience, sleepless nights and festering frustration.

It was heart-wrenching to know girls were already enslaved and suffering, and new girls would be taken before the wheels of justice ran down those responsible. Even if those wheels backed up and ran over Anatovich again and again, satisfaction would be fleeting because another evil bastard would pop up like a twisted game of Whack-a-Mole.

"Maybe a Samurai sword instead of a mallet?"

"Ma'am?"

Jeri looked up, unaware of her assistant's presence. "Just trying to kill that damn mole, once and for all."

The confusion in his eyes made her chuckle.

"Have a seat, Donald, and tell me what we know."

"A man and his family were murdered, wife and two daughters raped beforehand, house burned to the ground afterward. Looks like a home invasion, except..."

"Yes?"

"A fireproof safe contained video of dozens of young girls, minors, which is why we were called in. And get this – two of those girls were the ones who escaped a couple months back. In fact, the man who was killed owned a cabin in the woods twelve miles from where they were found."

"Have we searched it yet?"

"We're in the process. It's setup a lot like the former Director's – soundproof, cameras for recording, rooms for containment. We're bringing in cadaver dogs to search the woods as well, just in case."

Jeri nodded and asked if they'd discovered anything tying him to Anatovich.

"Not yet."

"What is it with traffickers having cabins in the woods? Maybe we should add that to the profile," she said as an off-handed remark.

"I have a cabin in the woods," Donald said.

"Huh. Are you keeping any girls out there?"

"No Ma'am. At least not until the cages get delivered. After that, I'll be good to go."

He gave her a grin, and she returned it. Gallows-humor. They'd consume themselves with worry and frustration without it.

"Thanks, Donald. Please keep me informed."

"Yes, Ma'am."

"Oh," she said before he walked out of her office. "Let's see if Anatovich, or any known associate, owns a cabin in the woods."

~~

Hale had never been so quiet. Ever since the police called and confirmed his suspicion, he'd hardly said a word – until he saw his friend laying in the morgue.

"God damn it, Brett."

Anger churned and soured his belly. He'd have driven a fist into Barbara's face when she put a hand on his arm if the detectives hadn't been there.

Tasha nodded and the intern covered the body.

"I'm sorry for your loss, Mr. Bedford. Mrs. Bedford."

She led them from the observation area to a small conference room down the hall. They sat at the long table and asked when the body would be available for burial.

"Tomorrow," Tasha said, although it could have been released today. She wanted answers before they left town.

"I apologize for having to bother you with questions. It seems insensitive I know, but your cooperation will help us find the person who did this to your friend."

She thanked Dominic after he got coffee for everyone, and then asked when they'd last seen Brett.

Barbara spoke up when Hale did not.

"The night of the Fourth. He left the beach house about a half-hour before Hale and I left for the Raw Bar. Said he would catch up with us later."

"What time was that?" Tasha now wondered if Brett's *won't be long now* text alluded to what she just learned.

Barbara looked over, but Hale was still within himself. First his sister and now this. Brett's death had hit him hard. He not only lost his closest friend but a brother as well, and she worried his cruelty toward her would intensify.

"About nine? Nine-thirty, maybe?"

"Did he say where he was going, what he was doing? Anyone he might have gone to see?"

Barbara remembered Hale telling Brett *good luck* when she walked in on them but had no idea of its meaning and, therefore, no reason to tell the detective.

"No. He just, uh . . . kissed my cheek and left."

Tasha noticed the blush and sipped some coffee to give her a moment's privacy, having seen the many ways Brett *kissed* Barbara Bedford. It couldn't be easy to relive those memories in the light of day. She framed her next questions carefully hoping to eliminate an improbability.

"Was there anyone Brett had a beef with, either up in Georgia or here in the Panhandle? Someone who'd want to settle an old score? Or he with them?"

Hale had been listening as they spoke, his calm exterior concealing the turmoil of his thoughts.

"No," he said. "Brett got along with everyone."

"What about Dax Palmer?"

He looked at her a few seconds before asking.

"Do you think he killed Brett?"

"Do *you*?" Tasha asked.

Fuckin' A, he thought. It was the only thing that made sense. Palmer must have caught up to him, somehow.

"Mr. Bedford?"

"He could have."

"Why would he do that?"

"Because he's an animal. Look what he did to us – beat up two innocent men, shot me and killed my sister. And y'all just let him go."

Tasha didn't waste time refuting his interpretation of the facts but rather kept him talking.

"But Mr. Palmer was playing at the Raw Bar when Brett was killed."

"When was that?"

She glanced at Dominic who told them what they knew.

"The medical examiner estimates the time of death was between midnight and four AM the morning of the fifth."

Hale saw a chance to muddy the water and maybe get that murdering son of a bitch another way.

"There you are then. How long did he play that night? Not until four, I'll bet."

"Well, Mr. Bedford, I don't know, but they usually close down around two or so. Earlier if it's slow. So, what are you suggesting? They ran into each other afterward, perhaps got into an altercation? Where would that be, I wonder?"

"I don't know," Hale said. "Where was he killed?"

"His body was found at the end of a trail used by local fisherman." Tasha pulled a couple photos from the folder but didn't see a lick of recognition in their eyes. "Do you have any idea why he would be there?"

Barb shook her head, but Hale looked at the detective. *What the hell was Brett doing in the middle of nowhere?*

"You said he was found there – but was he killed there? Looks more like a place you'd dump a body afterward."

Tasha thought to ask if he had any experience in that regard but didn't want to antagonize him yet.

"We considered it as a possibility, but we now believe that's where he died based on other aspects of the case."

She placed another photo in front of them.

Barbara's sharp intake of breath didn't disturb Hale's quiet demeanor as he perused the picture.

"Oh God. Is that him? Why is he wearing a mask?" she asked. "What's that in his hand?"

Tasha paused, but Hale didn't react or respond.

"A stun-gun. We were hoping you might be able to shed some light on what he was up to."

Hale took a last stab at incriminating Palmer.

"How would we know? Maybe whoever killed Brett is trying to throw you off his trail by leaving him like that. And how does this prove he wasn't killed somewhere else?"

"Brett's car was parked down the road a quarter-mile," Dom said, "so, if he was already dead, someone would have had to carry him because there wasn't any evidence of dirt, grass, or mud from the trail in the tire treads. It would have taken a strong man to haul him that far."

"Like Palmer," Hale barked.

"Also, blood from the head wound would've turned up inside the car or the trunk. If another vehicle were involved, I suppose it could have driven down and dumped the body as you suggest. But we don't think that's what happened."

"Why not?"

"Because three weeks ago, he purchased the mask, gun, and a few other items in Georgia using a credit card found in his wallet," Tasha said. "We think he was after someone and got himself killed. Any idea who that might have been?"

Hale shook his head, not because he didn't know, but cause he couldn't believe the stupidity of using a credit card.

Barb's head also shook, but hers was more a physical manifestation of denial. Hale's *good luck* now had meaning. They were after someone, someone they hated.

Tasha glanced at Dominic who shrugged his shoulder. She thought about bringing up the salacious videos but didn't when another thought interrupted. They all shared malformed sexual proclivities . . .

Could Brett have been trying to procure someone they could play with and discard after their appetite was sated? Was there a trail of dead and missing she could follow?

She would have to think on that but for now, a more serious concern needed to be resolved.

"Could Brett have been after Mr. Palmer?" Tasha asked. "Or his daughter?"

"Daughter?" Barbara turned toward her husband. "I didn't know he had a daughter?"

"That girl he found," Hale said without looking at her. "The one who killed the man from the FBI."

Holy shit! The girl who'd killed an FBI Director with his own gun after shoving an ink pen in his eye. Hale hadn't thought her actions to be anything other than a lucky set of circumstances, but now he reconsidered.

Did Brett take her there? Had she killed him too?

"I don't know, Detective. Whatever Brett was doing, he didn't share it with me. You?" he asked his wife.

Barb hadn't known anything before, but thought she knew something now. She just wasn't sure what.

"No. He was supposed to meet us at the bar, and we were all to leave the next day."

Tasha wasn't sure how much of the truth she heard, but nothing jumped out as problematic – except for Bedford's hostility toward Dax. Which, although misplaced, was understandable from his perspective. As she collected the photos, Hale stood and held out a hand for his wife.

"I don't believe there's anything we can add to help in your investigation, but we'll call if anything comes to mind. Feel free to do the same. Now, we'd like to see about making arrangements for Brett's return?"

Tasha looked at Dom, who shrugged his shoulders. She stood and walked them to the door.

"Thank you for speaking with us. I agree, some time to reflect might be beneficial in getting to the bottom of this. I'll speak to the coroner about the release of your friend."

Dominic waited until they'd left before saying anything. "You were kind of easy on them. How come?"

"I didn't want to spook them." She told him about the procurement possibility that occurred to her.

"Could be something there," he said. "I'll make some calls to the local PDs."

"What do you think? Do they know something?"

"The only thing that tweaked me was when she asked about the daughter. It surprised her. Might mean she's heard her husband talk about Dax in threatening ways. His hatred for him is obvious."

"Yeah, I got that too. Brett probably felt the same."

"You think? Busted teeth, busted jaw, busted testicle. Your boyfriend sure did a number on him. On all of them."

Tasha looked for an admonishment but saw a glimmer of admiration instead.

"First off, he wasn't my boyfriend at the time, so when I say they got what they had coming, it's not because I liked him like that. And boyfriend sounds so high school."

"So does *liked him like that*," he said with a grin. "Has he asked you to go steady yet? How about the prom?"

Tasha slipped the photos in the folder as a smile teased the corner of her mouth. "As a matter of fact . . ."

When Dominic raised his eyebrow, she shook her head. "What do you think about him?"

"It's really about what *you* think. Is he the one?"

"I don't know, Dom. Could be. There's something about him, but I can't put my finger on it."

"I'd have thought your fingers were already all over it," he said, trying to be funny.

"Well, sure, but I can't get a firm grip. He's too hard . . ." She stopped when Dom frowned. "What's wrong?"

"Sorry, Tash. My fault for joking around. But I really don't want to hear about his *junk*."

"What are you talking about?

"What are *you* talking about?

"Bedford," she said.

"Ah, well, your segue skills suck. I thought we were still talking about your boyfriend," he said and shrugged.

"You shrug your shoulders a lot, do you know that?" Tasha chuckled when Dominic shrugged his answer.

"I was saying, Bedford is too hard to read. It's not clear if he's hiding something or just hating."

"Probably both. Hard to imagine he wouldn't have a clue what his friend and fuck-buddy was up to."

"I agree. What do you think about his allegation? Dax killing Brett and dumping his body?"

"Ridiculous," he said. "But we still need to talk to him. Clear him as a suspect."

"I agree. Huh."

"What?"

"I agree about as often as you shrug. Probably a *partner* related phenomenon." She shrugged.

"I agree," Dom replied with a smile.

Tasha looked at the clock and pulled out her cell phone. "Let's see if we can get this done right now."

After three rings, he answered by singing a lyric from his *Pride and Joy* ringtone.

"Hey, girlfriend. Wassupwichu?"

"Now isn't that interesting? I was just telling Dom that calling you my boyfriend sounds high-schoolish. But how else can it be said?"

"Well, how 'bout what I was just singing at you – *I'm her little lover boy?* Except make it big instead of little."

"Would that I could."

"Funny girl," I said. "We could try the classics – Honey Dew, Sweetie Pie, Lamb Chop?"

"Those just make me want to smack you. Are you in town by any chance?"

"Yes. I'm at B.J. Auto having a valve stem replaced. Had just enough air to get the van here. I didn't see the tire until the girls took the truck to cut lawns."

"You let Mary drive?"

"No. She has a few weeks to go till she gets her license. I let Isabel."

"I can't believe you did that."

I couldn't believe it either. I didn't know what kind of driver she was, but I'd let them go anyway.

"Well, Mary wanted to show Isabel the *Quite Contrary LawnCare* business up close and personal. You know, get her mind off her troubles and onto some yard work. At first, I said no. But her rebuttal was compelling."

"What did she say?"

"Pretty please."

"Oh, well," Tasha said. "I guess you had no choice."

I heard the smile of her voice and asked if it was evenly distributed between laughing with me and at me.

"More at than with, but your love for her is very sweet. Listen, would you mind coming to the morgue? I'd like to talk to you about something. It shouldn't take long."

"Morgue, huh? Okay. See ya in a few."

"Thanks. Oh, and Dax?" she said, as Dom pantomimed a need for nourishment. "Could you stop by Subway? Dom is apparently at death's door from lack of sustenance."

"Sure. What would he like? And Tash? Tell him who's asking," I said suggestively.

"Dax . . ."

"Come on, now. It'll be fun."

"For you, maybe."

"Exactly."

When I heard her ask what her *big, lover boy* could get for him, his groan was worth the price of the sandwich.

~

We sat at the table small talking, drinking sodas, eating our subs. Dom finished first and burped his appreciation.

"Thanks, Dax. That hit the spot."

"You're welcome. It's the least I can do to show my gratitude for the good job y'all do."

"That's nice to hear. Now Mr. Palmer, can you . . ."

"Mr. Palmer? Why so formal? Is it because I forgot the hush-puppies?"

Tasha grinned and asked her partner for a quarter. Despite his confusion, Dom reached into a pocket for one.

"Dax, we need to ask a few questions. Usually we don't show our hand up front but I'm willing to compromise. Heads, we'll tell you what's up. Tails, you'll talk to us first."

I was intrigued and amused and curious as she moved the coin from one side of her hand to the other along the back of her fingers, something I'd never seen her do before.

"Do I need an attorney?"

"I don't know, Dax. Do you?" Dominic said.

I could see he was already in detective mode even as he licked the ranch dressing from his fingers. I looked at Tasha and cocked my head.

"You can call for one anytime you'd like," she said.

"Okay. Has to stay on the table, though."

"Go ahead and ask your questions, Dom," Tasha said before flipping the coin. She looked at me with a twinkle that only got brighter when it turned up tails.

"How many times is that now?" I asked in wonder. "Fifteen, sixteen?"

"Seventeen, but who's counting?"

I added cockiness to the list of things I liked about her. "Alrighty, then. Ask away, Detective Greer."

"What time did you leave the Raw Bar on July fourth?"

Well, well. Had Officer Hartley been telling tales?

"I don't know exactly, but I didn't close it down. One, one-thirty maybe? I remember being bone-tired."

"Even after your power-nap?" Tasha asked with a straight face.

"Yes," I replied and cracked a grin.

"Where did you go when you left?" he asked.

Let me see. After tasing, kidnapping, interrogating, and threatening a cop, I'd jogged back to my van and driven . . .

"Home."

"Any idea what time you got there?"

How long did I spend with Hartley? Thirty minutes?

"No. I talked with Mary for a while then went to bed. And no, I don't know what time that was."

"What did you two talk about?" Dominic asked.

I glanced at Tasha and then back to him. "Her friend tried to kill herself."

"Oh, right. Sorry. How's that girl doing? I heard she was staying with y'all."

"Better. She's starting to laugh more than cry. I think she'll be alright."

"That's good news," he said. "Did you see Brett Vander that night?"

Ahh . . . Not only had Hartley kept his mouth shut, I was being questioned about a killing I had nothing to do with.

"No. I haven't seen him since New Year's Eve. I did see his friend, though. At the Raw Bar with his wife."

"You didn't run into him on the way home? Maybe get into a scuffle?" Dom asked, but it was only a formality. He'd already dismissed Dax as a suspect.

I told Dominic I'd neither run into, around, or over him.

"Why would you think I might have?" I asked with the conviction of an innocent man. Which, for a change, I was.

Dom looked at Tasha and shrugged.

"Hale Bedford thinks you might have killed his friend. In fact," she said, "he proposed you killed him elsewhere and left his body down that trail."

"Why would he think that?"

"Bedford hates you. Reason and logic don't apply."

"Well, if I *had* done it, I'd have left him where he fell because I was too tired to move a body from here to there. Wasn't he killed where he was found?"

When Tasha didn't answer, I looked at Dominic who eyeballed the untouched half of my sub sandwich. When I pushed it his way, he told me about the car and the tires.

"Unless there was another vehicle," he managed to say with a mouthful. "Which would mean the killer had help."

"Well, let's see if I had any," I told him and called Mary. When she answered, I put her on speakerphone.

"Hey, kid. How goes the battle?"

"It's ongoing, but I expect to be done earlier than not. Isabel is surprisingly capable. She's weed-whacking as we speak. I might offer her a job if she hangs around."

"Great. Hey, could you help refresh my memory? Have we dumped any bodies lately?"

"You'll have to be more specific," she said without missing a beat. "Are you talking about the neighbor who sprayed water on Watson when he peed on his petunias, the old woman who got between us and our fried chicken at the Pig, or that boy who asked me how my garden grew and wanted to mulch me? Damn, he was cute. Wish you hadn't killed him."

"That boy had to go. You are too young, and he was too ... horticultural."

"Maybe," she said, "but he sure could hoe a row."

Tasha almost laughed out loud, and Dominic grinned.

"Did we have anything doin' on the Fourth?"

"Uh, no. That's when Isabel ..."

"Do you have any idea what time I got home?" I asked, taking a chance she'd been too distraught to know.

"No, not really. I didn't pay any attention to time until the alarm buzzed in the morning. What's going on?"

"I'll explain later. Any problems with the truck?"

"Yeah, about that. We kinda, sorta ... Oh, sorry. Gotta run. After while, Crocodile," she said and hung up.

"She's getting more like you every day, Dax. I hope you're proud of yourself," Tasha said with a grin.

"Yeah, the two of you could do stand-up," Dom added. "Like Dean and Jerry back in the day."

"She's a pip, that's for sure. And as quick-witted as they come. But she's going to be a handful come boy time."

I looked at Tasha for some empathy but saw little.

"You're on your own there," she said.

"Am I?" I asked, stung by the implication of our being together but separate.

"Well, thanks for coming in, Dax. We appreciate it."

"No problem, Dom. If anyone else turns up dead don't hesitate to call. I'm always available for questioning as a murder suspect," I said with a smile and a handshake.

"Will do," Dom said and told Tasha he'd be in the car.

"Hug or handshake?" I asked her after he left.

"As you have been so cooperative, Mr. Palmer, might I offer an alternative?"

Her kiss was slow and probing. When he groaned, she walked away knowing full well the dilemma he faced.

"Oh, sorry," she said but most definitely was not.

~~

"Hale," she said after working up the courage to ask. "Was Brett trying to hurt that girl? Were *you*?"

Barbara saw the truth in his eyes when he took them from the road to look at her.

"Of course not."

chapter twenty-four

Rice made a cast and waited for the net to settle before pulling it up and into the boat. He'd been a guide a few years now and still got a thrill from taking tourists out and putting them on some fish. Although his live-well was half-full, he tossed the net one more time. Better to have too much bait and not need it than to need it and not have it.

As he lifted the unusually heavy load, the reason for it became apparent when a boot broke the surface attached to a foot and leg. While unexpected, he wasn't surprised.

If you fished long enough, you'd see almost anything.

~~

"Can't say I'm sorry Pete's dead," Dominic said, "but the way he went gives me the heebie-jeebies."

"Yeah, that's a hell of a way to go. But every time I think about his calloused killing of that boy, I can't help thinking he got off easy."

"I don't know, Tash. Death by alligator seems harsh. At least with a shark you don't have time to think, you just react. But imagine the long few minutes of thought as that gator rolls you over and down before you drown. Eugh."

His shrug had some shiver to it.

"Well, if it *is* him, I hope that time was longer."

"Damn, girl. You're kind of a hard ass this morning. Everything alright?"

"I just want justice to have an element of parity. Sitting in a cell, even for the rest of his life, doesn't feel equitable with those parents having to suffer the loss of a child. He needs to suffer too."

"I hear you," Dominic told her and turned left. When he pulled into the driveway, she asked if he ever thought some people just plain needed to die.

"Sure, sometimes. But who makes that decision?"

Tasha tried but couldn't ignore a prick of conscience.

The obligatory 'No comment' was given to members of the media clamoring for information as they walked by.

"Please step back and stay off their property," she said as they climbed the porch and knocked on the front door. "We don't want to arrest you for trespassing, but we will."

When it opened, they stepped inside the house.

"Mrs. Hartley," Dom said with a tip of his head. "Dennis. Thanks for making time for us."

Dennis nodded and asked them to take a seat around an understated but beautifully carved coffee table.

"Would you like some lemonade?"

"You don't have to go to any trouble, Mrs. Hartley. We'd just like to ask a few questions is all. Before the arraignment this afternoon."

"It's no trouble, Detective. I was fixing to make some. And please, call me Jennifer. Of all the people on the force, you two have been the nicest to Dennis. Even though you didn't have to be," she said and left for the kitchen.

"Jen's right. You've both been kinder than I deserve."

"Maybe," Tasha said, "but I've never known anyone, cop or citizen, willing to take their full measure of responsibility regardless of the cost. Why *are* you, I wonder?"

Jennifer set the tray down and sat next to her husband, patting his leg. "He's trying to do the right thing."

"No, honey," Dennis said and placed his hand over hers. "The right thing would have been to hold my fire when Pete started shooting, or stop him from planting the gun, or come forward right away instead of trying to save myself."

He rubbed her hand and slipped his fingers into hers. "I missed my opportunity to do the right thing. Now, I'm just doing what needs to be done."

Tasha thought his words familiar. A movie maybe?

"We believe we've located your partner," she said.

"Really? Where?"

"Have you seen this before?"

Dominic passed him a picture of a tattoo, blown up and identifiable. Dennis nodded and handed it back.

"Pete has one like it. Left calf, I think. Oh," he said with realization. "He's dead?"

"It appears that way. He was, uh . . ." Tasha glanced at Jennifer who got up and went back into the kitchen.

"His truck was discovered this morning near the oyster house on Thirteen-mile road. But he wasn't in it."

"I thought you said you found him?"

"We found part of him. A leg was caught in a cast net yesterday, wearing a boot you patrol officers wear."

"Where's the rest of him? Another shark attack?"

"Alligator. That's what the coroner said. We're thinking Pete may have been wasted and wandered into the water, maybe passed out. An empty bottle of Jim Beam was on the ground near the shoreline. A search team is out looking now. Sorry, Mrs. Hartley," Dominic said as she placed a platter of coffee cake on the table between them.

Tasha noticed a look pass between Dennis and his wife that wasn't so much suspicious as niggling. When Jennifer sat down, it was a little closer to her husband.

"Dennis, this may seem like an odd question but did Pete ever express concern about what he did, or what might happen to him if it ever came out? Was he remorseful?"

"Pete remorseful? No, not at all. And the only time I asked why he wasn't afraid of being found out, he said, 'Pap's got it.'"

"You mean the captain?"

"I assumed so. When I asked, he told me to just keep my mouth shut."

"Did he ever threaten you?" Dominic asked.

"No, not in so many words. But I began to get nervous, until the second recording was released. Then he vanished. Or so we thought, I guess."

"I meant to ask you about that," Tasha said and reached for a slice of cake. She tried to tell herself it was only to put Jennifer at ease but her sweet tooth wanted a taste, plain and simple.

"Why didn't you release both recordings at the same time? You could have saved yourself some backlash."

Dennis nodded in agreement but couldn't tell her the truth, that he wasn't in possession of the second recording until it mysteriously appeared on his desk one day with a crayon-written note. So he told her some bullshit instead.

"I wanted Pete to share the responsibility willingly. But he wouldn't."

After the quiet became uncomfortable, Jennifer stood and took the platter into the kitchen. When she returned with cake to go, the detectives were standing.

"I don't know what else to say, Dennis, except good luck. Speaking for myself, I respect your decision to accept the consequences of your actions with such determination. Whether you realize it or not, your resolve will save lives. Maybe even help restore the public's good will towards us."

Tasha extended her hand, and Dom did the same when she finished, putting a hand on his shoulder as well.

"Keep your head up, Hartley," he said. "You look after yourself, and we'll look after your family. It's not their fault you fucked up. Sorry for the language, Mrs. Hartley."

After the door closed behind them, the reporters swooped and swarmed.

~

"Sounds like the captain might be blowing smoke up your skirt," he said on the drive to the station house.

"Could be, but damn if it won't piss me off if it's true. Why would he want to protect a Neanderthal like Pete? Is he one himself?" Tasha looked over at Dom who reached into the glove box for a tissue.

"He doesn't strike me as a racist lovin' asshole, but who knows?" Dominic cleaned the lens of his sunglasses and tossed the tissue back inside. "Hard to tell, sometimes."

"Did you find anything going on up in Georgia?" she asked, changing the subject. "Are Hale Bedford and Brett Vander serial rapists and murderers?"

"I spoke to someone who said there was some dead and missing around where they live, but those two are not on anyone's radar. Of course, they are now. The detective said he'd take a look. At least enough of one to eliminate them as suspects. He did mention something interesting."

"What?"

"Bedford is part of the 'swinging scene.' Vander was too. Said a friend of his had *participated* in the festivities. Apparently, Bedford's wife is a featured attraction."

"Maybe they don't need to grab up strangers, then. Brett may have just been scratching an itch of his own."

"It's possible, but why hasn't anyone come forward yet?" he said. "Looks like a clear case of self-defense to me."

"Me too. Don't know."

~~

The kayak was too long to close the back doors of the van, so I used some bungee cords to secure them. Watson and the girls left to mow lawns after Mary apologized again for teasing me about damaging my truck.

But I knew she wasn't sorry.

That girl would yank my chain whenever she could. And I wouldn't have it any other way.

I drove down the trail expecting to see other vehicles in the clearing but was pleasantly surprised to find it empty. My interest in seeing where Brett Vander had died paled in comparison to exploring the fishing potential of this previously unknown access point.

It was a sad commentary that, as I pushed off into the water, my thoughts centered on the possible honey-holes I'd find and not on the person who'd been attacked.

My juices began to flow, and I scanned around for spots that looked promising. The wind was light, so I let the kayak drift as I threw a topwater plug and *walked the dog*, making the lure move back and forth. Within minutes, the trout were biting and time seemed to twinkle in the morning sun.

I headed back to the landing after a few hours having caught thirty-two fish, releasing all but five kept for dinner.

The houses along the shore were an eclectic visual treat, full of color and whimsy and ranging from comfy cozy to ostentatiously ornate. Millions of dollars were on display in just a hundred yards with millions more beyond.

I often wondered what kind of jobs those people had to be able to afford them. My curiosity wasn't piqued by envy but employment. I didn't begrudge them their success, just wanted to know who was paying such exorbitant salaries. And for what?

Like the Sultan House. What did that guy do for a living? Or was it the Sutten. Sutter, maybe?

And the booby-houses – two domed edifices side by side wearing bright orange and lime painted attire. Others called them the titty-houses, but it seemed belittling to refer to that particular female attribute in that way. Their supple beauty had inspired a famous poem that said it best:

I think, I'm sure, I'll never see, a tree as lovely as a woman's breast...

As I paddled back to the van, it struck me that a lot of people had died recently. Three from drowning, one from heat stroke, the college kid who'd been eaten by a shark, Brett Vander, and Pete Miller.

Miller hadn't been found yet, as far as I knew, but that worked for me. The longer it took, the more he decomposed. Leaving clues of my involvement was always of primary concern, and I took some pride in being ghost-like in my evidentiary presence.

Pete surprised me by how fast he accepted his fate. Okay, he'd pitched a fit at first, but, given his limited options, he chose to suck bourbon through a straw instead of the instant death I offered as the alternative.

After three-fourths of the fifth was gone, I walked him through the foliage. He hummed a tune along the way, and I added some harmony until we came to the water's edge.

"Man, you kilt at the bar others night," he mumbled.

"Thanks."

I held him steady as he wobbled and sank to his knees and then cut the zip-tie I'd used to secure his hands.

"Last call, Pete," I told him and handed him the bottle. A few minutes later the gun was in his hand, under his chin.

I disliked his death seeming to appear as honorable as a drunken suicide after a bout of reflection and remorse, because he hadn't given one whit about that kid.

But he'd been held accountable.

And that was all that mattered.

~~

"Do you understand the charges that have been read to you, Mr. Hartley."

"Yes, sir."

"How do you plead?"

"Guilty, your Honor."

The spectators didn't erupt in jubilation but rather breathed a collective sigh of relief. An officer who'd gunned down one of their own would be punished – not hopefully, not eventually, but right now. For some, justice had never been as swift nor as sweet. A white policeman would finally pay for killing a young black man. A teenager.

A child.

While it was unheard of to see a cop so readily accept his fate, the satisfaction it brought caused many in the room to reevaluate America's broken promise of equality.

In an arraignment procedure, the accused was usually allowed to return to court at a later date for sentencing, providing a bond was posted for their release. But a judge could take those who pled guilty into custody immediately.

Judge Smith knew what the community wanted, maybe even needed, but he had to be true to himself. And his compassion applied to everyone equally.

"The Court appreciates your steadfastness in trying to right a terrible wrong. We'll reconvene in three weeks for sentencing, at which time you'll be remanded. Get your affairs in order, son."

When the gavel slammed, the gallery grumbled. They'd wanted him in jail, wanted to watch him dragged away, and the disappointment rekindled their frustration.

Within minutes, what transpired swept through the assembly of those waiting outside.

Dennis stood amazed and gazed out at the maddened crowd. At least a third of the multitude shouting for his head were white, and he was awed by the sight of it.

In that moment, he was grateful to have been given the opportunity to redeem himself, if only marginally, and bear witness to such a spectacle – black and white united in their desire for a better way and a better world.

When the cousin of the boy he'd helped kill shot him dead, Dennis' last thought was about that old chicken adage.

It had most certainly come home to roost.

~~

"What the hell's going on down there?" Jeri asked. "Y'all are in danger of losing your Forgotten Coast moniker with all the attention you're getting. Aren't you only two deaths away from a St. Vincent record?"

"No, we broke that last night an hour before the week ended when a family of four was killed by a drunk driver. Of course, *he* lived. Dammit."

"Sorry to hear that, Tash."

"Yeah."

Jeri felt the sadness in her friend's voice and let the silence go uninterrupted.

"How are things in your neck of the criminal woods?" Tasha asked.

"Same old soup warmed over. Too many people doing shit they shouldn't with too few of us to clean up after them. Makes me wish there were a reset button, sometimes."

"Yeah? What would you reset?"

"Men's attitudes. Speaking of which, how's yours? Behaving himself, I hope."

"We brought him in for questioning the other day."

Tasha grinned at Jeri's exclamation of *What?* and explained the *How come?* When she mentioned Dax and Mary's off-the-cuff comedy routine, Jeri chuckled.

"Those two. They're keepers."

"He asked me to marry him," Tasha said quietly.

"That's great! But why do you sound funny. What's up? What did you say?"

"That I wasn't sure."

"What aren't you sure about? It's obvious how much you care for each other. In fact, it's sickening to see, what with the two of you making goo-goo eyes all the time."

"I don't make goo . . ."

"Is it Mary? Does she want Dax all to herself?"

"No. Well, yes, I'm sure she does, but she'd share him, I think. She seems to want us together. All of us."

"Well then? What's the problem? Afraid you'll turn into a nagging wife and an evil step-mother?" Jeri said, with an added *hoo-hoo-hoo, ha-ha-ha.*

Her friend's cackle conjured up a fairytale about a lost boy and girl who'd found a hut of confection in the dark forest after their breadcrumb trail home was eaten by birds.

"I'm afraid, Jeri. I've never felt this way about anyone, never thought I could. And the strength of it . . . I'm losing myself, and it feels too late to get me back."

The solemnness of Tasha's tone gave Jeri pause. She had never heard a more mournful declaration of being head over heels, crazy in love.

"Do you want to, Tash? Get yourself back?"

"No," she said after a few seconds. "I can't imagine my life without him, both of them, but what if what we have gets messed up by making it something else? I don't know what I'd do if that happened."

"Well, the easy answer is – don't mess it up. You've found much more than you've lost. And Tash, so have they. You're a family waiting to happen, so let it. Give in and take the chance. You might just end up becoming the happiest version of yourself you never thought possible."

"That's a lot of wisdom in such a short exposition, Seven. It deserves some kudos – and some thanks. I will take your words under advisement."

"I hope it all works out, girlfriend. But if you decide to throw that man away, let me know," Jeri said with relish. "He'll need some comforting after you break his little heart."

"There's nothing little about him," Tasha replied. "And who'll comfort *you* when I break every bone in your body?"

"Nothing little, huh? Hmm. It might be worth it."

They laughed and made plans to visit before saying goodbye. Tasha set her phone on the table and thought about what Jeri said about her Forgotten Coast.

What the hell *was* going on?

A fifteen-year old boy had killed Dennis, who'd killed a fourteen-year old boy with his partner, who'd been killed by a large shot of bourbon and an alligator chaser.

Contrary to what she'd told Dom, the thought of Pete Miller dying like that touched an empathetic nerve. His gun was found in the water a few feet from shore, and, although bullets were missing from the magazine, when they'd been fired couldn't be ascertained.

After an extensive search, a suggestion was made to cut open a few alligators – and if it had been a child, tourist or innocent local, the proposition might have been taken seriously in order to provide some closure for the family.

But Miller wasn't innocent, and he wasn't missed. Once the leg was DNA confirmed, most folks preferred to let him *sleep with the fishes.*

On the bright side, despite the department's intention to fire him, Dennis was still employed when he'd been shot down, so his pension and benefits remained in effect.

While a poor substitute for a husband and father, Tasha was glad Jennifer wouldn't have to worry about paying the bills. But the long, lonely nights were going to be hell.

Dax . . .

How would she cope if *he* were gone?

Not at all well.

Tasha had been disingenuous with Jeri about losing herself for love of him because that battle had already been lost. She belonged to Dax in ways he would never know, as he belonged to her in every way there was.

He was hers, and she was . . . Still afraid.

This is bullshit. Some chicken-shit, scaredy-cat, bull. Words of encouragement she'd given another scaredy-cat a few weeks ago came to mind. 'Buck-buck, buck-oww.'

"Fraidy-cat, scaredy-cat, I love you. But what the hell am I going to do?" she said with a tinge of melancholy.

The files scattered on the dining room table needed her attention, but she filled her glass, took it to the sofa, and imagined herself a wife and mother.

Hoo-hoo-hoo, ha-ha-ha.

242

chapter twenty-five

After a fitful night's sleep, Tasha poured the first cup of the morning, sat down at the table, and shoved the yearbook aside to clear space for her elbows.

What the hell had that been all about?

She'd figured prominently in one dream after another – as a jealous, apple-wielding sorceress who repeatedly tried to kill Snow White, as the vain enchantress who kept her kidnapped daughter, Rapunzel, locked up and away in order to manipulate her, and as Cinderella's legal guardian who, while not quite the evil witch the other two were, was nevertheless a rotten bitch.

Why did so many fairytales have wicked stepmothers? And why had she been cast in that role?

It occurred to her she may be more apprehensive about accepting Dax's proposal than she thought, especially where it had to do with Mary.

Although she'd never been one, Tasha couldn't imagine being anything but a loving parent. What could ever happen to bring about the nightmare of her dreams?

Mary was a delight and hadn't displayed the slightest trace of teenage angst or rebellion – so far. But what if she turned into an obnoxious brat and caused all manner of trouble and contention? Maybe the fairytale stepdaughters provoked their mother's behavior by being rotten little pains in the ass?

Tasha chuckled, took a few sips of coffee, and looked at the papers cluttering the table. Now that Dennis and Pete were dead, the public seemed satisfied that justice had prevailed and frustration over the continued misuse of body cameras appeared to have dissipated.

Until the next time.

And there would be one unless a fundamental change took place in the way law enforcement did business.

We have to do better. For the people and for us.

She began to stack files and folders with the intention of taking them to the station house when she left for work. They consisted of notes, personnel files, and phone records of the dead officers, including a few items she and Dominic seized as evidence from Pete's home when he went missing.

In addition to trying to locate his whereabouts at the time, she had also poured over the information in an effort to find a connection between him and the erased SD cards.

Despite what she said to her captain about taking a look at both him and the Chief, all she'd been able to do was give them a glance.

Looking in full couldn't be done without creating a scandal that would probably tarnish the reputations of both men if a truth couldn't be found to exonerate either one. And she felt certain the captain wouldn't implicate the chief or anyone else without proof, so he would take the hit once the incident became known.

Tasha held onto the belief of his innocence, aided by the fact that he didn't ask her to 'drop it' after the Pete and Dennis were killed. And he hadn't needed to tell her about the memory cards in the first place.

Unless he was Machiavellian.

I wonder if he plays chess.

She leaned back in the chair and pondered the book on the pile. She'd taken it out of curiosity, wondering why Pete had a high school yearbook dated a year before he was born.

That question was answered when she went through his phone records.

He'd made a call to Alabama a little over an hour after shooting that boy, and she'd called the number thinking he might have been hiding-out there. It turned out to be his mother, and, while not entirely cooperative, the woman said Pete phoned to give her a heads up but hadn't called since.

When she tried to ask more questions, Miss Alcott, who now used her maiden name instead of Miller, said, "Sorry. I have to go."

At the time, Tasha called the Dothan PD, asking them to keep an eye out for him. But she knew where Pete was now. So did his mother, who'd hung up the moment Tasha gave her the news after saying she'd already heard he was dead.

How devastated she must feel.

Tasha opened the yearbook and looked for her inside. She read the congratulations and good wishes from those who'd taken the time to write them, and many had. Alicia Alcott was not only popular, but she had a boyfriend her classmates assumed she'd marry, according to comments .

She's pretty, Tasha thought, after finding her picture. Her smile was infectious and seemed genuine, making it easy to want to be her friend. Page numbers underneath led to other pictures – as editor of the school newspaper, playing clarinet in the marching band, and as a varsity cheerleader standing next to the boy mentioned by so many of Alicia's signatories.

Her eyes widened as she set the cup down hard enough for coffee to leap over the confines of the rim.

The boy was the spitting image of a young Pete Miller, but the name attached to the picture called him Billy. Tasha knew him as William Jeffries.

St. Vincent's Chief of Police.

~~

"Morning, Joyce. Are you having fun yet?" she asked the chief's secretary who was immersed in paperwork.

"Does a bear not not shit in the woods?"

Tasha grinned at the double negative and asked if her boss would have a few minutes after lunch.

"He's gone for the day. Had a golf outing to attend. Be back in the morning, though. Want me to pencil you in?"

"Let me get back to you, alright?"

"Works for me, Tasha. Everything good with you?"

"Yeah. You?"

"If I was any better, I'd die from sheer happiness," she said with a deadpan tone and expression meant to make Tasha laugh. It did.

"Thanks. I'll let you get back to your *good time.*"

"Nothing to it but to do it," Joyce said and gave a wink, returning to the task at hand.

Before leaving, Tash asked what course he was playing. "The National Golf Club up in Dothan."

~

"Okay, he's gone golfing," Dominic said and shoved the rest of the Bear-claw into his mouth. "So whatth?"

He licked the tip of a finger and pressed it onto her desk to reclaim the fallen crumbs.

"There's a funeral for Pete today at 11:00in Dothan." Tasha spoke quietly, indicating he should do the same.

"What does that have to do with . . ." He stopped talking when she pushed a yearbook at him after looking around to safeguard their privacy. He was struck by the resemblance – and the implication.

"Has this been substantiated?"

"My gut says it's true. What more do we need?"

They gave each other the eye, followed by a smile.

"If this is what it looks like, he's screwed. Might even end up doing time in jail," Dom said, shaking his head.

"Well, we can talk to him tomorrow, see where it leads. Even if Pete's his son, it doesn't mean he tampered with the SD cards. Could be somebody we haven't looked at yet."

They sat in silent reflection until Dom mused out loud.

"It's a tale of two Pappies."

"Huh?"

"Remember when Dennis told us Pete wasn't worried about what would happen if what he did came out? We thought he meant the captain because he said . . ."

"'Pap's got it.' Do you think he meant *his* pap?"

"Whose pap?" the captain asked. "And what's he got?" When neither answered, he said, "Y'all come into my office." He closed the door and gestured for them to take a seat.

"Well?"

Tasha handed him the yearbook and told him to turn to page seventy-two, offering her thoughts as he perused.

"It's a more tangible motive for him to destroy evidence than protecting the department from embarrassment. And, if someone knew Pete was the chief's son, they may have used that information to set him up. Did you? Know, sir."

Dominic looked at her with raised eyebrows, as did the captain who admired her keeping him dangled on the hook until she was sure he didn't belong there.

"No, Detective. I didn't. And we'll need to confirm your allegation before we get ahead of ourselves. No need to cast unnecessary aspersions."

"Tash's gut has already corroborated it, sir," Dominic said, grinning to lighten the mood.

The captain nodded toward a beginning to blush Tasha. "I appreciate your gut weighing in but let's try to verify it." His smile was almost apparent.

"We're talking to him first thing in the morning," she said and gave Dom an *I'm gonna get you, Sucka* stare.

"If you two don't mind, I'd like to talk to him first," the captain said.

Tasha didn't have a problem with him interrogating the man who might have tried to frame him, unless she believed he was involved in framing the chief – which she didn't.

When she asked Dom for his opinion, he shrugged.

"I concur with my partner's eloquent reply. Have at it. However, we reserve the right to question him ourselves, if we choose to. And you'll tell us what you learn. Agreed?"

The captain nodded.

"Just one more thing, sir," she said as they rose to leave. "Do you play chess?"

"A little," he replied.

"Are you any good?"

His smile suggested she might be making a big mistake.

chapter twenty-six

"Go on."

"You sure? I can dry."

Mary and Isabel giggled as they tuned the instruments and warmed up their voices by singing *me-me-me, you-you-you, us-us-us.* When a howl chimed in, they sang, *Watson-Watson-Watson*, trying to see who held the last note longest.

"Thanks, but I got this."

Tasha left me elbow deep in dishwater and joined them in the big room. She tuned the mandolin I'd borrowed to accompany Isabel's violin, and sometime fiddle. Although classically trained, Isabel also had bluegrass leanings. And she shared them with us to our amazement and delight.

After they played a few foot-tapping standards, a long, plaintive note pierced like an arrow as the horse-haired bow drew slowly across the string. I braced myself when Isabel began to sing *You Will Be My Ain' True Love.*

The song tells of a man who leaves the battlefield and struggles against all odds to find his way back to a woman he hardly knows but loves completely. But that wasn't what evoked my emotional response.

When Mary, and then Tasha lent a poignant harmony, my fingers tightened as the mournful melody breached the ramparts of my heart to lay bare my soul.

The haunting refrain always made me cry. Not in a sad or sobbing manner but in a manly way – a few tears from an over-abundance of coalesced condensation in the vicinity of the ocular region of the face.

Even Jesus wept. Or so I'd heard.

Finally, thankfully, my ordeal was over, and I applied the dishtowel where needed as they played another song. Fortunately, I'd been alone in the kitchen.

Except I wasn't.

"Any chance you'd keep this between us?"

His arched brow said *maybe*, but his eye said *no way*.

"There's a thick steak in your future if you do."

I held my thumb and finger about a half-inch apart, but Watson cocked his head incrementally until three inches of space lay between them.

"Really? That's about thirty dollars' worth of meat."

He looked toward the living room and then back to me.

"Okay, okay," I said and squatted to give a rub. "You drive a hard bargain."

He began to make an odd noise the more I scratched, one that reverberated and amplified.

"Is that . . . Are you purring?"

His face quickly changed to one of canine concern.

"Fear not, my friend. Your secret is safe with me. As mine is with you. Right?"

He nodded and nosed my face.

"Want to go for a walk, Watson?" Mary shouted out. "You're invited too, Dax."

"Y'all go on ahead. I want to finish these pots and pans."

"Alrighty, then. See ya in a bit."

After the door closed, footsteps crept toward me with silent intent. I pretended not to hear and continued to scrub a stubborn stain, looking forward to what Tasha had in mind while the girls were gone.

"Mr. Dax?"

"Oh, hey Isabel. Not up for a walk?"

"I wanted to ask you something."

"Sure. What's up?"

She couldn't ask while he looked right at her, so she grabbed the towel and started drying.

"Have you told Miss Tasha about Frank and me?"

Her affect was one of embarrassment, confirmed by the hue of her cheeks, so I rinsed the pan and handed it over.

"No. It's not mine to tell. Unless you're in danger. Are you, hon?"

"No. I . . . No."

She wiped the pan, put it away, and reached into the dishrack for another. A few minutes of stillness passed, interspersed with the clinking and clanking of dishes being washed, rinsed, and dried.

"I don't want her to think less of me. Or you."

The crack in her voice pierced as swiftly as her song.

"I don't, Isabel. Not even for a second. I do, however, think less of Frank. I hope you understand."

She turned my way as I handed her the last pot.

"I do, Mr. Dax. Mary feels the same way. And maybe someday, I will too."

"Would you . . ." I stopped, unsure of myself. Should I just keep my nose out of her business and out of her life? Was that best? For whom?

"What?" she asked.

"Would you let us know if he ever hurts you? If anyone does, for that matter. We're too fond of you to let others treat you badly."

Isabel unexpectedly threw her arms around me with pot and towel in hand. I felt her need to cry, and her effort not to, and held on as she wrestled with the two.

"Thanks, Mr. Dax," she said, her voice faint but firm.

"For what?"

"For caring. You and Mary both."

She squeezed before letting go, and I tried to change the tenor by praising her talent – which led to my undoing as I expressed my feelings about the power of music, especially when done to perfection.

"Your voice was like a bird in flight. And when Mary and Tasha joined you in sweet harmonic sorrow . . ."

I turned away when my voice caught, but she'd already seen what I tried to hide.

"Aww, Mr. Dax," she said and hugged me again.

"Something just got in my eye. Probably a dust mote."

"A dust mote? Alright," she said and started to giggle. "Do you need to go to the hospital? Should I go get . . ."

I gave her a look that exacerbated the situation, and her giggle grew in proportion to my frown. When I broke down and smiled, she cracked up.

Once again, I was in need of mercy.

"Isabellissimo? You don't have to say anything to Mary and Tasha, do you?"

"I don't *have* to, but . . ."

"Where's the fun in that?" I asked.

She nodded and put the pot where it went and hung the towel where it belonged.

"I could offer you the same deal as Watson's – a thick, juicy steak and my heartfelt appreciation."

"Your appreciation would be enough, but I'm sure they already know."

"Know what?"

"That you have *softy* tendencies."

"I do, do I?"

"Well, at least with the people you care about," she said. "What does Isabellissimo mean?"

"While not listed in Webster's, Dax's dictionary defines Isabellissimo as 'very beautiful Isabel.'"

She tried to hide but was as unsuccessful as I'd been.

"I'm sorry, Isabel. I didn't mean to embarrass you."

"You didn't. I mean, I am, but . . . I just don't see myself that way."

"Ever looked in a mirror? You're as pretty as you can be, Lissi."

"Really?"

Her face was beet red, but she looked at me intently. It tore at my heart to see such naked insecurity.

"Really."

Isabel took his words and fit them together with those Mary had given. Were they being honest or just nice? Was her true value higher than her low opinion?

"Lissi?" she asked.

"Well, Isabellissimo is long for a nickname. I figured Iz and Izzy were taken, and Mary calls you Belle, which only left Isa or Abel. So I took Lissi from bellissimo and, Voila."

"What about Sabel?"

"That's a good one. Sounds exotic."

We could hear Tasha and Mary laughing as they came into clearing a hundred feet from the house.

"Okay, Mr. Dax. I'll take your appreciation and the nickname in exchange for . . . What don't I remember again?"

"Exactly. See how you are? You're a good fit, Sabel."

"Lissi," Isabel said. "It has a nice soft cottony ring to it. Better suits my personality."

"I think so too, Fluffy," I said, and she beamed. "You can just call me Dax, you know."

"No sir, I can't. It's important to show respect," she said. "Especially to my elders."

Her eyes glowed with amusement and she left me with a grin on my face to join the others. I made root beer floats and was greeted with *oohs* and *aahs* in the living room.

"I'm sorry. Did y'all want one, too?" They gave me my *funny* and grabbed a mug when the tray touched the table.

I sat in the big chair, watching them talk and laugh with an affection they gave to one another easily, and then went to my room, returning with a manila-colored envelope. I set it down and pulled the coffee table from the couch to make room then stood in front of the girl with the spoon in her mouth before going down on one knee.

"Tasha, I like you. Quite a bit, actually."

"Would you say you might even love me?"

"I might."

"What, love me or say it?" she asked and looked at Mary and Isabel. Their faces were full of smile.

When I opened my hand, the girls said, "Ooooh."

"What, no *oooh,* too?" I asked Tasha.

"It's lovely, Dax. Who's it for?"

I was encouraged by the grin in her eye and put the ring on her finger with more confidence than I'd started with.

"I love you, Tash. Maybe more than what's good for me. I don't know if I'll make you happy, but I'll make you laugh – even if it's only *at* me. Having said that, would you be interested in being a wife?"

A well of tears sprung up and hid her thoughts, but I felt good about what her response would be.

"Uh, Tash?" Mary said. "Before you answer, did you hear him crack and pop when he bent down?"

"I did."

"I mean, he's a good guy and all, but it sounds like he's starting to fall apart. Have you considered your ROI?"

"What's that," Isabel asked.

"Return on Investment," Tasha said. "You bring up a good point, Mare. He's fit and firm now but for how long?"

"Well, to be fair, I don't know if you could do better. But you could certainly do younger."

The way they maintained their composure with eyes filled with unmitigated glee made me love them even more. I raised a brow for an answer to my hanging question, but Tasha asked for another minute to mull it over. When I tried to take the ring back, she told me to leave it be.

"It might help with my deliberations."

I smiled and stood and picked up the envelope. This time, I knelt on both knees and sat back on my heels in front of a wide-eyed Mary.

"Mare, I like you, too. A little less maybe than a couple of minutes ago, but not as much as I will in a couple more." She twinkled as only she could, and it never failed to please.

"You've given me more joy than I deserve, and I'd ask you to be my daughter but we both know you already are."

Mary nodded.

"Would you be interested in making it legal, sweetie?"

I handed over the folder and waited for her response. When she didn't answer right away, a pang struck me like a bolt of lightning. But after she teared up, her thoughts were as clear as a cloudless day.

"Shit, yes.," she said. "What the hell took you so long?"

"Florida state law, mostly. That and waiting for you to grow on me. Which hasn't been easy, let me tell you, what with your potty-mouth and all."

"Yeah, yeah. You've loved me since day one," she said with cocky certitude.

"You're only saying that because it's true," I replied and saw Tasha wipe her face with a sleeve. Mary, on the other hand, glanced back and forth at the folder and Tash's finger.

"Yes?"

"It's just, she got a ring."

"What, my undying love isn't sufficient?"

I winked at Isabel who wore a wide grin.

"Well, sure. But aren't you gonna give her your undying love as well?"

"First, the ring isn't hers yet cause she hasn't given me an answer. Have you?" I asked and shook my head as Tasha hemmed and hawed.

"And second, you might want to look inside the manila."

"Dax," Mary said, "I was just kidding. You don't have to give me anything."

"I know, hon. That's one of the things I like about you." When she opened it, her elation was priceless in its purity.

"Oh, Dax. They're exquisite."

Mary was not what you'd call a girly-girl. Things like make-up, frilly dresses, and jewelry interested her not at all – except for one small adornment she regarded as elegant. It was the only thing she'd even consider wearing.

Tasha mouthed a *very nice* to me, and Isabel said, "You'll have to get your ears pierced."

"Yup," Mary replied, holding up her new pearl earrings. "Thank you, Dax. I love them."

"And me?" I asked.

"And you," she said with a grin.

"And how about you? You gonna make an honest man out of me or what?" I stood and stretched my legs.

"There it is again," Mary said. "I don't know, Tash. He may need to be wheel-chaired to the alter."

"Yeah, we'd have to find a church with a ramp. On the upside, I suppose we'd get to park in the handicap spot."

I chuckled and pulled the table closer to sit on it.

"See what I have to put up with, Isabel? And they love me. Or so they say. Maybe you could help me out?"

Isabel had never known a family as playful and loving, and she would miss them when it came time for her to leave.

"How?" she said.

"Would you consider being an understudy?"

"What do you mean?"

"I love this kid," I said, nodding at Mary, "but she's a bit of a smartass. You've heard her pick on me. Now, if I had an understudy for her, a kind of back-up daughter to step in when she steps out of line, she might straighten up and fly righter knowing she could be replaced."

Tasha snickered, and Mary rolled her eyes.

"You've never had it so good, old man."

I cocked my head in a *see what I mean* kind of way.

Isabel giggled and asked Mary what she thought.

"He's right, I am a smartass. One he's nurtured with care, I might add. But having a back-up could come in handy. Especially after I run off with that sugar-daddy."

"You mean the man who pays you to cut his lawn even though he doesn't have one?" Isabel asked.

"No, that artist who asked us to pose nude."

"Oh, him. Where'd you two go the other day? I finished weed-whacking and couldn't find you anywhere."

Tasha heehawed and covered her mouth.

"It sounds like you've been corrupted, but the offer still stands," I said. "What say you, Fluffy? Want the gig?"

"Fluffy?" Tasha asked.

"That's me," Isabel said, smiling and having fun. "I'm collecting nicknames like charms."

"Funny you should say that. Will you stand in for my daughter should she be unable to perform her duties?"

"You mean cooking, cleaning, and general servitude?" Mary piped up.

Isabel hadn't felt as close to anyone as she did now. They really cared for her, and she loved them for it.

"Yes, Mr. Dax. I will be your back-up daughter."

Everyone cheered and welcomed her to the family. When I handed it to her, however, things got quiet again.

"Mr. Dax. You shouldn't have."

"Okay, give it back." I reached to reclaim it.

"Wait," she said, pulling the gold bracelet to her chest. "It's so pretty. How did you know I'd love it?"

Before I could answer, Mary said I'd probably sneaked up and listened through their door with a glass to my ear.

"Mary Jane, I did no such thing. I heard y'all fair and square one day when the door was wide open."

"I thought you didn't know my middle name?"

"I didn't, until I needed it for the adoption papers."

"How'd you come by it?"

"A pretty little bird told me."

"Uh-huh," she said and looked over at Tasha. "She's pretty all right, but not all that little."

"Hey. Is that any way to talk about your mother?"

"I don't know, Tash. Is it?"

We all looked at Tasha and waited for an answer.

Her feelings about marriage might be as conflicted as my own, and if she refused my proposal I wouldn't ask again – and not just because the ring had to be returned by noon tomorrow for a full refund.   We were happy now, and it might be best if I left well enough alone.

"Do you want one, Mare?" she asked in earnest.

"Only if it's you."

Tasha took Mary's hand. Despite her fears she wanted them both, to have and to hold.

"It could change things, hon," she said.

"Well, as long as you don't become a step-bitch, I think we are going to be as fine as wine. Speaking of which, how about some chardonnay to celebrate?"

"I don't know. It might not go well with the soap."

"Huh?"

"Children who swear need to be . . . discouraged. A nice, big bar of Irish Spring or Coast should do it, I think. You little shit."

Mary's eyes lit with merriment.

"Dad . . . Mom called me a little shit."

"Now, sweetie. I'm sure she meant it affectionately."

"But she swore. You going to make her eat soap, too?"

"Little girls get soaped. Big girls get spanked."

Mary and Isabel laughed when Tasha stuck out her tongue. What they didn't see was the look she cast my way. It was downright mischievous.

"Well, Tash? Are you going to leave me to raise this hell-child by myself, or grab a belt and help me before my back-up daughter follows her side-sister to Europe?"

"I . . ."

257

"Wait." Mary jumped from the couch, put the empty mugs on the tray, and then asked Isabel to accompany her. "We'll be right back."

Watson followed them into the kitchen and watched Mary take a bottle filled with amber liquid from the fridge while Isabel swapped the mugs for glasses. Seizing an opportunity, he asked for a treat or three as they prepared to celebrate the upcoming nuptials.

"Sure," Mary said. "Belle, would you give Watson some Snausages? Wine just makes him a silly goose."

Isabel found the snacks in the pantry and held some in her hand as he consumed one after another.

"He drinks wine?"

"Once. I tried to talk him out of it, but he insisted. Ended up howling at the moon."

"But that's normal dog behavior, isn't it?" she asked, rubbing and scratching his head.

"It was a porchlight."

Watson reached to bite her, but Mary saw it coming. "Sorry, Watson, but it's true. And it was cute. As were you."

Isabel kissed him on the snout and ruffled his ears.

"He can't help but be a cutie patootie."

Patootie? Watson thought. He was *not* a pretty girl, but a fine example of wolfish male magnificence.

Phooey on her patootie.

A stack of Solo cups snagged Isabel's eye as she slid the treats back in the cupboard, and images of what happened to her clashed with thoughts of who she wanted to be and what she would have to do.

"I can't just run away from what those boys did, or let them do it to someone else," Isabel said.

"Nope."

"Maybe I'll talk to Tasha tomorrow."

"Let's do it now," Mary said and turned to go get her.

"No, it's not the right time. She's getting engaged."

"She won't mind. Besides, it's always the right time to do what needs doing."

"Mare . . ."

~

After Tasha left to see what Mary wanted, I walked up the driveway to check the mailbox and watched another boringly beautiful sunset.

"Damn, Watson. I don't think that flash even exists."

I turned when he didn't respond and saw him smelling his way back to the house. As I followed down the driveway, a question I'd thought answered, asked to be reconsidered.

To kill or not to kill?

It would be much more difficult to continue doing so if Tasha lived with us. Where Mary might suspect but not ask, Tasha would. And then what?

I'd been foolish to fall in love in the first place and even more so to let her reciprocate before my vigilante ass was done doing what had to be done. The problem with quitting wasn't because I liked to kill, I didn't, the challenge and satisfaction notwithstanding. The problem was letting the wicked go scot-free and unchallenged, even though my efforts amounted to a drop in the bucket.

However, for a man who didn't believe in God, though open to the possibility, I'd been blessed with a daughter, a furry friend, and a maybe wife with extraordinary benefits.

Life was pretty damned good, and in order to make certain it stayed that way, I'd have to stop.

"I'm so sorry for what you've been through, Isabel," I heard Tasha say as I stepped into the clearing. "It's not easy to talk about, I know, but your telling will keep those boys from doing the same thing to another girl."

"I hope so."

"The boy who raped you in your dorm room . . . What's his name?"

"Troy Allison."

"The one who drowned?"

"Yes."

I didn't want to eavesdrop and scooted past the open window to the backyard.

"And when did Troy let those other boys . . . Where did that happen?" Tasha asked.

"A week later at the Sutter House, the night before y'all played the Tip. Then he sent me the video. That's why . . ."

I moved through the gate and made my way to a Rattan chair on the deck at the back of the house. The couch slid into view as I sat, the one I'd laid an unconscious Mary who, like Isabel, tried to kill herself because of the iniquity of another. My anger toward the boy who'd raped Isabel and later passed her around was tempered only by his death.

He already had an encounter with another predator.

Hmmm. What were the odds of him dying the same night Isabel tried to do the same?

And so accidentally?

If not a random act of divine justice, might he have died on purpose? My instinct said he had probably raped before, and perhaps a boyfriend, brother, or father had avenged a loved one. Could he have set aside the rage, I wondered, in order to execute a plan making his death seem unintended?

Probably not, especially if he wasn't in it for the long haul like I was. Used to be.

No, I'm not sexist, and yes, a woman could have taken him to task by surreptitiously taking his life. But it took a particular mindset to kill dispassionately, and most girls . . .

A feeling crawled over me like an intrusion of hungry cockroaches, and a thought I'd dismissed reemerged.

At the time, Brett's broken neck tweaked me because it was part of Mary's skillset, although I couldn't think of any reason she would be down that lonely lane. So I'd let it go. But what if she'd known what happened to Isabel?

I remembered smelling wet neoprene in the garage the night I'd *talked* with Officer Hartley but didn't think much of it – at least not enough to ask.

Did she wear the wetsuit to reduce her DNA profile, take a kayak to the Sutter House, and kill that boy for what he'd done to her friend? And what about Brett Vander? Had he been after her, after all?

A cold sweat beaded, and I kept my worry in check by taking deep breaths. As I found my calm, logic and reason were restored.

She wouldn't have had time to hustle from the hospital to the trail, paddle two-plus miles to kill one guy, another after returning to the launch, and get home before me, not knowing when that would be.

It was too risky a proposition, too improbable. Even I'd have trouble pulling it off. And besides, I would have known if she killed anybody. I'd have felt it.

The certainty of that belief vanished the moment Mary glanced at me from the kitchen table, and the longer we looked at each other, the harder it was to ignore the truth.

She'd done it. All of it.

A flashflood of emotion rushed toward me, the noise deafening as it approached, and I scrambled to find safety in the high ground of my mind. Her expression changed to one of trepidation as I left the deck for the enveloping darkness.

The first coherent thought didn't form until I came to the woods at the back of the property.

What did you think would happen?

I'd trained her to protect herself and others, honed her sense of justice, and encouraged her to do what had to be done when threatened or attacked. But I hadn't meant for her to go out and start killing.

It was too painful to think about the possible harm I'd done her by having me as a role model, and I tried to keep the recriminations to a minimum for the moment. There'd be plenty of time to castigate myself.

I always thought it a possibility she'd known what I'd been doing, but, if I were honest, it was more a probability. Still, it wasn't something I'd ever want her to be sure of.

What do I do? Not talk about what she did? Tell her to do as I say, not as I do, before she called me a hypocrite? I was nowhere near ready for that conversation.

As afraid as I was though, I couldn't help feeling a sense of pride in her accomplishment. She'd done something hard and made it look easy – no clues, no suspicions, no scrutiny.

That's my girl.

I wondered how she was coping. Did it keep her up at night or lay heavy on her mind? Planning someone's death was different than killing in self-defense, like Brett Vander.

That mother-f . . .

Had he acted alone or was his friend Bedford involved? If so, he would die. Period.

Sadness grabbed ahold of me. In trying to stand up against the butchers in the world, I'd inadvertently exposed Mary to risk and potential danger.

I'd failed her.

The taste of saltwater could have come from the bay when a gust of wind moved the moon across the water and made the palm fronds chatter, but I knew better and swiped at my face before Mary reached my side.

She looked through the trees with me, and after a while, took my arm and placed it around her shoulder.

I didn't ask, and she didn't tell as we watched the moonlight shimmer. When Watson barked from the deck, Mary leaned in and gave a long hug before heading back.

~

The girls talked Tasha into an impromptu sleepover, and I could hear them having fun in Mary's room as I sat in the dark and rocked with an ice-filled glass of moonshine a skydiving buddy had given me years ago.

I tried to confine some thoughts, like how Mary's life might be ruined because of me, while others I let run free.

Did Hale Bedford try to get back at me for killing his sister by coming after my daughter? Would he do that? How could I know for sure?

I could pay him a visit, but he'd call the police afterward because of the way I'd ask – guaranteed to garner the truth.

One of the girls squealed and the other giggled. I heard Tasha but not what she said. When the door opened, Mary's voice rose above the hullabaloo.

"Daaaad. Mom's swearing again."

Tasha chuckled and called them *damned brats*.

"See?" Mary shouted as the door pulled shut.

Laughter erupted from within, and I saw the reason for it as Tasha came toward me.

"Well aren't you a sight."

Her toes and fingers blazed in florescent splendor and her face was luminous. Literally. It was hard not to laugh when she sat on my lap.

"I know. Mary wanted to give me a spa treatment, but they gave me a redneck makeover instead. They really are a couple of little shits," she said.

I moved to avoid being poked in the eye by a hair-sprayed spike of torqued, twisted hair and ran my fingers along the nape of her neck.

"Isabel said I could tell you what happened, but if you don't mind, I'd rather sit and . . . Mmm, that feels good."

"Yes, it does. And no, I don't."

We rocked in quiet accord, the squeak of the chair the only sound besides the murmur of teenage voices.

"You never did give me an answer to my question."

"Didn't I?"

She found my lips and kissed me with the promise of a lifetime filled with similar moments. As my fingers tried to slip into her sticky hair, I knew we'd be together for as long as I didn't screw it up.

chapter twenty-seven

'Guess he liked it cause he put a ring on it.'

Before Jeri could respond to the text Tasha sent with a picture of her finger, another text followed.

'Thanks for your sage advice. I'm going with my heart like you suggested and then blame it on you if it goes to hell. Any idea who I could get to be my maid of honor? Maybe Marci or this woman I arrested the other day. She seems nice. Did I tell you about her?'

'Marci doesn't really like you much,' Jeri typed back, 'so she's iffy. As for your arrestee, I guess it depends on if she makes bail or not, right? In the meantime, I'll keep my eye out for someone who might be interested if you'd like. Would probably help if you threw in a few bucks.'

Jeri smiled when the phone rang. "Hello?"

"Would you do it for ten?"

"I'm sorry . . . Who is this?" They laughed and Tasha gave *thanks* to Jeri's *congratulations*.

"So, how did it go? Are you happy?"

"Too much so. And it went great. The proposal was sweet and funny and included all of us. Wish you had been there. You'd have had fun, maybe even scored a trinket."

Tasha filled her in, and Jeri felt left out.

"I'm sorry I missed it. Sounds like he did good. When are you tying the knot? Huh, funny expression, that. Like something you'd hear at a BDSM wedding."

"Gives being bound in holy matrimony a whole new meaning; that's for sure. And I've only gotten to the who and why of getting married, not the when and where part."

"Well, seeing how you two aren't really church-folk, maybe the beach could be the *where*? How about that sandbar island you spent the night on?"

"That's a great idea, Seven. It's intimate and private. I like it."

"As for the *when*, sooner rather than later, I think. Before you chicken-out. Or he gets cold feet."

"Oh, his feet aren't cold."

"I know, I know," Jeri said, chuckling. "There's nothing cold or little about him. I'd ask if there's anything else he isn't, but I'm afraid you'd tell me. Girls in love. At least you're not swooning."

"Yeah, but if I *did* faint, he'd hold me in his big, strong arms and give me butterfly kisses and tender caresses."

Tasha started laughing when Jeri said, "Oh, crap."

"I miss you, Seven."

"Me too, girlfriend. I'll get with you later and we'll talk about chiffon and flower arrangements."

"Uh, no. White bikinis and tequila shots, maybe, but no cookie-cutter ceremony for me. This wedding is going to be cool and casual. Like us."

"Y'all are surely that."

"Thanks, but I meant you and me – or is it me and you. You and I?"

Jeri was touched by Tasha's affection and appreciative of her humor to help ease a potentially emotional moment.

"Is it still I and thee for eternity, Lieutenant Yar?"

"That's affirmative my Borg friend. Resistance is futile."

Unspoken sentiment filled the empty silence.

"I have to get back to work, Seven. I'll let you know more when I do. Mary told me to say *Hey* to Aunt Jeri, and Dax says *Whazzup*."

"He may be cool," Jeri said grinning, "but he's neither hip nor hop enough to pull that off. Tell him to stick to words in his own lane. Like gooder and smartassitude. Although, that last one describes Mary to a T. Love that kid."

"Me too."

"Okay, then. Live long and prosper, Tash."

"May the force be with you, girlfriend."

"What the heck? You can't mix franchise tag lines."

~~

"What's that you got there?" Dominic asked when he sat next to Tasha's desk to drink his coffee.

"A pencil?"

"No. The sparkly thing on your finger."

"Oh that. It's just a little something from my fiancé."

"Really? What about that guitar player you've been dating? Boy, he must be bummed. I thought you liked him?"

"I do. That's why I'm going to keep on seeing him. Just don't tell my gonna be wife. She's a jealous lover."

Dominic managed to keep the coffee from spewing, but the hot beverage followed the path of least resistance. His eyes teared and he began to cough as the burning liquid dripped from his nose.

"Are you alright, Dom?"

He held up his hand to indicate he was and rode a coughing-fit bronco until it threw him off.

"Damn, Tash. That's some funny shit."

"Think I'm kidding? Said she'd *cut a bitch* if she ever caught me fooling around. I'm a little afraid of her."

The seriousness of her tone made him stop smiling and start wondering – until she burst out laughing.

"Now *that's* some funny shit. I had you going there."

"Not for a nanosecond," Dominic said. "But the picture you painted . . ."

"Okay."

". . . of you and another woman?"

"Alright, now."

"I'm going to need a minute to process that image."

He shut his eyes and pretended to visualize his partner and her make-believe girlfriend going at it.

"Mmmm. That's it. Right there. Oh yeah . . ."

"Detective?"

He opened his eyes and saw Tasha's grin juxtaposed with the captain's frown.

"Sir?"

"When you're done here, come to my office. And bring the Malcolm file with you."

"Well, that was embarrassing," Dom said after he left. "Why didn't you say something?"

"Good question. It was funnier not to? Besides, now you'll have another image to take the place of me and my Latin lesbian lover."

"Oh, so now she's Latin?" he said with a chortle and turned to leave.

"Don't forget the file, Dom."

"Right. Thanks."

After he left, she got up and filled a cup before making her way to Sam's desk, using a southern colloquialism to ask what's up, what's going on, or how they hanging?

"How 'bout it?"

"Not much doing. Things settled down after Pete and Dennis got killed, and I'm glad for that – the settling, not the killing. It kept people from getting hurt. Hell, the city might have burned to the ground."

"What do you think about Dennis coming forward like he did?"

"It was a hell of a thing. Of course, I'd have rather he exercised better judgement in the first place."

She nodded in agreement and brought up Troy Allison.

"I still don't know what he was thinking taking a midnight swim in shark infested waters. His blood-alcohol was high, but geez. Did he have a death wish?"

"I doubt it," Sam said. "More likely it was hubris. That boy had a lust for life, and a hunger for women."

"And girls?" Tasha asked.

"Well, he was only nineteen, so yes."

"What happened with the two who said he raped them?

"It was all too circumstantial and uncorroborated. Not enough evidence to make a case."

"Most rapes are, Sam. Uncorroborated."

"I know, but what made this kid's denial so credible was how many girls were just giving it to him. I stopped counting after seventeen."

"Wow. All from around here?" Tasha asked.

"Mostly, and no one said he'd forced or hurt them. Well, except from the sex itself. Apparently, he was big."

She nodded, recalling how Isabel had described him. "Did any of the girls say anything about feeling drugged?"

"Not that I recall. Why? What's this about, Tasha?"

She told him what happened to Isabel at her dorm, but not who she was, what the other boys did, or the video Troy made, preferring to keep that to herself for the time being. When she finished, Sam was as surprised as he was angry.

"That fucking son of a bitch," he said with disgust.

Tasha thought his outburst concise and accurate and couldn't have been said better.

"How come I didn't know? Or suspect something?"

"Sam, I don't know. The girl said Troy was kind, gentle, and respectful right up to the moment he wasn't."

"Yeah, but I'm trained to see through bullshit. Christ, he seemed like a completely different kind of kid. Makes me wonder whether or not I looked at him right."

"What do you mean?"

"Was I too quick to give him the benefit of the doubt based on all the girls who said they *weren't* raped? I didn't think so at the time, but now I'm not so sure."

"Well, it's something to think about, but don't be too hard on yourself. You're a good detective. Not as good as me, of course. Or Dominic, Winston, Rodriguez ... "

Tasha grinned as he tossed colored paperclips at her, eventually throwing the box itself.

"Would you mind if I talked to some of the girls, Sam? They may open up in a way they might not with a man."

"Go ahead. Just keep me in the loop, alright?"

"I will. Thanks." Tasha turned away then back again. "Did you happen to call Tallahassee, maybe speak to someone about other allegations?"

"Yes. The local PD said the university usually handled those kinds of things internally, so I ended up talking to a campus cop named Hutchins."

"See, Sam? You *are* a good Detective. What'd he say?"

"Nothing conclusive. Said a lot of girls saw athletes like Troy as nothing more than crotch candy and they would cry rape afterward to keep from looking skanky."

"Crotch candy? Hutchins sounds like an arrogant sexist creep with a penchant for baseless opinion – as opposed to my thoughtful condemnation of his character based solely on a run-on sentence by an okay detective."

"Okay? I was *good* a minute ago. What happened?"

"Just testing your detective-like reflexes. You did good. Maybe I should move you up in the rankings?" she said with a grin and left his desk for hers. "Thanks, Sam."

"You're welcome," he replied and then said, "Hold up. What do you mean detective *like*?"

Her expression left him no choice but to laugh.

~~

Dax had come along to cut lawns, and while she always appreciated his help. Mary knew there was more going on. He was worried about her. And she couldn't blame him.

She'd caught him glancing at her repeatedly, in addition to scrutinizing every vehicle that drove by, and Mary wished she could spare him the anxiety he must now feel.

On the one hand, he had to be concerned she'd been targeted by Brett Vander and what it might mean. But she would bet the farm, if she had one, that what frightened him most was what she'd done to Troy.

And what he thought it might have done to her.

Even though he would never broach the subject with Isabel in the house, Mary had half-expected him to wake her early and ask for a walk and talk before dawn. But he didn't.

Maybe he was afraid talking about it would somehow change things between them in a fundamental way? She didn't think that possible but would rather not find out if it could be avoided.

Maybe he plain doesn't know what to do?

Mary wasn't foolish enough to think Dax was perfect, but she thought him pretty darn close. She smiled, knowing kids believed their daddies knew everything and could do no wrong. But she was sixteen going on twenty-five and thought *hers* was the smartest – and right in most things.

If he needed to have the *Troy* conversation, she would willingly oblige. But until then, she would let him know all was well with her through humor and affection, like always. Because if she was okay with it, he would be also, in time.

Hopefully.

~~

A text from Tasha asking if I'd like to go for a ride was a welcome reprieve from the morning's work and worry. After hours of deliberation, I wasn't any closer to knowing what to say to Mary or even how I'd do that.

Troy had it coming, end of story. As did Brett. She hadn't done anything wrong, not by my standards, but she could have been hurt or killed. Maybe even caught.

Do I tell her that's it, no more? Or modify her training?

The girls began to wash the riding mower when I made my apologies for not pitching in.

"Tasha will be here in a few minutes to pick me up. I'm not sure where we're going, but I need a quick shower."

"Well, we can help you there," Mary said.

She sprayed me with the hose, and when I moved her way, Isabel tossed the bucket of soapy water.

"Oh, I'm sorry, Mr. Dax," she said but clearly wasn't. "Here, let me."

I stood still as she used the sponge to great effect while Mary laughed and rinsed me down afterward.

"You missed a spot," she said and pointed, but Isabel retreated, not wanting to get gotten.

I smiled and thanked them with a look that promised to return the favor when they least expected it.

Their snickers lifted my spirits and allayed my earlier apprehension. When I turned toward the house they turned their attention to Watson, who ran past me and through the front door as soon as it opened.

~

"We need to get them back," Tasha said, a grin forming.

"Why?" I asked but already knew the answer.

"For my redneck makeover and your redneck shower. I can't tell anymore if the instigator is Mary or Isabel, but I know who's to blame."

She looked at me with raised brows and a cocked head that left no doubt who the culprit was.

"What did *I* do?"

"Encourage those girls to like themselves, live life to the fullest, and to have all the fun they can along the way. Is it any wonder they behave as they do?"

Her smile was full of affection, for them and for me. "Maybe I should arrest you for contributing to the reckless well-being of a minor?"

We turned onto Cape San Blas Road and the crosswind stirred up the pleasant aroma emanating from the backseat.

"Mmm. Is that Piggly Wiggly chicken I'm smelling?"

"I thought we'd have a little picnic first," she said and pulled into the entryway by the volunteer firehouse that led to the beach along the Gulf of Mexico.

"First?"

She angled the truck so the breeze would flow freely through the open windows, an attempt to keep them cool while they ate their lunch and watched the blue-green water without having to use the air-conditioner.

"Yes. Then I'll tell you what Isabel told me last night," she said and reached in the back for the plastic yellow bag.

My mouth watered in anticipation as she handed me a salad spork and a Styrofoam container.

"A couple of breasts. I know how much you like them."

I took the sparkle in her eyes the way she intended; I did like them – hers and the Pig's.

"There's a cooler on the floor behind my seat with cans of cold beer on ice. Would you get me one, please?" she said.

I reached back and grabbed two A&W's, popped the tab for her as any gentleman would and handed it over.

"If you didn't already have me, I'd think I was being courted, what with the good view, good food, good drink, and your, as always, good-lookingness. You know, it just occurred to me that you must get hit on a lot."

Tasha tried not to laugh with a mouthful of macaroni salad but had to settle for an uncontainable chuckle.

"It just now did?"

"Is that going to be an ongoing problem?"

"Not for me. You?"

Her voice resounded with playful mischief as I picked a piece of pickled pepper from her chin.

"I can't hardly hold that against them, Tash. I mean, look atchu? But so long as I get to hold *you* against *me*, I'm all kinds of okay."

Tasha found his funny routine devastatingly endearing and wondered if she could ever love him more. They watched the waves roll in one after the other and listened to the rhythmic slap of water on the shore. After the last bite of Piggly's finest fare, she told him what all had happened to Isabel. His eyes narrowed when she mentioned the video they'd made and sent.

"I know. Makes you want to kill them, doesn't it?"

She may have meant it as a figure of speech, but I did. I'll bet Mary did, too.

"The problem will be proving she was drugged and unable to consent," Tasha said with trepidation.

"You don't think she was?"

"No, I do. She doesn't strike me as someone who'd choose to be passed around like that. And the desolation in her eyes when she talked about it was genuine, I'm sure. But the girl in the video seems willing. I'm afraid the state's attorney will need more to support Isabel's allegations."

"Allegations?" I said.

"Yeah, sorry about that. It's just cop-speak."

"How can you find *more*?"

"Legwork," she said and shook her empty can.

I replaced it with a colder, fuller one and received a smile with her thanks.

"After I drop you off, I'm going to stop by Sacred Heart Hospital, see if anything other than her mother's sleeping pills turned up on the toxicology report the night Isabel tried to kill herself. Then we have to identify, interview, and investigate the boys on the video. She only knew the names of two of them. Isn't that sad?"

I nodded and looked out the side-window so Tasha couldn't see my anger. Those damned boys needed to . . .

"That was a nice thing you did yesterday, by the way – asking her to be your back-up daughter. I think it meant something to her."

"To me, too," I said, leaving those boys be. For now. "She's got a good heart. And an appreciation of my humor. Unlike some others."

Tasha chuckled, like I knew she would.

"Mary and I laugh at you all the time, Dax. *All* the time. You're a funny ha-ha, ho-ho, hee-hee kind of guy."

The song in my head best described my feelings for her. Not Brick House, although she was indeed *mighty-mighty*. No, it was a tune by the Stylistics about feeling brand new.

"I like you, girl."

"I know."

~~

Mary was playing her Martin and singing a song she'd written when I walked through the door, encouraging her to continue by rolling my fingers and lifting the Epiphone from its stand to accompany her.

The ballad had an inspirational chorus with haunting underpinnings, and the lyrics were particularly poignant. She nodded as I harmonized every now and then, only a word or two where it felt right, and after she finished, we let the quiet have its way until her eyes opened.

"That was beautiful, Mare. Really. What do you call it?"

"Why?"

"So when I ask you to play it sometime, I won't have to say, 'You know, that song you played that day.'"

"Why?"

A single tear glistened from the corner of her eye.

"Honey, what's wrong?"

"Nothing. It's Why?"

"What's why?" I asked, concerned and confused.

"It's just Why?" she said and grinned. "No What."

"Oh, I get it. *Why?* is the name of the song."

"That's what I said," she said.

"Yes, you did. Sorry." I waited for her tear to fall, but it held its position. "Your song is both sad and encouraging. Is it about Isabel?"

"It's inspired by her experience and some of mine," she said, dabbing the tear with a knuckle. "You're in there, too. In the major chords that rise from the minor."

The significance of her meaning wasn't lost on me. She saw me as a positive influence in her life, one that lifted her out of darkness and would forever keep her in the light. At least, that's the spin I put on it.

"Where's Isabel?" I said.

"She went to her house for a visit."

"What about Frank? Should we be concerned?"

Mary shook her head and placed the guitar in its stand. "She said that was done with."

"And Watson?"

"I asked him to go with her."

"Just in case?" I asked, smiling.

"That's affirmative."

"You care about her quite a bit."

"She's alright," Mary said, and added with a grin, "For a blind-sided, saddled with, side-sister."

As I smiled back, I considered asking about what she'd done despite my fear of what would happen if I did. Maybe she needed to tell me, to unload and get it off her . . .

"I like what you did with my song," Mary said, taking the Martin from the guitar stand. "Your judicious harmony added a plaintive quality I hadn't imagined when I wrote it. Want to play it again, Sam?"

Whether she interrupted my thoughts fortuitously or intentionally, my courage faltered. Hell, maybe she wasn't any more ready to have that discussion than I was.

Are you, sweetie?

One and a half seconds later, she cocked her head to acknowledge she received my telepathic inquiry, or to ask if I was going to play the song with her. I'm not sure which.

The twinkle in her eye indicated the former.

chapter twenty-eight

"It's pretty thin, Tash," Dominic said and entered some information into the search engine. When she lifted her brow along with the toxicology results, he nodded and said, "Yes, some so-called recreational drugs were found in her system, but how they got there is the rub, as the Bard put it. Is she a party girl?"

Tasha was more surprised he quoted Shakespeare than upset he'd questioned Isabel's sexual character. It was his job to be objective. Hers, too. A professional detachment kept one from reaching an emotional conclusion.

"She says no, and for what it's worth, I believe her. But we can't really know until we look into it, can we? I'll talk to her tonight."

"Well that was easy enough," he said and turned the laptop so she could see. An internet search using the names Tasha was given led to a webpage with biographies and pictures of fraternity members, past and present. They identified the boys on Isabel's video and Dominic pointed to the bio of one of them.

"See that? He's majoring in Chemistry and has a 4.3 GPA. He's not just getting straight A's, he's getting A-pluses."

"Smart kid," Tasha said.

"Maybe too damned smart. Makes you wonder."

"What?"

"He could be manufacturing what they're using. Then they wouldn't have to expose themselves by getting drugs on the street. Hell, maybe he designs his own."

"What do you mean?"

"Some recreational drugs have date-rape qualities, each with a specific advantage and disadvantage – from a rapist's point of view. And it's the disadvantages, passing out or permanent memory loss of the event, that make the attacker's claim of consent suspicious."

"Go on," Tasha said, anticipating where he was heading.

"What if a drug could be designed that combined things you'd want – euphoria, hallucination, short-term amnesia, lowered inhibition, heightened arousal – and eliminated the tell-tale signs of a non-consenting crime?"

"That would be a nightmare. Is that even possible?"

Dominic shrugged.

"Don't know. But the girl in that video not only didn't resist; she didn't protest. If you know what I mean."

"Yeah, I know it looks bad. But she's innocent until proven otherwise."

"And those boys?"

"The same," she said, though not feeling much for them. "Let's run their names for priors."

As they read the results, the door to their boss' office opened and he walked out with the chief who stared at them a few seconds before leaving. Captain Doyle waived them in by cocking his head.

"Well, you were right," he said after the door closed. "Pete was his kid."

"He copped to it, just like that?" Dominic asked.

"Not at first but eventually. He was very candid."

"So do we arrest him?" Tasha said.

"I'd like to hold off on that. The public needs time to recover from the death of that boy and something like this could set them off, maybe blow the lid off the city."

"But he put lives at risk to protect a murdering racist. Not to mention tarnishing your reputation," Tasha said.

"He didn't do it for Pete. Didn't even know he was his father until the mother told him the night of the shooting. She left town without an explanation soon after their high-school graduation, and he's been heartbroken ever since. Apparently, she was the love of his life, and when she called, sobbing hysterically, he was *overcome with emotion*, as he put it. According to him, he didn't even think about erasing those cards until he saw me heading to the bathroom. Said he must have temporarily lost his mind in his anguish to help her."

"And you believe that shit?" Dominic said.

"I think so, Dom. He was very demonstrative," Doyle said, unwilling to tell them how the chief had cried openly when expressing his feelings for her.

"But Captain, his actions could have hurt a lot of people, not the least of which is you," Tasha said. "If Dennis hadn't come forward with a confession, if Pete hadn't turned up dead, then police and protesters alike would have suffered, maybe even been killed. Are we just going to let that slide?"

"I'm proposing we set it aside, for now. What the chief did was wrong, and if I thought it malicious, we wouldn't be having this discussion. Yes, things could have happened, terrible things. But they didn't, thank God. And because they didn't, perhaps a measure of compassion could be given here. After all, to err is human."

Dominic shook his head, not at all happy about letting the chief get away with trying to incriminate his captain. He would rather have beaten the crap out of him and arrested his ass in front of the whole department.

He looked at Tasha and saw she was of a similar mind. But she was more inclined to make lemonade out of lemons, a characteristic that both vexed him and bolstered his admiration for her. So when she gave a shrug, he returned it. If Pap and Tash thought it worthwhile, he'd go along.

"Alright. We just let bygones be bygones then?"

"Not quite, Dom. The Chief is going to take some accrued vacation time, a leave of absence for introspection. When he returns, we'll make a hard decision about whether he stays or goes."

"And what if he recants and tries to make trouble?"

"I had him sign a statement. It might interest you to know he seemed relieved to give it and didn't equivocate in the least. I think his apology is sincere."

The room fell silent, each coming to terms with what the chief had done and what might happen as a result.

Afterward, Tasha told the captain about Isabel. When finished, he asked if the girl claimed they drugged her.

"No. She'd never done anything like that before. But after trying to kill herself, she thought they must have."

"What *had* she done before?"

Tasha's face grew warm as her anger flared, but she kept her composure and answered him.

"We're in the preliminary stages of our investigation, but we'll know more as we go forward. Any chance we could get search warrants?"

"Have you run them through the system?" Doyle asked.

She nodded, but shook her head when he said, "And?"

"Then, no. Not yet. But you knew that already."

"Yes, sir."

"Don't look so glum, Tasha. I have every confidence you'll find what you need to nail those bastards," he said and handed her the yearbook she brought in two days ago. "Is there anything else, Detectives?"

They said no and turned to leave.

"Tasha, wait. You asked me about chess the other day. Do you play?"

"I've dabbled."

"How about a game, sometime? Might be fun."

The glint in his eye stirred her competitiveness and she accepted his implied challenge by making the first move.

"e4."

She'd hoped to unnerve him by playing without board or pieces, but he just smiled and replied, "c5."

"Knight to f3."

Dominic shook his head, preferring checkers to chess, and left the room.

"d6," Doyle said as he sat on the corner of his desk.

"d4."

"Pawn takes pawn."

"Knight takes pawn."

"Knight to f6."

"Knight to c3," Tasha said, curious about his capability. Not many people could play a game of chess in their head, and, if not for her eidetic memory, she probably couldn't either. After preparing to fianchetto his bishop by playing g6, one of the sharpest lines in the Sicilian Defense known as the Dragon Variation, she grinned.

"You're right, Captain. This is fun."

~

On the way to see Dax and Mary after work, a smile crossed her lips as she recalled the captain's utterance.

"Oops."

Based on his play up to that point, she knew his blunder wasn't tactical but forgetful as the piece he moved on the imaginary board was needed where it was to guard a rook. She'd been impressed with how far he'd gone in the game without making a mistake, even more so when he rejected her offer to take back his move.

"That's not how I roll. Consider my King toppled. Good game, Tasha. Can't wait for the rematch."

She was pleased with the win but now realized some of the satisfaction of beating him stemmed from irritation, first with Dom and then the captain. It was unreasonable, she knew, even unfair. She respected them, and their questions and comments about Isabel were appropriate. But why did there seem to be a double-standard in the way a woman's sexual history was perceived and interpreted?

Maybe because there was.

If a man has casual sex long enough, he's called a stud. His exploits are considered adventures and told with pride to peers who applaud and admire his manly conquests.

He is elevated.

By contrast, a woman is put down, scorned, dismissed. Her character is impugned, and her activity derided.

She's called a whore.

How is that fair? Or right?

Tasha worried how Isabel would hold up once her story became known. Until evidence of non-consensual drug use could be established or other young women came forward with allegations to support her own, Isabel's name would probably be dragged through the mud.

As she thought about the struggle that lay ahead, she unknowingly turned right instead of going straight, and a few miles later found herself driving up the sandy driveway to the Sutter House. Two cars were parked, one behind the other, and she positioned her truck so as not to get boxed in if another vehicle should arrive.

Tasha glanced in the cars as she walked by out of habit and didn't see anything helpful like drugs on the dashboard or a girl passed out in the backseat. On the way up the porch, she thought of a reason to be there that wouldn't tip her hand about the upcoming investigation – one that might get her inside the house, maybe even catch them doing the very thing they were accused of.

Wouldn't that be nice?

A young man opened the door after the third knock, and the unmistakable odor of cannabis assailed her senses. But it was the way he looked her up and down that gave her pause. He was brazen in his assessment, and she could almost feel his eyes unbuttoning her blouse.

"Well, looky here," he said. "Aren't you as fine as wine? Come on in. What's your name, darlin'?"

Tasha did a quick assessment of her own.

He was about six-foot tall and looked athletic. Though not one of the boys in Isabel's video, it wasn't much of a stretch to think he might be in someone else's. While she didn't find his interest in her at all flattering, it did present an opportunity to *catch more flies.*

"My name is Detective Williams," she said, expecting him to rescind his offer to come inside. Before he did, she extended her hand and gave him a smile. "And you are?"

She upped the wattage of her *sparkle* as Dax said she had the first time they met, thereby entrapping him. If the boy had any reservations, they must have been dismissed because he took her hand and pulled her through the door.

"You can call me Jimmy."

Tasha let him hold onto her hand a few seconds longer than he should have before retrieving it from his grasp. She could smell the beer on his breath.

"Thank you, Jimmy. This won't take long. I'd like to ask you some questions, if that's alright."

For the first time, Tasha saw hesitation in his eyes.

"What about?"

"Troy Allison. Did you know him?"

Sure," he said, the cloud of concern dissipating. "He was a good friend. Hey, would you like something to drink?"

"No thanks. Can you tell me . . ."

"You sure? It's no problem?"

"Maybe later. I'm very sorry about your friend. It must be tough. I'm curious why he went swimming that night. Is that something he'd ever done before?"

"Sure."

"Seems, I don't know, reckless. What with the sharks."

"Yeah, I wouldn't do that shit, for sure. But he wasn't afraid of much. He was a King Kong kind of guy," Jimmy said and gave a kind of wink.

The word lascivious lept to mind, but Tasha grinned to keep him talking. After a few more innocuous questions to gain his confidence, her inquiries began in earnest.

"So Troy was quite the ladies-man, huh?"

"You know it. All he had to do was snap his fingers and they got in line to spread 'em."

It amazed her how crass he was, and, while difficult to put up with, it did hold out the possibility of some truth spilling from his boorish mouth.

"Do you know if Troy ever hurt any of the girls?"

"You mean other than *effing* their brains out?"

"Yes. Other than that."

Tasha marveled at his behavior, hoping it was alcohol induced but surmising it probably wasn't. She thought it funny, no, quirky, that he talked about girls spreading them but wouldn't say the F-word.

Maybe his mother raised him not to use that kind of language in front of a lady? But given the way he'd been eye-balling her, she doubted he thought of her as one.

Jimmy shook his head. "Those girls were just lying – to their parents, to the police, and mostly to themselves. Because they wanted it."

The girls he referred to were the ones who came to the station months ago to make an allegation of rape, and she pretended to understand how 'bitches be crazy sometimes' by nodding in agreement.

"What about his girlfriend? Is she lying too?"

"Girlfriend? Hey, how about that something to drink? A soda, maybe? Or something stronger?" he said with a leer.

Tasha almost laughed, fascinated by his hitting on her. She was almost old enough to be his mother. Nearly almost. Alright, there was no *almost* about it.

"Just a glass of ice water will be fine, Jimmy."

She looked around after he left and wondered if they were alone in the house. When he returned, she thought of asking but took a long drink from the glass he handed her.

"Hmm, that hit the spot. Thanks."

"You're welcome, uh . . . What's your first name?"

"Detective," she said and grinned to let him know they were still friends. "Now, Troy's girlfriend?"

"Troy didn't have a girlfriend."

"You sure?" Tasha asked. "She'd been seeing him for about a month or so and thought he was a good guy. Then he raped her in her dorm room. Know anything about that?"

"No, I don't. Why would he do that when he can get . . . could get it for free? Girls threw it at him all the time."

"She doesn't seem like the type to *throw it*. Or give it away to just anyone. Her name is Isabel Chambers. Do you know her, Jimmy?"

"I've known too many girls to remember their names, Miss Detective. But I don't think I'll ever forget yours."

Tasha found his smile disarming and thought his inability to keep his eyes off of her amusing, if a tad creepy.

"What about faces?" she asked and handed her phone over when she found a picture of Isabel.

"Yeah, I've seen her hanging with Troy," he said, giving the phone back. "She's been with other guys, too."

"What do you mean?"

"Since you've shown me yours, I'll show you mine." Jimmy stood and slid a hand into his front pocket, drawing attention to himself by taking his time to pull it out. After a few seconds of scrolling, he sat down beside her and said, "Looks like she's giving it away to me."

Tasha expected to see the video she'd been given but instead saw one of Isabel making out with a different boy on another bed. She didn't resist, protest, or appear to be drugged, and a twinge of doubt emerged.

As the boy fondled her naked breasts, someone banged on the door shouting Isabel's name.

'Christ, Jimmy. Take care of that,' the boy said, and the picture pointed at the door.

"Is he talking to you?" Tasha asked and Jimmy nodded.

A girl walked in, yanked the boy off Isabel by his hair, and escorted him out of the room. When the video ended, Tasha asked if he knew who the girl was.

"She's that tease from the news who did her dad."

Tasha cringed hearing Mary described that way but kept it together and asked if he had any videos of her.

"No, nobody does. But she's a primo TILF."

His crude objectification of girls in general, and Mary in particular, eradicated whatever charm she thought he had going for him up till then. He was a pig, plain and simple, but one that might inadvertently squeal on his friends out of arrogance and sheer stupidity. Just as she was about to hand him his phone, she glanced at it.

Tens upon tens of thumbnailed videos stared back at her and continued to add up as she scrolled and scrolled. She was holding a veritable treasure trove of potential victims, assailants, and witnesses in the palm of her hand – and couldn't think of a single legal reason to hang on to it. And then it came to her.

Tasha experienced an out of body incredulity when he smelled her hair, but the oddest sensation came from the expulsion of his breath on her neck. Her skin felt singed and crackled with electricity.

What the hell was that?

"Jimmy, we have a problem here," she said, standing up.

"And what would that be, Detective?" Jimmy's smile reflected his impure thoughts.

"I didn't hear Isabel give her consent."

"What are you talking about? She was all over Jason. You saw her."

"Well, he was all over her. Not the other way around. But I meant you needed permission to record them. I didn't hear you ask for it or her give it."

"You're kidding me, right? It was an effing party, man. Everybody was shooting everybody."

"As long as you are recording someplace a reasonable expectation of *privacy* doesn't exist, it's all good. To a point. But this was shot in a bedroom – where it does. I'm afraid I'm going to have to place you under arrest."

Tasha stepped back to give him room to rise and pulled the handcuffs from its pouch.

"Aw, hell no. Give me back my phone."

He stood and stepped forward but stopped when her hand fell to her hip. In all the time he'd been feeling her up with his eyes, he hadn't once noticed the gun.

"Come on, Jimmy. Be nice. Don't make me shoot you."

"But . . ."

"Turn around and put your hands behind your back."

After a minute of pissing and moaning, he reluctantly complied. When the cuffs clicked into place, Tasha patted him down for weapons, taking a little too much pleasure in telling him to *spread 'em*. A giggle escaped her lips, which was way out of character. Not to mention unprofessional.

The foggy feeling she felt after Jimmy first sniffed at her became more pronounced, and she reached for the glass of water he'd given her to quench an overwhelming thirst. Only after a long swallow did the thought occur.

Geez Louise, he couldn't be that stupid. Could he?

Could she?

chapter twenty-nine

James Stanton, aka Jimmy, had indeed been that stupid. He spiked Tasha's water with a synthetic drug in the hopes of 'bagging' a much older woman so he could check that off a list of sexual endeavors many of his fraternity brothers had already completed – two having done it twice. Troy held the record at four.

His lawyer claimed Jimmy's impaired judgment due to alcohol and other substances made his intent unknowable and therefore unprovable.

The state's attorney, however, dismissed his argument as bullshit, said she liked her chances in court, and gave him a one-time only offer. In exchange for dropping the more serious charge of assaulting a police officer with intent to do grievous injury, his client would plead guilty to the lesser felony of illegally recording a sex act for the purpose of distribution, as well as cooperate fully in the investigation and prosecution of individuals involved in any form of rape, drug-induced or otherwise.

Jimmy took the deal, and, in the end, might have got the better of it.

Although there was plenty of sexual activity on the confiscated phone videos, determining consent, or its lack, proved difficult. Any drugs that might have been in the body were long gone, and search warrants only turned up those Jimmy used on Tasha. Nothing was found at the fraternity house in Tallahassee.

All of the girls interviewed over the next couple weeks either drank before, had sex before, or took drugs before, some having done all three.

Most were afraid to be seen doing *those things* by their parents and almost all refused to press charges, not wanting to be held up to public scrutiny and ridicule.

Unfortunately, the prosecutor agreed it would be an uphill *he said-she said* battle for many of them. And even if Jimmy testified against a particular boy as an assailant, without more compelling evidence, his unsavory character would create plenty of reasonable doubt.

She decided to start with the boys who'd raped Isabel. They'd been identified in eight other related videos, and she felt confident a jury would see a pattern of abuse that could only be biochemically coerced. After all, how many girls really wanted that kind of attention?

It seemed like a slam-dunk when the *deal* was made but bringing those boys to justice wouldn't be easy.

In fact, it was much harder than it should have been.

~~

The day after receiving her driver's license, Mary sat behind the steering wheel with Isabel in the passenger seat, Watson and I behind them. She'd driven me from Panama City once, but this was the first time she'd done so legally.

It was also the first time she'd done it as my daughter.

As I half-listened to Isabel talking, I saw a smile in the rearview when Mary glanced at me. It mirrored the one I'd been wearing since the judge made it official. Yes, I'd thought of her that way for a long time, but there was something about having it *decreed* that lifted the corners of my mouth into what seemed like their new digs.

It was hard to believe she was mine all mine all mine!

"How you doing back there?"

"I'm good," I said more nonchalantly than I actually felt. "You?"

"Couldn't be any gooder," Mary said.

She beamed at me reflectively, and I didn't have to be a mind-reader to know her happiness matched my own.

I wished Tasha could have shared it, but we'd celebrate tonight when she returned from Tallahassee after arresting the *fuckers* who'd drugged and violated Isabel.

While the girls chitchatted, I became agitated thinking about the boy who'd slipped something into Tasha's water. In my mind's eye, I'd already tightened the noose around his neck, but, before I could kick the chair out from under him, Isabel said something that made me stop.

"... can't wait till we're roommates. It'll be so much fun! Maybe we can take some classes together?"

"Uh, wait," I said. "What am I hearing?"

"Now, Belle, I ..." Mary said and glanced in the mirror. "Dax, we've just been talking about it. Nothing is decided."

"Hmm."

"Really. Even if I did go, it wouldn't be this semester."

"Uh-huh."

"That's right, Mr. Dax," Isabel spoke up. "Mary said she couldn't leave just yet, at least not until she got you and Miss Tasha settled in as newlyweds. But after that ..."

It sounded like my not quite an hour-old daughter had already made plans to strike out on her own after she tucked her new mom and dad away in a retirement home.

I grinned at Mary who twinkled back a *gotta love her* look as Isabel went on and on about how cool things were going to be. It was easy to understand her excitement in their living together and sharing their lives. Believe me, I knew how much fun Mary could be.

But I was nowhere near ready to let her go.

chapter thirty

"You know, he never really makes that much noise, but it sure seems quieter."

Mary nodded and stuffed a few things in her backpack.

"I thought I'd be okay with his being gone, after all it's only for a week. But the house feels so empty."

"That's it. It's not quieter but emptier. You can almost hear an echo. 'Here, boy, b*oy*, *boy*.'"

She grinned.

"How 'bout a snack, sn*ack*, *snack*."

We listened quietly, almost expecting Watson to come down the hallway to her room.

"I wonder if he misses us, too?" I asked.

"Sure. But Isabel needed him to help settle back into the school thing. They've become really good friends."

"Not worried she's going to steal your dog, are you?"

"No, and I don't mind sharing my family with her. She's a good kid and deserves better than what she's had."

"Kid? Isn't she almost a year older than you?"

Mary gave me an *Oh, Dax* eye roll and shook her head.

"Chronologically, maybe, but she's just a youngster."

"And you are?"

"An oldster, I'm afraid. Kind of like you," she said, "but faster and in much better shape."

With unexpected quickness, she pushed me on the bed, jumped on my back, and made a full-nelson in half a second.

"So, you went and got yourself a back-up daughter. Contingency planning, were you?"

When I chuckled, she applied a smidgeon of pressure at the base of my neck.

"My back."

"What about it?"

"You're a little high, hon."

"What?"

In a flash a few milliseconds slower than hers, I swung my legs up and we tilted forward. When the tipping point was reached, I threw my legs down and let the pendulum of us swing me to my feet.

"Watch your head," I said and swiftly stepped back and hit the wall, not hard enough to hurt too much but enough to break her grip. It was not altogether unsatisfying to hear her say *oomph*.

"Are you okay?"

"Yup," she said. "But I'm flabbergasted. Where did that come from? I had you good."

"You did and you didn't," I said and looked her over to make sure nothing was bent or broken.

"It had to do with specific conditions in relation to your attack, which was nicely executed by the way. If you'd taken me down on a flat surface, my counterattack wouldn't have been successful. But the bed gave me an opportunity to use it as a fulcrum, one you might have negated if your weight was more evenly distributed."

Mary's eyes shined with enthusiasm. As much as she liked to use her skills to *get me* from time to time, she liked learning how to hone those skills even more. She was the most exceptional person I knew, young, old, or in between. Which reminded me . . .

"Flabbergasted? Maybe you're an oldster after all. I don't think you got that from me."

"Not from you, but because of you," she said and picked the backpack off the floor. "I came across it when I couldn't find *fidgetarian* in the dictionary.

"You sure it wasn't there? Should be after *fibologist*. Maybe you could look for that, as well?"

"I'm looking at one right now."

She grinned and twinkled or twinkled and grinned. Either way, she did cute proud.

"When are you heading over to Tash's?" I asked.

"Anytime now."

"You driving over wearing that?"

"Yup."

My forehead furrowed of its own accord as I regarded her short flannel bottoms and bright yellow tank top.

"I don't know, Mare. It's a little too casual."

"It's a sleepover. And when attending any elegant affair, proper attire is required. See, I'm wearing my pearls."

She showed off her earrings by fake smiling and using her hand to display them like a game show model

"Could you maybe wear a jacket at least, or better yet some clothes until you get there?"

"I thought it might feel fun to drive around in PJs. You know, kind of like sneaking around in your underwear."

"Yeah, but . . . Wait. What? No."

She laughed at me, but I wasn't sure why. Maybe my expression had set her off, or my befuddlement in general, but it was still light outside and there was no way I'd let . . .

"Don't worry, Dax. I'll wait for the sun to set first."

While Mary could have read my mind, her knowing my thoughts probably had more to do with my stammering. She called me sweet, kissed my cheek, and punched my arm.

"Don't you have a long way to go and a short time to get there? The blues aren't going to play themselves; you know. Of course, if the audience wants to hear the good stuff, they could just put a quarter in the jukebox."

Her jibe put a smile on my face, and I looked at the time.

"Shit, you're right. I gotta be gettin' gone. See you tomorrow, hon. Like you."

"Like you back."

Just before I pulled out of the garage, she asked me to roll down the window with a gesture.

"What, miss me already? I've only gone ten feet."

"I'm curious. If little girls get soaped for swearing, and big girls get spanked – what do big *boys* get?"

That kid. She wasn't just the apple of my eye; she was the whole damned tree.

As I drove down the drive, I thought about how much more fun it would be to join their pajama party instead of heading up to Georgia to play for one night. But I'd wanted to try out a few new songs, and the club manager helped scratch that itch by offering to pay me double and telling me how great I was. I didn't believe him, but my ego told me not to harsh its mellow. So I took the gig.

After turning left at the mailbox toward St. Vincent and beyond, I didn't make it a quarter mile before pulling into an opening between some trees. A car sitting in a makeshift driveway for a house that had yet to be built caught my eye and pricked rather than piqued my curiosity.

Wasn't that car on Indian Pass Road yesterday when I'd interrupted Mary's mowing with some lunch from the Pig?

It wasn't so unusual to see it again as it was suspect. Why was it so close to my house? Had it been stalking her?

I reached for the binoculars knowing I might be a little paranoid. But as that old saying went, even if I was, it didn't mean they weren't out to get me.

After finding a line of sight through the trees, a man smoking a cigarette came into view. He looked peaceful, without a care in the world, and the hairs on my neck stood as I watched him blow smoke and flick ashes through a slit of opened window.

He had the appearance of a person waiting but never consulted a watch, phone, or dashboard clock. Instead he peered through the windshield and occasionally glanced in the rearview mirror at the soon to be setting sun.

I can't explain how I knew, but I did. Maybe because of my own experience of waiting in similar situations.

After sliding between the van's buckets seats, I selected the right tools for the job, donned a DNA neutral jumpsuit, and flipped a switch that disabled the interior lights before opening the door. When my feet hit the ground, I hurried through the foliage and crawled the last hundred yards to within forty feet of his vehicle.

I brushed my face of sweat and mosquitoes, wishing I could've applied a bit of bug-spray but knowing the smell might have been detected. The gun in my hand held steady at the driver's door, and I turned to watch the sun as the last of its light reflected off the rear bumper of his car.

A bright-green flare winked at me as it slipped below the horizon, and I smiled in disbelief.

Well, what do you know?

I'd watched decades of sunsets looking for that flash, and the fact I'd seen it while lying on the ground in the woods with a snake crawling across my leg didn't diminish the wonder of it. Perhaps my perspective had needed some alteration in order to behold that fleeting phenomenon?

Looking for flash in all the wrong places hummed in my head as I waited for the man to move or the sky to darken.

The critter chatter paused when the engine stopped, then resumed. While he'd been enjoying the comforts of air-conditioning, I'd been sweltering in high-humidity and was more than ready to get on with it. Whatever *it* was.

Maybe this had all been an over-reaction to a suspicion run amok? If that were true, I pitied the boys who'd try to date Mary. They didn't stand a chance.

The porchlight from my house became brighter as the night set in. I was only a few minutes from confronting him when he stepped out of the car. It didn't bode well that the dome light was out. He reached inside and brought out a gun of his own with a suppressor attached, just like mine.

When Mary's voice carried on the breeze, we both looked over and listened to her sing a few bars of Christina Aguilera's *Beautiful.*

"She's pretty good, isn't she?"

The man didn't jump or jerk but said *yes* and turned toward me ever so slightly.

"Don't move."

"Mister, I don't . . ."

He must have needed to know for sure cause he moved. A whispered bullet grazed his ear and stopped him cold.

"You going to answer my questions?"

"Sure."

His composure was that of a professional which made him easier to deal with. And more dangerous.

"By yourself?"

"Yes."

"Who sent you?"

"Hale Bedford."

"What's the job?"

"Kill Dax, daughter, and detective. Not necessarily in that order."

I appreciated his humor. And his candor. He was cooperating to buy time, waiting for an opportunity to strike but not willing to risk his life by lying.

Mary drove from the house up the driveway with the headlights on and the radio blaring on her way to Tasha's.

"What about the dog?" I asked out of curiosity.

"Him too. But I wouldn't have. Not unless I had to. Fuck Bedford."

"I'm with you. Fuck him. Set the gun on the roof, put your hands in the air, and get down on your knees."

He hesitated but did as instructed as I got up, walked over, and shut his door.

"Keep your hands above your head and lie face down." When he wavered, I pressed the gun to the base of his skull. "Now."

We were on the ground before Mary could see us, and I asked him a work-related question.

"Is that your personal car or a rental?"

~~

Jeri turned the key and yawned, exhausted beyond what she normally felt this time of night. Despite bringing work home with her, all she wanted to do was take a shower, relax with a glass of wine, and go to bed.

The beep of the alarm was particularly grating tonight, and she told it to shut up while entering the security code. It obeyed after pressing enter, and she wished a few other problems could be as easily solved.

Like Dimitri Anatovich.

In addition to his being a pedophilic scumbag and a procurer of children for other despicable degenerates, she was convinced he killed the kids who caused trouble, tried to escape, failed to satisfy, or got too old.

Her frustration began to spin like a playground merry-go-round, and she jumped off before the centrifugal force threw her into a tizzy.

I'm going to get that murdering son of a bitch.

But right now, she needed to undress and unwind. The shower soothed, and her thoughts turned toward Tasha. She would be a married woman soon, and Jeri was glad one of them was going to give it a try. She hadn't given up on becoming one herself, but how would that come about? Her days, and too many nights, were taken up by work – and thinking about work. Where would she ever find someone? Or the time?

Perhaps an *occasional* husband would work best? Someone whose life was as busy as hers or lived far enough away to keep him from wanting more than she had to give.

Jeri grinned and turned off the shower. Maybe she and Tasha could work out a time-share plan with Dax? They could be sister-wives.

She toweled herself dry, threw on a Georgia Bulldog T-shirt, and left her bedroom to pour a glass of wine. When she entered the living room, one was sitting on the stand next to her cozy-chair.

"Have a seat, Miss Ryan."

The hairs on her arm raised, and she stepped toward the desk where a gun sat in a drawer for quick access.

"It's not there. Neither is the one in your bedroom nightstand, the kitchen pantry, under the couch cushion, or your purse on the dining room table. Seems like an awful lot of firepower for such a respectable neighborhood."

"The neighborhood is fine. The rats are the problem."

She walked over to the chair and sat down, reaching to adjust the skewed lampshade meant to shine its light on her.

"Leave it. Unless you want to see me."

"Sounds like you're not going to kill me right away," she said and took the wine from the stand.

"Not right away, no. Maybe not at all."

Jeri lifted the glass and looked at him as she took a long sip. He was a sitting silhouette without definition or detail, except for the gun held in his equally blurred hand. When the ceiling fan reminded her she was naked under the shirt, she crossed her legs.

"What do you want?"

"Consideration," Anthony said.

"About?"

"Sometimes what you're after is better left alone. Because while you're trying to get it, *it* gets you instead."

She tilted her head and tried to see him more clearly, but the effort was wasted.

"That's a bit cryptic, but I get your point. Who are we talking about here? Wagner? Anatovich? Stillman? There are a lot of ass-wipes that cross my desk. Whose balls are you licking?"

Anthony smiled at her pluck. He didn't come across many who talked to him like that, at least none he let live. And never a woman. He looked her over with a discerning eye and found her doable.

"How far would you go to save your life?"

"Probably not as far as you'd think," she told him.

"Would you take off that shirt, come sit on my lap?"

"No."

"Not even to keep me from killing you?"

Jeri didn't respond and sipped her wine.

"I could just take you. Maybe you'd like that?"

"You could try. But I'd break it off and feed it to you."

Anthony enjoyed the back and forth with her. It was like foreplay. But he wasn't here for that.

"Would you shut down an investigation if your life depended on it? Because it does. Right here, right now."

Faced with no other alternative, Jeri told him the truth.

"No."

His gun spit and a bullet passed through her hair, hitting the back of the chair. "You sure about that?"

Like her Borg pseudonym, her response to imminent destruction was measured against the cost of trying to prevent it. In the final analysis, holding on to her integrity mattered more than losing her life.

"Absolutely," Jeri said with more calm than she felt.

Another bullet followed another spit and stirred the hair closer to her neck. Anthony waited for her to break down but instead got attitude.

"You're kind of a piss-poor shot, aren't you?"

He noticed a slight shake of the glass when she brought it to her lips and found himself admiring her nerve. Most others would have been begging by now.

"Aren't you afraid to die?"

"Sure, but whatcha you gonna do?" she said and emptied the glass.

Her life didn't flash before her eyes, nor was she riddled with regret as the last of it approached, save for that of leaving Tasha the pain of her loss. She'd miss her terribly. Thank goodness she wouldn't have to bear it alone.

"Okay, I'm ready. Try not to miss this time. Asshole."

~~

"Hey, it's me," Mary called out, walking past the giant fern to the living room. She heard the muffled shout to run but didn't move, even when a man came out of the kitchen with a mouthful of sandwich.

"Com hare," he said, pulling a gun and swallowing.

"No."

"I said come here, damn it. Before I shoot your ass."

She looked from him to the sofa. Another man sat next to Tasha, whose hands and feet were bound. A piece of duct tape covered her mouth, and a discolored bruise sat high on her cheek. The anger began to build, but Mary tamped it down to keep a clear head like Dax had taught her.

"No," she said and slipped the backpack from her shoulder and sat across from Tasha.

"Tie her up," the man on the couch said.

Mary had no intention of letting that happen. *If she was tied, she died*, according to one of his many Daxioms.

And in this case, Tasha would too.

"I don't think so."

Sandwich-man took a step toward her, but couch-man put his hand up and a gun to Tasha's head.

"I'll kill her."

"Isn't that your intention anyway?"

Mary saw a glimmer of something in his eyes that was confirmed when he looked at his accomplice. They were waiting. For what?

299

"I mean it, kid. I'll blow her brains out right in front of you. Do you want that?"

She blocked the image of what that would look like and hardened herself for what had to be done.

"Stop being such a drama Queen. If you're going to kill us, kill us. Otherwise, cut the *I'm gonna kill your mom if you don't do what I say* crap. It just pisses me off."

The men looked at each other in disbelief, and Tasha's heart filled with pride in spite of the dire circumstance.

That's my daughter.

~

"You surprise me, Miss Ryan. Is your life so unfulfilling you'd give it up just like that?"

"I'd rather be in the ground than under your thumb. Or any other piece of shit's."

Anthony shook his head, impressed by her defiance. "It would be simpler to kill you and start fresh with a new Deputy-Director . . ."

"*Assistant* Deputy-Director."

". . . but I'd like to try once more to persuade you. Maybe this will help." He reached inside his jacket, tapped the screen, and said, "Catch."

Jeri had no idea what he was talking about until something sailed into the light. She snatched it out of the air with cat-like dexterity before the iPhone hit her chest.

"Nice reflexes," he said and meant it. "Would you keep your nose out of my business to save her life?"

Jeri didn't have to look to know who *her* was. Only one person meant enough to matter. She flipped through the pictures with mounting alarm, noting the bruise on Tasha's face and the anxiety in her eyes. Was she afraid?

Was she alive?

Fear stabbed without warning, and she jumped from the chair toward the shadow.

"Stop right there," he said and shot her in the leg when she didn't. While she writhed on the floor, he went to the kitchen and returned with some dishtowels, a few aspirin, and the bottle of chardonnay.

"Here you go, tough guy."

Anthony tossed her the towels then put the aspirin on the stand and poured some wine in her glass. He shifted the lampshade and watched her attend to her wound. He'd only meant to graze, but, with her sudden lunge, the bullet left a bloody mar on an otherwise fine-looking leg.

"Now, get up and sit your pretty little ass back in that chair. We're not done."

Jeri took a moment to pull down her shirt, her modesty more insistent than the pain, and as she sat, an odd, errant thought spoke up without any regard for couth or context.

He likes my ass.

His intention to kill her and Tasha didn't register with the section of her cerebral cortex that, like most people, wanted to be perceived of as attractive.

Dumb-ass brain. How about a more helpful insight? I'm in trouble here.

"I assume she's still alive. If not, we *are* done."

"Except for the blow to her cheek, she is unharmed and unmolested. For the moment."

"You'll forgive me if I don't believe you, but I'll need proof of life and limb," Jeri said and picked up the phone.

Anthony nodded then recoiled when she threw it back.

~

"Just keep an eye on her," the man on the couch said. "If she tries anything, we'll deal with it then."

"Why wait? I'll just take her in the bedroom and put that smart-mouth to good use."

Tasha yelled when he moved toward Mary and tried to stand as he got closer.

"Leave her alone," Lucas told him, but his associate kept walking. "Jack," he said more sternly. "Knock it off."

A Darth Vader ringtone emanated from Lucas' pocket, and Mary couldn't resist.

"Oh, that's cute. You must be Storm Trooper number one, cause your buddy here is a real number two – if you know what I mean."

Jack looked at his partner who shook his head.

"Come on, man. She's asking for it."

"Put your gun on her, Jack, and shut the fuck up," he said before answering the phone. "Yes, sir?"

~

"Show me," Anthony said, and smiled when the girl came into frame. This made things much, much easier. "Alright, good. Now let the detective's see the phone."

He got up and gave his to Jeri.

"Take a few minutes. And feel free to speak your mind."

Jeri felt like crying when she saw her, but Tasha wasn't so neither did she.

"Hey, girlfriend. How they hanging?" Jeri asked.

"One tight to the right and the other lefty-loosy."

They grinned at their use of colloquialisms to impart information, something they'd been doing for years. Jeri now knew how many there were and their relative position. Her grin vanished when she saw the multi-colored bruise.

"I'm sorry I got you involved, Tash."

"Why is it always about you, Seven? Why can't it be about me, me, me?"

Jeri smiled at her reference to a popular country song, and for a moment, life was good again. After she recounted the night's events, Tasha summed it up perfectly.

"It's the *Kobayashi Maru* scenario."

"It is."

The *Kobayashi Maru* was a training exercise on Star Trek designed to test Starfleet cadets in no-win situations.

"If it's just me, Tash, the choice is clear."

"Well, if it were just me and you, I'd say *fuck 'em* and start the auto-destruct sequence. But Mary's here."

Jeri's heart sank, and plummeted even further when Mary said, "Hey, Aunt Jeri. I'm with Tash. Fuck 'em."

"Let's wrap this up," Anthony said, annoyed at their seeming willingness to die for something as trivial as honor. *Honor don't mean shit when you're dead.*

They didn't say goodbye or love you, but they did.

"Live long and prosper, girlfriend."

"May the force be with you, Seven."

"Tash, dammit . . ."

"You mess with the bull, you get the horns," Mary said before Anthony took the phone.

After leaving instructions with his men, he sat and gave her some time to think it through.

"The girl wasn't supposed to be there, just so you know. Although, from my standpoint, I'm glad she turned up. Your detective friend is as stubborn as you are. The kid too. So tell me. Do you still prefer death to cooperation?"

If it were her alone, yes. Her and Tasha, maybe. Mary?

"No. You win."

Jeri's gut turned and twisted, knowing the decision would ultimately be her undoing. But what could she do? Let Tasha and Mary be murdered? Or worse?

"Good. I'm glad we've reached an understanding. It's important that you keep your word. Someday you may try to extricate yourself by hiding your friend and . . . niece. And you may succeed for a time. But we'll find them. We always do. And then, well, you know what'll happen."

She nodded in defeat and tightened the dishtowel around her leg, exchanging her sorrow for pain.

"Who are you working for?"

"Later for that," Anthony said and stepped forward. "Let's get that wound cleaned and dressed before infection sets in. You have what we need in the middle right drawer of your bedroom bathroom."

He extended his hand, but Jeri swatted it away

"I can do it myself. Just leave."

"The night isn't over, Miss Ryan, and I have yet to let your friends go."

His tone was benign but his inference was not, and Jeri reluctantly took his hand to expedite Tasha and Mary's release and get him the hell out of her house.

When they reached the bedroom, he told her to sit still while he got the supplies.

"And lose the shirt."

~

Mary felt sandwich-man's eyes all over her and better appreciated Dax's concern about the outfit she'd worn.

There wasn't enough of it.

Granted, she hadn't expected to run into anyone at Tasha's, but what if she'd been pulled over by the police or got into an accident? Apparently, there was a down-side to driving around at night in your pajamas.

It could have been the loose flannel shorts and long legs that captured his attention, but it wasn't. What had him so worked up was her big mouth and bigger breasts. He wanted to get his hands on both, so she encouraged his prurient interest by yawning and stretching before leaning forward to give him all the cleavage he could handle.

"I'll bet you enjoyed every bit of it," Jack said to her. "Probably couldn't wait for him to give it to you."

She knew what he was talking about without asking. "Sure. What little girl doesn't dream about her father raping her repeatedly someday? It's an uplifting and magical story. I'm surprised Disney hasn't made the movie yet."

Her sarcastic retort threw cold water on the flame of his desire, and the fantasy of her begging for it flickered.

"You're a smart-ass little bitch, you know that? But you won't be much longer. As soon as we get the word."

"Yeah, well, until then? Fuck off," Mary said, surprised at how much she liked using the word – even though it was only for effect. It felt powerful and badass.

"I have to pee."

As soon as she stood up, everyone became tense.

"Sit down."

"Or what? You pussies can't do anything till you're told to." She set her plan in motion by walking away.

Lucas nodded at Jack who moved with purpose. Just before he grabbed her, she accidently tripped and fell.

When he reached for her as she knew he would, Mary rolled and drove a heel at his chin, swept his feet from under him, and then planted a fist to the testicles as he hit the floor. It was fast and furious and she pointed Jack's gun at two pair of wide eyes. But Lucas already had his own in Tasha's ear.

"I'll kill her. Orders or no."

"Maybe," Mary said and re-assessed the situation.

Sandwich was down, maybe dead. Couch-potato posed a problem, though. He was serious about killing Tasha, and it rattled her nerve.

"If you don't put down the gun, she's a goner."

"And so are you," Mary replied. The man on the floor moaned, and she saw him move out of her periphery.

"I'm done fucking around. Drop it before Jack picks his sorry ass off the floor, or else."

The man's trigger-finger tightened, and Mary's fear began to build. She had to tell her before it was too late.

"I love you, Tash. Always have. You've been a great friend to me and would've been a super mom. I'll miss you. I'll miss us."

The duct-tape muted Tasha's words but not her tears, and Mary nearly lost it. If the man had kept his mouth shut, she might have faltered.

"Now isn't that sweet. Did you hear that shit, Jack?"

A switch flipped inside of her and the fear was gone.

"If you kill her, you'll die – but not all at once. If you take the gun off her, you'll still die."

"Why would I take my gun off her?"

Mary put two bullets in Jack's head and then just as quickly brought the gun back on him.

Lucas pulled Tasha over and moved behind her.

"Who are you, kid? Where'd you learn all that?"

"From my dad. Isn't he cool?"

"I thought he raped you. Over and over you said."

"That was my father. And that *sumbitch* is long gone," she said and shot him just below the elbow.

chapter thirty-one

One of the many problems of an *on-the-fly* alibi is the incessant second-guessing. Is it plausible and feasible? Should I have done this instead of that, or maybe . . .

Self-doubt can have an adverse effect on even the most well-thought-out plan, let alone one as hastily thrown together as this.

Creating the time and space was easy enough. I called the club manager and told him I had a flat tire but would still be there in time to play,. Which I wouldn't. Later I'd follow-up to apologize and bitch about my damned van quitting on me in the middle of nowhere. He would be hard pressed to find a replacement on such short notice, but my angst and sincerity would be conveyed to whatever law-enforcement agency might speak to him one day.

The thing bugging me for the last fifty miles though, was having to leave that hitman's car so near to my house. Especially with him dead inside of it.

But my choices were limited.

I'd flirted with the idea of bringing him along and trying to stage a double murder of assignor and assassin. While it appealed to my sense of poetic justice, there were too many variables – Bedford, his wife, and the hired gun who'd try to kill me at every turn, to name a few.

If I handed him to the police, he would deny he was there to kill my family and tell them some crazy guy jumped out of the woods and forced him from his car at gunpoint. 'I just told him what he wanted to hear to stay alive, Officer.'

Not only would it expose me to all kinds of unwanted scrutiny, but he'd eventually be released and come back for us with a vengeance. His ego would demand it.

More importantly, Hale Bedford would escape justice and get to live another day. And that I would not allow.

By leaving that guy in the trunk, I hoped to give the police some kind of connection between him, Brett Vander, and the other dead-man I was on my way to see.

Bedford would be anxious to hear the *good news*. And I'd be there before long to give it to him.

~~

When she reached for the weapon he dropped, Lucas kicked at her, something he wished he hadn't done after she shot him again. With a gun to his head, the girl grabbed his hair and pulled him to the floor. Despite his howling, he heard her voice above the din.

"Who sent you?" Mary asked.

"Fuck you." A bullet to the knee changed his refrain. "Oh, Christ," he cried. "Stop. Please!"

"Who sent you?"

"Mary, don't," Tasha tried to say through the duct tape, but it was unintelligible.

The ominous ringtone beckoned from his pocket, and, instead of removing her binds, Mary reached for his phone.

"Who's Darth Vader?" she asked. Tasha was trying to talk and trying to get up, but Mary pointed the gun at Lucas. "Answer me."

"I can't. He'll kill me."

"Not before I do."

Tasha told her to stop, but Mary shook her head.

"I can't. Not yet. He needs to tell me."

The phone quit ringing, and then started again.

"Well?" she asked and moved the gun to his crotch.

"Anthony," he said, "Anthony Ferrelli."

The pain was an insatiable beast needing to be fed, and if she shot him again, it would devour him. He answered all her questions. And then she shot him dead in the head.

Tasha was shocked, but the phone rang again before Mary could untie her.

"Hang on, Tash. Let me. . ."

Mary sent Anthony a text, one she hoped sounded right. 'Sorry, sir. Damn phone rings but hangs up when I answer. Can you try texting?'

"Maybe that'll work," she said and released her.

They held on to each other for a long time, the intensity of their hugs saying things too difficult to voice. The little girl in Mary who'd stepped aside so her stronger-self could do what needed doing began to tremble, and Tasha pulled her closer – if that were even possible.

When Lucas' phone chirped, Mary read the text.

"Guess we get to live," she said and looked around a room inundated with blood and flashing patrol-car lights. "For a while at least."

~~

Anthony drove off with the window down, perturbed by the vagaries of cell phones but pleased with how well the night turned out. Not only did he have an Assistant Deputy-Director in his pocket and the leverage to keep her there, Ryan was an invaluable asset with an incredible ass who'd given more than he'd expected.

He smoothed his moustache and smiled as she wafted on the wind.

~~

Hale watched Barbara attach the cable from the pully system to the collar around her throat. She tested the remote's asphyxiation button after getting into position then pulled down the mask, locked her wrists in place, and let her elbows sink into the padded leather bench before pushing back and pressing another button. The whirring sound of the machine was soon eclipsed by groaning as she manipulated both depth and speed with her finger.

A chain between her breasts swung back and forth giving pain and pleasure while it pinched and pulled, and the motion reminded him of a psychiatrist's oscillating timepiece. Its effect was similar to hypnosis in that his loathing for her was temporarily suspended.

There's something to be said, he thought, about a beautiful woman who'd do anything and everything she was told. Something raw and powerful. And he both exploited her need to please and prized her obedience.

There was also something to be said about a woman who betrayed her husband by defending the man who killed his sister. And something to be done about it.

He'd heaped humiliations galore upon his wife and cast her into a pit of depravity of which she'd yet to find bottom. And he would have DaxPalmer dead, tonight. And his family. And his fucking dog!

Why is it taking so damned long?

Hale checked his watch and reached for a phone that wasn't there because he had set it on the kitchen counter downstairs to pour the brandy he was now drinking.

Barbara began to draw the collar tighter in anticipation of what was to come, and, while he wanted to see if she'd strangle herself to death this time, he needed to know if Palmer had been dealt with.

The stairs creaked and the marble floor felt cool on his feet as he walked into the dimly lit kitchen and retrieved his phone. A dark shape loomed when he turned around.

"Who the . . ."

~

Unlike the movies where the villain is made aware of the who and why before his *has it coming* ass is riddled with bullets, I put one in Bedford's heart and head and called it done. Simple, neat, professional.

But believe me, I had a clip of hate-filled projectiles with his name on each one of them. If he'd even so much as twitched, I might have unloaded them all.

The house was quiet except for the increasingly louder moans she made upstairs. Nothing in her cadence indicated she heard anything or cared if she had, and my instinct said she hadn't been involved in trying to murder my family.

A family that had, ironically, killed hers.

I removed the suppressor and left the man in the trunk's gun on the counter; the same one I'd used on him. Ballistics would form the convoluted connection between the two, but how it played out after that . . .

After making up the mileage between Bedford's house and the club, I turned on my phone, having shut it down to prevent cell-tower pings. I'd intended to stop in and maybe get in a song or two before they closed the joint, until I glanced at one of Mary's texts.

'Call and let me know you're okay. ASAP.'

Well, that seemed to answer that. Because if she *could* read my mind then she knew I was. And what I'd been up to. Unless she was just playing with me, or her capabilities were limited or based on proximity.

I slammed on the brakes after reading another text and pulled over. I think I stopped breathing until she answered.

"Hello?"

"Mary," I said with relief and an expulsion of air.

"This is Mary. May I ask whose calling, please?"

"Mary." My eyes teared up at her humor.

"Huh, how 'bout that? How can I help you, Mary?"

"Mary," I said with some tone that made her chuckle.

"We're alright, other than a few nicks and bruises. Our guests, however, have a case of terminal headache."

She acted a tough little shit, but I heard the tremor in her voice. I needed to hold her. Maybe she needed it, too.

"Tell me, Mare. All of it."

"Hang on, okay?" she said and went outside for privacy. "Tasha's still in the house talking to the police."

"Is she good?"

"Yes. Except she's been looking at me funny."

"What do you mean?"

She told me everything from beginning to end without hyperbole like she had been taught. When finished, I asked what I needed to know most.

"How was it for you?"

"I did okay, I think. It was risky, but I figured . . ."

"Sweetie, I meant, how *are* you?"

"Oh. Well, I'm a lot of things. A bit shaky now that the adrenaline is gone, but mostly I feel . . . Capable. Thanks."

"For what?"

"For teaching me the ways of the force. No girl ever had a better Yoda. Or Dad."

It was impossible to explain how that simple three-letter word could be imbued with so much power. But its impact was not. And I'd kill anyone who threatened her. Every last one of them.

"Did Lucas . . ."

I wanted to know where he might be or if she knew who'd sent him but couldn't ask without telling her why – a dilemma rendered moot when she told me anyway.

"Lucas didn't say much about Anthony other than he was afraid of him. Same for his boss, a man named Dimitri Anatovich."

I recalled where I'd heard that name and why. As I considered a hasty course of action, I let her know I knew. "You did it again, by the way."

"What?"

"You know what I mean."

"Now, how could I know without reading your mind?"

"Exactly." I knew she was smiling as well. "We can talk about it later."

"Talk about what?"

The lilt of her voice both pleased and perplexed, and I was as sure and uncertain about her ability as ever.

"Could you ask Tasha to come back with you? It'll be pretty late by the time I get there."

"The van still giving you fits?" she asked.

Her omniscience gave me an eerie feeling until a more practical explanation came to mind.

"You called the club?"

"Yes. The manager said you were having a night."

I was indeed.

"It seems to be running fine at the moment," I told her, "but you know how it is."

"Yup. I do."

Mary knew what he had in mind and almost asked him to come home instead. It was dangerous and made more so by inadequate planning and hurry. But she also saw the wisdom of his thinking – they wouldn't be expecting him. And that could make all the difference.

If he could get them now, tonight . . .

Otherwise, we're sitting ducks in someone else's pond.
How he'd find them she just took for granted.
"You'll be careful, right?" she asked, suddenly afraid.
"What, don't you think I can handle an unruly van?"
I sensed her apprehension and it tugged at my heart. "Don't forget to clear the house, hon. Okay?"
"Copy that."

~

I stopped by the club for alibi's sake, apologizing for not showing up, and then again for having to leave for the same reason – unreliable transportation.

My odds of finding Anthony were slim. I hadn't even heard of him until tonight. Finding his boss, on the other hand, was at least a possibility.

Dimitri Anatovich.

I'd overheard Jeri talk about him to Tasha on the beach before their trip to Mexico. He was an evil man in an evil profession, the trafficking of human flesh for consumption by other equally evil individuals who needed to die slow and painful deaths.

Surprisingly, his identity and location had been easy to discover. Too easy in fact, which made the information suspect. At the time, I'd just typed his name and *sex offender* into a search engine and there he was.

How could the police fail to arrest a man the internet so clearly espoused as guilty?

That last was rhetorical sarcasm as that same internet had claimed a former presidential candidate ran a child sex ring out of a pizza parlor. And as crazy as that sounded, a man with a gun went to investigate.

Much like I was doing now, racing sixty-some miles away that may or may not house the man I was looking for.

And after I got there, then what? Wouldn't a man like that have people to protect his sorry ass? Was I going to kill them to get to him? Were they as deserving of death as the man they were guarding?

My phone chirped as I drove to this longest of shots hoping to work out the ifs, ands, and buts along the way. Mary's text said *I love you, Dad.*

Were sweeter words ever penned to paper? Or text?

I smiled and turned the phone off to keep from pinging.

~~

Anthony wasn't worried, not really.

He hadn't told Ryan who he was or who he worked for, and, though surprising, his men getting killed shouldn't alter their arrangement. But he considered the possibility she might now feel emboldened to do what he warned her not to – try and save her friends.

He'd kill them all if she did, but it could take months, even years if they went into hiding. Unless his mole inside the Bureau got wind of their whereabouts.

It was the mole's call that informed him Jack and Lucas had been put down, by a child no less. The same one who'd killed the former Assistant Deputy-Director. He started to think Robert Thompson's death wasn't just a fluke; that kid might have been trained.

By the cop? Could be.

She'd killed those morons in Mexico easily enough.

An incoming message interrupted. The boss wanted an update. Anthony was already heading to his estate knowing he would want to hear bad news right away.

He texted he'd be there shortly and checked his gun. Dimitri wouldn't kill him for an unexpected turn of events.

But his temper might.

~~

After securing him to the tree, I stuck the needle in his neck – a pine needle, but he didn't need to know that.

"Ouch!"

"Shut up and listen. The nearest hospital is forty-three miles away, and it'll take hours to figure out the poison coursing through your veins before they find the antidote. But it won't matter, because you'll be dead in thirty minutes, Unless you answer my questions. Then I'll give you the cure when I come back."

"How do I know that?"

"You don't. But the longer you dick around, the less time I have to *get 'er done* and return before you die an excruciatingly painful death in . . ." I glanced at my watch. "Twenty-nine minutes."

He spilled his guts and begged me to hurry.

"Don't call for help now, or I'll break the capsule. And don't try to wrestle free. The poison will pump through the blood stream faster if you exert yourself."

"Please, go," he said in desperation.

I taped his mouth shut and left with trepidation, not because of how many obstacles stood in my way but how few. Security was lax and seemed incongruous for a sex-trafficking crime lord. The grounds should have been patrolled by armed personnel carrying radios, and I began to doubt if I had the right Anatovich. The guy at the tree only started a few days ago and didn't know an Anthony.

Maybe Dimitri's enterprise didn't appeal to his criminal contemporaries who preferred to sell drugs and not people, making it unnecessary to staff soldiers to safeguard against a hostile takeover.

I took the route suggested to avoid detection and came to the backyard pool and patio area. A light shone through the sliding doors of his easy to access *ground floor* bedroom, which made him stupid, fearless, or the wrong man.

Familiar sounds emanated from inside.

A man smoking a big cigar sat in a big chair watching two girls actively engaged on a Super King-sized mattress. Teenage girls. Barely.

I slid the screen door open and sidled up behind him, halting as a girl on her knees came into view. When she glanced up at me, I was taken aback. Her face was the most angelic I'd ever seen, and the innocence in her glazed eyes was perversely incompatible with what she was doing.

"Don't stop, Princess. I'm almost there," the man said and took a puff from his Cohiba.

I put a finger to my lips and motioned her away. Maybe she was afraid of the mask I wore or of what he'd do if she tried to leave, but she didn't move.

"I said don't stop, dammit."

He put his hand on the back of her head, and I hit him hard with the butt of the gun.

"Don't touch her."

The little girl fell back, and the two on the bed stopped and stared.

"Get up, hon, and go sit with your friends."

I pulled back the mask and lifted her by the elbow. The other girls took her in their arms when she reached them.

"I'm not going to hurt you. Only him. In fact, if you'll let me, I'd like to take y'all away from here to someplace safe. Would that be alright with you ladies?"

I didn't know how I'd make that happen, but I wasn't going to leave without them.

They looked at each other and nodded.

"Are there other girls here?" I asked.

"No," said the older looking one who couldn't be more than fourteen. "It's just us."

Her words slurred some, and I suspected they'd been given something to make them more compliant.

God, I hoped so.

They were scantily adorned, and I didn't want them to be seen that way if we managed to escape.

"It's getting chilly out, so y'all need to put on something warm. Where's your bedroom?"

They pointed, and I opened a door that connected his with theirs. It was a gilded cage with the basic necessities but none of the amenities. The convenience of having those little girls so readily available for his pleasure sickened me, but that expediency would now keep us out of the hall and out of sight.

Anatovich started to come to, and I needed to attend to him before he made a fuss.

"As quickly as you can, get dressed, put your shoes on, and come back here. Okay?"

While the girls hurried, I closed the vertical blinds and turned off all but one light before slapping that *sonofabitch*. His eyes spewed hatred.

So did mine. And I asked the only question I would. "Where can I find Anthony?"

His smile was twisted and malevolent. "Fuck y . . ."

I didn't give him the satisfaction of finishing the sentiment and put two in his head, two in the heart, and the rest between his legs as the quiet whisper became more pronounced with each shot. After replacing the empty clip, I turned to grab the blanket before the girls came out. But they were standing still in the doorway.

I covered him up, wishing they hadn't seen that. And if I'd kept my emotions in check they wouldn't have.

"I'm sorry, girls, but . . . He needed to die."

I didn't have anything better to say and turned off the light so our eyes could adjust to the darkness.

"We'll have to hurry. So let's stay together and be quiet. Are y'all ready?"

They were, and we ran into the night hand in hand.

~~

He took the safety off the gun before knocking. When Dimitri didn't respond, he spoke up.

"It's Anthony, sir. I need to speak with you." After a few seconds, he placed his ear to the door and knocked again. "Sir?"

With weapon in hand, he turned the knob. The room was quiet, dark, and smelled like death. Anthony found the light switch and saw the bloody blanket sitting in the chair.

The door to the girl's cell was wide open, and, after a quick peek inside, he went to Dimitri, pulled back the cover, and checked for a pulse.

He was dead but still warm to the touch. A cool breeze rattled the sliding door blinds, and Anthony walked over and looked out across the grounds.

There.

A light-colored object moved in the distance, and he called Yuri before it disappeared into the trees.

"Dimitri's dead, and I think his killer is heading North through the woods. Get over to the access road. Take him alive if you can. If the girls are with him, kill them."

~

Headlights appeared in the distance just as we reached the dirt road. Any hope of it being coincidental was dashed when a powerful spotlight began to shine through the trees. I looked for a place to hide the girls.

"See that group of trees with the hanging branches in front? Get behind them. Don't move or make any noise no matter what you see or hear."

The angelic one started to cry and hugged me hard.

"Don't leave us. Please."

I put my arm around her and glanced back. The vehicle was moving slowly in a hurried fashion, the light scanning both sides of the road.

"Honey, I'm not going to leave you. I just have to take care of something and then I'll be right back."

"You promise?"

"I do." I hugged her soft and kissed the top of her head. "Now go hide."

The oldest reached for the little girl and pulled.

"Come on, Angela. We have to hurry."

How about that? She was an *angel* after all.

I put as much space as possible between them and the oncoming vehicle by running toward it. Before reaching the outer range of the headlights, I ducked into the woods and hid behind the biggest tree I could find. After evaluating my options, a thought occurred that scared me to death.

What if it was just a truck full of good-ole Georgia boys spotting for deer? If true, they would be unarmed, right? Unless they were poachers. Or were given permission to hunt the wide expanse of forest in the middle of the night.

Improbable as it might be, it was not at all impossible. Georgians did whatever the hell they wanted, whenever they damn-well felt like it.

Well, shit. I couldn't safely eliminate the threat without the element of surprise, but, without knowing who they were, I couldn't just kill them outright. Which was exactly what I'd intended in order to save those girls.

As if by divine intervention, but more likely not, a stout branch materialized in my peripheral vision. I pulled it onto the road, blocking just enough to require its removal. Hopefully, this ruse would save lives. Or cost others theirs.

When the lights got closer, I amended a favorite movie line to help keep my shadow from being seen. I had *to learn to think like a tree. And, whenever possible, to look like one.*

"Goddammit," I heard as they came to a stop. "Get that fucking thing out of the road."

First one and then another jumped from what sounded like a truck. A sweeping light kept me from a quick look-see, so I'd have to step out soon to determine who was what.

"Hurry up, dammit, or we'll lose that fucking buck."

Hunters. I relaxed as they dragged the limb *out* the way. When they continued on their quest for meat and antlers, I'd follow them in case they stumbled across the girls.

"Do you think Anthony cares if we have at 'em first? It'd be a shame to throw away all that sweet young 'tang before breaking off a piece and havin' a taste."

"I don't think he gives a shit what we do with them girls, as long as they end up in the ground when we're finished. There's plenty more where they came from. Now, get your ass back in the truck. If the buck that killed the boss gets away, Anthony might just put us in the ground too."

I stepped out and did a quick assessment. Instead of going left-to-right with the men who'd moved the branch, I'd have to go right-to-left so the guy in the truck bed didn't blind me with the spotlight once the shooting started.

So I killed him first, then the driver, the man beside him reaching for a gun, the guy by the ditch as he raised his own. When the last man turned to run, I fired and then swapped out the clip before walking over.

"Where's Anthony?" I asked.

"You shot me."

His voice was surprisingly serene given the situation. "This is true.," I said. "Now answer me before I do it again."

"Back at the house. He's the one who found Dimitri. Hey . . . I'm bleeding," he said with incredulity.

"Yeah, that happens sometimes when you get shot. Where does he live?"

"How the hell should I know? It's not like we hang out and shoot the shit over a few beers. He's a killer."

"Me too," I said with whispered lead and ran off.

Leaving Anthony unfinished, especially when he was so close, filled me with frustration. I didn't know how I'd find him, or if I'd be able to before he came after Mary for killing his men. But the girl's hiding in the brush needed me now. We had to leave while we could.

When I was within a hundred feet or so, the oldest said, "Anthony," and pointed across the road.

What felt like a giant fist hit my chest accompanied by a sound of thunder, and I fired a couple shots at the muzzle-flash before my ass hit the ground – followed by the rest of me as two more slugs whizzed by my head. As I laid there, I couldn't help thinking his aim was for shit. At least one of those shots should have found its mark, and in the dark, maybe he thought they did.

Fortunately, I hadn't moved or moaned, and my gun was on the correct side of my body relative to his position.

As cliched as it was, my best chance was to play dead – which might become a reality in the next few seconds. Or the next. Or the . . .

What was he doing? Did he want me alive? Was he waiting to see if I was? If so, why not put a bullet in my leg to get a reaction? What the hell was going on?

There hadn't been any sign of movement, and the only sounds I heard was a night owl and a child's whimpering. After a minute, I fired all but four rounds in his direction, and then rolled from the road to the ditch.

Ohhh, man. That hurt.

The Kevlar vest had done its job, but my rib felt broken.

"You girls stay put and don't move till I tell you," I said, wincing from the effort.

Three minutes later, I found him hunched over behind a tree peppered with bullets. My bullets.

"Now that's how you shoot, asshole."

His arm was bloody but what killed him was the bullet that nicked his Femoral artery, leaving him to bleed out.

Luck? Is that all it was?

'Well, that and some mighty-fine marksmanship,' my ego told me. Still, it was hard to accept.

I gave him a *terminal headache*, as Mary had called it, to guarantee he'd stay dead.

"Come on, ladies. Let's skedaddle."

chapter thirty-two

Tasha jerked and opened her eyes, but her alarm was allayed when Mary snored again. She smiled and nudged with a foot until it stopped.

They decided to wait up for Dax and hunkered on the couch with pillows, blankets, and wine. When Mary filled their glasses for the third time, Tasha thought about saying something but didn't, given the night they'd been through.

Mary's courage and calm saved them tonight. Tasha watched her lure the man in like an expert, using the right bait and presenting it effectively to agitate that fish to bite.

That same calm, conversely, had an ice-covered core.

From an objective point of view, her decision to kill the man on the floor seemed justified. He had been a threat behind her that needed to be neutralized so she could deal with the one in front of her. And if it had stopped there, Tasha could have lived with it, like she did after Mary killed her uncle last year when he tried to kidnap her.

But what Mary did to the other man was worrisome. She'd tormented him for information and then killed him, all with cold-blooded efficiency.

Technically, she murdered him. But that's not what Tasha told the officers who responded to the 9-1-1 call from a neighbor who'd heard gun shots. In fact, it was Mary who first explained what happened. And when it came to killing the man who sat on the sofa, she said he'd kept fighting even after she kept shooting.

She lied – and Tasha hadn't contradicted her. Nor did she mentioned the names Mary recovered.

'It's better the men they work for don't know we know who they are until we talk to Aunt Jeri," she'd said before letting the police in. And Tasha just nodded along.

Her composure was unlike anything she'd seen before, made even more astounding because of her age. But how could she condone her actions? Mary killed those men as if it were nothing. How could she do that?

Was it in her nature? Or nurtured?

What is Dax teaching her?

"To protect myself and others if needed. Why? What's wrong with that?"

"Sorry, Mare. I didn't know I said that out loud. There's nothing wrong with it. It's just... I can't stop thinking about what you did. How composed you seemed to be."

"That's because of the training. We've run hundreds of simulations and scenarios to cover a wide range of *what-ifs* to find optimal solutions in confrontational situations."

"What ifs?"

Mary's eyes lit up as they always did when strategizing.

"Take tonight. *What if* you're confronted by jerks who mean to do harm? By itself, that's easy enough to overcome providing you have the skills. But, as more variables are introduced – weapons, intent, others to protect – it becomes more problematic. Of course, that can also lead to some intriguingly creative resolutions. Like..."

Tasha couldn't help smiling at Mary's enthusiasm. She was in computational heaven.

"... But the most important variable is also the most difficult to train for. And according to Dax, it can't be taught. Only learned."

"What's that?"

"Fear. And he's right. When I saw that man meant to kill you, I had to suppress the panic to keep thinking clearly. Otherwise, I couldn't have eliminated the threat."

"Like Dax taught you to?"

Something about her question made Mary uneasy.

"What are you asking, Tash?"

"I've always thought his training you was a good thing. You're a stronger, more confident young lady because of it. But the way you..."

"Yes?"

Tasha saw irritation in Mary's eyes and was hesitant to proceed, but too afraid not to.

"Why did you kill that man, Mare?"

"Which one?"

"You know which one. He was no longer a threat."

"Do you think I wanted to?"

"I don't know. Did you?"

"No. But I had to."

"Why? He would have gone to jail for a long time."

"Maybe," Mary said, her voice tempered. "Maybe not. But he came to kill you, and he was never going to get that chance again. Ever."

Tasha was touched by her fierce affection but troubled, nevertheless. "But Mary, it's wrong."

"Why?"

"Because he was unarmed. It was over."

"I disagree. It wasn't over until he was dead."

"Why?"

"I told you. He came to kill you. They both did."

"Is that the only reason?"

Mary paused to consider her response. She recognized the significance of the moment as the worry in Tasha's eyes asked to be addressed.

"He also had to be kept from harming others."

Tasha remembered that Dax said something similar on the sandbar and it raised the level of her concern.

"Does Dax talk about people who need to die?"

"What? No. Well, not in that context."

"In what way then?"

Mary told her about the time she got the best of him in a confrontational-training exercise.

"It led to a *what if* about people who'd try to rape, take, or murder me. 'You kill them,' he said. 'Otherwise, they'll harm you or someone else another day.' And Tash, he's not wrong. Just look at the news."

"I don't know, Mare," she said, shaking her head.

"Do you think that man would've quit his evil ways?"

"That's not the point."

"Tell me. Please."

"I don't know. Probably not. But we can't know for sure. And if he were in prison, it wouldn't be an issue."

"Maybe. But after he served his time, was paroled, or escaped, what then? Think he'd never come after you or me? Never kill anyone else? Do we just go about our lives and *hope* he doesn't? That's not fair. And before you say *life isn't*, maybe the reason it's not is because we don't do what's needed to make it that way."

Tasha took a deep breath and exhaled slowly, unable to fault her reasoning or refute its truth. While conflicted, she was relieved those men were dead. Still . . .

"It's not right, Mare. It's just not. Life and death decisions are not yours to make. Don't you see that? You can't just take the law into your own hands."

Mary lifted the glass to her lips and took a long sip.

"Just for the hell of it, why not? I mean, the law is just a compilation of opinions from people like you and me based on our feelings, experiences, and beliefs. It's subjective, relatively speaking, and therefore may be inadequate for its intended purpose."

"You sound downright professorial at times," Tasha chuckled. "Do you know that?"

"I blame Dax. His articulation pattern is rubbing off. You know – so many words, so little time to use them all."

"Where is he, by the way? Should we be alarmed?"

"Not yet," Mary said, grappling with worry of her own. "Consider this, though. One state has capital punishment while another doesn't. Why is that? If killing the guilty is wrong then why the discrepancy? I'm talking undeniable guilt, like tonight, not assumption of. For me, the matter is unambiguous – if you want to live, don't try to kill my mom."

Tasha smiled and thought about Mary's musings. They had merit in that well-meaning individuals couldn't always agree on what was right – or even what right *was*. A few minutes passed before she tried again to understand.

"What you did . . . Does it bother you?"

Mary nodded. "But it had to be done. And I can live with that. What bothers me right now is, can you?"

'How can I not?' Tasha asked herself. Hadn't she made a similar decision by killing the boy who molested his little sister? Did their two wrongs inexplicably made a right? Both were contrary to the law as written but correct in its intended purpose – to hold people accountable.

"Maybe I shouldn't question how you saved my life and just be grateful you did. Which I am. I'm also proud. You were remarkable, honey. Disciplined and fearless."

"Disciplined, maybe. Thanks to Dax. But fearless? Only on the outside. Inside, I was . . ."

Her phone chimed and she read the text from Dax.

"He'll be here in a few minutes."

"Good," Tasha said. "I'm not ashamed to admit I need a hug from that man."

"Me, too. But he made us worry, so . . ."

Tasha raised her brow and Mary grinned.

~~

Jeri leaned back against the chair and felt a bullet hole left by the man who now had a name. He'd been arrested twice, once for aggravated assault when he was seventeen, and eleven years ago for murder. Both cases were dismissed when the complainants accidentally died before testifying.

Yeah, right.

She reached for the glass but didn't lift it, twisting the stem back and forth between her thumb and finger instead, waiting for the phone to ring.

It was a risk with terrible potential consequences, but Tasha agreed he would probably come after them anyway now that his men were dead. So she'd sent agents to bring Anatovich in for questioning and arrest Anthony Ferrelli for a litany of illegalities – save one.

Jeri was unwilling, as yet, to tell what she did. What he made her do. Despite the gentle dressing of her wound, Ferrelli was a malevolent man who demanded everything from her to keep Tasha and Mary alive.

The evil of his want was only surpassed by its form. She'd expected him to be blunt, brutal, and hopefully, brief. To her dismay, he'd taken his pleasure by taking his time, deliberately trying to evoke a response.

The phone was cold against her too warm cheek when she answered it. "Talk to me."

"You're not going to believe this," her assistant said. "Are you sitting down?"

"Yes, as a matter of fact. Why?"

"Anatovich is dead."

"What?" Jeri stood up and cringed as her leg protested. "How?"

"Someone punched his ticket along with six of his men. Mostly head shots, if you can believe that."

"Damn. Do we have any idea who the shooter is?"

"Big guy dressed in black, wearing a skeleton mask."

"We have witnesses?"

"A man tied to a tree gave us that, but he was freaking out about some poison the guy gave him. He seems alright, but we sent him to the hospital, just in case. Special Agent Hicks is with him."

"Well, damn." Jeri didn't know what to think, but what she felt was crystal clear. Absolute satisfaction. That waste of space finally got his.

"What about Ferrelli? Has he been arrested yet?"

"No need. He was one of the six."

The joy she experienced was unprofessional but more powerful than any she'd known before. All the people she loved in the world were now safe, and what he'd done to her could remain unreported.

"Donald, are you sure about Ferrelli?"

"Driver's license says it's him, and the mugshot looks right. Even with the head wound. We'll verify the prints to be sure."

Jeri couldn't wait to give Tasha the good news and said she would call him right back.

"Wait, there's more."

Holy crap, she thought, as Donald continued.

~~

For the umpteenth time since dropping them off, I tried to find relief by adjusting my position and rubbing my rib. It wasn't broken, but it wasn't not, either. At least that's how it felt. Hiding my injury would be tough, and the phony-baloney reason I'd come up with so far needed refinement.

Such were the shortcomings inherent in *fly-by-the-seat-of-your-pants* plans. Sometimes shit happened. Shit not easily explained. Like being shot in the chest

As luck would have it, as it had so many times tonight, I'd found a safe place for the ladies. Or rather one found me.

I couldn't trust leaving them with local police without knowing if the cops were in Anatovich's pocket or not, and the only place I could think of where responsible adults worked so late at night was a hospital. The staff could notify the authorities and look after them until they arrived.

When I told the girls what I intended to do, Angel said, "Why can't you take us home? I miss my mom."

She began to cry, and I saw the other girls comfort her in the rearview mirror. Before I answered, I asked.

"Where do you live?"

"Arizona," the older girl said for her. "Glendale."

"How about you two?"

"Emily's from Ohio, and I'm from Florida."

"Where in Florida?"

"Wewahitchka."

"What's your name, sweetie?"

"Leigha Taylor. My dad calls me Lela, though."

I looked up and into the reflected eyes of a child who'd gone missing in Wewa three years ago, abducted when she was not quite eleven-years old.

"That was a brave thing you did back there, Leigha. Warning me about that man in the woods."

She shook her head. "I was scared."

"That's what makes it brave."

After some thought, I tried to ascertain the possibility.

"Leigha, did your mom and dad treat you right?"

"Yes. They loved me very much. Mama used to pretend to get upset when Daddy said I was his most *specialist* girl. He even made up a poem about me once."

"Will you tell me?"

She shook her head but said okay when I said please.

"No one can compare to your purity and flair, and no one can deny you're a beaut. But if anyone should try, I will look them in the eye and tell them at best they're just cute."

The way she beamed assured me I'd be leaving them in good hands with her parents. They'd see that Emily and Angel were reunited with their families.

But Leigha's smile faded.

"What's wrong?"

"He won't think I'm special now. Not after the things I've done."

Despite my efforts to prevent them from seeing me too directly, I pulled over and looked her in the eye.

"Don't do that to yourself. None of you. What y'all did, you were forced to do to stay alive. None of it was your fault and all of the blame is theirs. Always and forever. Try never to forget that. Okay?"

They nodded, looking like the children they were.

"And Leigha? Your daddy will always think you are special. He loves you no matter what. Believe me."

"You think so?"

"I know so."

I told them I was heading to the Keys – a lie to give the police a place to look – and Wewahitchka was on the way.

When it came time for them to leave, they hugged me so hard it hurt. And not just my rib.

~

When I reached the driveway, a car flashed its lights.

"Hey, Dax."

"Dominic. Man, I'm glad it's you keeping an eye out. Sorry I'm so late getting back. Damned van's acting up."

"Yeah, Tasha mentioned it."

"How rattled was she, if you don't mind me asking?"

"Why would I mind?"

"You're her work-husband. I'm only the fiancé."

He chuckled.

"You know her, hard as nails when the shit hits it. She was more scared for Mary than herself. That's a tough girl you got there."

330

"Yes, she is. And I appreciate your sharing her. Not many husbands would be as generous," I said with a grin.

"You're welcome, but I was talking about your kid. She's got what the teens today call, *mad skills*. Is that you?"

"The training, yes, but the fortitude is all her."

He nodded. "Thank God for it."

"Amen to that," I said, anxious to get inside. "Thanks again for looking out, Dom. Give my best to Carmen."

"Will do. Alright, then. I'll leave ya to it."

As I drove down the drive, I watched him pull away only to see him stop by the car up the road. Given the events of the evening, he might check it, run the plate, and follow-up in the morning. Unless a smell emanated from the trunk.

After the garage door closed, I walked into the kitchen expecting to be met with hugs and kisses. But they must not have heard me come in. With my shoes discarded, I poured some moonshine over a few cubes of ice and listened to the girls talk trivialities.

How could I ever survive without them? Or them me? I left the kitchen to find solace in the arms of my family.

Still no hugs, no kisses.

Maybe they hadn't noticed me, but how could they not? I walked over to the big chair.

"Oh. Hi, Dax," Tasha said, continuing her conversation with Mary, who gave me a *What's up* nod. I stifled a grin and played along by sitting down.

As they discussed the pros and cons of this and that, I set my glass on the coffee table, sans coaster, and then shut my eyes expecting their discourse to come to an abrupt halt. Mary would undoubtedly say something to me now.

But her game was strong, and I said so to the multi-spotted drum swimming alongside my yellow submarine. He agreed and introduced himself.

"Fisch. Redd Fisch. And you are?"

"Dax," Mary said, incredulous that he wouldn't answer. She picked up his glass and placed it on a coaster – not wanting to but inexplicably unable to keep from doing so.

Have I gone and developed an eccentricity?

331

"Damn it, Dax."

"Honey, I think he's sleeping."

"No, he's just faking." But Tasha was right. "Well, hell."

"You sure are swearing a lot tonight," she said as Mary took a blanket and tucked it in and around him. "We're going to have to put you on a soap-bar diet."

Mary grinned and settled back on the couch. "So, you're going to be a do as I say not as I do kind of mother?"

"What do you mean?"

"You said fuck earlier."

"No, I . . ." Tasha said before remembering. "Oh. I did. Well, you said it twice."

"Yeah, but you said it first. And I'm just a sweet, impressionable young girl."

Mary gave an expression of innocence that would've fooled anyone who didn't know better, and Tasha chuckled.

"Okay. No soap."

"And no spanking for you."

They looked at Dax, but he showed no sign of being anything other than asleep.

"Damn, Mare. I really wanted that hug."

"Sorry about that. But you have to admit it was fun." She scooched over and put her arms around Tasha. "I know it's not the same."

"It's only different, sweetie, but every bit as wanted."

Tasha stroked her hair as Mary snuggled.

chapter thirty-three

A gentle breeze blew as the morning's dew kissed my cheek. I basked in rays of affection from a sun that warmed within and without – until I opened my eyes, temporarily blinded by the dark.

Mary lay asleep on the couch in blissful repose, looking like a little girl. Albeit one with a killer personality. A chill ran down my spine. She could have died tonight. Tasha, too. I glanced around and became agitated.

Where was she?

The shower sounded in Mary's room, and I relaxed and checked my watch after a struggle to free the arm from an overly tucked blanket. It was the middle of the night and my curiosity got the better of me.

I opened the door and walked by a semi-filled suitcase of things Tasha must have brought over with her. When I reached the bathroom, I knocked. Not so loud as to be heard but enough to satisfy the courtesy police.

"Tash?" I whispered and stepped inside. The night-light cast an ethereal glow in the cloud of condensation. "Tash?"

A bruised but beautiful face appeared from behind the curtain. Her eyes said she was glad to see me.

"Sorry. Did I wake you?"

"I don't know. Did you smooch me in my sleep?"

"A lady never kisses and tells." She smiled and said, "Gimme."

After quenching her thirst from the fount of my lips, she patted my face. "Now, let me finish up. I have to go."

"Where? Why?"

She ducked back inside and told me what I already knew – the people who tried to hurt my family were dead.

"Man, that's convenient."

"I know, right? With one fell swoop all our worries seem to have disappeared. Jeri said it was a professional job – in and out, no fuss, no muss."

While not meant as a compliment, I took it as one.

"Well, there was some fuss, and he did leave a mess," she said and turned off the water. "But damn if our killer doesn't have a conscience."

Tasha reached for a towel that wasn't there and opened the curtain to find it.

"How so?" I asked, holding the sought-after item.

"Gimme."

I moved in to receive another kiss, but she shook her head and indicated the terry cloth.

"He essentially rescued three girls," she said and began to dry off. "One held captive for years."

Even as I reveled in the vision that was her, a bad feeling came over me. "A hitman with a heart?" I said. "Huh. How 'bout that. Are they alright?"

She told what she knew, where she was going, and why.

"Jeri's flying down on the *corporate* jet with a couple of Special-Agents, but it'll take hours before they get here. So she asked me to drive to Wewa and stand guard until then. Maybe help question the girls."

What had been a bad feeling became a foreboding. In retrospect, I should have left the ladies at the hospital. Had I considered that Jeri might interview them personally?

Yes.

And that she might talk with Tasha afterward?

Yes. That's how I knew about Anatovich.

Did I give one thought to the possibility of Tasha ever seeing or talking to those girls?

Uh, no.

Or the likelihood of Leigha recognizing me one day getting fried chicken at the Piggly Wiggly only twenty-four point three miles from her front door?

Oh, shit.

That hitman had a heart and a modicum of courage. But what he really needed was a brain.

"Would you like me to come with you?"

"Yes, but no. I'll be acting in an official capacity," she said and started to wrap the towel around her body.

"Can I hug you real quick before you do that?"

"I don't know," she said with a knowing glint in her eye. "Can you?"

Tasha had my number, for sure. I took her in my arms and kissed her battered cheek.

"Thanks for not getting yourself killed."

"You're welcome, but that's Mary's doing. You should have seen her; it was incredible. But Dax, she . . ."

"Can we talk about it later? I just want to hold you for a bit."

"You sure? Seems more like you're feeling me."

My hands had drifted to the contour of her behind.

"Sorry," I said with a chuckle. "Want me to stop?"

"Mmmm, no. But yes. I need to get that ass in gear. Later maybe?"

"Maybe. If I'm still in the mood."

Tasha gave a *when are you not* look that tickled me. Yeah, she knew who she was dealing with.

I just hoped she didn't find out who I *was*.

~~

Watson watched Mary fly in circles before sitting down on the upper branch of the tallest tree.

"Are you going to mope or come get some lovin'?"

"I'm not moping," he said. "I'm thinking."

"Well before you hurt yourself, get on up here."

"Oh, ha-ha."

With a flap of his ears, he rose in the air and joined her.

"Look what I have for you?" She reached into a pocket and came out with Snausages.

Watson's worry wandered as he licked his lips.

"You mean to tell me that all the time we've been dreaming together, we could have been eating as well?"

"It's news to me, too. I just wished I had some treats for you and there they were. Cool, huh?"

She rubbed his head while he enjoyed his snack. "Want to see if we can rustle up a T-bone?"

Watson's eyes filled with elation and then emptied. "Are you trying to distract me with visions of sugar-plums dancing in my head?"

"Oooh, I like that poem a lot. Can you recite it for me?"

Mary moved her fingers to *the spot,* but he pulled away. They looked at each other in stunned disbelief.

"Wow," she said. "You must really be upset. Okay. But what else could I have done? Let them kill us?"

"No, of course not," he said. "But you're going to get yourself hurt if this keeps up. Why is this happening?"

"It's not like I'm inviting people to come and get me, you know. I'm only glad I can do something about it. Something significant."

"Like you did with the boy who hurt Isabel?"

Mary got quiet and looked at her dangling feet.

"Are you judging me, Watson?"

"No. Animals don't judge. But we are pretty protective of those we care about."

"You know what else animals don't do? Prey on their own for sport. Or perverted pleasure. Or..."

"I get it. Sometimes people suck. But you can't put them down without losing a part of who you are. Or will be. Can you?"

His question was sincere, but her answer was vague.

"I don't know. Guess we'll have to wait and see."

Watson laid his head in her lap, and she scratched. And scratched and scratched.

~~

Thanks to the thermos of coffee Dax gave her, she was wide awake when the man walked up and raised a shotgun just as the dawn began to break.

"Who the hell are you?" he said.

The double-barrel loomed through the windshield and wavered in unsteady hands.

"My name is Tasha Williams. I'm a detective from St. Vincent. Are you Mr. Taylor?"

"Can you prove it?"

"Yes sir. I have identification in my purse."

He kept the weapon on her and moved to the window.

"Show me."

"Are you Leigha's father?"

"Yes."

"Mr. Taylor, I appreciate your apprehension. I do. But would you please take your finger off the trigger? At least till you're absolutely sure I need shooting."

He lowered the gun after seeing her badge.

"I'm sorry, Detective. I just . . . I can't lose her again." The anguish in his haunted eyes was palpable.

"I understand, sir. I have a daughter of my own. Well, I will in a few days."

He nodded in kind and then in confusion.

"Why are you here?"

Tasha told him about Jeri – who she was, why she was coming, and when she'd arrive.

"She asked me to keep watch over your family. I'm sorry if I've caused you alarm."

"It's alright," he said and glanced around for any sign of anyone who'd try to take his child from him. "You hungry?"

"I . . . No. Thanks for asking, though."

"Please. I'm too afraid to let Lela out of my sight, and you can help me keep an eye out over breakfast."

Her stomach *growled* she hadn't eaten since yesterday noon just as her mouth began to decline yet again.

"Well then, yes. Thank you, Mr. Taylor."

"Paul," he said and hurried back to the house.

Tasha's expectations were turned on its head when she reached the door. The scene wasn't solemn but festive, with girls laughing and playing in makeshift pajamas. A smile lifted with her spirits.

"Mother, this is Detective Williams. She's okay."

"Tasha," she said to the woman in front of the stove as her husband sat in a chair positioned to keep an eye on the door and his daughter with the shotgun across his lap.

"I'm Nadine," she said wiping her hands on a dishtowel. "Very nice to meet you. Is this your doing?"

"No, ma'am," Tasha said. "But I'm so happy for you."

They watched the girls murmur and giggle like sisters.

"It's amazing."

"It's a miracle," Nadine said with heartfelt sincerity.

"Yes, ma'am. It truly is."

"Tasha, I know it's the southern way, but could you please stop ma'aming me? It makes me feel like an old lady."

"Yes, ma'am," she said, but caught herself after the fact. "Sorry."

Nadine grinned and returned to her cooking.

"Nadine? Which one is Leigha?"

"The redhead," she said and flipped a flapjack.

"She's beautiful."

"Yes, too much so. I think that's why they took her." She glanced at her daughter and forced herself not to cry. "Do you have kids, Tasha?"

"Not yet. But soon."

Nadine glimpsed and said she didn't look pregnant. "Are you?"

"No. The man I'm about to marry has a daughter."

"Tell me about her."

"I don't think . . ."

"Please. It'll help. Would you pass that plate there?"

Tasha handed it to her and watched it fill with pancakes as she talked about Mary.

"What?" she asked when Nadine started laughing.

"You sing her praises like a new mother in love – she's the smartest, prettiest, funniest, cleverest."

Tasha laughed along and helped her set the table.

"I haven't even mentioned the coolest, the toughest, the bravest. She actually saved my life last night."

"Really?" one of the girls asked.

She was a pint-sized pixie with big Bambi eyes, and Tasha thought her the cutest little thing she'd ever seen.

"It's breakfast," Nadine called out. "Y'all come and eat." She made the introductions when they came to the table. "Girls, this is Detective Williams."

"Please, call me Tasha. What's your name?" she asked the pixie.

"I'm Angela. The quiet one is Emily. And the brave one is Leigha."

"I'm not brave."

"Uh-huh," Angela said. "The man said you were."

"Paul? Are you going to join us?"

He shifted his chair to keep both daughter and door in view. "Not right now, Mother."

"Why did the man say that, Angela?" Tasha asked.

"Because she stood up and warned him. But Anthony shot him and he fell to the ground."

She stuffed her mouth with syrupy cake and continued. "I started to cry, but he was just pretending."

"Pretending?"

"To be dead."

"Oh, I see," Tasha said.

"He killed Anthony. And the bad man in the bedroom. Said he needed to die cause of the things he made us do."

"Alright, Angela" Leigha said, trying to discourage her. "Let's not talk about that."

"But it's not our fault, remember? The man said so. And that your daddy would love you no matter what."

"Angel, please." Leigha's eyes began to fill with tears. "Daddy, I . . ."

"It's okay, Carrot-Top. The man's right. I'll always love you. And this was none of y'alls fault."

"See?" Angela declared and started on some bacon.

Tasha was struck by the compassion the killer showed the girls, reminding her of Dax's when he found Mary.

Perhaps last night had been a rescue mission?

"Did any of you see the man's face?"

"Yes," Angela said. "He wore a mask but took it off."

"Had you ever seen him before?" When they all said no, she asked what he looked like.

"He was very handsome," Emily stated and blushed.

Tasha did her best to stifle a grin that fought back hard. It's always the quiet ones, she thought.

"Really? What color eyes did he have, Emily?"

"A beautiful Azure," she said with a dark red hue.

"No, they were green," Angela countered.

"Leigha? What do you think?" Tasha asked.

"Why?"

"What do you mean?"

"Why do you want to know?"

"Well, we'd like to find him if we can."

"What for? So you can put him in jail?"

When Tasha didn't respond, Leigha did.

"Whatever else he did, he saved us, and we can't help you catch him. We won't."

The other girls nodded as Nadine patted her daughter's arm and looked at Tasha, one mother to another.

"I understand, Leigha," Tasha said. "And I respect your feelings. All of yours. We need to know everything that happened and everything he did. But we don't need you to tell us what he looked like. Can y'all do that?"

Emily and Angela looked to Leigha who looked at her mother who nodded.

"That sounds fair, dear. Tasha has a job to do, but I think she'll keep her word."

Leigha said okay and the others did, too.

"Good. And thank you. When my FBI friend gets here, we'll talk. And then we'll *all* talk. Her name is Jeri Ryan . . ."

Tasha read the incoming text on her beeping phone. "She's outside in the driveway. Please excuse me."

Jeri greeted her with a hug.

"How are you holding up, girlfriend?"

"I'm good, Seven. You?"

"Better than I was a few hours ago. Is Mary alright?"

"She's great."

"She sure is. I'm looking forward to hearing the uncut version of what happened."

Two well-groomed agents stood quietly behind her.

"Tash, these are Special-Agents Reid and Moore. Special-Agents, Detective Williams."

Tasha smiled and shook their hands.

"Seven, can I speak to you before you go in?"

"Sure." Jeri asked the agents to walk the perimeter. "What's up?"

"First, I apologize for going inside. The father made me an offer I couldn't refuse."

"Bathroom?"

"Breakfast."

Jeri grinned. "And second?"

"I've already talked with the girls a bit."

"Good. Helps break the ice. I trust your judgement, Tash. You know that."

"Thanks. Let me fill you in."

When she finished, Jeri asked her opinion.

"They're pretty protective of him, so I'd let that go for now. And considering the kind of empathy he displayed, I don't think he's a risk to the general public. The most helpful information they can give will be things that could get you inside Anatovich's operation. How they were taken, where they were kept, who they know and can identify . . . But I don't think that's a conversation for today."

"I think you're right. The other parents have already been contacted and are flying into Panama City. Agents Reid and Moore will accompany them home for protection, and then interview them more fully when appropriate. So for now, we'll just focus on last night."

"The younger girls take their cue from Leigha, but Angela is the most talkative. Wait till you see her, Seven. The expression 'cute as a button' was coined for her."

As they walked to the house, Tasha noticed the limp. "What's wrong with your leg?"

"Ferrelli shot me."

"Why?"

"To keep from getting his ass kicked," Jeri said with more bravado than was true. She didn't tell Tasha what else he'd done but thought she would eventually. Someday.

"Don't worry. As the hero always says in the movies – 'It's just a flesh-wound.'"

She saw her joke register but Tasha didn't smile back. "Shall we proceed?" Jeri asked and knocked on the door.

~~

I awoke with a start from a dream without end.

It took place at a county carnival. After knocking down all the targets at the shooting gallery, I collected my three Kewpie-doll prize and turned to leave.

At first, I thought the thwack on my back was just me patting myself for not missing a single shot. But as both my hands were holding the dolls, I guessed not.

When something whistled past my ear, I squatted and shot from the hip at a target shooting at me.

Bullseye!

No, I was not three-handed but such is the nature of dreams. Although I did safeguard the Kewpies as one target after another began to shoot.

The sound of ting, ting, ting kept sounding as I shot each one in turn. Except now, they weren't going down. And they were multiplying. I kept firing even though there were way too many of them . . .

There were always going to be too many, I thought and laid in bed for a few minutes before looking at the clock.

But did that mean the effort was wasted?

If Michelangelo had let seeming futility overcome his attempt to free David from that large block of marble, we'd all be the less for it.

Now, I'm not saying I'm as significant as . . . *Jesus*!

I'd only meant to catch a couple hours but had been asleep for almost six. I jumped out of bed, donned shirt and shorts, and hurried to get to it before Tasha got back.

The house echoed as I casually called out her name. "Mary? Oh, Maaary. Come out, come out wherever you are."

A touch of fear flickered until I saw her note.

I peeked in but you were snoring, hence
the note. I felt the fish mocking me, so
I went to show them what's what
before the press and paparazzi descend
like a pox upon our house.

I assume Tash is doing something work
related because she is g-o-n-e.

According to the news, seven men were
killed at the estate of one Dimitri Anatovich,
so don't worry about me being out and about.

Looks like we got lucky.

The smiley face mocked me. Not derisively like her fish, but in an *I know what you did last night* kind of way.

And she might.

But even if she didn't, Mary wouldn't give a second thought to my cleaning the van after a gig because I always did – whether or not there was a DNA concern.

The ladies may have left some of themselves inside, so it was imperative to start there. As for my on-the-fly alibi, I *did* have to change a flat tire. Because I'd punctured it. And the mechanical component? Hose and wiring issues I knew about for weeks but kept to myself, just in case.

I am a contingency planner after all.

chapter thirty-four

Tasha yawned for so long she almost pulled over. She was as tired as she'd ever been, and the thought of lying down felt like a little piece of heaven.

The forensic team should be at her place by now, and she thought about pulling into the station house to find out but decided to call the captain instead.

"An Assistant Deputy-Director from the FBI called to thank me for the loan of one of my detectives," he said.

She explained and then asked about her house.

"Forensics is done. Dominic is at the morgue. That was a hell of a thing last night. You alright this morning?"

"Yes, sir. I need to grab some shut-eye, but I'll be in after a few hours."

"No, I think not. Take the rest of the week off."

"Sir, I don't . . ."

"Detective, that is not a request. You have things that need doing – getting some rest, getting your house in order, and not getting killed before your wedding day. A wedding I wasn't invited to, by the way."

"It's just a small affair, and it didn't occur to me you'd be interested in going. Would you?"

"Are you still having it out on Bird Island? I hear the Tarpon are jumping all around that sandbar."

Tasha smiled with a better understanding. "I am. And they are. You're welcome to attend. It's BYOB, though."

"You're making your guests bring their own beer?"

"Their own bait, Captain."

"Thanks, Tasha," he said. "I'll see you on the sand. Oh, how is that young girl doing? She sure is something. Think she'd like a career in law-enforcement someday?"

"Maybe."

Her excitement began to build as she drove out of town. Tasha would be a married woman in three days, and on her honeymoon for ten more. Or less, depending on how much they missed Mary.

If she were any other teenager, they wouldn't think of leaving her home alone. But she wasn't, and she wouldn't be. Not with Isabel and Watson keeping her company.

Rather than fly, and in case they needed to return in a hurry, they planned a romantic getaway in the state, the location her idea because she'd never been. They'd explore the Florida Keys, culminating in a stay at the southernmost point of the Continental United States. Key West.

Maybe we'll run into our killer?

Tasha guffawed, too tired to know if it was out loud or in her head. She didn't believe *the man* told the young ladies the truth about that. More likely it was a wild goose asking to be chased. And even if she tried to pursue it, how?

The girls wouldn't say what he looked like and couldn't agree on the vehicle he'd driven. Emily thought it was a van, and Angela said it was more like a really big car. Leigha of course, didn't confirm, deny, or offer an opinion.

Tasha no longer thought them rescued on purpose. If so, *the man* wouldn't have said he'd leave them at a hospital. No, he was there for Anatovich and saved them by accident.

He killed another six and could've died himself, just to help those girls. What kind of murderer does that? Was he, as Dax joked earlier, a hitman with a heart? And where was her indignation? Why wasn't she more upset by what that man did to those men?

Maybe because those three little girls were forced to do unspeakable things and *those men* got what they deserved. Didn't they?

The niggle that began at the Taylor home returned, and she rubbed the back of her neck to relieve its irritation.

According to Angela, the man said, '*He needed to die.*' The words were only slightly different than what Dax said, and while he didn't have exclusivity in speaking them, the coincidence unsettled her.

Maybe it was because she was dead tired and couldn't think clearly, but the similarities between Dax and *the man* seemed a few too many. She pondered some particulars as she drove past the abandoned car a few hundred yards from his house.

Their attitude
Their compassion
Their training
Their vehicle
Their eye color
Their being very handsome

Tasha chuckled at her silly supposition and quit trying to connect elusive dots as she pulled into the driveway.

What was she thinking anyway? That not only did Dax think some people needed to die, but he acted on it?

The house was quiet except for running water in the main bathroom. She saw Mary's note and went to the fridge and poured a glass of wine with the intention of sharing Dax's shower before crawling into his bed.

The niggling asked her to hold up for a few seconds. 'Let's take a quick look in the garage.'

'*That* coincidence is too ambiguous,' she replied. Yes, hypothetically, Dax had the time and the corresponding opportunity, but his van had been appallingly unreliable – what with everything he said happened with it.

It was the smell of clean that sparked her suspicion. The side door of the van stood wide open to facilitate drying, she assumed, and the carpeted floor inside was still damp – and so was the bench seat behind the driver's, a seat similar in description to where the girls sat and saw the man's eyes in the rearview mirror.

'Hold on, now,' she said to the niggle. 'This doesn't have to mean anything. It probably needed to be cleaned because of the music equipment. And the tire change.'

She stepped back to confirm her conjecture and saw a flat against the wall and a spare on the van.

'Maybe,' the niggle said. 'Or maybe not.'

Tasha examined the Wet-Dry vac. Like the interior of his van, it was also thoroughly cleaned. And dried.

'Uh-uh,' she said to the suspicion that asked to escalate. 'This is just senseless speculation based on circumstantial coincidences fueled by a state of exhaustion.'

'You sure?' the niggle insisted. 'Anthony and Anatovich just happen to get killed right after putting you and Mary in danger? That's one hell of a timely twist of fate.'

'How would he even know who to look for?'

'Didn't Mary make it a point to find out? Maybe . . .'

"Enough. This hypothesis is rife with ridiculousity," Tasha said out loud.

As she left the garage for the kitchen, a smile traced her face. Couples who'd been together a while started to look like one another, she heard. But speaking the same dialect?

After emptying her glass, and hopefully her mind, she filled it again and went to see him before Mary got home.

"Dax?"

"Lisa," he said with a sense of urgency from behind the shower curtain. "What are you doing here? Look, it's been fun and you're a great gal, especially in the sack. But I'm getting married and we can't do this anymore. Please, you have to go. I hope you understand."

"Why her, huh?" she said, trying not to laugh. "What's Tasha got that I don't?"

"My heart, for one thing."

His head appeared with a goofy grin in his eyes, and she thought them more Cobalt blue than Emily's Azure.

"You know what'll happen if you ever cheat, right?"

"I'll end up buried in Money Bayou?"

"Just so we're clear," Tasha said and set down the glass. Her kiss was slow and his response sure and satisfying. She hoped it would always be so.

"You must be dog-tired, girl. Why don't you go lay down and I'll come rub your back till you fall asleep?"

Thoughts of a shower gave way to those of drifting on a slow boat to Slumberland while his fingers rowed the way.

"That sounds like a plan. See ya in a bit."

I turned off the water and stepped out of the tub with a feeling of relief. Nothing in her demeanor implied a shift in attitude toward me, and I thought it safe to assume her time with the ladies hadn't raised her suspicion.

Maybe it was all over – the worry of her finding out and the fear of losing her if she did. Last night was my *last* night. Unless, of course, someone else tried to hurt my family.

But who'd help those other families now? I was lost in thought, conflicted about their need and my own for Tasha, when the door opened.

"I forgot my glass of . . ." She stopped and stared.

At first, I assumed the magnificence of my nakedness left her speechless and in awe. Okay, I'm not all that, but it was fun to imagine – until I tracked her gaze.

When she looked in my eyes, I could see the wheels of her curiosity spin. My original stupid explanation about the bruise on my chest had been exchanged for one marginally more believable, so I was ready for her question.

But she turned and walked away without saying a word while I hurried to get dressed.

~

Tasha stood in the living room with her arms folded. 'He was just pretending,' Angela said, after he'd been shot.

What if he was wearing a bullet-proof vest?

It would explain why *the man* didn't get up right away, though how he'd kept quiet and still was beyond her. It hurt like hell when she'd been shot wearing one, and her wound looked a lot like Dax's.

At what point does a confluence of coincidence become something more substantial?

That old observation about investigation came to mind – *Once you eliminated the impossible, whatever remained, however improbable, had to be true.*

"Tash, what's wrong?" he asked from behind her.

What's wrong? She felt the first stirring of the surreal. What's *wrong?*

"Do you know that thing you and Mary do where you tell the truth no matter what?"

"Yes?"

"Do we have that?" His silence said they didn't. "Can we have it now?"

I was caught in a trap of my own making – not cause I couldn't lie to her, but because I couldn't lie to her anymore. *Isn't love fucking grand?*

"Sure. What do you want to know?"

Even before she turned to face him, Tasha knew. She heard it in his voice.

"Did you kill those men?"

"Which ones? Could you be more specific?" I asked, trying to be funny in a last-ditch attempt to dissuade her. But her eyes said this was serious, and boy, didn't I know it.

"Did you kill Dimitri Anatovich?"

"Yes."

Perhaps it was the fatigue or the sense she was sound asleep and dreaming, but his admission didn't unravel her. It wasn't as if she'd never given any thought to his capacity to kill or his rationale if he did. Dax didn't suffer from the illusion of a legal system that functioned properly to protect its citizens, and he wasn't going to rely on its empty promise to keep his loved ones safe from those who didn't give a shit about the rule of law.

What surprised her was the admiration, misplaced as it might be. His actions not only saved them all from reprisal, but he rescued those poor girls from unimaginable abuse.

'That doesn't matter,' the cop inside her asserted. 'He stepped way outside the law.'

I know . . . But she would rather a hundred, a thousand evil men met similar fates than another child should suffer. *At least those Dax killed won't harm anyone else ever again –* something another little girl tried to tell her last night.

"And Mary's father?"

"Yes."

Tasha had long suspected but must have always known because she wasn't shocked and didn't care. Maybe because she knew what that man did to his daughter.

To *her* daughter.

Dax looked at her in a way she could never replace or live without, and feelings of right, wrong, life and death, love and duty swirled into a whirlwind of troubled thought. She put her arms around him and held on, afraid of being torn away by the fear of losing him. As the maelstrom began to dissipate, Tasha loosened her grip but not her embrace.

"Emily has a crush on you."

"Do tell."

"She thinks you're very handsome."

"Well, that's true."

He winced when she poked him in the ribs, but her kiss was tender and her eyes a misty pool of hazel-green.

"What am I going to do, Dax?"

thanks for reading

It's a funny thing, writing. A thought turns into an idea that could evolve into an interesting story, and you set out with a kinda plan and a sorta map on how to get there. That's what *I* do, anyway.

Along the way, what is envisioned and what is written can change significantly as the characters begin to do what they want instead of what they're told. As a result, they take you places you may never have gone otherwise, places that both excite and disturb.

It's a wild ride. And as you're driving down the literary road with the top down and the wind blowing through your hair, you hope those who join you have at least half as much fun reading as you've wholeheartedly had writing.

Thank you for spending time with me.

larehalebooks@gmail.com

Made in the USA
Columbia, SC
26 June 2021